THE DRAGON ORACLE

ERICA DERETZ

The Dragon Oracle

Copyright @ 2023 by Erica Deretz

All rights reserved.

Cover Illustration by Luisa Galstyan

ericaderetz.com

First Edition: 2023
Second Edition: 2026

 Formatted with Vellum

For Betty, who shares the most beautiful songs.

UNDER ANOTHER'S MOUNTAIN

The marble prison gleamed with my dying queen's blood, even as our newfound salvation crumpled from her efforts. She was... had performed an impossibility. She had mended- *healed* a dragon. In my queen's wretched and ruined state, she called for blood, demanding death even for the one that saved her. Maybe she was right. Maybe she saw something that I could not.

Disobeying an order from one's queen may be unwise, but it was my birthright as her brother to ignore her. After all, this woman had just saved Thea's life. Stumbling upon us, she'd been mortified at her discovery. Finding us in this cold, sterile dungeon underneath her own queen's Mountain had clearly unnerved her. Never mind finding one nearly in-step with death. Timely though for Thea that she had.

She was foolish though, this woman, recklessly so. She had mended my sister in a way that I knew, or rather- *had* known wasn't possible, not anymore. Besides that marvel though, something still was not right. The task had been too big. Using too much of her own energy... she had faded while bringing a seething Thea back to us. My sister was frantic for blood- *any* blood that was not her own. Our tormentors had overdone it, even for them. And now their *wizard* was gods knows where with his pitiful vials, taking his gods damned time slowly getting around to playing his part in this cruel nightmare.

I moved this faded woman's body only an instant before my sister's jaws would have found her. My dear Thea was desperate. Anyone in her position would be. Still, best to avoid ill fortunes when and where we can.

And there was something about this one, this... bewilderment. Something in her blood was calling to something in mine. I didn't understand it. I couldn't explain it. Thea wouldn't have listened, or cared, even if I could. But I knew I needed to help her, to save her. She didn't know what kind of danger she was in. The imminent threat of my sister- Anthea, the Dragon Queen of the Green Mountains, really was the least of it.

Thea was still snapping and snarling at me as I drew this woman onto my lap to protect her. Her body was as ice, undoubtedly from using enough of her energy to fade away and lose herself. As I ran my hands over her extremities to warm them, her dark auburn curls fluttered with the movement, reminding me of autumn winds as they move through the trees back home.

I couldn't help my smile, even here.

Thea, sneering as she spoke, hissed, *"She reeks of him. He'll kill you for looking at her. Never mind you holding her like that."* Despite her demeanor, it was clear she was still somewhat pleased. No doubt hopeful this encounter would especially trouble our principal tormentor.

It was nice to see her spirits improving.

I remained silent, of course. Saying anything would only fuel her animosity, and she might keep pushing me to end this one's life. Not that I would. Not that I even could. Moving the curls out of the woman's face as I held her, our salvation nuzzled into me reflexively, trying to likewise warm herself. Looking down at her, I felt my breath catch. Quickly I prayed to the gods that remained *and* the bastards that left for Thea to have not noticed.

Naturally my prayer went unheeded, just like all the rest and all of Thea's had. My sister's transformed voice lit up the room, "Is that your plan then?! Steal her from him? He'd kill her before letting her go! Let alone be yours!" The amusement in her callous tone was palpable. "This one might be too much for even you, dear brother!"

For the first time in weeks Thea was actually laughing. It was a crazy, despairing laugh, but I heard the hope behind it. She'd say I was foolish. Admittedly a part of me was, but I took it as a sign that I'd been right not to kill this strange and beautiful creature now resting in my arms. Even if that embodiment of petulant evil had claimed her, I'd simply end him and set her free. Nothing would make me happier.

But this, whatever *this* was that had taken hold of me, truly wasn't about him.

Her heart was starting to beat faster. She'd be awake soon. I didn't know how she'd react to finding herself in my arms. She needed to be able to move away as quickly as she wanted to, not that I wanted her to. I found myself barely able to let her go. For the first time since landing in this gods-forsaken kingdom I too found myself feeling something akin to hope. I wanted to hold onto it for as long as I could. I wanted to hold onto *her* for as long as I could.

Calming myself and adjusting my hold on her, my eyes began to linger. Her bodice had fallen noticeably. I'd been as careful as I could, but my moving her around to save her, well, it hadn't helped the situation. A small marking at the top of her left breast caught my eye. I shouldn't have, I do know this, but my curiosity got the better of me. Glancing over I saw Thea turned away, nursing what remained of her physical wounds. I peeled this wondrous creature's top down no more than an inch. (I swear it!) Only enough to see the rest of the smallest of marks.

A little rose.

It suited her.

Smirking, I admired the cute little inking for one stolen moment, just as Thea turned back to us. Instantly the room filled with her suffocating ferocity. "What are you *doing*?! We're going to be slaughtered down here. And you—" At the first sound of their wizard finally making his way down the tunnel, her words and anger fell.

After they finished with Thea for the day he'd come *repair* her. Only to the point where she wouldn't die, of course. Couldn't do anything to minimize our suffering, now could they? Their fun would have ended before it served their purposes after all. Then they'd have no way of justifying any of this to themselves, their people, or their gods.

My eyes locked on the doorway as I listened to his steps, holding tight to my Little Rose. A soft touch startled me as tender fingers brushed my face. I looked down sharply to see the loveliest moss green eyes staring back up at me. Surprised herself, she pulled her hand back quickly as if she'd been burned. A familiar flash of gold rippled through her eyes. I must have frightened her, but in truth, as I looked into those eyes, what I myself felt could easily be likened to fear. She was beyond tense, but I couldn't take my eyes from her.

Still a bit dazed and drained, she warily moved from my lap to the floor before slowly standing. Her eyes never leaving mine. I didn't want to let her go, but I knew better than to try and hold on. I needed to warn her, but the words wouldn't come. Not lost as I was.

Shattering glass and billowing clouds of red smoke startled her, forcing her to turn from me. The wizard had arrived to see her backing away from his victims. His precious, broken vials forgotten, he took a moment to look between the three of us. Little Rose, befuddled, concerned, and livid. Myself, lamenting ever letting her go as my eyes still held to her. And Thea, sitting on her haunches, calculating. He grabbed Little Rose and dragged her away as quickly as he could.

He said nothing as she barraged him with question after question about who we were, why we were down here, what they were doing to us.... My heart raced hearing her lilting voice and then fell as it trailed off. I could feel Little Rose's fire flare once more as echoes of her carried until they were out of the tunnel. I smiled bitterly to myself, regret filling me.

Thea hissed at me again with newly heated aggression, "If we survive this and you don't kill her, if you don't kill **all of them** when you have the chance, I swear on the gods that remain that I *will* kill you and find myself a new commander."

She was lying. Thea didn't trust anyone enough to replace me. Although I could easily imagine her killing me out of spite alone. It wouldn't matter. That Little Rose was going to engulf our world. I could still feel her fire. Our world of indifferent deities had all but died. We'd been waiting on the spark needed to ignite its rebirth. Some of us had grown tired of waiting. We'd started looking for the Fated Fire. And as Fate would have it, as it always has it- it had found us.

CHAPTER
ONE

It'd been over a year since my fiancé's charred body was brought into my trauma center. Of course the occasional nightmare still visited me, but those weren't what really haunted me, not anymore. The thing of it that *really* got to me? Those sickly stenches that lingered all day after one of those damned dreams. Illusory scents of burning flesh and hair, tinges of iron strong enough that you could taste it, wafts of putrid meat- those were what really gutted me. Never had a smell accompany a dream like that before.

I didn't recognize him when they brought him in, not with what was left of him. He'd lied about his last name. It meant nothing to me when I heard who was coming in over the radio. By the time I knew it was him, he was gone. That's how I found out he was already married- his wife came in after him.

The engagement ring he'd given me rested at the end of a delicate chain around my neck. Just low enough for my scrubs to cover it. The weight of it suddenly became far too heavy as I began to suffocate underneath it all. For three years I had loved that man. I had been making a life with him, planned on having kids with him, trusted him......

What happened to the ring or the necklace or how- I do not know. I remember it nearly burning itself into my flesh, grabbing for it despairingly, flashes of pain and rage and fury- and then there was nothing. It was gone.

And so was I.

After that... I simply kept freezing at all the wrong moments. Maybe I was expecting another cruel twist of fate to come around one of the already too crowded corners or through the automatic glass doors. At some point I realized I couldn't put one foot in front of the other and do what needed to be done anymore. Or maybe I just didn't want to.

Some of the other nurses suggested I take some time off, talk to my therapist, work back into it slowly. I knew none of that would make a difference. You can't want what you don't want. After a particularly bad night, one of the old crotchety doctors told me with a warmth that betrayed him, "You're not cutting it anymore, kid."

He was right, of course. My indifference at hearing this truth spoken aloud told me everything. Besides, I'd known it already- when I stopped seeing my patients as puzzles worth solving, as pieces worth putting back together, as people worth healing, I knew. I just needed to hear it from someone else, to be confronted with the reality of it all. It's not that people weren't still puzzles. That will never change. Puzzles just weren't worth figuring out anymore, not to me.

FOR A TIME, far too long of a time, I did nothing. When that became unacceptable, my parents suggested I volunteer at the nearby botanical garden. After all, gardening couldn't possibly be that stressful.

That's where I met Jen. She was a different kind of puzzle all in and of herself. Her novelty intrigued me, sparked something in me. I think that's why I clung to her so fervently.

Jen had been helping out in the gardens longer than anyone could recall. She even had her own little niche area with some of the more particularly nasty plants. People knew not to bother her; she could be a bit prickly herself. Talking with her, you might get the false impression that her crotchetiness was simply an affectation of her old age. She seemed to like me though. Maybe it was pity. That was one of the oddities of Jen- she seemed to know everything about everyone. Either way, I was grateful for what she had to teach me. She showed me a new way to heal. Not just a new puzzle, but a new way to solve it entirely. I needed the distraction.

Admittedly my puzzles... patients were now plants, so the stakes didn't seem as high, but I was using my hands to fix things again. It wasn't as singularly dimensional as most puzzles either. Now I was working with an internal pattern, more of a multi-dimensional tapestry. I had threads of energy to move around and wind through, in and out, connect, replace, rearrange. Nothing was finite or rigid. It took a different effort, a different energy. And I had an instinct for it that surprised us both. Not to mention the best part- plants don't lie to you. And they rarely do anything unexpected.

After I quit the trauma center, spent the appropriate amount of time wallowing, and then crawled through to the other side- I took a regular nine-to-five in medical billing. Wonderfully mundane, and I made sure to find a position with the same parent company as the trauma center, so I was able to keep most of my benefits. "Nothing if not practical," as my sister would say. Although I do think that's one of the nicer things Lark would have to say about me. At least lately. It'd been several months of this gloriously monotonous routine, and I couldn't be happier. Happy as I defined it, anyway. Still, I was a bit happier that it was Friday.

Friday meant what it usually does, that tomorrow would be Saturday. My Saturdays were now for gardening. Fall was in full swing and I really needed to step up my winterizing. It may sound a bit desolate to you, but in the middle of the woods, in a well-cared for garden... well, that was about the only place I actually wanted to be anymore. Most other places I simply didn't want to be. Not that I told this to most people. Not anymore. That sort of thing worries most people.

These particular gardens belonged to Jen. Had belonged. She passed away a couple months ago now. Her heart had simply stopped. It had seemed a bit odd to me. But what's the saying? No one dies of old age anymore. That's all anyone really said about it.

Jen with her grouchiness always kept everyone at arm's length. Except me. I found her grouchiness endearing, if not amusing. And either in spite of or in tolerance of my own affections towards her, she became like another mother to me- one that didn't sugar coat a damn thing. We'd gotten pretty close in the months we'd known one another. In her will she'd left a small allowance and requested I tend to her gardens for however long it took for her prodigal son to come deal with her estate. Now I readily looked forward to spending my Saturdays fulfilling that obligation.

Even knowing I was getting up early tomorrow, Lark was again nagging me to go socialize, texting every half hour or so since lunch. I was almost thirty, but apparently I acted closer to forty. At least that's what Lark kept saying. I suppose that's what happens when you see more storms, you become more weathered. Besides, I liked getting an early start. Jen's house was way out there in the heavily wooded wilderness of the pacific northwest. She had spent her every spare moment on these gardens and there weren't nearly enough hours in a Saturday to keep up. Though I did try.

Lark was too young to call in response to ignored texts, but that was Lark. I was already driving home when she put in that last-ditch effort and called. Not that she actually wanted a conversation.

"Frankie," she whined endearingly, "you never come out with me anymore. You're starved for affection; you do know that. Right? And Joe asks about you every frickin' time I see him. Give him a chance! He's a nice guy. He has a successful business. And he's cuuuute." Joe wasn't just cute. The man was hot, in that gruff, lumber jack sort of way. But that was neither here nor there, and certainly not the kind of fuel I needed to give Lark to feed this little imaginary fire of hers.

Besides, I'd slept with Joe a few months back. Something else she very much didn't need to know about. It was only ever going to be that one-time thing. My numbness had assuaged itself momentarily, letting grief hit me squarely in the face, as it does, and in that moment I needed a warm body to help me feel again. Joe was a good friend. That was all he was ever going to be. He checked in on me occasionally. That was it.

"Yeah..." I drawled, knowing how this was going to go, "I'm good, Lark. Thanks. Maybe you and I could watch a movie tomorrow night?"

"It's been what? Over a year now?" she scolded. "When are you going to stop all this and just be *you* again?"

The silence between us fell heavy. Lark was waiting for me to get upset, desperate for hysterics. No such response would come. Mom worried about it too. But none of this actually mattered. They worried I hadn't grieved properly because I hadn't lashed out. They were hoping, waiting, for some kind of outburst or meltdown. Apparently I didn't work that way. As if

I needed one more thing to point to and wonder what the fuck was wrong with me.

"I didn't mean it like that," she said quietly, flatly. I knew she'd feel guilty later on, but she shouldn't. I simply... didn't care anymore. We'd both been abandoned as children, more or less, by our own biological families. That's how we came to be sisters. We're some of the lucky ones, our adoptive parents are wonderful. But we all still had our moments when we'd tiptoe around one another, for better or worse.

"Don't worry about it. Have fun tonight and be safe. Love you, La—"

She hung up. Our conversation was over, and Lark never let anyone say goodbye. She could be a bit dramatic that way, but did anyone ever bother her about that? No, of course not.

It's not that I hadn't grieved or that I wasn't over it. It's just that some things happen in your life that change who you are. They are quite literally life changing events. You go through the thing, it changes you, then you're changed. You're different. No big deal. Those that really love you, will still love you. No one else in our family seemed to mind as much. After a few months they'd stopped asking me how I was doing in that god forsaken, sympathetic tone that made my skin crawl. I was still at family dinners every Tuesday night. I'd gotten a new job. I paid my bills. I took care of myself. I attended their celebrations. I just didn't invest in anything anymore. I didn't need, anymore. It was fine.

I was fine.

CHAPTER

TWO

The couple of hours before sunrise are an inimitable time reserved only for those willing to put up with the asininity of getting up so damned early. It's magic in a way though and can feel like you're stealing time. It's also quite solitary. But I never was much of an early bird. Not before I had my reasons to be. Reasons that are hard to remember when your alarm starts going off at 4 a.m.. There's a trick to it though- don't think about it.

Once upon a time I would drive with my music playing so loudly that I could feel it in my bones. The noise would drown everything out, and I'd find this oddly peaceful contentment. It was like its own kind of Zen. Now? Now there wasn't anything to drown out.

It was barely dawn as I turned down the long, dirt drive that led to Jen's house. It wasn't the roughest road around, but it wasn't far from it. Bordered on both sides with a dense forest of conifers, two cars could barely pass without brushing up against one another or a tree or two. This is not a road to go quickly down. My little hatchback didn't have the suspension it once did, so it wasn't an issue for me regardless. I still had to hit my brakes agonizingly hard when a large mound of red, illuminated only by my headlights and just a hint of sunrise, suddenly appeared in the middle of the road.

A heap of antlers crowned the mass of fur as it lay clustered up together in the middle of the road. He wasn't sprawled out, so I didn't think he'd been hurt. I gently honked my horn at him, well, as gently as one can do such a thing. He didn't even flinch. Nothing. I didn't dare drive around him. Elk can be extremely aggressive, and I mostly knew not be stupid trying to get him to move. I opened my door, standing behind it, one foot out of the vehicle and one still in, thinking I could slip back in pretty quickly if need be. "Hey buddy," I cooed at him, assuming we were on friendly terms, "this isn't the best place for naps."

Having somewhat stepped outside of my vehicle, I could see him more clearly. I still couldn't believe what a deep and dark red coat he had. It gave the impression of dried blood, even in this lighting. Picking his head up, he looked over at me and slowly decided to stand, the ground practically shaking as he did. Never in my life had I seen an elk this massive. To be fair, this was also the first time I'd ever been this close to a live one. His shoulders alone must have been seven or eight feet tall. Through the narrow opening of the road and framed by the lining from the trees, his antlers seemed to stretch up into the strip of sky and still visible stars.

I probably should have been much more afraid than I was. Taking only one step towards me before stopping, he barked at me, firmly elevating my level of fear. There was something otherworldly about it though- it was deeper than a normal elk bark, and I swear I could actually feel the vibrations from it as it rippled through the air towards me. I was stupid for getting out of my car. But I wasn't *that* stupid. I fell, quite inelegantly, back into my seat, keeping my eyes on the elk until turning my head for a mere second when I couldn't seem to grab the buckle. When I looked back, he was gone. I let out a long and exaggerated breath, letting some of my anxiety go with it.

A few minutes later and I was finally at Jen's house. I loved this house. Macabre Victorian is what we'd call it now. I think it was just Jen's style. Dark, elegant, and foreboding, in a cozy way. The whole house was painted gray and had darker gray shingles and matching shutters. On the left side there were bay windows on the top and bottom floors. On the right, the first floor was recessed with a covered porch and a walkout balcony above it. Her solar powered motion sensor light that kicked on as you pulled in was beside that porch. There was a sunroom on the back side with another walkout balcony above it and the whole house was surrounded by a variety of gardens bordered by dense forest.

Jen's Jeep had been parked about as close to the porch as you could get. Both the house and her sideview mirror had the marks to prove that sometimes she would get even closer. Now it was parked far enough off that I could see the old tire indents. Apprehension blew through me like a cold breeze as I got out of my car. I'd dressed light for the weather, knowing I'd warm up once I got going in the gardens. Black leggings with pockets large enough that they were my go-to pair, and starting to get a bit worn as such, a somewhat distressed tank top under a well-worn hoodie that mostly covered my ass, and a headband that kept my fly away curls out of my face. I looked a mess, but I hadn't expected to see anyone. One of the perks of this obligation.

I let myself into the house that had at one point felt bizarrely, innately like home. The electricity had since been turned off, and it was still too early for any outside light to be penetrating through the windows. I was a little on edge as I timidly called out into the dark, "Hello?"

I didn't really expect an answer as I crossed the threshold. Maybe I'd somehow moved Jen's Jeep and had completely forgotten about it. That could have happened. Maybe.

An answer came though. A bit apprehensive itself, it was deep, melodic, and a little unsure itself. "Hello?" Something screamed inside me to turn back the way I'd come. Something else held me in place. An obnoxiously bright light appeared and slowly drew near, accompanied by steady footsteps. "Can I help you?"

"Oh," I hadn't actually expected anyone to be here, let alone someone with a sense of ownership. "I'm sorry. I take care of the gardens. I noticed—"

Walking out of the darkness like an apparitional beacon of destiny, a concurrent warning and calling, he held a camping lantern up to inspect me. All I could see with the light shining in my eyes was that he was taller than me and had the kind of rugged nose that might have been broken a time or two.

"You're Frankie? The lawyer mentioned you come out on the weekends." He extended his hand which I silently, reluctantly took. "I'm Jen's son, Briar." His tone softened drastically, and I could feel the tension leave my shoulders as he shook my hand. His skin was noticeably, almost uncomfortably, warm. He must have had a fire going in whatever room he'd just come from.

"Yeah, hi... I noticed the Jeep had been moved and thought I'd—"

"What? Make sure there wasn't a burglar in the house?" He snorted at the idea as I rolled my eyes in the lantern light and turned to go back outside.

"Hey! Apologies, I wasn't trying to be an ass," he halfheartedly apologized. Yeah, he was Jen's son alright.

I cursed silently as he followed me outside. It was still dark out, but not as dark as it was inside. "I've been here a couple days now, packing up. If there's anything of hers you're interested in, feel free to grab it. I'm pretty much getting rid of it all."

His indifference didn't sit well with me. This was his mother's home, after all. It'd been a few months since she passed, yes, but I still couldn't imagine this not being her home. Admittedly I hadn't known her for very long, but that woman had saved me.

"I took a couple of pictures already. I can make you copies?"

"That's okay," he laughed. I could tell I was being weird, but I couldn't seem to help it. "You were close with my mom." He wasn't asking.

"I guess? We didn't know each other for very long." I wanted this conversation to be over. "Well, if you need help or anything let me know. I'll be out here most of the day." I could see him better now. I must have woken him up. He was only wearing sweatpants, walking around barefoot and shirtless in the cold, crisp fall morning. Odd marks marred his chest and arms and I tried hopelessly not to stare. His short black hair was messy and laid weird in certain spots and his dark eyes seemed to find something funny about all of this. I think he must have been desperate for some company.

"Isn't it a bit early? The sun isn't even up yet," he asked hesitantly.

"I can see fine." I knew my tone was getting a little short, but something about him made me nervous.

We stood for a moment, awkwardly looking around. Neither of us knowing what to say or do to move this along. The open space and blue light of the early morning were working to put me at ease. He wasn't as tall as I'd thought, but his broad shoulders made him still somewhat intimidating. He made no move to leave, and I thought I should try to be amiable for Jen's sake. "Jen said you work in the military or something?"

"Or something. Yeah." His small smile annoyed me. I didn't know what he found so amusing. Jen didn't talk about him much. Why did he have to follow me out here?

"Well, there's a lot to do, so I'm gonna get started." I headed to the shed to grab my supplies.

He called after me again, "Could you use some help?"

I turned to look at him. I didn't understand why he'd want to. He seemed nervous as he crossed his arms over his chest. I didn't answer immediately, wondering why he was anxiously tapping his fingers against himself. He tilted his head down as he peered up at me and I realized he was asking for my permission. He casually looked away from me as he explained, "Mom never liked me in her gardens. It'd be nice... to help take care of her last one."

With my hands on the ground, working, I felt at ease. It was soothing to me. And I liked being left alone as I worked. This could very well be the last day I'd be wanted here and I wasn't quite ready for that. Especially to have my last day here preoccupied with someone else. Even still, I could tell this meant a great deal to him.

"Sure," was all I could think to say. I hate that word. It means yes, when the answer must be yes. And if ever an answer needed to be yes, it was here.

There were about four acres of gardens encircling the house, all laid out and productive right up to the edge of the woods. Our winters weren't terrible but there was still a lot of work to do to prepare, and I didn't entirely know what I was doing. But there was something about being involved in the process that made my heart happy, even through my comfortable numbness.

"If it's a bother...."

His strong voice, now smaller, brought me back to my senses. Just because my day was disrupted didn't mean I needed to be an asshole. I don't know what happened between the two of them, but she was still his mother, and this couldn't be easy for him.

"It's no bother, really." I forced myself to give him a small, but genuinely warm smile. "And I'm sure your mom would have appreciated the thought."

He nodded and ran back into the house to get dressed. I thought about texting Lark that I wasn't alone out here. Not that it would matter. The text would never get through until I got back to the main road, or my body was found miles away, possibly months later, if ever. But he didn't really seem like a sociopath. Then again, it wasn't like I had the best track record when it came to identifying psychos.

Briar and I set to work with enough distance between us that general conversation felt forced. We worked all day like that, section by section, mostly in blissful silence, trimming, removing the tops of some plants for the compost pile, and leaving the roots to nourish the soil. I'd planned on mixing in some ashes later on as well, but we'd see what time allowed. Dropping armfuls of plant matter into the compost bin was the only time we really interacted.

"Not sure if there's much point in adding to this," I mused aloud, curious if he was relocating or selling. He simply smiled at me before going back for the last of the compost. I think he knew his presence was somewhat intrusive, and it was kind of him, in a way, to try and preserve what I loved about this.

"I'm gonna head over to the rose garden," I called back to him.

Jen's rose garden was a small area she'd made for no reason other than to have a place to sit and relax. It was the most uncharacteristic thing I'd ever known her to do. This particular garden was outlined with juniper bushes as a way to further separate the area. Walking over I noticed one of the bushes had nearly all brown needles. A wild ivy had been strangling it. I wasn't sure how I hadn't seen it before. This sort of thing doesn't exactly happen overnight, or over the course of a week, and I was certain it hadn't been like this last Saturday. I pulled the ivy off of the juniper and pulled as much of it out of the ground as I could. The juniper needed healing the way Jen had taught me. I had to redirect its own energy and likely put some of my own into it. She'd compared this technique to talking with your plants, aggressively. I knew that was bunk and that this wasn't normal. That it didn't make sense. The word *magic* had crossed my mind more than once, but I never did ask her too many questions.

My mother would have called her a forest witch, if I'd ever told my mother about any of this. I'd learned not to talk about the crazy people in your life. Some people just liked to live in the middle of the woods and didn't want to be bothered. It sounded lovely enough to me, but I don't think I'd survive well away from everyone for too long. Even if that was what I wanted. But what did I know.

Briar was still over at the compost pile. I didn't know what he knew, so I needed to act quickly. I knelt down in front of the juniper and placed my hands in the dirt on either side of its trunk. Closing my eyes, I pulled the energy from myself as Jen had taught me. Letting it travel through me, out to my hands, through the soil, and into the plant. Examining at first, restructuring, reweaving its life tapestry. Then forcing it to grow back healthy under my fingers. Just enough so that it could come back the rest of the way on its own. Eyes closed and wholly occupied in my endeavor, I saw my energy flowing through it, browned needles turning a fresh, vibrant green.

"Not bad." I jumped at his voice behind me but quickly settled myself, trying my damnedest to not give him the satisfaction of catching me off guard. "But if you place your hands like this," he knelt beside me and laid his hands on the soil. Only slightly differing from where mine had been, though at a sharper angle to be sure. "It'll be easier for your energy to flow." I glared at him, annoyed at him for sneaking up on me, suspicious that he knew anything about this. His mother didn't seem to trust him. I was surprised she'd taught him this. He ignored my glower, and I eventually resumed my position, careful to place my hands where his had been. I moved more energy into the plant. He was right. It was easier, faster, more efficient.

I managed to mumble, "Thanks," as he stood and offered me his hand. I didn't take it.

"You know, there aren't many of us that can do that anymore." I could feel his eyes on me, unperturbed at my attempt to keep my distance.

"I only know what your mom taught me." I crossed my arms in front of myself and began walking away.

"I could teach you," he called after me. I took another step before my feet failed me and I froze, considering. "If you want." I did want to know more. Jen had said there wasn't anything else. I knew she was lying. Still, I didn't trust this man.

I turned back to him slowly. He knew he had me. Hesitantly I probed, "Jen told me not to do too much, to not overdo it."

"Yeah, that sounds like mom." He clicked his tongue and seemed to question if he should go on. "You can build up your heart's energy though. It's like building up any muscle. You need to push yourself a little to create microtears and it will heal back stronger so you can endure more, build up your ability, push more, do more. But yes, you have to be careful to not overdo it. You can seriously hurt yourself if you're not careful."

"What did you call it? Heart's energy?"

"What *did* she teach you?" He squinted his eyes at me in disbelief at how little I knew as the familiar sound of disdain echoed through my head. Right.

Don't ask questions.

Before my now family I'd get in trouble for asking questions. I began explaining all over myself to him, hoping to not come off as too pathetic. "I think maybe she just needed some help, so she taught me a weird thing to help her plants. She never really went into it. I didn't ask any questions. I was worried she'd stop teaching me if I asked the wrong thing. By the time I worked up the nerve to, it seemed... well, it seemed silly when I'd seen for a while that it worked, and that I could do it." I was angry at how defensive and frustrated I'd become. Nearly on the verge of tears and not really sure why, I spun away from him, hoping he wouldn't see.

Kindly, softly, he affirmed, "You're upset."

Fuck.

I never have been good at hiding my emotions.

"I'm not. I just... need a minute." I walked off towards my car. I knew it was ridiculous that I was feeling overwhelmed like this, but it happened so easily anymore. It was as though I couldn't even handle the smallest feeling. I lived in a state of masked numbness, going through the motions mostly. I didn't even notice it anymore. I preferred it that way. There'd be the occasional spark of sentiment, and everything would suddenly be too much for me to manage. I'd tried some anti-anxiety meds but none of them had really agreed with me. I didn't hear Briar follow and I didn't turn around to check either. I thought about getting into my car and leaving for good. Again, something stopped me.

Instead I veered toward the front porch as though I'd planned to all along. I glanced over to see him still standing where I'd left him. He was facing away from me, watching the sun start its descent into the tips of the trees. It was only late-afternoon, but the house was in a kind of valley surrounded by these wooden giants and this time of year the sun would dip down for an hour or two before technically setting, giving us a couple hours of light limbo.

After a while, with a relaxed, slow stride, hands in his pockets, he made his way to the front porch. I suppose he didn't want to catch me off guard. I'd pulled myself back together by then, but his consideration annoyed me. And feeling had exhausted me.

He walked up the porch steps and sat down in the patio chair next to me. I would have apologized, but he spoke before I had the chance.

"She told me about you, ya know? She talked about you a lot in her letters. That's why I was surprised. By how little she told you, I mean. That's on her, not you. I guess it was her way of trying to protect you, but it feels dangerous to me. And wrong. If you want to learn, I want to teach you. I could show you what else you can do with your energy. There's so much more to it than just healing some garden plants. I can stay longer, take more time off. I'm in no rush."

It'd be a lie to say I wasn't tempted. But I didn't need anything to change in my life. "That's sweet of you, but I don't want to be a bother."

He smiled at me, returning my words. "No bother." He'd leaned forward in his chair, relaxed but still fidgeting with his hands.

"Your mom meant a lot to me." He looked at me with a tender smirk and said nothing. "She could be... surly, but she was a sweetheart, deep down." He reactively snorted and I laughed in turn. "Once you got to know her!"

We smiled at each other for too long. I knew most people didn't see that side of Jen. I really hoped he had.

"I know she didn't exactly exude kindness," I said, "But she didn't want anything from me except my company. There aren't a lot of people like that. She really did just want someone around to pass the time."

"She didn't just want *someone* around. She wanted *you* around. She liked *you*." He was being sincere, but there was something else to it. Still, it was nice to hear.

"Yeah, I don't get that."

"You will." He watched me intently, trying to gauge my reaction I suppose.

"Funny. She said the same thing," I recalled. Missing her was annoyingly painful, and I was ready to change the conversation. "So how long are you planning on staying?"

"Uh... I'm here until I find what I'm looking for."

"And what is that?"

He went along with the change of topic hesitantly. "A, uh... signet ring. Family heirloom sort of thing."

"I don't think Jen ever wore any jewelry."

"No, she wouldn't have." He offered no further explanation.

We spent hours talking about her as the darkness around us gradually deepened to night. It was clear he missed her too, but they'd had some kind of falling out. I didn't want to pry, but it did explain why Jen had rarely mentioned him and why I was just now getting to know him. He was funny in the same way she was. It kind of took you by surprise as they masked it behind mild exasperation. A bit crass, they'd make the sort of jokes that made you blush and wonder if you understood them all at the same time. Jen had always been amused with her ability to make me blush. She'd smile to herself, and that was always accompanied by this little heartwarming chuckle. It seemed to light up Briar's face in its own way, which only made my face redden all the more.

When I heard his stomach grumble I mentioned a pizza place not terribly far away. We took my little hatchback and headed that way, discussing the sorts of things that are easier to talk about when you're not looking at the other person. Who needs therapy when you can burden a stranger with your innermost demons and dilemmas? As awful and selfish as it sounds, I was pleased that it was reciprocal.

The pizza place was mostly for takeout, but they had a couple of booths and tables crammed into a small corner. They brought our pizza out to us, already boxed up with a menu and magnet jammed into the edge of the box. Briar grabbed them and studied it for a moment while I watched him, amused.

"Mind if I keep this?" he asked sincerely.

"What? The magnet? Knock yourself out. Not sure what good it will do you though, since you're not staying." He smiled to himself, a wistful kind of smile as he pocketed the magnet, and we dug in.

On our drive back he was mostly silent. I was surprised by the quick comfortableness of it. I went slower than usual down Jen's driveway, just in case my red elk had returned. We parked and neither of us made a move to get out. After a few moments I noticed him fidgeting with the magnet. I asked him outright why he'd wanted it since he hadn't responded to my curiosity before. He wasn't from around here; he had no plans on moving here. I didn't see the point.

"It might sound strange, but I collect memories within objects like this. When I'm home I can pull this physical piece of here out and I'll remember so much more of this place, and of you."

I rested my head back against the headrest and looked over at him. "That's a rather romantic notion. I'm a little surprised Jen's son would be so sentimental."

"There's a lot about her, and me, that would surprise you."

Laughing, I dared him, "Try me."

He turned in his seat towards me. The only light came from the motion sensor light off of the porch. It was behind him, and I could just barely see the dark of his eyes. A flash of glowing gold warmed his irises and before I could question it, he was kissing me. That had certainly taken me by surprise, but it wasn't unpleasant. His warm lips pressed against mine, waiting briefly before mine parted. His hands moved gingerly as he cupped the back of my head, shifting and angling just so as I inhaled his scent, a deep musk with a hint of smoke and leather. He was intoxicating and my hands found themselves likewise wandering to him. My heart was racing and so much of me wanted this, but enough of me knew better. It was getting too impassioned, too heated, and I had to pull back.

I fell back into my seat and turned to face forward. Biting my lower lip, I nodded slowly, unsure of what to say, but certainly surprised. He got out of the car first. I sat still, jumping when he opened my door for me. I should have just left. It was late and I had no reason to stay. But I chose to, and I let him take my hand and lead me back up to our spots on the porch there we sat, talking at times, and other times not.

CHAPTER
THREE

Moonlight gleamed on every surface that would have it as the last of the evening's clouds rolled off. I'd gone from my comfortable cold numbness to a concerned hesitancy around Briar's warmth. I knew better. This wasn't the first time, and I knew better.

The actual temperature was dropping, and I absentmindedly rubbed at the goosebumps on my arms. "We could go inside?," he offered, seeing me shiver. "Let me get the generator running and I'll turn on the heat. I need to stop into town tomorrow anyway. I can grab more fuel then. Or I could start a fire?"

"I can't believe how cold it is already. How are you not freezing?" I'd put my worn hoodie back on earlier, but he still only had a shirt on.

He shook his head, slightly boastful. "I run hot. It's got to be a lot colder than this before it even touches me. Where I'm from this would be one of our warmer days." I was about to ask where that was when we heard a vehicle coming down the drive. Unusual for a house so out here to have drop-in visitors, especially considering no one actually lived here.

"Expecting someone?" I asked, curious and slightly perturbed at the disturbance, even if it was for the best.

"You're the only one that even knows I'm out here," he said with a confidence that annoyed me. He was more intrigued by my tone and implication than the actual intrusion, which like-wise annoyed me.

"Must be nice," I mumbled as I recognized the lights of my dad's truck rambling towards us. He cocked an eye at me as I buried my face in my hands. Looking up at him I explained, "It's my dad. I'm not sure why he's here, probably checking on me. They... worry about me."

He returned my embarrassed expression with a concerned one. I shot him a warning glare not to ask when it was clear his curiosity was getting the best of him. I very much was too old to be checked in on like this, and Briar was making no effort to hide his amusement at my mortification. When he stood to get a better view of the quickly encroaching vehicle, I swear I heard a muffled laugh. It was only slightly endearing.

"Ah, fuck!" I groaned and joined him at the top of the porch stairs. "It's my sister." He nudged me with his elbow and shot me an earnest grin as Lark jumped out of Dad's passenger door. Even in the dark she noticed Briar right away.

Of course she did.

"Frankie! So this is how you've been spending your Satur-days?!" A salacious grin spread easily across her face. She was dressed for a night out, her flashy little dress complimenting her petite figure. Her golden-brown hair had been straightened and landed low on her back, swaying as she walked up to us.

"Lark, this is Briar- Jen's son. He's here packing up the house. We just met today, so don't be an ass, okay?" He wasn't exactly her type, but I didn't need the barrage of inevitable innuendos. "Care to tell me what you're doing all the way out here?"

"It's late! I've been texting you for a couple of hours and you've been ignoring me," she chastised before turning to unashamedly look Briar up and down again. "Nice to see why though," she said in a voice that had turned honeyed and hopeful.

Lark, always the dreamer.

"You *know* I don't get service out here. I'm fine! And did you really have to drag Dad along?" It was my turn to lecture her, and it needed to be done before the situation escalated.

"What is your problem?!" she scoffed. "There are bears and things out here! I didn't know what had happened to you. Mom and the boys said I was being crazy, so I asked Dad."

"Dad thinks you're being crazy too, he just spoils you. I am *fine*. Just heading out actually." I made a point to not look at Briar as I said this and tried ushering Lark away from the porch, and him. Dad was leaning against his truck, wearing his usual jeans and flannel. He was looking away from us, not wanting to intrude but making sure his presence was known by all. "Hey Dad!" I called, settling down somewhat. "Sorry to worry you."

"Y'alright there?" he asked flatly with the barest touch of concern. The way he was leaning exaggerated how slim of a man he was and for a moment I couldn't help but see how much older he'd become.

"Yeah, Dad. I'm fine. Come on, Lark. Time to go." I tried pulling her away again to no avail.

"Don't be rude, Frankie. Introduce us," Lark teased.

Unfortunately I had enough manners to know I actually should introduce Briar and my dad to one another. I hesitated, desperately not wanting to prolong this interaction any further. Shoulders slumped, I sighed heavily as I did my mother proud and followed through. "Dad, this is Briar, Jen's son. Briar, this is my dad, Teddy."

Briar descended the steps briskly and both men took long steps towards one another. They shook hands and there was a sense of rigidity in the air as Lark and I watched, both of us trying our best not to roll our eyes, as the two men sized one another up.

"And I'm Lark. Frankie's favorite sister," Lark sidestepped me and scurried towards Briar to take his hand.

"Only sister," I chimed in unnecessarily. Briar's half smile nearly undid me, and I had to look away.

Lark ignored me, as she does. "Briar, Frankie and I are going out for drinks tonight if you want to join us?"

I shook my head and started walking to my car. Dad was wise enough to not get involved and retired to the driver's seat of his truck.

Lark was practically staring Briar down as I called to them both, "Don't believe a word she says! Goodbye, Briar. It was nice to meet you. Good luck with the house."

"Frankie." The way he said my name as he nodded farewell sent a shiver up and down my spine. Some part of me hoped I'd be seeing him again. I bit the side of my mouth, hating myself for wanting. Lark talked to him for another minute before going over to the driver's side of Dad's truck. He turned his truck around as Lark walked towards me and I not-so-silently wondered what the fuck she was doing.

"Relax. You're giving me a ride and we're going out tonight. I saw how you two were looking at each other." She buckled her seatbelt and turned to me, beaming at my scowl.

"You don't know what you're talking about. Besides, he's Jen's son. It'd be... I don't know, kinda weird." Briar was now watching us from the porch; his arms again folded across his chest. I waived one last, subtle goodbye and he nodded in response.

"See?" Lark chirped as I started my car.

"Huh," I muttered, "Do you think he can actually see me? It's so dark out."

"Now *you* are being kinda weird. Girl, let's go!"

I didn't go quite as slowly down the lengthy drive as I should have, relishing all the grumbling maybe a bit too much.

"Seriously though, he is Jen's son and there are so many similarities between the two of them. I don't know, it just doesn't seem like a good idea to me."

"Why? Because she's dead? If she wasn't it would seem pretty kismet to me. You two look good together."

"He's leaving in a few days."

"That's perfect! I didn't say fall in love. He's handsome, in that rugged man sort of way that you like. Have some fun!"

"Why are you so interested in getting me laid?"

"It's an important part of the healing process, Frankie." Lark was working on her PsyD and had this annoying psychologist voice she'd fall into once in a while as if we were her patients. Hearing her use it now as she was talking about me sleeping with Briar was one of the funniest things I'd experienced in a long while. I broke into an old, uncontrollable laugh that she always found contagious. I couldn't remember the last time I'd laughed with her like that. It used to happen so easily before. I could see what my laughter, and hers, meant, what moments like this meant to her, and it hurt.

We went to my place after I reluctantly agreed to go out. While I showered the day off, trying very hard to not think about Briar, Lark tried to pick out the most scandalous outfit of mine that she could find. Much to her chagrin, it wasn't really all that bad. Just a dark green skater dress that worked with my ample curves, low cut, and with an obnoxiously short hemline.

The color really made my copper curls and green eyes pop. She was shocked when I agreed to wear it, but her face fell seeing me grab a pair of leggings to go underneath and a black wrap to cover up with. "You're no fun!" she not-so-playfully admonished. I shrugged it off as I fought with my hair and put on the barest of makeup. Realizing how hopeful of seeing him again I was becoming, I thought about calling it off. As if I even could. Lark would never have forgiven me.

Joe's Hookah Lounge was just down the street, so there really wasn't any good reason to go anywhere else. At least not one I could think of to tell Lark that wouldn't give me away. I counted my lucky stars that Joe was out of town that night. Introducing him and Briar would have simply been too awkward. We'd gone upstairs to the lounge and took a spot near the windows. By the time I'd had two drinks, the coal on the hookah needed ashing. My spark of hope was dying down too, and I was ready to call it. I told Lark I'd be leaving after the next drink.

"He'll be here." She smiled at me in her own kindly reassuring way that I hadn't realized I'd missed. "It's nice to see you acting more like your old self."

"And what exactly does that mean? Maybe I'm just getting too old for this?" I didn't mean for it to sound as snide as it did.

"Okay, well, right this minute you're anxious, clearly. But you know that's not what I mean. You're hopeful! Before, you were just kind of existing. Going through the motions only because it was easier than not. Now you're excited and I can see the life in your eyes! Just remember- he is a stepping stone, not the landing. I won't have you breaking again."

"I would hope I wouldn't need someone to be happy." I leered at her. I knew what she meant, and she knew me.

"Look, I get it. You've been hurt. A lot. Like, a lot a lot. More than any... well, I've had to watch you give up, more and more.

Or at least, I did. You don't seem like you've given up now, and that's enough for me." She leaned over and hugged me. She wasn't completely wrong, but I wasn't about to admit that to her.

Another hour passed without him showing up. I could feel myself getting buzzed, and hurt, and angry. "Alright, Lark. I'm done now. Really."

"Frankie, it doesn't make sense! We should go check on him. You should have seen how his eyes lit up when I promised I could get you to go out." I couldn't look at her. I didn't believe her, and I didn't want to hear it. I couldn't believe how stupid I'd been, again.

We walked back to my apartment, the cold sobering us both. As well as the truck tacos we picked up outside of the bar. Lark seemed more upset than I was. "You should go give him a piece of your mind!" She kept huffing as she paced around my apartment.

Her anger overwhelmed mine, and I was again letting go of my own emotions. It was easier this way. "Don't be silly. He's here packing up his dead mother's things. Maybe he thought better of going out to drinks with some strangers."

"Yeah, but we're cute strangers! And you spent all day with him, and apparently Jen told him all about you, whatever that means. That's not what I'd call a stranger!" I glared at her, not entirely disagreeing with her reasoning.

"Just drop it. It doesn't matter and I'm tired." And I really didn't want to think about it or him or anything. Honestly that'd been the first time in a while that I'd had a chance to really catch up with her. Yes, I was hurt. But I didn't regret having gone out for one minute, and I was too tired to dwell on any of it.

· · ·

THAT NIGHT I had a dream about my red elk and Briar. I was following above from the sky. Frightened, but I didn't know from what. Maybe I was afraid for the elk, I wasn't sure. Briar was frightened or furious and running. I could hear Lark calling to me. And then she was shaking me awake.

"It was just a weird dream," I kept trying to convince her. I was covered in sweat and had apparently been calling out to someone.

"Maybe you should call Mom and tell her about it?" She looked concerned, which annoyed me.

"No. You know she always sees the worst in all my dreams. It would just make her worry." Mom could be a bit out there, goddess bless her! But something was off. I couldn't shake it, parts of the dream kept creeping back in.

"I think I'm gonna go out and make sure he's okay."

"Frankie, NO! Don't waste any more time on that guy." Her voice was dripping with incredulity.

"What the hell?! You told me yesterday I should go give him a piece of my mind!"

She frowned and grumbled her frustrations. We were having a hard time finding one another again and I couldn't help but blame myself. It didn't help that I was pretty sure she was doing the same thing. We'd get there eventually- we always did. That was one thing about Lark and me, we never gave up on each other. Never, ever.

After she left I debated for another hour about whether or not I should go back out to Jen's. I still couldn't shake my dream; it had felt too real. An hour after that I was turning down Jen's drive, slowly, shifting between anxiety and anger.

When the jeep wasn't in the driveway, I thought about leaving.

Almost noon when I found myself again apprehensively calling out as I stepped into the house. "Hello?" I nearly left after a few moments of silence when I finally heard him coming from down the hall.

"Frankie?" His voice was rough, and he looked worse. Shirtless again. He was bruised all up and down one side with a black eye, dried blood on his face, a mangled hand, and an arm that wasn't laying like it should be.

"Briar? What happened?" I asked flatly as I moved towards him, the familiar sickly-sweet scent of iron filling my nose. My *handle-it* mode leftover from my days as a trauma nurse had been activated. I guess some people were still worth fixing to me. He seemed completely at ease being this battered up. Almost as if he was used to it.

Reluctantly he explained, "I'm not sure. I was heading to town, and something hit the jeep. Hard. It rolled into the woods and stopped against one of those huge trees." My dream flashed through my mind, and I felt my stomach drop.

"Jesus, Briar, why are you here and not the hospital?! Come on." I grabbed the hand that wasn't mangled and tried pulling him with me. He didn't budge. Instead, he pulled my hand towards him and kissed it gently. My eyes widened in disbelief as I felt my cheeks flush. He winced as he tried to smile at me.

He was a lot calmer than I would have expected him to be. I'd seen a lot of people with far less damage act hysterically. It didn't seem to bother him. Military, or something. Right. I kept forgetting that.

"I'm not going to the hospital. I just need to rest. I'm sorry I wasn't there last night." His voice was still rough, but gentler now. "I didn't know how to get a hold of you."

"Don't be stupid! You're lucky to be alive." I moved around him to look him over more thoroughly. "I think your arm is broken."

"It was. I set it already." He leaned against the wall, his eyes heavy.

"If you didn't do that properly—"

"I know, Frankie. And I did it properly. Believe me."

"You're sure you won't go to the hospital?" I knew better than to argue with a child of Jen's. That woman was the definition of stubborn.

"It's hard to tell you no, but no." I couldn't believe he was actually still flirting given the amount of pain he had to be in.

For what little good it would do me, I bristled at his stubbornness. "Come on then, you need to rest. You won't go to the hospital? Fine- but I'm not leaving until I know you're okay."

He nodded somberly. He wanted to argue, but he likewise knew better. Really I think he just wanted to get the last word in, but he let it go. Walking down the hall I put an arm around his waist and his arm over my shoulder to stabilize his movements. He grumbled a bit but kept walking towards the bedroom he'd been using.

"Are you sure you set that right?" I eyed his arm suspiciously.

He gave me an amused look as he answered, "Yes, I'm sure." He seemed confident enough that I wasn't going to push it again, for now.

Jen didn't have much in the way of a first aid kit, but I kept a decent one in my car. He was nearly asleep when I got back to the room, but his eyes never left me. I sat on the edge of the bed, careful not to brush up against him as I cleaned his wounds, washing off the dried blood as I went. I could feel myself blushing as he watched me. I'd meet his gaze every once in a while, but I was always the one to look away, feigning the need to continuously be cleaning him up. I worked in silence, not knowing what to say. I felt an odd kind of ease with him, just as I had with Jen.

His face cleaned, I broke open a cold pack and gently placed it on his black eye. He groaned from the contact. "Sorry. Is it okay?"

He took my hand and kissed it again. "Yes, thank you," he whispered as he held the pack to his eye. "Lay down with me?"

I laughed nervously and shook my head. "Get some rest. I'll be out in the sitting room if you need anything."

"I don't want you to go." He barely knew me and was already able to play me like this. I cursed myself for it, but couldn't stop myself, or didn't want to. I was still thinking about that kiss last night.

"Fine," I mumbled as I laid on my side, facing him as I stayed as close to the edge as I could without falling off. He looked perturbed. "What?"

"*Fine.* That's not what I want to hear the next time you lay down with me."

I couldn't help but roll my eyes at him through my inadvertently coquettish laugh. What the hell was wrong with me?! I really was too old for this shit. "You're supposed to be getting some rest," I playfully chided him and his charming but bruised smile.

"You could try to heal me."

I choked down a laugh remembering Lark's plan for me to heal myself.

"I'm serious. You have a gift for healing plants. We're not so different. And I really could use some help." The blood drained from my face. He was actually serious. "You didn't know you could heal us." He wasn't asking.

My answer came slowly. "No. I wasn't kidding when I told you everything Jen taught me or even told me was how to align my energy and help plants."

"I am sorry. I really do think she was trying to protect you."

"You keep saying that, but you want to teach me and have me get stronger. So what? You don't want to protect me? Not that I'm buying *any* of that. Besides, what on Earth would either of you be protecting me from?" I'd hoped to mask my hurt with genuine curiosity. He had the wherewithal to at least go along with the facade, even if it wasn't successful.

"I want to protect you from the world, which means making sure you get stronger. Mom was trying to protect the world from you, which means stopping you from trying to heal every single thing you come across that needs it. Promise me you won't use this to heal like that? Not everyone. Not everyone deserves it."

"You know none of that makes sense. But if you're not full of it and I can actually heal you, then yes, I promise I won't use it all the time."

"Okay then. Now get on top of me."

FOUR

"It's easier than me sitting up," he offered defensively, as if I was ever going to buy that.

"Mhmm," I hummed as I sat up in the bed and scooted closer to him. "I'm sure this will be fine."

"It won't be as effective, but that's fine. Suffering and I are old friends," he said, his sly expression showing just a hint of bruised ego. Seeing him lay there, vulnerable, and still being cheeky, forced a small, playfully derisive laugh out of me. His eyes lit up as he held my gaze. "Even your disdainful laugh is beautiful," he teased, moving his hand to rest against my outer thigh.

"I'm sure it is," I said, picking up his hand and returning it back to his chest. "Shall we begin?" I wasn't exactly in a rush to call him out on his bullshit, but I was curious to see where this was going.

He lifted his good hand and offered it to me. "Relax. I'm going to guide you, and you need my hand for that. We're going to start with some simple meditation. To start you just need to listen to my voice. Once you're comfortable we can begin sensing your energy, pulling at it, and we'll see what we can do." I was beyond nervous. Why, I couldn't say. With more than a little hesitation, I did as he asked and took his hand. "Good. Now place your other hand on my broken arm."

"Okay. I'm ready," I said as I shifted myself more towards him to get a better angle. My mouth felt dry all of a sudden and I could feel my pulse quicken. Briar's subsequent smirk did not go unnoticed.

"I told you it'd be easier if...." He wisely let it go after seeing my glare. "We'll start with some awareness. Close your eyes. Breathe normally, make sure you're comfortable." His voice slowed and his tone lowered. "Be aware of how you are, what your body is touching, the air as it brushes over you, your hand in mine. Notice the warmth and coolness of these sensations. Be aware of the pressures in and on your body. Start to notice any internal energies, where they are, how they're moving." He slowed even more as I actually began to notice... *something*. He started giving longer and longer pauses between his instructions. "Breathe deeply as you continue to notice these things. - Keep breathing deeply and settling into yourself. - Take note of where your energy is flowing to and from. - Follow the flow of your energy as it moves with your breath. - Notice the movements as you pause between inhaling and exhaling. Watch it. Be aware of it within you."

My body had relaxed. I could sense my energy and follow its flow in a way I never had before. Jen had taught me enough about feeling for my energies and aligning them that I'd been able to sense mine, but never observe it like this. With Briar's help it became so much more corporeal, so much more *real*. I could see it as flames of gold inside my chest that would rise and expand before falling and retreating with each breath. "Is it weird that I see it as a color?" So much of this work only appeared as a scale of gray.

His gentle grip tightened. "It's not weird at all, Frankie. That's fantastic." I could feel the blood rushing to my face. Then it hit me, again- how much I was feeling. It wouldn't end well. That realization gave me pause and of course Briar noticed. He always seemed to notice everything.

"Keep breathing naturally. Stay aware of your body. When you have a thought, welcome it, experience it, observe it, then let it go. Air brushes over you, let the thought brush over you. Don't evaluate. It's not good or bad. It doesn't need to be dealt with now. Right now, breathe. Follow the flow of energies."

He was silent for a while as I kept watching my golden fire move through me, rising and expanding, falling and retreating. I was becoming more aware of the cold in the room, and I could feel the temperature drop on my arms. Maybe I should have thought to start a fire. "You need to go deeper. Follow your energy to its center. Don't get distracted." I tried to follow it, but it felt forced and the closer I got to it, the more it felt like it was burning me. "You need to relax. Remember to breathe. Loosen up your body. Let the stress melt away."

I tried again and only got minimally deeper. "You've done so well, Frankie. Let's stop here for now." I didn't want to stop. I hadn't done anything to help him yet. Maybe he didn't think I could.

When he went to let go of my hand I grabbed onto his. "I want to keep going," I said, opening my eyes to plead with him. "I want to see if I can do it. Unless you really are full of it...."

He acknowledged my goading with a smirk, but I hadn't needed to convince him that way. He wanted me to keep going, but he wouldn't push. "Breathe out the stress and let yourself in," he resumed. I kept trying over and over and could only make it an imperceptible dash deeper. I was beyond frustrated. "If you'd like, I could help."

"Yes!" My answer came out louder than I had expected. "Please," I whispered modestly.

"You'll have to let me in. You'll feel it where our hands meet. It will be a different energy. Mine will be a different color. Are you ready?"

I was a little uncomfortable, unsure of what was to come. Nevertheless, I was excited for it. "I'm ready."

Instantaneously an unnerving warmth radiated from his hand. It moved swiftly like my own energy, but it wasn't a fire. Not as concrete as mine either, and it didn't move the same way. Not exactly. It seemed to *fly* more than *burn* and his was more copper than my gold. Not huge differences, but clear and distinct ones. His energy crept along mine. I tensed up and he stopped. "We don't have to do this. Ever. If you don't want to. We can also try again later, if you decide that's what you want." He squeezed my hand reassuringly.

I let out a long breath. "No, I'm okay. It just... is it supposed to feel so intimate? I didn't expect that, just give me a moment?"

He pulled his energy back a little. "It is a very intimate thing. To let someone else's energy inside you like this." He began to pull it back completely.

"WAIT!" I reached out with my own energy and entwined it with his. He made a soft, almost painful gasp. "I'm sorry! That wasn't okay of me," I said timidly, not really sure how this worked. I didn't want to stop. It was uncomfortable, but not unpleasant.

His voice was huskier when he answered me, "That was... fine, but please don't surprise me like that again."

"I'm so sorry. I'm not sure how I did that! Or what I even did?"

"Frankie," his voice was low, "I think we should stop now."

"But we haven't even tried to heal you yet!"

I could sense his contemplation as he went back and forth trying to figure out how to proceed. *"Fine,"* he finally grumbled.

Amused at his diction and excited to possibly learn something new, I let out an obnoxious, "ha!".

He sweetly grabbed my hand tighter for just a second. "It's a similar process to healing plants. Sense the layout and see how the tapestry is meant to exist. With us it's important to be a bit more precise. Plant tapestries aren't always as specific as ours, they are simpler in many ways, but we also don't often worry about killing one or two of them. I would very much prefer it if you don't kill me." I tried taking my hand from him and he laughed a full laugh before reeling from the pain he'd caused himself.

"You're not going to kill me. I'll be guiding you. We can't use our own energy on ourselves, not to this extent, it becomes... unsound. But we can guide others to help us. Frankie, I got you."

"You better," I said, hating myself for it.

"Always," he promised. "Let's focus on my arm. See its tapestry. The weave, the pattern, the weft and warp, the threads within threads that make it what it is. Sense it. Can you see how it's not as it should be right now?"

"It looks angry at the points where it's messed up, red and tattered. But the pattern seems clear enough. It's like your body has already started to heal itself, your energy is trying to pull everything back into place."

"Good. Move those threads as you do with the plants. Guide them while giving as little of your own energy to heal them as possible. And be careful. This is somewhat painful for me."

"Okay," I said shakily as I began mending the innermost threads, working my way out. The realigning was easy enough, moving his body's smallest structures to where they should be, where they wanted to be, but there were so many broken and missing pieces. Creating and replacing those took a lot of my own energy as I healed him. It actually felt good to be this exhausted again.

"Don't push yourself, Frankie."

"How does it feel now?" I was nearly done with his arm.

"Good as new," he said. My eyes popped open feeling his once mangled hand move to cup my face.

"It worked?!" Shock unashamedly permeated my words. I couldn't believe it.

"It worked," he mused. "You did well." He moved his hand from my face, and my eyes followed it as he stretched out his arm and fingers, demonstrating just how well I had done. I looked down and he met my gaze. My smile faded as I watched his face darken, his eyes growing hungry.

I leaned down and kissed him. Between his palpable desire, me not being able to forget the kiss from last night, the adrenaline from this newfound knowledge- I didn't even think about it. Maybe that was the trick here, too. I could feel our energies all over again. Fire and wind whirled together and became entangled. He put his arms around me, pulling me down on top of him. As I submitted, feeling his too warm chest against me, a muffled groan of pain escaped him. "You're still hurt," I said as I sat back up, much to his protest.

"I could *not* care less right now," he insisted. "Please come back." When I refused, he tried sitting up. The task made arduous by unmistakably broken ribs.

"Let me finish healing you," I begged as I tried placing my hands on his bare chest. He grabbed them before I could.

"You can't. Believe me. With what you've already done- it would be too much. I can deal with the pain, I promise." He'd stopped trying to sit up and was again urging me to come back down to him. I obliged and as I kissed him again his hands got lost in my hair, holding me to him. Carefully I straddled him and moved my hands to his chest. "Frankie," he growled my name with just a trace of exasperation. "What are you doing?"

"You said yourself it would be more effective this way. Now I won't be using as much energy, right?" I sat up to let him think it over.

"That's not fair," he said, staring up at me. "You're not going to take no for an answer, are you?" His hands were clasping my thighs on either side of him and he was absent-mindedly rubbing his thumbs against me as he considered the situation. "When I say stop, you *have* to stop, yes? You don't want to use too much. Trust me, okay?"

I was literally giddy about trying this out again. Exhilaration outweighed the drain I could feel on my body. He moved my hands to his chest, leaving his on top of mine near his broken ribs. "I'm going to let you take the lead. Remember, not too much. When you're ready."

Closing my eyes, I began feeling his energy. It was dancing like wisps of wind, moving through the center of his body, very close to the three broken ribs. I focused and began examining those ribs, seeing what needed to be replaced and what could simply be woven back together. I began weaving back in what I could. If I wasn't allowed to give much, the least I could do was set right what I could, while I could. Then I started in on the first rib. They were really just cracked, but I had underestimated how drained I was.

"Stop," he called, his body tensing underneath me.

"Just one more." I started working on it.

"Frankie- *STOP*." I didn't want to, but after another moment I did. I opened my eyes to see him glaring up at me, painfully angry.

"What? I stopped."

For a long moment he just stared at me. "If I'm going to teach you, I need to know you trust me."

"I do trust you, but it—"

"I need to be able to trust you, too," he admonished.

"I'm sorry." It stung to have him reprimand me like this. I looked away from him, wounded. I chastised myself for caring about him like this so quickly. But he felt different to me. He felt like a home I'd never known before. I slid off of him and stood up.

He swung his legs over the side of the bed and ran his hands through his hair. Taking my hand, he simply stared at it for a while. "Don't be sorry. Next time, listen."

"Next time? You're still going to...."

"What? Did you think I wouldn't teach you anymore?" He stood quickly and wrapped me in his arms. Surprised, I stood still, shocked for a moment. I slowly returned the embrace and nuzzled into him, inhaling deeply, trying to memorize his scent. His bare skin was so warm, too warm.

I frowned as I felt his forehead. "You have a fever."

"I don't. I run hot, remember?" He took my hand off of his forehead and kissed my palm and wrist slowly, his eyes never leaving mine. An anticipation was growing, and I began to feel lightheaded. He kept an arm around me and pulled my head towards him as he kissed me again, deeply, heatedly. He sighed huskily as I leaned into him, our bodies flush with one another. He backed me up to the bed and the room began to spin. "What's wrong?" he asked as the room began falling up and away. "Frankie?!" His hold on me tightened as my hold on the world disappeared.

~

I ROUSED SLOWLY to a crackling fire and the smell of burning wood. Realization that there were arms around me, holding me firmly, woke me up much more quickly. He spoke softly, reassuring me, "you're safe – you're okay."

"What happened?" I asked, not sure if what I was remembering was the whole of it.

"You used too much energy." There was no malice in his words, only kindness. Lark would have tormented me endlessly for having not listened. I would have deserved it.

"I don't feel right." My stomach was in knots, and even though I was under a pile of blankets, there was still a chill in my bones.

He held me tighter to his bare chest as I shivered. "I wasn't trying to be untoward. Your temperature was dropping. I made a fire and grabbed every blanket I could find. You still weren't getting any warmer. It's from using too much of your energy, but nothing was... I *had* to do something." His nervous explanation was beyond frazzled. And adorable.

Despite myself, I kissed his chest in an attempt to validate his actions. He quivered around me as he sighed deeply. "You need to eat. You'll feel better." I didn't want his arms to leave me, but I wasn't about to argue.

"I'm sorry," I whispered.

He whispered back, "Stop saying that. You have nothing to be sorry about."

"I'm sorry I didn't listen!" I shouted. "I'm sorry to be a bother. I'm sorry for passing out right when...."

He chuckled kindly. "You'll listen next time. I hope." I let out a little snort, and he kissed the top of my head. "You are never a bother that I don't want. Not to mention you saved me months of healing. And... there will be time, later."

"You're leaving in a few days though."

"One less than that, I'm afraid."

"What?"

"It's Monday. You've been out for nearly a day."

Shit.

Reactively I tried jumping out of bed, but my body failed me.

"I called your work and told them you had a fever. It wasn't exactly a lie." He tucked me back in as he got out of the bed. "I'm going to get you something to eat." I made a mental note to call work later and take the next couple of days off. I could hear my gleeful, childish coworkers now, asking who the guy was that called in for me. He kissed my forehead before leaving and a deep sleep came hurtling back onto me, taking my worries away.

I woke with him tracing his fingers through my hair. It was calming and I felt a contented smile cross my lips, just before my stomach threatened to turn. His face contorted into something like guilt. "Come on. You need to eat." I sat up in bed as he brought me some rather dry oatmeal.

Sitting at the end of the bed, facing me, he looked anxious as he watched me, not entirely present himself. I wanted to apologize for being a bother again but thought better of it. "Penny for your thoughts?" I asked, hoping he didn't regret letting me heal him.

He answered although his mind was still elsewhere, "I still haven't found the ring. And I can't imagine where it might be. She would have had it with her when she passed."

"How? She never wore jewelry."

He shook his head at my comment. "It would have been with her."

"I was actually the one who found her. She was sitting in front of the fireplace in her study. I thought she had fallen asleep; I hope that's what happened. Asleep in front of the fireplace and passed peacefully." Death was so familiar to me that

I said all of this rather nonchalantly and regretted it immediately, realizing he likely didn't have the same experience or attitude towards it as I did.

"I'm glad she had you. I often worried she'd be alone. We didn't always get along, but I did love her." He turned to face away from me. "Thank you for taking care of her."

I gave him a moment before pressing on. "If the ring would have been with her, we should check the study."

"It's not there. I've looked thoroughly, several times. I also called the coroner and anyone else who handled her remains. It's a plain stone ring, not much monetary value. I don't believe anyone would have stolen it." He'd started tapping his thumb again. "No need to worry," he said, his tone shifting. "It'll turn up. How are you feeling?"

"Better. Thank you." I was amazed at how much better actually. "I know this is going to sound absolutely awful, but when I would spend time with Jen, working and being around the plants, feeling them, using my energy, that's the only time I've felt like I really, truly belonged. I've been searching for that feeling for as long as I can remember."

"What's awful about that? I think everyone goes through that, at one point or another."

"But my parents... you don't understand, they took me in. I'm only okay because of them. And I still never felt like I belonged. It wasn't anything they did. I'm just... damaged. I mean, I have to be, to be unloading this onto someone I just met, right?"

He smiled, strangely sanguine. "We may have just met, but there's clearly something here. For me- it's as if I've known you for ages. As cliché as that sounds." I nodded solemnly at his words. The feeling was mutual, and that wasn't sitting well with me.

Staring out the window into the forest he looked exhausted

for just a moment before turning back to me. "Come on. I want to show you something. Let's build a fire."

I followed him into the sitting room at the corner of the house. My favorite room. There was an embellished black marble fireplace with a metal grate that was held in place by cast iron figurines. I never truly appreciated those I'd cleaned out all the fireplaces after Jen's funeral. I'd done a lot of little things like that- put away the dishes, emptied the trash, that sort of thing. I'd left some wood in the fireplace. We wouldn't be able to start a fire like this, but aesthetically it looked nice. And that was how Jen had kept it.

I knelt down and began to remove the bigger pieces of wood.

"What are you doing?"

"Starting a fire," I said blatantly. He shook his head and extended a hand to help me up. "You don't need to coddle me. I feel fine."

He walked me over to the couch and we both sat facing one another. "You need to know some things before we begin. With healing and a few other things, it's all about alignment, seeing the tapestry, knowing and being able to see what belongs where. With other things, like starting a fire, you need more of a framework of your intent. Fire should come naturally to you as your energy has a fire source.

"With living things there is a tapestry. It's easiest to start there because of it. With everything else, there is a blueprint, but you won't be able to see it as such. Mind you we call it that because it's a blueprint of our intent, which we've designed. For this, you're not realigning or mending. You're pulling from yourself, creating with your own energy. I should show you."

He went and grabbed a pen and some scratch paper from the kitchen. I sat motionless, trying to figure out what the hell he was talking about. "Fire is a fairly simple glyph." He drew a handful of lines and then drew a circle around them a few times. "The more complicated ones we normally draw out. For something this simple we can commit it to memory. You *draw* it in your mind and then you *engage* it. Some find it useful to use a word to set it off. For us, pulling like this uses the same energy, our heart's energy, so be careful with that."

"You want me to start a fire? With those scribbles?" I genuinely couldn't tell if he was kidding.

"It's a glyph. Focus, intend, and draw it with your energy, as the designed glyph." He seemed so sure of himself that I half believed him. He was watching me patiently when I burst out laughing.

"I admit the tapestry stuff seems like magic, but the flow, the energy, it makes sense in a weird way. With the healing energy alignments I'm taking from me to give to something else. But this glyph stuff? You're actually talking about magic. Like magic-magic. Abracadabra, hocus pocus, poof! Something from nothing, which isn't possible. Funny, but I'm not buying it. What are you trying to...."

He rubbed his hand over his mouth, his attention turned towards the fireplace. He looked back at me with a suggestive grin. I started to laugh again, thinking I knew what was going through his head. An immense wave of heat began emanating from the far wall before I knew what had happened. Flames were enveloping the wood inside the fireplace and in my awe I barely registered Briar closing the distance between us.

"Briar...." The fire was mesmerizing, but I could still feel the weight of his eyes on me. "How did you do that? You put something in the fireplace when I wasn't looking."

"You know I didn't." He put a hand out towards the fire and pulled it back towards him slowly. The fire died down correspondingly. He pushed his hand back towards the fire and it roared again. He did this a few times, still watching me patiently. Waiting.

"Stop," I whispered with a mix of terror and wonderment. My heart was racing again. I was painfully aware of each breath as I took it. He lowered his hand and the fire burned evenly. I wanted to be excited. Wanted to be ecstatic. But I was scared. Something was off. "Why are you showing me this?"

After a long, heavy silence he slowly answered me. "That is a very big question, Frankie." His arms were crossed over his chest as he settled back into the seat next to me, giving me some space. I watched the fire, waiting for a revelation. "I'm showing you this because it's your birthright. You should have been taught how to do this all ages ago. Given how you've taken to aligning I imagine you'd be quite the force. You still will be, in time."

I scoffed and turned to face him. He wore determination well. "It's not something from nothing. It still takes energy to do this. Some energies are more concentrated than others, that's all."

"Why are you here, really?"

He grumbled a bit under his breath. "I really am here for the ring I told you about. It has its worth. But no one around here would know about that, not really. Owjen knew about you, but she was here to get away from the politics of our world, not set right a wrong you didn't even know about. Stumbling upon you, that was all the damned Fates. Owjen knew I'd come eventually and wouldn't be able to turn a blind eye like she had. To say I'm furious that she denied you for so long would be an understatement. If I'd known how little she was teaching you...." I didn't hear anything else he said after that as my brain froze. He was still watching me. My face could have gone through a dozen different reactions or none at all. I wasn't aware of any of it.

"Owjen?"

"Jen. Owjen isn't a very common name here, so Mom chose not to use it."

"Wait. One thing at a time. You're saying I can do that?" I was still staring at the fire as the realization finally hit me.

I heard the lilt and relief in his voice. "Yeah, you can. You'll need to learn some of the basic forms. It's a language that can dance and we put our energy into those words to create the movements. It's mostly interpretive. You'll learn it easily enough. There are a few that become so fluent they make new words, but that's rare."

"I'm not saying I believe you, about any of it, but it's clear that you believe what you're saying." He nodded with an understanding and grabbed the paper and pen. He drew the glyph he'd made earlier again. Taking it slightly more seriously, I saw that it resembled a simplistic wave of fire with things resembling atomic structures intertwined. He circled these over and over again.

His hand paused and he asked without looking up. "How do you feel? Energy wise?"

"Oh. I'm not really sure? I don't feel weak like I had, if that's what you're asking."

"Check in. If you can see the center of your energy, you're too weak to do this now."

I couldn't even get close. Telling him this, he hesitantly proceeded. He opened his hand towards the fire and closed it quickly in a fist, extinguishing the flames completely. He stood and offered me his hand. As I took it, he quickly pulled me to him, kissing me deeply as he held me tightly. In that instant I could feel a heat drawing me towards him. His lips left mine and greedily I wanted them back. I'm not sure when I'd closed my eyes, but I found myself opening them slowly.

"Tease," I mumbled.

"You're the one that fell asleep," he said with a wily tone. I opened and shut my mouth a couple times to respond, but none came. As I stood there, resembling a fish gasping for air, he led me over to the fireplace. He knelt down in front of it, and I followed his lead. "I see two possibilities," he confessed. "You will either be successful and knowing that I am not crazy you will be as... *fond* of me as before. Or you will not succeed and deem me a psychopath or pity me and leave as quickly as you can. Apparently selfishness runs in the family." He looked at me with sad, sultry eyes. "I wanted one more kiss. Just in case."

"Briar, I wouldn't just—"

"Take the paper," he commanded, willing destiny along. I did, timidly. "Aim it in the direction you want it to go. It can be a bit unpredictable until you have more control. Gather some of your energy. In your mind, use it to fill in where the writing is. You should only see your energy, no pen marks. You'll eventually get to the point where you know the symbols and won't need to draw it out. For now, I need you to believe me, and this is easiest.

"See the images. Use your energy. Intend for the wood to catch fire again and release it. Quickly. Forcefully." I hesitated for a moment. Looking between the paper, the fireplace, and Briar. I closed my eyes, took a deep breath, pulled my energy, opened them, and began tracing the lines in my mind using my energy.

Nothing.

I looked over at Briar as his face began to fall before he caught himself. "Try again."

I kept staring at that paper. Kept tracing the images and every line, over and over and over again. Even if I did think this was all bunk, I was determined to give it my all, to actually believe. Wasn't that always the trick after all? You had to really believe it. I heard him clear his throat, uncomfortable with how long this was taking.

"How do I... I don't know, release it?"

"Send it like an arrow or a shot in the direction you want it to go. You can use a word to send it off." His voice was clipped. I wasn't sure what was worrying him more.

I giggled having found my word. I whispered it and suddenly felt a tickling sensation flit over my body. I barely heard Briar calling my name as a wave of liquid light flared before me, nearly blinding me. I turned to him and felt all the air being forcefully, agonizingly pulled from my lungs as I fell to the floor. In another instant the tickling sensation and blaze were gone, but my panic remained as I struggled for air. Briar was holding me up as I coughed and wheezed, trying desperately to breathe again. His hand was on my chest as I felt his energy surge through me. And then I was... fine. Confused, but fine.

"What *was* that?!"

"That was the fire that was supposed to engulf the wood, not you. But that was different. That shouldn't have happened."

"Is that a good thing? Or a bad thing?"

"It's not... something to worry about now." A bad thing then.

I thought about this as he continued to hold me, my chest heaving against his palm as my breath regulated. His hand bolted off of me quickly, surprising me. I looked up to see him blushing. He mumbled a "sorry," and wouldn't look at me as we got off the floor.

"Briar," I purred at him, my voice almost a whisper. Finally, his eyes met mine. Now I was ecstatic. "It worked. You weren't... *I did that.* I know I did. I know that was me!"

His whole body relaxed as he let out a heavy breath. I threw my arms around his neck and kissed him. I smiled against his lips as he tensed up momentarily before kissing me back. He moved me up against the wall and his lips began making their way down my neck, his hands under my shirt, on my waist. He took a hand away for just a moment and the fireplace leapt back to life. I could barely feel the flames as I held onto him, even though we were only a couple feet from it. There was a fire in my blood, pulling us together, a warm, substantial pull.

My fingers were in his hair as his kisses trailed down my chest before he quickly came back up to my lips. "Do you want this? Be sure," he asked as he searched my face for his answer.

"You only have a couple of days here. And maybe that's for the best." His dejected look told me he felt differently. I kissed him lightly and whispered, "Make them count."

Taking it as a challenge he picked me up and twirled me around. I squeaked, surprised at how easily he moved me. He laid me down in front of the fireplace and in a frenzy we undressed one another.

He paused to admire me as though I were a piece of once lost art. I tried covering my face from embarrassment as he stared at me and my naked body, but he gently held my arms. I wasn't used to people looking at me the way he was. He whispered something that I heard clearly, although I had no idea what it meant. The way he said it was in this hauntingly deep, raspy whisper, "*Bellus.*" I looked at him, questioning, watching his chest rise and fall when I that familiar flash of gold cross his eyes again. Just as he came crashing down to me.

Laying on top of him, listening to his heartbeat, watching the fire- I was beyond content. Our breathing had long since calmed, but neither of us dared move. He'd been so tender and passionate, he'd surprised me. I surprised myself, giving into my feelings like that. The flames in the fireplace were already burning down to embers. A few sparse cinders remained, the last flecks of life beginning to leave them.

It was the closest I've ever come to having a vision. I wouldn't have even thought of it that way if not for my flower child of a mother. But in this fireplace, the one I dreamily stared at as I savored his warmth beneath me, I saw what looked for all the world to be a ring, embedded in the ashes. I blinked and it was gone. Picking my head up to get a different view, I couldn't shake the feeling that I hadn't actually imagined it.

"Hmm?" He was curious but hesitant. Neither of us wanting this moment to move on.

"It's nothing," I cooed. It wasn't exactly a lie. I didn't want to lie to him, but it was my turn to be selfish. I had an idea of where Jen's ring might be. Where it *had* to have been this whole time. But I wasn't ready for him to go yet, and there was a very real chance that he'd disappear once he found what he came here for.

He kissed the top of my head again as I settled back down against him, staring back into the fire. I hated the idea of him leaving, but couldn't really picture him staying, and instead focused on the present moment. I turned to look up at him and moved forward to kiss him. I'd only meant for it to be a little thing, but he didn't let go. I could feel him under me, ready again as I sat straight up. His eyes never left mine as his hands moved to my hips, guiding me onto him.

We moved together- slowly, rhythmically, as we held one another's gaze. Watching the fire dancing in his eyes, his desire for me kept growing, even as I freely gave myself to him. I treasured this moment, and how he made me feel. I needed to remember this. As I neared my climax I began calling out his name, the word quickly morphing into nothing but sounds of pleasure. The melody of his rough breaths became deeper, raspier- sending me over the edge as he ardently groaned out my name with his own completion, grasping my thighs even tighter. That concurrent bliss was a first for me. Sweaty, spent, smiling to myself, I collapsed on top of him and he wrapped his arms around me, holding me to him, kissing me ceaselessly.

The unique scents of burning wood, sweat, and sex filled the room. I started to fall asleep on top of him, eliciting a warm chuckle that reverberated from his chest. "Come on, let's get you back in bed." I grumbled my protest, not wanting to move. And then I promptly, soundly fell asleep once more.

Again I woke with his arms around me. Fleetingly I wondered how I'd gotten here. I knew I should tell him about the ring. Still, it wasn't as if I *knew* where it was. It had to be more of a hunch. Why couldn't it wait until tomorrow? Turning in his arms to face him, he appeared to be sleeping soundly. Wanting to see just how soundly, I began slowly kissing his chest, tracing those scars of his with my lips. When he didn't move, I progressed upwards. By the time I reached the crook of his neck his arms were tightening around me as he made a happy grumbling noise. I lightly nipped at him and could feel his whole body shudder.

Smiling into his chest, our bodies pressed against one another, his still half-asleep, raspy, deep voice mumbled, "I could get used to this." My smile fell as my body stiffened. He finished waking up, realization dawning on him like the memory of a forgotten and unpaid parking ticket. He held me tightly and said nothing.

"I think I know where to find the ring." I'd decided to rip the band aid off quickly. His hold on me didn't loosen as he kissed the top of my head. "Jen was sitting in front of the fireplace when she passed. When I cleaned up the house after, I emptied out the ashes from the fireplaces. I'd never done it before, but it seemed simple enough. Dump the stuff in the metal bucket. Carry it out to the pile next to the compost heap. I... I think the ring might have been in with the ashes."

He sighed deeply into my hair. "And we can't forget about that for a few more hours?"

"Come on," I said, turning away from him as he barely let me go. I wanted it done. All of it.

It took me a minute to remember where my clothes had been discarded. Thankfully he didn't follow me, but a part of me wished he had. In my earlier excitement I'd forgotten what he'd said about some kind of birthright with the energies. It had all seemed so... unreal. Now didn't seem like the time to bring it up.

We walked to the back of the shed where Jen had kept her ash heap. She had a metal burn barrel full of the stuff, a little ways off from her compost pile. Grabbing a shovel and some gloves, we began digging out the barrel, bit by bit.

He'd shovel out a few piles and drop them beside the barrel. I'd sift through as he continued making other small piles. It didn't take long. A decent sized ring, made from some kind of rough, variegated stone. I wiped away as much ash as I could and held it up. There was a coarse design to it. No, not a design. A sort of texture. It'd been made from an odd sort of stone, had to have been, but it hadn't been polished completely. There was an almost animal skin-like quality to it, reminding me somewhat of alligator leather if that were to harden without cracking. The grooves and spaces played tricks with the light, making parts of it look copper and other parts black.

I offered it to Briar. He looked at it and then looked at me, indecision clouding his face. He dropped his shovel, brushed my arm and the offered ring aside and came to me, zealously kissing me, pulling my body to his. Clutching the ring in my hand, I threw my arms around him as we lost ourselves in each other, kissing and nipping, grabbing and pulling. He was so warm. There was a spark of some strange fire in him pulling me to him. It was as if I needed him.

I suppose that's why I didn't notice it getting warmer and warmer until he pulled away subtly, whispering with controlled ferocity, "Frankie, you *need* to listen to me and do as I *damn well* say. Run to the house. We're not alone out here. Get there as quickly as you can. There's a safety perimeter around it. The back porch is closest. Get there. NOW!" He all but roared the last word as he pulled away from me, pulling me up off the ground and pushing me towards the house as he turned.

I didn't really register what he was saying before I found

my footing and for whatever reason, perhaps the urgency in his voice, I did exactly as he said. I ran as fast as I could to the back porch. It was only a few dozen yards away from where we were. There'd been a wave of heat at my back shortly after taking off, but it wasn't until I hit the wood of the porch that I dared to turn to see what was happening.

Briar was standing with his back to me, facing the great red elk. MY great red elk. The one from my drive the other day. The one from my dream. It was aggressively approaching Briar as he was trying to back up towards the house. If Briar tried to run it would be on him before he could take another step. Elk can be aggressive, but where had this one come from so suddenly? Why was it attacking us?

Briar was talking to it, much like I had when I'd encountered it in the road. But for all the world I'd swear I heard it *respond*. But it wasn't hearing the way you normally hear things. I could feel the words as it spoke them, almost like they were crossing through me. But what it was saying made no sense. It was as if I was catching fragments from another language. The only word I did understand was **leave**. It kept saying it, at least that's what I thought it was saying. I couldn't make out any of what Briar was saying.

The red elk would *speak* and rush forward a step, forcing Briar to take a step back defensively. Then it would react to his movements even more violently, shaking its head and trying to pass him, as though it was trying to get to the house. Each time Briar would quick step to keep himself between the beast and me, and again it would stamp up and down as if it were about to attack. The elk couldn't be after me, but Briar seemed to think it was. They're smart creatures to be sure, but even if there was a reason for one to hold a grudge against me, they simply don't do that. I had no idea what to do or how to help.

Cold sweat covered my shaking body as the sounds of my pounding heart ran through me.

I genuinely didn't know what to do. Why was I freezing like this?! This wasn't like at the hospital. Or just... life recently. This was different. It was actual ignorance and I hated myself for it. A helpless rage began to swell just as the beast charged Briar, knocking him to the ground. The elk began violently stomping and pawing with those unbelievably massive hooves. I couldn't tell if it was actually making contact or not. Panic won out and before I realized it, I was running to him. Briar somehow either heard me coming or caught a glimpse of me. I ignored his pleas for me to turn back. He could be angry about it later- if we survived.

The shovel he'd been using earlier was nearby and I grabbed for it. Brandishing it towards the elk I tried to force it back, hoping the movement and aggression would be enough. Unbelievably I surprised the damned thing as it paused its attack. Shovel in hand, I wedged myself between Briar and the elk. The crazed creature eyed me but remained still. I could hear Briar moving behind me and I began stepping backwards, reaching for him. He grabbed me around the waist and quickly yanked my body behind him, again putting himself between me and the elk.

It was a blur. Briar threw a hand down and just as swiftly the ground before him rose up, the earth beneath our feet trembling, then sliding. He moved as though he was pushing this wall of dirt and rock, with pronounced effort, towards the elk as it reared and stomped against the moving barrier. I was clinging to him for dear life as his arm remained protectively around me.

The elk spoke its words again before retreating into the woods and I could feel them all the clearer. Briar watched it until he was sure it had gone. Turning to me with rage in his now solidly golden eyes that truly frightened me, he roared, *"Why won't you listen?!"*

"You needed help! I wasn't going to leave you to—" He cut off my thoughts as he grabbed me, holding me close as though he was never again going to have the chance. My arms came around him and a moment later he'd picked me up and was carrying me into the house. I wasn't fond of being carried like a child. I wasn't exactly a slip of a thing, and I didn't care for it. The lack of control was... unsettling.

We got to the porch, and he put me down. Opening the back door, he shooed me in, careful to lock it behind us. (As if the elk were able to turn the doorknob, if only for that darn lock....) He busied himself checking the windows and watching where the elk had disappeared to. "Briar, did... did I hear it speak? Not quite *hear*. But sense?"

"What did you hear?" he asked tensely. He seemed surprised I'd heard it.

"It was telling you to leave here? Leave something? Maybe just leave? Something like that- it wasn't English, was it? Not completely anyway. What does it think you're doing?" My voice started to break, giving away my anxieties. "Briar, what is going on?! What *was* that?!"

"I'm not sure. I came here for the ring. It doesn't seem to want me to have it. I'm not entirely sure what *it* is."

"Why would it not want you to have your mother's ring?" He was tapping his thumb again, pacing the kitchen. I could see he was shaking slightly and far away in thought. I stopped his pacing. "Briar, are you okay?" I cupped his face in my hands as I asked. He calmed, letting out a heavy breath and settling into my hands.

He brought his own hands up to mine and a peace seemed to wash over him. "I forgot about all the little gods your world still has." I quirked my head at his comment, and he shook it off as he gently took my hands from his face. His own hands moved to either side of my head.

His energy was pushing in.

The world was fading out.

I was fading out.

In the darkness came a whisper, "You really are going to have to start listening to me."

CHAPTER

SIX

The high, sharp din of footsteps clacking against a stone floor pried painfully into my skull. The noise translated to a tumultuous thunder raging inside my already aching head, jolting me back into consciousness. It felt like the worst hangover of my life, if I'd also been hit by a bus. Trying to remember, well, anything, was like grasping at bubbles, as soon as I thought I had one it'd pop and disappear. I'd been in the kitchen. With Briar? Now I was in a bed, but certainly not one of Jen's. Even with my blurry visions I could tell the dark wooden posters were ornate and over the top, as well as the drapes around the sides.

I'm sure the linens would have felt luxurious, but all I could feel were my burning hands. Moving them felt as though I was pulling flesh from muscle. Confusion temporarily over-whelmed me as I realized they, and my wrists, were bound in some sort of rough twine. Several people were walking around, muttering to one another in too severe tones. A memory started to worm through the fog- Briar *had* been there.

A voice called out, "My Lady!" and the noise reverberated

through me, intensifying the agony cracking into my skull. Clattering steps grew painfully louder as these terrors hurried towards me. Hoping that any modicum of pressure might extinguish some of my pain, I reflexively grabbed for my throbbing head. As I fought against the bindings, a fresh jolt of pain echoed through me. The cords were biting into me, deepening sores and blisters underneath the bindings. How long had I been bound like this? How long had I been out?!

In a hushed whisper a woman scolded them, "*Silence!* Can't you see she's in pain?" There was a familiarity to the voice that I couldn't quite place. She was close, but I still couldn't see well enough to say if I knew her. I could smell her floral fragrance, some kind of pungent jasmine. That I knew I didn't recognize.

"You're okay, Frankie. You're safe," she whispered. "I'm going to help with your pain." She was trying to be a soothing presence. Trying. And failing. "But I need to feel it before I can take it away." She laid a hand on my head, and I thrashed myself away, desperate to avoid her touch. The last time hands touched me like that, I blacked out and still didn't know what was happening. The few others surrounding us moved in and held me still as I screamed out every profane thing I could think of. Once she was able to keep her hands on me, it only took a few seconds.

The pain crept away. My vision slowly adjusted as I took her in. She was beside me still, her broad, locked smile beaming down at me. Smoky blue eyes, porcelain skin, luscious blonde curls that adorned her narrow shoulders, and a waspy waist that accentuated her hourglass figure. She looked like she was about Lark's age, but her demeanor aged her significantly.

"What the fuck is going on?" My painfully strained voice cracked as I demanded an answer for the unreasonable position I found myself in.

"Ooho, I like angry!" I could almost recognize that smile, now that it seemed sincere. My confusion had turned to rage, and she knew it. "Don't look at *me* like that. I didn't choose to do this to you. He was supposed to kill you. It's his own damn fault for falling in love with you. Well, his and Owjen's of course. If she hadn't been so fond of you, written about you like she had, you probably wouldn't be here right now. Although, judging by those marks on you," she winked at me as she quickly tugged at my shirt, revealing more of the speckled marks Briar had left, "maybe you would be." I glared as I tried to collect my thoughts. I had no idea what was going on, but I knew to stay calm. Panicking would do no good.

"You were taken to that world for a dryad's damned reason and that world is where you should have remained. Dead or alive, if you ask me. But no one did and no one is, so here you are. Come on now." I couldn't help but gawk as she stood.

Dressed in some dark silver nouveau riche ball gown she glided towards the other side of the room. Her impatience was restrained, but only barely, as she tried to move me and this whole fiasco along. "You're filthy. You've been out for a couple of days and procedure is procedure. You need to bathe and dress. Your queen still needs to see you for tea before she'll unleash you into our world. Again, no one asked me. No arguing now. Rache and Malk are here to help with anything you might need." I still didn't have any answers to my questions as she gestured impatiently to the doorway off of the room. "Girls, bath."

For the first time I could clearly see the other people around me as they again closed in on me. There were only two of them, both dressed in gray, floor-length tunic dresses. One was rather short, with a round face, and wore her dark hair in a substantial braid straight down her back. The other one, also short but heavier, wore her hair in tight curls close to her face.

They quickly approached with their determined eyes glued to the floor.

When I didn't budge they began to pull me with a precision and speed you wouldn't expect from these women. My calm wavered and I begged for answers. "What the fuck is going on? Please? Where am I? Who the fuck are you people? Where is Briar? Did he do this?!"

"You're in our peoples' home. You're safe. But you do smell awful. Please wash up. I have other things that demand my attention and would very much appreciate your cooperation instead of you exhausting us all." Blondie was losing her façade of patience, but I was losing my mind. I'd been kidnapped, and whoever did it had a lot of help. I wasn't stupid enough to think I'd be able to escape right away. My mind was reeling as I tried to assess the hellhole of a situation I'd been pulled down into. If I figured out why I'd been taken- it might help in some way, but I couldn't think of a single damn reason. I was no one to anyone. Would it even matter though? I didn't know. All I did know, was that right now, I just needed to breathe.

"Fine. But untie me. I need to be able to move my damn hands." The women looked up at Blondie for the first time that I'd seen. There was a palpable hint of fear. I guess they didn't like how I was talking to her. Neither of them would be any help in escaping, not with that level of loyalty. (Or fear.)

Blondie looked at them and nodded slowly. They approached apprehensively and worked to untie my hands. The rope had been wrapped around my embraced hands repeatedly, my palms facing one another before being bound together. As they removed the cord, the last layer of rope stuck fast to my flesh. The women looked at one another before continuing to pull the rope off, taking too many layers of skin with it. Angry, split blisters and weeping wounds adorned my swollen and bizarrely colored hands. After Blondie's intervention they had been manageably numb while wrapped. With the rope off the blood was once again flowing, and so was the pain. It was almost enough to make me keel over, not to mention the smell.

"Let me see those." She moved towards me, her sparkling dress a world apart from the two women doing her bidding. The skirt's hem kissed the floor as she walked and the little light in the room reflecting off of it shone like starlight. "We'll heal them right up."

"NO!" I shouted, my hands recoiling as she reached for them. This wasn't to be washed away. I wanted them to have to see what they'd done to me. I wanted them to see the raw ugliness and pain.

She hesitated for a moment, pursing her lips. "You want the pain? Fine! I expect not to hear another word about it. Now go wash, you little masochist." Again the two women moved to withdraw me from the bed. I managed on my own and they didn't dare press.

The three of us walked to the far end of the room, passing through a heavy wooden doorway. My eyes stung as they adjusted to the light of the comparatively well-lit washroom. I was barefoot and the warmth coming from the marble flooring surprised me. Even the walls of the room looked like cold stone, but I could feel a heat coming from them. A large porcelain tub in the center of the room drew my attention, already filled and egregiously aromatic.

Walking to the tub I noted a door to the left, closed, and another to my right that opened out onto some kind of balcony. I could see the night sky and a little banister behind loose curtains that fluttered with the breeze. One of the women, the one with the curly hair, noticed my gaze and rushed over to shut the door as a strong gust blew over us.

That wind, the temperature... it was too cold for this time of year. Had we gone further north or very far south? Either could be the case if I really had been out for days. They all had slight accents, but nothing I could place.

"Shouldn't let in that draft, now, should we?" She chirped, trying to cover up her obvious effort to prevent an escape. My attention turned back to the tub. The same woman asked, "Do you need help disrobing?"

I was beyond annoyed. "Do I need... NO! I do not need help disrobing! I'm all set. You can leave now." My intolerance was evident, but they held their positions.

"We have been tasked with keeping you safe, my lady." The woman with the braid finally spoke. She'd been the one that alerted the others that I had woken.

"Tasked?" I asked sarcastically. "Who *tasked* you? Safe from what? And just how do you plan on doing that? And from whom?!" I'd started out angry but again devolved into pleading for answers.

Blondie yelled through the closed door that led back into the bedroom. "They won't be answering any of your questions. Not unless they're hygiene related."

Rolling my eyes, I ripped my robe off quickly, too quickly. I figured there was no sense in trying to be modest, but I regretted it immediately as more pain shot through my hands. The swelling was getting worse and opening and closing them was excruciating. Blondie banged on the door muttering something about not hearing any water yet. Incensed and fuming I tried to calm myself. Raging against psychopaths wasn't going to do me any good. Carefully I stepped into the chilly water.

The one with the braid cursed under her breath when she saw me shiver. Grabbing a jar of what looked like oversized magnolia petals, she dropped one into the water. There was something written on it and curiosity got the better of me as I grabbed for it. She caught my hand a second before the petal started sizzling. I jerked my hand away, the pain making me sway with nausea as I noticed the water in the tub heating up.

"Heat glyph," she offered. "Starts to burn the moment it's in enough water to dissolve. And this one," she pulled a petal from one of her pockets, "has a healing glyph. Won't wash away your wounds, my lady, but it will help," she said, dropping it in before I could stop her. I huffed at her as she turned her back to get more supplies to make me presentable for her mistress. My once painfully parched mouth and throat, as well as my hands, began to feel some relief. But maybe that was just in my head. Or maybe the steam coming off of the water was more than just relaxing. Maybe it was restorative. But I was still going to be bitter about it.

I don't know how long I'd been soaking before the apparent shock of it all started to really weigh on me. I'd been kidnapped. But why? I still couldn't dwell on it. My reality was that I was surrounded by strangers that had harmed me and were making demands of me. What had happened to Briar? Did I finally have a full-on breakdown and just imagined him? But—

"You still need to dress!" Blondie called out to me, pulling me from my reflections.

Standing and stepping out of the tub sheepishly, the women wrapped me in a peculiarly smooth silk towel that proved implausibly absorbent. Blondie opened the door from the bedroom and without a glance our way walked through and entered the room on the left. She sounded exasperated and bored at the same time as she explained my next steps. "It's tea with the commander and the queen. It's very much a formality, but it'll go a long way toward pleasing her. I doubt there will be any actual tea, but as a newcomer you will need to get used to this sort of thing. At least for a while."

I scowled at her as I struggled to wrap the towel around myself. I was surprised the water had somewhat soothed my hands, or the glyph or whatever. But they still weren't working like they should. I began to get angry all over again. I didn't care about whatever game they were playing other than trying to get away from them all. I kept wondering about Briar. This had to be his doing. But why? Where was he? "Wait, did you say queen?"

The women ushered me in behind their mistress. I was expecting some equally extravagant closet. Instead it was a mostly dark room lined with deep shelves filled with long, narrow boxes and a small pedestal in the center of the room. The only light was coming from a surprisingly modest chandelier dangling above the pedestal.

Blondie searched the shelves as the ladies dried my hair and I tenderly clung to the towel wrapped around me. "Here we go!" She pulled one of the boxes out. I was trying to watch her, but the ladies were moving me and moving around me despite my outbursts and attempts to get them away from me.

They had finished drying my hair and had moved on to putting oils into it. I stopped fighting them, realizing it would be quicker, and less painful, this way, even as they battered my head every which way. Blondie handed me some undergarments that they again tried to help me with until I slapped their hands away. I knew it was going to hurt me more than them, I just hadn't realized how much more. A stabbing pain dug through me, deep in my discolored hands. They didn't exactly laugh as I stifled my pained groans, but there wasn't an ounce of sympathy for me either.

The undergarments looked... archaic. How far could they really have gone with me? Far enough to be in a world apart from the modern one I was used to? One more thing that didn't really matter in that moment. The undies mostly resembled antiquated boxer shorts and an oddly long slip camisole. There was another piece that looked similar to a corset, but not really rigid. For all I knew it was a corset. That particular piece I did allow them to help me put on. It tied up in the front, but I'd never worn anything like it before and didn't know how to do it properly. Not that my fingers could be anything close to nimble enough in their current state anyway.

"Isn't this all a bit much?" I thought the idea of me being abducted and then expected to have tea with a queen and her commander was utterly ridiculous, but whatever they wanted to believe I suppose. I wanted to hurry this along, find a way out, and get home.

Blondie shushed me as they laced up the corset-like garment. Tight, but not uncomfortable. It felt similar to a tank top that was a size too small. Everything was snug but secured in place. The next layer were black linen pants that were warmer than I expected. They were like leggings, but a bit looser and they tied at the top. The next garment she lifted, slowly, from the long box she'd pulled. It was a bright, cardinal red gown with black lace embroidery at the hems and edges. It was mesmerizingly opulent. My eyes followed it closely as it very nearly gleamed. "She likes that one," Malk (I think) chimed in. I glared at her as she looked away with a nervy smile.

"And why shouldn't she?" Blondie shot her a look that no one would envy. Something had happened that I wasn't quite picking up on. I kept my mouth shut. The best way for me to get away from these lunatics was to bide my time, make them believe I was enduring this whirlwind with the patience of a saint, figure out my location and surroundings, and escape while their guard was down. If I fought with every tooth and nail I had right off, it would only take longer for them to relax around me. Besides, what other choice did I really have?

The women eased me up onto the pedestal as Blondie helped me with more layers. First into a plain, full skirt with a thick lining, then the luxuriously ruby-colored gown she'd pulled, and finally the corresponding top that laced up the back. It was all made of some kind of thick, stiff wool. Low cut, snug to my arms, chest, and waist, but it left enough room to sway around the hips. I felt as though I'd died and been reincarnated into some dread-filled renaissance festival.

Stepping down from the pedestal I gestured to myself and asked, "Happy now? Can I have some fucking answers? *Please?*" I wasn't going to trust anything they'd tell me, but I knew they'd be suspicious if I was too compliant.

"My! You do like that word," she mused while looking me up and down before declaring, "Good enough." I'd said it to my reflection a million times, but it hit differently coming from someone else.

I followed her out of the dimly lit closet, through the washroom, and into the bedroom. I'd been so out of it when I was ushered away earlier that I hadn't taken proper stock of the space. The bed I'd been in was indeed a large four poster, raised up on a stone dais in the center of the room. The wood of the bed frame looked beyond ancient. You could practically smell the antiquity of it. The whole room reeked of another time. There was an oversized mirror beside the door we were leaving through. And another opened balcony door on the left. Outside the window I could see down and into a courtyard. I was on the second floor, at the very least.

Blondie yelled at me to hurry along. I reluctantly followed after, pausing as I passed the massive mirror by the door. The oils they'd used in my hair made far more perfect curls than I'd ever been able to manage. My skin even seemed to have a glow to it, despite the way they'd been treating me. The dress flattered my curves in a way that distracted me from my still discolored and swollen hands. Something in that water really had diminished the damage. It was the dress though that I couldn't keep my eyes off. The sumptuously deep color was so rich and vibrant. I hadn't noticed the intricacies of the lace embroidery along the hemlines and seams.

Blondie snapped at me again and I acquiesced, following her down a wide hallway lined with pastoral paintings. I had a difficult time keeping up, enchanted as I was by the artwork and their elaborate frames. This all seemed like a dream, or some bizarre afterlife. Maybe I was in a coma? Whatever it was, I could have spent days here. All of the paintings had a sort of Rococo inspired style with their soft colors and fluid lines.

We eventually stopped in front of a suspiciously plain black door. "What, no guards?" I asked with a smirk. She held her hand at the ready to open the door, absorbed in her own thoughts as she stared ahead of her.

Sighing heavily and looking down, she began to speak so quietly I could barely hear her. "He genuinely cares for you. Truly, he does. But he *must* be what his position demands of him to be able do anything about it. This will be difficult for him, too. Know this- you are alive now only because *he* cares for you. More deeply than he should be able to, really. He has risked everything he is, *for you.* She wants you dead. They all do. They always have. They think it'd be easier. They're... they're not wrong. Be careful who you trust. I'm only telling you this because I love my brother. Even if he is an idiot." Before I could react she pushed open the door and walked through. Her face had turned to ice, callous, masking any sign of her confession uttered mere seconds before or the tempest of emotions that must lie beneath.

The intimacy of the room surprised me. This space too was poorly lit and there was a small round table. A woman and man were engrossed in a conversation and had yet to turn to acknowledge us. The queen and her commander, presumably. Blondie waited, straight backed and patient, as the two spoke words in hushed, hurried tones that I couldn't quite hear. The only thing apparent to me was that the queen was angry, very angry. I stood next to Blondie, wondering if her anger was because I was still alive and how I mattered to anyone that much. Realizing this all must be some terrible nightmare, that there must have been some kind of mix up, and that even if that were or were not the case, I was likely dead either way- I soothed myself by fidgeting with the bottom of the corset top that overlapped the skirt almost seamlessly.

The queen was breathtaking, even furious as she was. She wore a dandelion yellow dress similar to mine, though hers was accented heavily with gold embroidery and looked to be made of silk. It all draped beautifully over her dark skin. I found myself staring at her more than once as we waited to be acknowledged. Silk ribbons of gold were woven into her gathered box braids that fell over her right shoulder. She was fuming and her eyes looked like they were glowing gold. I'd seen Briar's do something similar, but not like this. Hers looked like molten gold, dangerous and moving. It wasn't faded and it wasn't disappearing. I was transfixed and unaware I'd been gawking again when she looked directly at me. The man had his back to us but had visibly stiffened when we entered the room. All of it put me on edge in a way I hadn't known possible.

Blondie noticed the somewhat diverted attention and began her introductions. "I would like to introduce, uhm, Frankie... unearthed from... Earth." Her nervous laugh echoed through the otherwise silent room. "Frankie, it is my great honor to introduce you to your sovereign, Queen Anumonwo." She bowed as she said the queen's name. I may have scoffed.

The queen watched me for a moment as my eyes darted

between them all. It was clear she wouldn't be the first to speak, and I was done waiting for my answers. "You're going to be the one answering my questions?" It came off as less of a question itself than I would have liked, but this whole mess needed to come to a head.

Her anger morphed into annoyance as it found a new target- me. I should have been more apprehensive. Turning her attention towards me, her high cheekbones and sharp, well-defined jawline made her look all the more intimidating. She had a regal manner of speaking with crisp, clipped words setting her accent apart from the rest. "No, Francesca, I will not be the one to answer your questions this evening. I am sorry for what you have been put through. Here, and on your Earth. Know that we are doing what we feel needs to be done for the good of our world. I will leave it to the commander here to answer your questions." She stood and left too quickly, yet somehow wasn't running away. I don't believe that woman had ever run from anything in her whole life.

I was still looking at the door the queen had vanished through when Blondie began to slink away silently. She glanced at the commander once with a wretched look before nodding to me and disappearing herself. I wanted to ask her about Briar again, but I knew I'd get that answer sooner or later.

I turned on my heel to look at the commander that still wouldn't face me. He wore a fitted suit of armor that left only his hands and head exposed. The armor looked like leather, but what little light was here made it appear like a weathered metal- a gunmetal gray that seemed to suit the mood. All I could really see of him was that he had dark hair. It looked black but in here I couldn't quite tell, and I didn't really care. I wanted my answers. He stood, still keeping his back to me, resting a hand on the back of his chair.

"You're the commander, right? So where am I? What is this place? Why did you people kidnap me?!" I screamed only the last question. I imagined I saw his hand tremble before he clenched the chair tightly.

"Frankie...." His voice was deep and solemn. I knew that voice, but I didn't want to.

"Look at me," I demanded coldly, my small voice cracking. He didn't move. He didn't even start. "Briar?" My voice had gotten even smaller, weaker. I knew he was involved in all of this, but I didn't know to what extent. I suppose that wasn't true. I knew, only, I didn't want to know. I didn't want one more person to have outright betrayed me. I was trying to keep my wits about me, and I was failing. They'd clearly set this up to mess with me and had succeeded. I wasn't sure who *they* were yet. None of this was making any sense.

He turned around when he heard me, frail and imploring, utter his name. We stood there staring at one another for a forever of one kind or another, a moment lost in some void of time. His guilty expression enraged me, even as his eyes appreciated the grandeur Blondie had dressed me up in. Of course he'd had his part in this, but I'd hoped against hope it wasn't what I thought, what I knew. Yet here he stood, before me as their commander, whatever that meant, being the one to answer my questions. I wish I was the type of person that didn't cry when I was angry.

"What is going on? *You* kidnapped me? Why?!" My throat burned as I screamed. Hot tears seared as they fell. I hadn't eaten in the days I was passed out, and now as I raged at the culmination of it all, my body began to fail me. Or I was simply overwhelmed by the emotions of it all. I'd need to sit soon or collapse on the floor. My legs wobbled, about to give out on me. I wasn't sure what was making me weaker, my emotions or my body. I felt myself sway and Briar swiftly moved towards me. "Don't you fucking *DARE!*" I shouted when he was inches away from catching me. I forced myself to stay standing. "Answer. Me. **NOW.**"

"I will! Just sit down, damn it!" My heart ached at his voice. It had all been an act. Back at Jen or Owjen or who-the-fuckever's house. He'd done this to me, and it had been nothing, meant nothing, to him. It didn't matter. *I didn't matter.* I sat in the seat closest to the door. He took the seat next to it, turning it towards me. He brusquely ran his hands over his face and through his hair. I could feel my eyes burning as I willed myself to stop crying.

His anger and impatience took me aback as he snapped out his defense. "I didn't kidnap you! I returned you. I brought you back. You belong here. You were born here. This is your home!"

"Where is *here*?" My awareness was starting to come back as my tears slowed.

"You're in our world, Visnatura. It's different here, Frankie." His demeanor started to soften, and he seemed almost glad in that moment. "You really will love it. Give it a chance and look at it with an open mind. You can use your energy here in ways you never imagined." His voice was full of wonder and apprehensive excitement, even a bit of hope had seeped its way in there.

"Are you serious right now?!" I snapped at him. His face blanked in an instant. "You took me from my family, from my life, from my... *everything*, and why? Because we fucked a few times?! Do you really think you mean *anything* to me?!" He meant something to me, had meant something, but I couldn't tell him that. I didn't need to. But I couldn't think of any other reason why he'd take me. I'd never known my biological parents, but it had been conveyed in hushed and accidentally overheard conversations never meant to be heard by my small ears that they weren't the kind of people that anyone would miss or care about or even notice had gone missing.

My words to Briar had done their damage. His face became ragged as he looked away from me. "That wasn't part of it. We... that shouldn't have happened." I felt a small stab in my chest as his wounding words caused their own harm before I stole myself away again.

I brought my hands up to apply some pressure to my eyes. Something I'd done since childhood. The compression helped soothe me. My hands were still swollen and the pressure I used, while helping my nerves, sharply reminded me of the damage they'd inflicted.

My head jerked up at the sound of his chair moving abruptly, scraping over the rough stone floor. A blur of gray-black moved past me. "GALE! Who?!" he bellowed through the hall. I ran after him as best I could, the threat in his voice and my adrenaline willing me to move. He was charging through the halls, and I wasn't able to keep up. They'd given me a slipper type shoe when I refused the ones that clacked. Now I was sliding all over the hallway's polished stone floor, clearly moving faster than their decorum permitted. Kicking them off I could finally feel my feet on the ground. I caught up moments after he found Blondie, or Gale, apparently.

"WHY?! She knows nothing. The most dangerous thing she could have done was grow a dryad's damned rose bush and nick them!" His rage was suffocating. Gale was regarding him with wild and apprehensive eyes.

"We didn't have a complete briefing! She wasn't exactly expected, Commander. We were being cautious. If there's anyone to blame, it's you for being reckless and impulsive!"

"Choose your words wisely, sister," he threatened through gritted teeth.

"Briar, knock it off. I'm fine. It'll heal." He gave me a look so cold I felt it in my bones. I didn't know what was going to happen, but I was done with the showmanship. "Come on, calm down and I'll let you heal me." He was staring daggers at Gale who hadn't relaxed an iota despite her defiant words.

Gale tried to defend herself, scratching at a pitiful scrap of her previous composure. "I offered to heal her as soon as she woke." She knew he'd wonder why I hadn't already been healed. Still, I detested something about her means of self-defense. She turned towards me and curtsied. An actual, full, nearly to the ground curtsy. I was speechless. Gale was not. "Apologies for my team's carelessness. It should never have happened. The one who tied your hands will endure the due consequences."

"Why was I with your... team? Briar was the one who knocked me out, right?" I tried to take out any affect in my voice, not wanting to outwardly tout the betrayal I felt.

Gale answered, "When you were brought over from your world—"

"*This* is her world, Gale." His words came through almost as a growl, though he did seem to be trying to calm down.

"When you came over from Earth...," She stood upright, her vibrant blue eyes darting between Briar and me as she continued talking, "my kingdom is between the closest gateway and here. I am the commander of my kingdom and Briar is obligated to obtain my permission to pass through. My queen insisted our team escort you here while Briar's was to go on ahead to brief Queen Anumonwo of the situation." She bowed again as she finished her explanation.

"I don't have a queen, or a commander for that matter. Why am I here?!" They'd finally started giving me answers, as bunk as they had to be. Foolishly I hoped they'd continue.

Gale responded, "That is not for me to answer. I am sorry." I believed she was, actually. I turned to Briar. He wouldn't meet my gaze as he stared painfully at my blistered and discolored hands. "He can't heal you. Not here. He's on duty, as you can see by his armor. There are strict rules about what he can and cannot do as commander with his energy."

"So even if he wanted to, if he did, he'd what? Be punished? How?"

He finally looked at me, his voice steady and matter of fact. "I'm as responsible for your hands being injured as my incompetent sister. It's not punishment in any sense you'd appreciate right now. We are told what our duties are, and we are compelled to follow them. Know that I avoid it only because it would bring more hardship to you. If it were lashes, I'd take a thousand to take your pain away." His eyes quivered as he stopped himself from coming to me. "You may well hate me, but I am not the villain you are imagining me to be. You know I care for you, and you know I want to take that pain from you." I resisted the urge to mockingly laugh. I'd been played with enough before. He was going to have to up his game if he thought sweet words would ever convince me he was different.

I'd been staying at a sensible distance from him given the glacial look that was seared in my mind. Now I walked over and stood squarely in front of him as a smile crossed my face. I pulled my hand back and as fast and as hard as I could, I slapped him. Gale quickly clipped her gasp while Briar rolled with it. He knew it was coming and still took it. My mother would have been disappointed in me, but I wasn't thinking about that now. The pain in my hand assured me that if it hadn't been broken before, it was now.

He wasn't angry. He just sounded tired. "Gale, take her to my place."

"I am not going anywhere! Why did you kidnap me?! Why am I here? What are you going to do with me?! Let me go!" My voice had begun with a sense of resilience that quickly dilapidated into whimpers as I began to fall apart. I lowered myself to the ground, unable to stand any longer. Gale came to my side and put her arm around me as I buried my face in my broken hands. I shook her off and continued sobbing.

Gale crouched next to me, her voice nonchalant, "Come on, princess." My face still covered, I didn't see anything between them, but something was happening. She was talking distinctly to Briar now. "What? You want me to call her by her actual title? Wouldn't that just open up another bag of sprites? One she certainly doesn't need tonight. Come now. We'll all feel better away from these stone walls."

Gale offered to help me up. I should have been curious about her strength as she effortlessly pulled me to my feet. But I wasn't. Not now. Briar was gone when I stood, but so was I. Again. That old familiar numbness had returned, enveloping me whole. I thought of the pain I'd gone through before that had led me to this level of emotional anesthetization. I'd experienced more than my fair share of trauma. Abandoned, betrayed, left to try to be human still, to go on. I hadn't done well. This, with Briar, was actively happening to me, but my mind was elsewhere. Or nowhere. I was walking through these things, and I was numb. I felt a nothingness, a void. And that was fine.

I stared blankly, waiting for direction. "He really is why you're still alive. If you want to stay that way, you'll listen to him." I didn't care to. She stared at me for a moment before clicking her tongue. "I need to find Helen for a moment." We walked back down the hallway in silence. Gale kept fidgeting with her hands.

"Wait here," she said as she disappeared behind a painting, leaving me alone. She knew I wasn't going anywhere. I wouldn't get far and had no idea how much time I had. I could try to run, but I knew I wouldn't so much as get out of this building. And in that moment, caring was beyond me.

My numbed mind stared blankly for a time at the painting Gale had disappeared behind. Through my unfocused gaze the ill-defined shapes began to develop as my eyes continued washing over them. This one was in more of a baroque style, dramatic and powerful in a way the others weren't. There were two dragons winding around one another as they flew through a dusky star-filled sky. Their wings contoured to one another in either a dance or a fight. One of the dragons was snow white and the other onyx black, only visible in the night sky where it blacked out the stars. There was an intimacy to it that I could feel but didn't understand. When I could no longer look at it, compelled to avert my gaze, I didn't question why. I didn't care. It was as if the painting wanted me to turn away, and so I did.

The painting opposite it was in a similar style. One dragon, onyx black again, reflecting what looked like a fire that wasn't captured in the painting. Her scales were uniform except for a noticeable gap and discoloration under her raised right claw. It was elevated as though she was trying to take something or stop something with that outstretched appendage. There was a reflection in her eyes. I moved closer, trying to see it. "Beautiful, isn't she?" I stopped and turned slowly at the queen's voice.

"Yes." I didn't meet her gaze. I didn't know what was proper, but I couldn't seem to make myself lift my eyes. She stood beside me in silence, admiring this solitary dragon. "She's heartbroken," I whispered. The dragon's sadness felt contagious, though I could not tell you why. At that moment I could not care. I couldn't really feel it, not anymore. I just knew it was there, like a heaviness of the world. And I could see it. I knew her story. I knew it in my blood and in my bones, yet I could not seem to recall it.

The queen spoke slowly and with intention. "Someone she loved very much is about to kill her for the very thing that gave them their freedom. She is about to be killed for being a good mother, for providing, for protecting."

Gale cleared her throat. I wasn't sure when she had joined us, but she had piles of dark fabric resting in her arms. She spoke hesitantly. "We should be going." She was noticeably worried, and the queen eyed her indignantly. She handed me half of her pile. I watched as she put a dark gray wool cloak around herself before mimicking the act myself.

"I will see you soon for tea." The queen gave Gale a look, though it was clear she was talking about/to me. Ephemerally I wondered if there would actually be tea next time.

Gale curtsied to her before pulling me along back down the hall and out of this suffocating palace. We made a few turns before Gale slipped behind another hinged painting and pulled me along with her. We went down a tight spiral staircase that seemed to last forever. It felt like maybe three or four floors at least. I hadn't realized we'd been up that high.

Coming to a large door that had no handle, she knocked in a rhythmic pattern before it popped open. We came out into an intricately manicured garden and Gale relaxed a bit as she wound around a path. It was too dark for me to see past a few feet and Gale slowed her steps.

There was a solid hedge wall and Gale walked up to it and promptly disappeared into it. I stopped in my tracks. Looking around I could see nothing but a few sparse lights from the building we had just left. I tried counting the floors. It seemed to go up forever and stood alone, like an oversized obelisk of contradictions. Being outside of those foreboding walls did actually make me feel a bit though. Odd.

It was cold here, frigidly so. The chill from the ground crept into me as a burning sensation on my bare feet. Then on my chest as the wind blew, taking what little warmth I had off of me. I pulled the cloak around me, the effort and bitter cold biting at my wounds. Gale grabbed me by the arm, startling me. "You need to keep up."

I didn't move. This was all too much. She looked back at me, somewhat sympathetically. She took her hand off of my arm. "I am sorry. I don't trust you and none of this was my idea. Now please, follow me." Reluctantly I obeyed. What else could I do? She continued talking in a more hushed tone. "It's cold and we need to get you inside. No one knows who you are right now, but it won't take long. Better for there to be nothing they need be curious about than try to deter it."

"Better for who? Who do you people think I am?" She ignored me and kept walking at her steady pace. I followed more closely as she slid through one of the bushes that I now could see had been grown slightly out of line from the rest. We came up to a solid wall and she slid a finger over one of the bricks. What looked like one of Briar's glyphs lit up in the dark and the wall pushed forward just enough for us to slip past. And then we were out on a cobbled street. These stones were much colder and harsher on my feet than the frozen lawn had been. I turned back towards the wall to find it was flush once again. I eyed it suspiciously, knowing I should examine it further, but needing to keep up with Gale.

Ahead were rows of dark houses with brief flashes of color under scant lights. My feet were getting cut and scratched up on the rough cobblestone, but even that pain barely touched me now. The slightly too long linen pants mostly covered my feet but offered little warmth. With the cold still leaching away my heat, I better understood the layers of fabric and thought of my shoes from home. More had been demanded of my weakened body than I was aware, and I could again feel it failing me. I was okay with that now. Okay with being done. I could stop now, stop everything. That'd be okay. Lovely, even.

SEVEN

Not even the glacial air cutting at my face could compel my unwilling spirit to keep moving. Gale, however, lived up to her name as she grabbed me by the arm and carried me away with her like an unwelcome gust of wind. Block after block we walked in this polar atmosphere through alleyways and across streets until Gale finally stopped in front of one of the houses. Absently I noticed a green door and ornate opaque windows framing it. "Here we are," she exulted.

It was a two story structure built right up next to the ones on either side of it, like all the rest of them. Light blue, light enough that it would likely be a different color in the daylight. I didn't notice much else right then. Even the cold was finally leaving me alone.

At least, it was, until she ushered me inside and a wave of heat washed over me. There was a fireplace across from the doorway and the familiar scent of burning wood became a temporary salve for my soul. It reminded me of my parents' home. Their wood stove would be going as soon as even a hint of a chill set in. Briar was standing to the side of the fireplace, frozen mid-pace where he'd halted at the sound of the door opening. No longer in his leathers, he was now wearing linen pants with a sage green tunic shirt. A more relaxed look to be sure. Not that he was.

"I'll grab you two dinner before I retire for the evening. Unless one of you needs anything, I'll be staying at the Mountain tonight." Briar shook his head and looked away. Gale nudged my arm and it occurred to me that she hadn't really been asking him.

"I would rather sleep in the freezing stree—"

"You're his responsibility now. Take your issues with your lodgings up with him." I wanted to ask why she bothered asking then, but I was certain I was missing something. "She needs to see Helen for tea in a couple of days," she directed to Briar. He made no response, verbal or otherwise. I watched Gale go and stared at the door for another minute, wondering what would happen if I followed. Their message was clear- I was a prisoner. Briar my warden.

I waited for him to say something, but no words or sounds or even grumbles came. I turned around, looking over the room slowly. A dining table and chairs occupied a good deal of space to the left with an archway behind them. On the right were bare walls with another archway leading towards the back. In front of the fireplace was a huge shaggy rug with a couple of worn leather chairs and a couch placed around it.

"Frankie, sit down," he directed in a flat voice. The idea flitted across my mind that I should refuse. Possibly try to run. But I couldn't. Broken, I obediently took a step, wincing from the pain in my feet. I hadn't noticed it as much while moving, or with the bitter cold dulling the pain-filled sensations. Now that my feet had warmed and I'd stilled, every movement sent waves of agony rippling through me.

I sighed heavily in my frustration as I tried to find the words to explain. Timidly I muttered, "I hurt my feet." It was all I could manage. He didn't ask for an explanation. Picking me up he carried me through the door on the right. I didn't care to fight with him. I'd resisted putting my arms around his neck to stabilize myself, forcing him to work a bit harder to balance me. He didn't need to get the wrong idea. It occurred to me allowing even this much was likely sending that message already, and I needed to stop it. "Put me down," I said with an edge that gave him pause, for a moment, before he continued on ignoring me completely.

He shook his head at me as he scaled a flight of stairs. "Don't be stupid, Frankie. Hate me- fine. But let me heal you. You won't be able to run away with injured feet anyway. Right?" Carrying me through one of the doors into a sparsely decorated room, he laid me down on a bed and knelt beside it.

"What are you doing?" I asked, sitting up, as he pulled my layers of clothing up and away from my feet.

His eyes searched mine with trepidation as he placed his elbows on the bed. Again he ran his hands over his face and through his hair in frustration. "You're not going to believe me, but I'm trying to save you." He placed his hands on my feet and instantly I could feel his energy. I thought about stopping him, but it was hopeless, and I was exhausted. I laid back down, waiting for the pain to go away. The wave of warmth that came with his healing surprised me and elicited a small sigh before I realized what was happening. He took his hands off of me as he scoffed quietly.

He stood and looked down at me as I stared off at nothing. "Care to tell me what happened to your shoes?"

"Why? What does it matter?" I mumbled as I rolled away from him.

"I need to know if Gale wants you dead, too."

"She does."

Walking around the bed, he sat down next to me. He went to take my hands in his and I pulled away. "Let me make it better," he begged as his eyes scanned my face. My pain seemed to bother him. I wouldn't have let him if I hadn't agreed to it earlier. He could lie to me all he wanted, but I'd hold to my principles and keep my word. I held out my hands and felt that same warmth flow through them. I sneered at his little smile before looking away.

He was still holding my hands. "Frankie, you're freezing."

"It's cold here. Wherever *here* is." I pulled my hands away from him and sat up, putting my legs down the side of the bed. I wrapped my arms around myself, both for comfort and because I really was freezing. Briar moved to the other side of the room cursing under his breath. I looked over to see a huge burst of flames ignite a small stack of wood in the room's modest fireplace.

He came over to the bed and pulled the blankets up, wrapping them around me. "I'm sorry I keep making a muck of all this."

Coldly I asked him, "What do you mean by *this*? My kidnapping? Or my life?"

"Come sit by the fire." I rolled my eyes at his intentional lack of an answer. "I can carry you, if you'd prefer." He was looking down at me, stone faced until we heard the front door open and close a moment later.

I stood up, holding the blankets tight around me, and shuffled over. "You owe me answers."

"You'll have them. Let me grab dinner and get rid of Gale. Then I'll answer what I can." Hurriedly he disappeared back down the hallway. He was barely gone a minute and brought back a large bowl filled with some leafy greens, vegetables, and a generous heaping of some kind of meat. He'd brought some mugs, which seemed to be filled with a kind of red wine. "It's not quite the same as what you're used to." He was rubbing the back of his head nervously. "It's not poison, I swear."

"Sounds like something you'd say if it was, in fact, poison." He seemed to relax immensely as a smile flitted across his face.

"Is it terrible?" he asked after I'd taken a few bites. A sad hope filled his eyes. I didn't want to hate him. Hate took too much from me. I'd just lost all hope of being able to trust him. I'd let myself be blinded before. Never questioned anyone that seemed to care for me. It was too risky. But what if Gale was telling the truth? If I really was in danger.... But why would anyone want me dead? Because I could use my energy? It wasn't normal, but even that I never questioned. None of this made any sense.

"It's not terrible. A little gamey, but the wine helps."

"I wanted to show you this world under different circumstances. I wanted—"

"Why did you kidnap me?" I knew he'd hate me asking it this way, but it seemed only fair to be accurate.

His brows furrowed. "Again, I didn't kidnap you. We brought you home. It wasn't supposed to happen like this."

"*What* wasn't supposed to happen like this? Gale said the queen wants me dead."

"*Wanted*. Not anymore though. And Gale needs to keep her damn mouth shut."

"She also said you're the only reason I'm alive right now." He nodded somberly, giving me my answer without emotion. "You know I don't believe any of that."

"I do. But you should. You will. I'll tell you what I know. I'll prove to you what I can. The rest you may have to learn the hard way."

"Fair enough," I conceded, taking another long drink of the

wine. I'd learned plenty of lessons that way already, no point in stopping now.

"Since you were discovered it had been my mother's plan to have you return to our world. Visnatura. Think of it like a sister world to Earth. Our magical creatures weren't hunted to extinction, we didn't forsake the old ways, and our magic became stronger instead of fading away. We have some doorways to your world that we've maintained. They aren't readily accessible, but there are some who can and do travel between the worlds."

"Would you take me back home?" My words pained him, and I hated that I cared.

"I need you to see and know your world first. You need to know what you're giving up. If, after you've learned what you need to here, you still want to go back, I will take you. I'd need to make it safe for you first though."

I wasn't sure how long Stockholm syndrome took but that was the least of my current concerns. I also wasn't buying the second world thing. Although, there was something undeniably different about this place. There was something *more* in the air, but it wasn't as simple as that.

"Why should I believe you?"

"I have never lied to you, Frankie. And I never will." He stared into my eyes as he said this, and for a moment, just a moment, I believed him. Not that he didn't have plenty to account for, even if he was being honest.

"You've never lied to me? You stole me, had my hands broken, brought me to a strange world which you have to know I don't buy, but lying? No, of course not."

"You're a smart woman. Right now you're thinking you'll bide your time until you come up with some way to escape. I assure you, it will fail for one simple reason- you're not accounting for the possibility that this is all real." His voice and expression were both level, patient even. "I swear no harm will come to you. If nothing else, enjoy this adventure, let go for a bit. Think of it as a little frolic into the fray." He seemed amused with himself. "When it's all done I'll take you back, if that's what you still want."

"Fine. Let's get on with it then. What do you want from me? What do I need to know?"

"I want you to know who you are. And selfishly, I want to know you, too. I want to know why you were taken from this world. Your mother likely left shortly after you were born. I need to know why. When we find one of our own on Earth it's protocol to kill them."

"That's so fucked up!" I was horrified, and nervous again.

His face hardened, knowing this would be how I would react. "We have our reasons. I don't expect you to understand, not yet anyway."

"Why wasn't I killed then?"

"My mother left this world for her own reasons, but she was given permission and protection. Owjen left you alive because she was ordered to do so. You are a bit of a mystery to us, after all." I scoffed in disbelief. Jen wasn't like that. Not the one I knew. But maybe I didn't know her at all either. One more person that did nothing but lie to me.

"Something is missing. I worry the queen knows, which is why we need to be careful. But she swore to me she wouldn't let you be harmed. It's a delicate relationship, queen and commander. Neither of us would outright stand against the other. She has sworn to protect us, all of us. But it will serve us to remain vigilant."

"Vigilant about what? And who is *us*? I can't imagine I count if she wants me dead."

"Again, *wanted*. Past tense. You're here now, so until we know what you are—"

"What does that mean? What do you think I am? Is this what Jen was trying to protect me from?"

"The easy answer? Yes. And it all has to do with your lineage. You're in Heartwood now though. Even if your father was what I think he was, you're safe here. Our sorcerers would lead an uprising if we killed you because you're not pure."

"I'm sorry, *sorcerers?!* How strong is this wine?" The food and wine had done me a world of good, in many ways, but this really was too much to take all at once. "And wait, is me being killed still on the table?!"

"Of course not! But that wine is actually pretty strong, be careful. And yes, you'll eventually run into some of them sooner or later. Those damn wizards are always butting into business that isn't their own. Err, don't call them wizards though. I shouldn't have, given how willing they've been to help us recently."

"Am I a prisoner?"

"No!" His outrage at my question surprised me, all things considered.

"All this because I still wanted to heal," I mused in disbelief. "Or is it because of that ring?"

"Not exactly." His tone and sadness surprised me, wounded me. "Owjen, Jen- she really did write to me about you."

"She wanted you to come kill me?"

"No!" His wounded expression made my heart ache. "Not at all." He moved as though he wanted to touch me, to comfort me, but he stopped himself. "She loved you. She wanted me to know you, not to kill you. She disagreed with how our queen does things, and she trusted... she trusted that I'd take care of you."

I shook my head in disbelief as I mumbled, "Fine job you're doing."

"I did what I had to. Believe that, if nothing else."

I pushed the blankets off of my shoulders and stood. "I don't need to believe any of it. It's late and I'd like to get some sleep."

He hesitated, seemingly unsure of himself in that moment. "Can you ever forgive me?" He asked as he stood up. Stepping towards me, close enough his scent faded in and out, I could see the desperation in his eyes. Seeing the pain on my own face, he seemed to resign himself of that hopeful reassurance. "I'm sorry. It isn't fair to ask you to accept all that is happening. I'll give you some space." He stepped away and put his hands behind his back. "This will be your room. Mine is across the hall. There is another room on the other side of the house if you don't want to be this close to me. Tomorrow—"

"No." My certainty staggered him. "I don't want to stay here. I *want* to go home. But if I must be here then I want to stay anywhere else."

His face darkened and he spoke coldly. "I am the only one here you know. I'm trying—"

"You've lied to me, tricked me.... You can't keep me like some pet. You cannot dictate where I go, what I do. If I'm not a prisoner, and you won't take me home right now, then I should have some say in where I stay."

He let out a heavy and aggravated sigh as he appeared to think it over for a moment.

"Give me three days. There are things you don't know. We are connected in ways you cannot understand. If after three days, you still want me out of your life, I will arrange other accommodations."

"I only *don't know* because you're not telling me. Two. I'll give you two days if you swear to give me the answers I need AND to take me home." I didn't relish the idea of knowing no one, but how could I ever trust him? He was no better than a stranger. Worse, even. I wouldn't change my mind in two days, regardless of what he had to say or show me, but if he truly believed he hadn't lied to me, this promise would prove useful, one way or another.

"Thank you." His cold voice cut through me. Guess I was more than he'd bargained for. "I'll get you some clothes to sleep in." He went across the hall, returning a moment later with a long shirt and linen pants, similar to what he was wearing.

"Thank you," I said as I took the clothes from him. He held onto them for a moment until I looked up at him again.

"I...," he started. His eyes trembling as he looked deeply into mine. I knew I was close to tears again.

I looked away and he let go of the clothes. After he left I tried taking off the bodice and realized I couldn't get the laces behind my back undone. I thought about sleeping in it but knew that would be too uncomfortable, even with how exhausted I was. I went to find Briar. His door was ajar, but I didn't dare enter. Clearing my throat loudly, I heard him scramble to the door. My lips twitched despite myself.

He swung the door open with a speed that startled me. "Frankie, is everything okay?"

He'd taken his shirt off, revealing the marks across his chest that were a world apart from what they'd seemed at Jen's- scars so faded they looked to be from a lifetime ago. "What are these? They didn't look like this before."

His bearing softened at my concern. "Worried about me?"

I scowled at his cheeky grin. "No, I, I just...."

He tried to muffle a laugh until he realized I was actually upset, my arms crossed in front of me. "I'm sorry. But you're adorable when you're flustered." He brought his hand up to brush my cheek and I didn't immediately pull away. "They're scars from my youth and my training. They have elements to them that require they be hidden in certain circumstances, certain worlds."

For a moment I stared at his bare chest and what looked like white claw marks. "You've been hiding who you really are this entire time," I whispered more to myself than anything.

His mood shifted back to anger. Exasperated, he spoke through clenched teeth, "They're just markings. They aren't who I am. They mean nothing to you. It was that damn elk, it knew. I hid these to protect you!"

I finally snapped. "Damn it, Briar! You don't even know the worst part of all of this! I *want* to believe you! I want to believe *in* you! But how stupid would I have to be to believe the man that knocked me out and took me from my life?! My family? My sister?!"

I'd been betrayed and abandoned too many times. I couldn't trust anymore, not if I wanted to survive. And somewhere along my path, without even realizing it, I had chosen to want that. As pathetic as my life was, it was mine and I wanted it. I'd hoped my heart would become callous to the world in some way, but it never seemed to. I wanted to slap him again. At least my anger was back now. That felt good in its own way. He stood there, unflinching, waiting. My pain reflected in his eyes. I wasn't a violent person. I didn't believe that was the way to go. I'd been so desperate earlier. And now there was so much guilt and a part of me wanted to apologize.

I turned to hide my face, letting the heavy tears that had been swelling fall. Immediately his arms were around me, and I let myself fall back into him. Permitting myself to forget, but certainly not forgive, for just a little while. He was so warm and still smelled of leather and the smoke from the fireplace. The strength and devotion I could feel as he held me melted what little resolve my exhausted body still had.

He untied the bodice and pulled it off of me, letting its

beauty fall to the floor. He did the same with the skirt and the pants, leaving me in the undergarments they'd given me. Carrying me to his bed he laid me down and climbed in next to me, pulling a heavy comforter over us both. I fell asleep with his arms around me. Again.

That night I dreamt of that elk. It was heartbroken. And furious.

CHAPTER
EIGHT

S unlight shining through peculiar green windows woke me the next day. The rays invading the room, and my sleep, were oddly unaffected by the glass's color. There was no tinting or green shadowing whatsoever. Just very, very bright light. It felt far too early. Looking around at the warm clay-red walls and his chocolate-brown bedding, I got the distinct impression that Briar was just as Spartan as his mother.

His arms were still around me and I turned in his hold to face a sleeping Briar. For the first time since I'd been abducted, I *really* looked at him. He had more stubble than I remembered. It suited him, but I didn't expect it to last here. I loved how his hair was a bit messier now, like it had been. Not that prim and proper look he'd sported while in his leathers. I wanted to touch and trace his newly revealed scars. I wanted to discover more about him.

Then I remembered my own wounds. And his promise.

I was thinking things I shouldn't be when he began to stir. "Go back to sleep," he grumbled. "It's still early. I'm not going to try anything, I promise." I scoffed at his words and closed my eyes, falling back asleep quickly, despite the intrusive light.

WHEN I WOKE AGAIN, I was alone. Though the sounds of running water assured me that I wouldn't be for long. Lying there, listening, I could feel the tiredness of my muscles weighing heavily on me. Rolling onto my back I threw the blankets off as they'd become uncomfortably warm. Still wearing the linen boy-short type of underwear and the slip from yesterday, I didn't feel entirely untoward. My mind began to wander back to home. Lark would know by now. She'd be freaking out of course, giving everyone who would listen Briar's description and swearing vengeance.

The water stopped and a moment later a clean shaven Briar came in with nothing but a towel wrapped around his lower body. Seeing me, his stride paused before he looked away quickly. He sat at the end of the bed, facing away from me.

"How do you feel?" he asked gently.

"Is this real? Any of it?" I asked, dazed, still not feeling quite right.

He brushed his hands through his damp hair. "Let me show you our world. You'll see. I won't forget my promise." I put my arms above my head, stared at the ceiling, and let out a long, tired sigh. I looked down the bed towards him and caught him staring ravenously. He turned away quickly and stood, letting his towel fall.

"You said you weren't going to try anything," I grumbled after him.

"And I'm not. You're in my room. I need to get dressed." He shrugged. "Besides, it's nothing you haven't seen before." I watched his bare ass retreat into what must be his closet. I grabbed my own clothes from last night and crossed from his room to mine.

There was a cloth-wrapped package laying on the bed and a pair of boots on the floor beside it. Supplies from Gale. Inside the package was a change of clothes and some bathroom essentials. I was more grateful for the boots than I would ever tell her. The clothes were of the same style from yesterday, except more muted and far less luxurious, a sky-blue wool dress and gray wool leggings. Opulence was apparently no longer required of or for me.

Hands healed, I was able to clumsily tie up the corset-like stays that served as a rough replacement for a bra. The top part of this dress blissfully tied up in the front and I found I could manage it as well. Still, I took my time getting ready.

Gale and Briar were standing by the main door when I came down. Briar was dressed in his leathers but now had a long wool cloak that covered most of it. I wondered if that made a difference in what he was allowed to do while wearing them. Gale now donned a similar type of armor, but it was nearly all white. "Frankie, it was... *interesting*... meeting you."

"You're forgetting something, Sister." Briar stared at her heatedly.

Gale cleared her throat and straightened herself. "Frankie, I am sorry my unit acted hastily. We have no excuse and I take full responsibility. Whenever you may be in need of it, if it is within my power, I owe you a debt of service." She bowed again and quickly left before I could respond.

"She's your sister!" Briar half-smiled at my revelation. "I knew there was something familiar about her. I'm guessing it was from Je... Owjen. She even sounds a bit like her."

"We were young when Mom left. Gale doesn't... didn't have the same sentimentality towards her that I did." His guilty expression was fleeting, though recognizable. "I thought I'd show you some of the city today. Then the animal sanctuary. If you're feeling up to it? It's a bit much for one day, but I am apparently on a time crunch." He eyed me, hoping I'd changed my mind about the third day.

I looked at him grimly, annoyed at us both. I knew that no matter what he showed me, I didn't want to stay under this roof with him. At least I shouldn't. I wouldn't let myself get used and manipulated like this, not again.

I sat down at the table without further acknowledging his hope, and he hesitantly joined me. "Why didn't you tell me about all of this back on Earth? Why kidnap me? If you would've told me, if I'd known, if I'd had a choice- I might have willingly come with you. And everything could have been different."

"I'd planned on telling you! But that elk, it... it was there for you. I couldn't take the chance after you'd found the ring. I should never have told you about it. It's my fault and you have every right to hate me."

"I don't hate you!" I glared as he fought the corners of his lips and looked down at the table.

His voice was a little lighter now. "I didn't have the time or resources to figure out what was going on well enough to keep you safe. Not with how aggressive that beast had become. He'd tried to kill me a couple of times while I was there. Having connected with the ring, I imagine it had realized what you are as well. I barely survived its attacks. I couldn't simply hope that you would too if I were to leave or if you dismissed me, thinking me insane." I eyed him apprehensively. "Wouldn't you have? If I told you about all of this, could you see any possible way that you would have believed me?" He was looking at me in earnest and I knew he was right. I would have put as much distance between us as I could. And whatever that elk was, it may have eventually killed me. It certainly wanted to that last day.

~

EVERYONE WALKS IN HEARTWOOD. The city is concentrated enough that it's practical and to watch everyone commuting- you'd think it was some kind of social event. Everyone seemed happy to see everyone else, and they all seemed to be checking in with one another. It was... odd. Possibly a byproduct of the close quarters. There was a carriage or two and a handful of people riding horses, but nearly everyone seemed to be walk- ing. It was a slow sort of bustle, and all in the same direction. It was really kind of bizarre, like a sort of migration. The only thing that seemed even remotely magical about any of it were the three central buildings that spiraled up to unimaginable heights in the middle of it all.

"Those are the pillars of Heartwood- the Spires. Buildings made with magic more than anything else. They belong to and are run by some of the more influential sorcery families. They're vital to the city and deserve our respect. Remember that and you'll do alright with them." We walked at a relaxed pace, Briar letting my curiosity lead us this way and that as he acted as my tour guide and answered my questions.

"Heartwood?"

"The name of this kingdom. Admittedly kingdom might seem an antiquated term to you, but it serves its purpose. Our people have a queen and a commander, but the kingdom also has a council of Eldors that are made up of less magical people that have sorcerer advisors. It's very involved and political, but if you're interested...."

"Does everyone have magic, energy, whatever?"

"We are a minority, but we have our strengths, obviously. Everything is still pulled from something though, in all matters. To not know where it's being pulled from is dangerous. For the sorcerers that's all about lineage and it's more about borrowing magic than using their own energy. They pull from around them instead of creating from within. Here's an Earth analogy, it's as though they're able to use a bulldozer, but we *are* the bulldozer. Admittedly they're able to do more, but only if they have their tools. We are our own tool and therefore are never without our power. You should be able to build up your power, your energy, far more quickly now that you're here."

"Really? Does *here* matter?"

"We're stronger here. I've watched you notice the gold in my eyes. You'll see it's brighter here. You and I can utilize energies, unlike regular humans. We create our energy within us and can use it as freely as it will allow. Sorcerers manipulate the world, using it, pulling from it. We don't always agree with their methods, but they are essential to our way of life here. Everything and everyone deserves their own place."

"Prove it to me then. Show me." I stopped walking and we turned to face one another.

"Why is it you only believe what my mother has told you? Don't you believe that your healing with the plants, even just being able to see life's tapestry, is beyond the capabilities of most?"

I simply shrugged. "Some magics are easier to believe in than others. You said you'd prove to me what you could."

"All I can do is try and trust that you'll believe me or at least believe what you know to be real." He seemed exasperated, but I could sense a modicum of doubt. "Speaking of trying." He buried his head in his hands and rubbed his face roughly before looking at me again. "I am trying for full disclosure here. I know you value complete honesty. No one calls me Briar. Everyone calls me Thorn. You can imagine the jokes."

"Yeah, I'm not calling you that. But thank you... for trying."

"Frankie, call me whatever you want. As long as you keep calling."

I smiled awkwardly and began walking again. "What are we then? If you and I are the same, what is that?"

"Magic. Fire. And so much more. I cannot wait to show you, but for now...."

"For now I have to trust you. Got it. So, what does that mean- *Commander*? What is it that you do?"

"Don't say it like that!" His faux exasperation was endearing enough that I began to relax. "I command Heartwood's military. I keep us safe."

This revelation genuinely shocked and stopped me in my tracks. He was too young to command an entire military. It seemed absurd. I was about to ask how that was possible when something flying above us caught my attention. Nearly noon, the sun was almost directly above us and there were no clouds in sight, just beautiful blue sky. What I'd seen was mostly white against the blue background. Finding it, my gaze locked on it, trying to register what I was seeing.

I was peripherally aware of Briar following my gaze and turning back to watch me. I could feel his eyes on me, but I wasn't going to look away from the flying wonder I'd spotted for anything. It looked like what I imagine the underside of a white teddy bear would look like from this distance, all rounded and fluffy, but with wings. Large wings. The wingspan was at least double the length of the would-be teddy. And it *was* flying. Actually moving its wings and literally flying above us. I couldn't believe it.

Without realizing it I was moving around trying to get a better angle and nearly lost my balance. Briar caught me and held my hand as I kept looking, following its path as best I could, trying to see it for even a moment longer. "Briar, what *was* that? Did I really just see what I think I saw?" He was smiling at me as my mouth gaped open still in amazement. He pulled me closer and put his arms around me. Staring into his eyes, I could feel the rip in my reality that would ultimately tear it all apart.

I had just seen a griffin. Yes, it had been flying above me. But like the vision in the fire of Jen's ring, I'd had a similar one of this creature at a different angle and knew what it was. And in my bones I knew I'd be seeing it again, soon.

For a moment it seemed as though Briar was about to kiss me. "Do you believe me now?" Instead of answering I straightened myself back out, suddenly unsure of what I had actually witnessed. The visions I'd been having, both awake and asleep, could be a trick of the mind. I crossed my arms in front of my chest, looking around, as I shivered slightly against the chill of the wind. "Come on, we need to get you a coat. I won't have you freezing on my watch."

I didn't argue and followed behind him. "Where are we, in relation to Earth?"

"So you believe me now?" His seditious question was met with an icy stare that he quickly shook off. "Northeast from where you're from. About a fifteen-hour drive. But it doesn't exactly match up the way you're thinking." His pace slowed and he offered me his arm. I took it, a bit uncertain, and we continued walking side by side.

"Why was I unconscious for two days then?"

"It's not exactly a straight route when you need to jump worlds. Not to mention we had to go through Gale's kingdom. They're a bit chilly, that bunch." He snickered to himself at whatever joke he'd just made. "No one thought it wise to have you aware while there were so many moving parts."

"How considerate...," I drawled. "So how do I get home then?" His step paused and I tightened my hold on his arm. I wanted to tell him it wasn't personal. But the thought occurred to me that it should be.

"I said I'd take you back once you know this world, if that's what you still want."

"Promise me. Promise you're not lying to me. Promise me that you will actually take me back. I need you to promise." I was desperate and begging and knew that of course his word could still mean nothing. I was trying to keep my hopes from rising and my fears from falling, but still, I needed to try *something* to reassure myself as I felt the safety of my numbness falling away.

"On my life I swear it to you. And I swear it on one I value more than my own- yours." He took my hand and kissed it as he promised.

I'm an idiot and I couldn't help myself. I wrapped my arms around him and held him close. Against my better judgment, I believed him. He hesitated for a moment before letting himself melt into my me and hold me tightly against him. "Thank you," I whispered in his ear. His body went stiff feeling my breath on him. He quickly let me go and grabbed my hand, leading me back towards the buildings that twirled up towards the heavens. The outside city with its plethora of homes reminded me of one of those Italian coastal villages with all the houses slightly staggered and painted in an array of happy colors. Except these all had oversized windows in uniquely unusual and rounded shapes and all with that peculiar green glass. They were all the same, but each had some element or another of uniqueness, as though each had its own tiny bit of agency.

The streets lined with these houses finally opened up to a large plaza with the spiraling towers in the center. What I'd seen of this world appeared mostly to be from ages and eras long forgotten, but these buildings far and away surpassed any technology I'd ever seen. The buildings themselves were massive, cylindrical, and... gleaming. The walls looked as though they were built of diamond rods and beams with swaths of curving glass between them. Boulders rose up, spiraling alongside the entirety of the buildings, flush against the glass as if they were gravity defying stairways. These impossibly large stones were crowned with lush greenery, and from my point of view it all appeared to go inside of the buildings as well. "How does a structure like this exist in a world that's so far behind mine?"

"This *is* your world," he said stiffly. "And why would you assume we're behind Earth? We have technologies that are far more advanced. Yes, magic helps facilitate such things, but we have also borrowed quite a few inventions and ideas from Earth. Having not shut ourselves off completely has given us a step up in many arenas. There are reasons why we keep the gateways open after all. Using minimal land coverage, we think up, not out. Most of our vital operations are housed here. There are several levels and varieties of gardens, libraries, and there are recreational areas higher up that I think you'll enjoy. I'll give you a tour tomorrow. I'm afraid we don't have time today."

As we walked through the open plaza, I couldn't help but feel a bit unsettled. It was a bustling area with an excess of people coming and going. The cobblestones we'd been traversing had turned into large, seamlessly connected flag-stones and there were vendors selling nearly anything you could think of- fabrics, foods, books, trinkets. It was an entire marketplace spread out around these three buildings.

I could smell some kind of meat and my stomach growled more audibly than I thought was necessary. Briar directed us to one of the stands and we each got a meat kebab. Dinner had been edible. This had been juicy and succulent. Phenomenal, and exactly what I needed. Briar seemed to have a knack for always knowing what that was, and making sure I got it.

"How are these buildings so tall? And why didn't I see them last night? Shouldn't they have been pretty well lit?"

"One of the sorcery families specializes in turning things to a diamond like state, allowing for nearly unbreakable materials to be made relatively easily. Buildings, tools, weapons, that sort of thing. But one of them, ages ago, had some unique abilities with rocks. The families are nothing if not diligent with putting their skills to good use. And these have proven very useful to us.

"Of course, there are also protection barrier protocols in place. Mostly for weather related incidents but for security safeguards as well. They're designed to withstand everything we could think of, and a few other things as well. They're enchanted to not throw off light. It's not good for the wildlife, and we do share this world after all. Besides, it would destroy the view of the night sky. Not to mention make us a pretty big target.

"Now come on, we do have a schedule to keep since you're only giving me two days." He looked at me pointedly, still holding out hope.

"Well, best get to it then," I chimed in, giving him the answer I knew he didn't want. To say my curiosity was piqued would be an understatement. He'd brought me to a world of magic, and I'd seen, *felt*, enough that I no longer needed to have faith. But there was still something off here, I could sense it. And I wanted for nothing but to wake up back home from an overly vivid dream and have Lark harangue me about something or other.

Briar offered me his arm and again I accepted. A few people

were eyeing us. I noticed, so Briar must have as well. He didn't seem to mind though. It made me uncomfortable, but I wasn't sure why.

The inside of the spire we entered was lined floor to ceiling with pristine white marble. There was a distinct lack of any kind of scent. Odd and stark enough that I noticed. It didn't even smell sterile, just... nothing. Briar led us to a large, opaque, glass column in the center of this bizarrely futuristic lobby. He waved his arm in front of something on the cylinder that I hadn't noticed. A door on the side opened and we walked over to it.

A young woman stood inside, smiling pleasantly as we entered. "Welcome to LaFaye Spire. Where may I take you today?" She looked between us expectantly and I turned to Briar. He had his hands behind his back again, trying to make me take the lead.

I sighed heavily, not a fan of this game, before addressing her. "I need a coat, I guess."

"Of course!" She was very cheerful and reminded me a bit of Lark, when Lark had to be nice. "There are several ateliers that will have just what you need. If you could tell me a bit more about what you're looking for I can help direct you. Or I can take you to where the shops start, and you can look around."

"Something *really* warm. I'm not sure besides that. The start sounds like a good idea. Thank you."

The doors had already closed seamlessly. Her hand moved over the wall before her, and an intricate design of spirals and slashes flashed, glowing over where the door had been. Her face went blank, and she murmured a word I couldn't quite make out. We stood silently for just a moment, only long enough for me to wonder when something would happen. When the doors opened back up, it wasn't to the white marble lobby. There was more white marble, but only for a few feet outside of the elevator. Past that were multiple store fronts along a rounded wall of glass, all with their own aesthetic and complimenting entrances.

Briar followed me around the shops like a lost little puppy. The selection was adequate, though nearly everything stayed within a certain style. I ended up picking out something pleasantly warm despite how thin the material felt. Of course it was wool- everything seemed to be made from some kind of wool around here. But it had to have been magicked somehow to be this excessively warm. The coat was long, nearly down to my knees, with enough pockets to make me happy. The front of it overlapped each side and there were loop ties in a few places instead of any kind of zipper. I also picked up another pair of boots that fit better, and a couple outfits for lounging and a few more for day wear. Mercifully, I wasn't expected to wear these cumbersome dresses at all times.

For the most part I was only looking at the essentials, but there was one nightgown the associate brought along after seeing me eye it a few times. It was a succulent red and around the hem, which landed only halfway down my thighs, it had embroidered dragons in a repeating design. It reminded me of a rustic Viking pattern. The fabric was as smooth as butterfly wings. And given how low cut it was on the top as well, it clearly wasn't meant to be worn for very long. I couldn't get the design out of my head. Not that I wanted any Visnatura lingerie. I had no use for it. Regardless, I was grateful for the associate's discretion because I could have never picked it up with Briar watching so closely. I wasn't really sure how their money system worked since I was yet to see any exchanged for anything. And I didn't want to ask Briar in front of anyone. Something told me these people weren't used to outsiders, especially those coming from another world. Or maybe they were. I'd have to ask him about that later, too. My list of questions was growing longer, and the answers weren't coming nearly fast enough.

When we were away from everyone else, I had to ask, "Are you sure this is all okay? I mean, how do I pay you back?"

"You don't. Didn't I steal you away from everything?" he goaded. "I owe you."

"You're mocking me." I turned away from him, not wanting him to see the emotion in my eyes. If either of us had a right to be annoyed, it certainly wasn't him.

"*Teasing* aside, don't worry about it. You have always been nothing but kind to me and I'd like to reciprocate wherever I can. Our disbursements are very unlike what you're used to. Everyone takes part in society, and everyone gets what they need. You're under my protection, and I'll make sure you have whatever you want." I still wouldn't turn towards him. I didn't want him to see my face glowing with curiosity and interest. And I hadn't always been kind.

We went back to the elevator. We were at least twenty floors up while we were shopping based on the view from the glass walls around the outside of the shops. After Briar told the attendant where we were going the elevator went up another forty. I asked. There was only one door on this level- dark wood embedded with a handful of gemstones in a celestial pattern. The wall next to it was adorned with a handful of simple runes.

Now Briar took the lead without asking for my arm. I chided myself for missing the contact. He'd taken me to lunch at what seemed like a very posh place. A quick word to the host, and we were led through a handful of crowded rooms to a private one. It was a cozy setting against the outside wall of the tower. The view was outstanding. I could see the other towers to the side and all the rest of the kingdom as it lay before us. Stone walls encircling us, a river running through the land, rolling hills of golds and greens, snowy mountains in the distance, all looking rather peaceful and picturesque.

A few stories down there were commuting tubes running between each tower. As I watched the people walking through the somewhat transparent cylinders, fascinated, he continued his self-imposed tour guide duties. "The other towers have different purposes. One is basically a hospital. Another is used for government departments for the kingdom. Our people have the Queen's Reign. It's our own governing body, basically. Those dealings occur in the Mountain, the castle-like building you woke up in. Our dealings with the rest of the kingdom occur over there, along with the rest of the governing bodies and their works." He motioned to the tower on our left. "They all have a few restaurants up higher, greenhouses, gardens, and various recreational structures at the top. They each have different libraries as well. Most professions have their practices here as well. As I said, nearly everything is housed in these towers."

"Do all the kingdoms have these?"

"These are unique to Heartwood. It all has to do with what sorcerer families reside where, and where the kingdoms spread out their own resources. Here we reserve more of our livable space for the forest."

"Livable space?"

"Our world only permits so much space to each region. We have more sentient species than Earth and we try, not always of our own will, to leave enough room for all. It's a matter of practicality. Not all the kingdoms take this obligation as seriously as they need to, and we all pay for their malfeasance. That's another part of my responsibilities, reining them in for the betterment of our kingdom, and our world." He looked grim but I didn't want to poke into politics just now.

"How many kingdoms are there? Could I see a map?"

"I would love to show you a map. On day three." He winked at me, and I pursed my lips as I rolled my eyes at him. He enjoyed teasing me too much.

I couldn't get the idea of *permitted space* out of my head. "So who decides? Where your livable space is, I mean?"

He looked at me hesitantly again. "You're not going to believe me. Not yet."

"Try me? The worst that happens is I think you're crazy and you just prove it to me later."

He nodded dourly. "Our gods tell us. The ones that are still here, anyway. We have gods that play a much more active role than your own and they designate certain rules, limitations, that sort of thing. Their presence is very physical and tangible, as is their power. Given the ones you're used to, it may be difficult to understand, or believe."

I nodded but kept my mouth shut. He was right, I didn't believe him. My questions would be answered in time, and it was all growing fantastical enough that I was rethinking my coma explanation.

Lunch had resembled old world Italian cuisine, but with a bit more kick. In a word- divine. Briar relaxed noticeably over the meal. Afterwards he took my hand as he led me out of the restaurant, and again I let him.

A carriage was waiting for us when we left the tower. An actual horse drawn carriage- although the eyes of these horses looked far wilder than any I'd ever seen. Practically buzzing, I was visibly excited about going to the animal sanctuary. I love animals and as a child always wanted to take care of them. I felt protective of most things, although they generally didn't care for me. My mother used to take in all sorts of strays, and they would consistently litter my room with tiny dead things. Briar had an amused look as he helped me into the carriage. "The sanctuary has to be outside of the security walls. We could never appropriate the space needed inside. It's not as secure, but it's workable."

The carriage took us away from the Spires, down street after street. I wondered if the kingdom had been designed to confuse people. I'd never be able to navigate with how the streets looped and turned back on themselves. Eventually the houses dissipated, replaced with a manicured clearing bordered by a stereotypical castle wall- complete with....

"A moat and drawbridge, really?"

"Water is very powerful and cleansing. You'd be amazed at how well it can protect. Besides, we needed the stone wall for a different kind of barrier. One you can't see."

Another plethora of questions populated, again, but I was distracted by the area coming into view. It was the densest forest I had ever seen, and being from the Pacific Northwest that was saying something. The trees were wider than most houses. They were also taller than any I'd ever seen, and I'd seen the tallest ones Earth has to offer.

Simply existing amidst these arboreous giants, as they began to surround us, a rush of joy and happiness overtook me. I wanted to run through this mystical forest and literally hug a tree. They were so thick it was nothing but gloriously textured bark wherever you looked. The canopies shadowed our path, making this surreal play place for us. Being here... my heart felt happy. My mind soothed. My fire steadied.

I was vaguely aware of Briar watching me again. "I don't think I've ever seen you this happy. And all it took were some damn trees," he scoffed. Despite his cynicism- I can't explain it, I had this overwhelming desire to hug him.

As I joined him on his side of the carriage, he turned towards me, curious but guarded. His arms were still across his chest when I embraced him. "I don't know why I'm here," I whispered into his ear, "I don't understand any of it. I don't believe most of it. I know I should be angry and rage and try to get away. But...." I wanted to thank him, but I didn't know why or for what. I had this... gratitude towards him. If I believed in souls, I'd say my soul knew his and was happy to be by his side in this place. But I didn't believe in all of that, so I had no idea what was happening. I was simply happy, present in that moment.

He unfolded his arms between us and wrapped them around me, pulling me closer to him. "It feels like home, doesn't it?" He cradled his face into the crook of my neck as though it was the most natural thing in the world for him. His breath on my skin made me quiver. I pulled away before I felt too much. I kissed his cheek as I let him go. He looked at me and I held his gaze for a moment as I nodded my answer. An explanation I hadn't been able to put into words myself. One I wasn't sure of until just then. Home.

I had to look away, checking in with myself to make sure I wasn't being led astray again. It always hurts infinitely worse when you're not expecting it. I wouldn't survive the hurt of trusting someone again, and it needed to stop. He didn't say anything as he placed his arms across his chest again. I stayed next to him as I marveled at this new world around me.

After a few minutes I felt him put a hand over mine and I didn't pull away. Something akin to butterflies in my stomach started up as we rode along, and the thought of the pain that was going to come from this made me want to cry. We stayed like that for a time until the forest opened into rolling fields. A large series of barn-like structures started to come into view, and he laced his fingers with mine. I squeezed his hand to let him know it was okay. A while later we arrived at the stables and again he helped me down.

"I have a surprise for you," he said, long past ecstatic.

"Isn't everything a surprise to me right now?"

It was his turn to steal a quick kiss on my cheek. "You saw her earlier and the look on your face.... It's been a challenge keeping quiet." He led the way into the largest barn with an endearing spring in his step. For the size of the barn there were only four colossal stalls, each bigger than most houses.

Inside the one at the far corner, preening her feathers, was the snow leopard griffin I'd seen earlier up above and in my quasi-vision, or whatever those were. I gasped seeing her so close, and so real. She had the body and rump of a snow leopard, but her head and forelegs resembled a snowy owl with intricate and pristine feathers. I could see black talons at the end of fuzzy white legs in the front and white furry paws in the back. "I knew you'd like this," he beamed as I fought to control my excitement.

A stout, older woman in hide-leather pants and a graying blue sweater walked up to us. "Commander!"

"Stable Master!" Briar said. "Frankie, I'd like you to meet

Voula. She oversees everything here. Voula, this is Frankie. She's quite fond of your creature here." It had been clear from Voula's demeanor that she was in charge, but it still took some effort for her to not look too prideful.

"Frankie." She nodded politely and I reciprocated the gesture. "Here to meet Brynn?" She was unlocking the stable door as she asked. "Had her first long flight this morning. Already a yearling now. She'll be going to her own aviary soon enough." Voula handed Briar a brown sack that was dripping something dark and foul smelling. We followed her in, and she latched the door behind us.

She walked up to Brynn and after preening the griffin's head and scratching her hocks for a spell, she brought her over. With an unnerving nonchalance, Voula took the bag back and pulled out a dead rat by its tail. "Here ya go." She extended the rat out to me. I stared at her, mortified. "It's her favorite. Toss it over. Quick like!"

Biting my tongue to still my revulsion, I took the not-so-tiny carcass and tossed it. Brynn caught it midair, swallowing it whole as she moved it down her throat with a crunching noise that sent a shiver down my spine. Voula and Briar shared a laugh as Brynn walked up to me and began rubbing her head into my chest. I scratched it the way Voula had, and Brynn chirped her approval. I couldn't believe I'd finally found an animal that actually liked me! I didn't even care that I'd had to bribe it first.

As I kept petting and preening Brynn, Voula and Briar discussed some other business with the sanctuary, the aviaries, and other overhead issues that couldn't compete with the chirps and nudges of a living, breathing griffin. Every once in a while their conversation would become a bit more tense and hushed, which naturally interested me. They'd notice and their voices would return to a normal register as they presumably changed the subject.

I was letting myself get swept away by all of this. He had promised to take me back, at some point. The specifics needed to be nailed down. I wanted to trust him, but I'd been burned enough to know better. Would he still take me back if I continued to insist that I didn't want to stay with him? When I knew everything he needed me to know? Why didn't I already?

Brynn eventually tired of my attentions and went to lay in some bedding to preen herself. Guess I ruffled some of her feathers the wrong way, I thought to myself as I fought back a smile. When I approached Briar and Voula, it was clear I was interrupting something. They'd been odd enough with their business I didn't think much of it.

When Voula said, "Let's go see the rest of my babies!" I forgot all about their private conversations. I was no one in this world, but Briar still had to keep it safe, even as he showed it to me.

THE SUN WAS SETTING as we left. By the time we entered the forest we couldn't see anything for the dark. It didn't deter our driver as he continued at his steady clip. The quick drop in temperature surprised me though. Sitting next to Briar, I let him put an arm around me. I should have kept my distance.

"Are you feeling okay? You're very warm. Not that I'm complaining."

He chuckled at my question. "More than okay. You'll acclimate soon enough. Was... Frankie, was today okay?" His voice was tinged with a nervous energy.

I took a minute to answer. "This world is intricate and involved and complicated. There's also still a lot you're not telling me. But today... was okay. And I still want to go home."

We rode for a while in silence as he held me, warming me, and my head gradually came to rest on his shoulder. "If I told you everything all at once, you wouldn't believe any of it and very little of it would make sense. I don't want to keep anything from you, but some things you're not ready for."

"Is that what you told yourself about lying to me before?"

He let out a long, slow breath. "I have never lied to you."

"You didn't tell me about this world. Keeping things, things this *big* from someone, is tantamount to lying."

"I *tried* telling you. In front of the fire that day. You didn't want to hear it, and I knew not to push. I've never lied to you, Frankie. I know what it means to you and whether you like it or not, you mean a great deal to me. I care about you. I know you're not going to believe me, but I'm not going to hurt you."

I looked up to see a flash of gold radiating in his eyes as he stared down at me, brighter here like he'd said. I believed him, for better or worse. I believed him.

Fuck.

I believed him. I laid my head back on his shoulder as he kissed my forehead.

BRIAR MADE DINNER THAT EVENING. I'd offered to help but he insisted on doing it all himself. It was cute, in a way. Conversation came easier. Everything was starting to feel less heavy with him. "Well Commander, what's on the docket for tomorrow?" He smiled and gave a little laugh, relieved that I was easing into it all.

"Since it may be my last day with you, I wanted to start with the greenhouses the Medela family uses for their healing practices. Then I'd like to show you Owjen's ring. *Really* show it to you. It is yours after all."

"I just want a little agency here, that's all. I'm really not trying to hurt you. I still want to know you, to see you. And wait, why is the ring mine? It should be yours, or Gale's?"

"My mother left it for you. The intentions in the energy she's left on it are clear. It belongs to you. You should keep it with you. But it's too big for you to wear as a ring. I'll get you a necklace to put it on, if you'd like?"

Attempting to hide my smile I nodded. I didn't know why, but I wanted that ring. Inexplicably it meant something to me. A flash of another ring I'd once worn around my neck came to me, one that had nearly destroyed me, making me shudder. I shook it off, thinking of things to contend with presently.

"Where will I stay? After, I mean?" I asked quietly. My mind already made up, but he didn't know me well enough to know what that meant.

Eyes pleading, he cleared his throat. He wanted to argue with me- ask why I would still be thinking of leaving. He put on an emotionless mask before answering me. "While this has always been your world, you are considered a new citizen to Heartwood. As such you will be given accommodations like any new arrival. There are apartments set up in the Spires for newcomers. They will help you get on your feet, without me, if that is your wish."

"Aren't you going to threaten to abandon me or not take me back?"

His emotionless eyes curved into a dejected expression. "No, Frankie. I will always be here for you. Whether you want me to be or not." I could feel my face warming at his words.

"What do you want from me?" I asked.

He shook his head in understanding. "Nothing. You don't need to do or be anything for me, for anyone. I don't want anything from you, other than for you to be happy. Even if it's not with me." He stood calmly and left the table. Maybe I should have gone after him. I just watched him walk upstairs. We'd had such a good day, and of course I had to ruin it.

After dragging myself upstairs to my appointed room, I took a very long bath before crawling into the cold bed. My body was exhausted. I had pushed myself too hard after being abducted and still had not completely recuperated. The cold here seemed to be getting more unbearable with my overtiredness. Still, sleep evaded me. I couldn't seem to relax in this bed. I walked out of the room with the intention of going downstairs to sit in front of the large fireplace.

Briar's light was still on, and I decided to check on him. I cleared my throat outside again. No response. Creeping along to the door I slowly pushed it open. He was nowhere to be seen. I should have looked through the rest of the house. Instead I climbed into his bed and curled up under his heavy blankets. Sleep came quickly after that.

Light coming through his window woke me again. He wasn't here. I lay on my back, staring up at the ceiling. He must have found me in his bed and decided he didn't want the trouble. I heard the front door open and close and someone clearing the stairs to this level in seconds. Briar opened the door and for a moment we just stared at one another.

"Frankie...."

"I was just getting up."

"I had an errand.... I should have said something." He couldn't seem to find the words.

I shrugged. "It's fine. It's your life. All I care about is that you keep your word and take me home when you're done toying with me."

Anger flashed over his face before he regained control, removing any hint of emotion. He nodded grimly and walked into his room as I made my way towards mine. I could smell something on him that wasn't him. A floral scent mixed with possibly a waft of liquor. A vice tightened around my heart. He'd gone out with someone. Why was I so upset about this? He wasn't mine and there was no expectation here. We'd only slept together a couple of times before all of... this. There was really no need for even a courtesy heads up. *You stupid girl*, I thought to myself, not for the first time.

I walked into my room and hurried to close the door so he wouldn't see me cry. The recent influx of emotions that I couldn't handle had continued to build. I cursed myself, knowing tears were imminent. I was a mess and knew it and had no idea what to do about it. I stifled my sobs hoping he wouldn't hear. A moment later he was at my door. "Frankie, talk to me," he pleaded. "Frankie?"

I said nothing and went to the bathroom to turn on the water, desperate to drown out the noise. Pulling myself together, I hated how foolish I was being. I wasn't his and I didn't want to be. I dressed quickly and laid a cold washcloth over my eyes for a few minutes, hoping the swelling would become less noticeable. I was surprised he hadn't just barged in. I guess he really was trying. Or didn't actually care. Funny how either seemed plausible.

I walked downstairs like nothing had happened. He was sitting in one of the chairs in front of the fire, tapping his thumb. "Frankie?"

"Ready to go?" I asked as my stomach grumbled at me. "Maybe after breakfast?" I laughed it off. "Why don't I make something this time?"

"Frankie...."

"Look- it's fine. Neither of us expected this, right? Anyway, you won't have to babysit anymore after today. So come on. We're burnin' daylight!" My false bravado was wearing thin.

"DRYAD'S DAMN IT ALL, FRANKIE! STOP! You have no idea what you're talking about. You have no idea how I feel about

you. You don't *know* what I was doing last night! You want people to be brutally honest with you, but you make all these assumptions without ever trying to communicate yourself!" I hadn't heard him yell like this. I'd never seen him this angry. Not like this. His eyes were that same molten gold the queen's had been. He started to storm off towards the front door.

"BRIAR! You can't scream at me like that and then storm off! It isn't fair that you can run away whenever you want and just leave me. Stop it! Stop abandoning me!" I hadn't realized that's how I felt until the words forced themselves out. Had he ever really abandoned me before? I'd known this man for a little over a week and been unconscious for a good deal of it. I guess some part of me simply couldn't handle the idea of him being like all the rest.

He froze in his tracks. As he turned to look at me, I could see the gold in his eyes tremble. His voice followed suit. "I never meant to abandon you."

There was a stillness. A gap in time as we stood, frozen, emotions churning and thoughts flying. I relaxed my body and let out a sigh alongside my apology. "I'm sorry I yelled. And that I got upset because you... no, that's not... I'm sorry I got upset." I wanted to ask where he had been last night. But if my assumption was even close, I didn't actually want to know.

"Come with me." Against my better judgment I complied. My stomach again grumbled as I trailed behind him. "We'll get you something on the way," he murmured back to me. His kindness aggrieved me. He was angry with me and still cared. It had never been that way before. I hated how kind Briar could be. I wanted to hate him.

We walked directly to the Spires. It took about fifteen minutes, and I was starting to get a better feel for the streets.

"This is the spire that the Medela Family runs. The green-houses are mostly for medicinal plants. The library is a medical one. The Medela healing center is here. Research and Development for nearly everything is here, too. You get the gist. Given your knack with plants and mind for healing I thought you'd be intrigued by what they do." He still looked and sounded miserable.

"Thank you, Briar." His lips twitched every time I used his name.

"There's also something special I'd like to show you." The inside of this tower mirrored the other one with the elevator in the center. We went up higher and higher, only perceptible through the short amount of awkward silence between us all.

"How many floors up are we?" I asked, nervous at the idea of being so high up.

"We are going to level 127." This attendant wasn't what I'd call friendly.

We stepped out of the elevator and Briar grabbed my hand. "This entire level is dedicated to one tree. It's the only plant that can heal a dragon." I gave a little laugh, and he froze in his steps. Without turning back to look at me he spoke quickly and quietly, "Frankie, there are things I need to tell you that you do not yet know. Things that have escaped me, mostly for my own selfishness. For now, while we are here, please play along with everything. You'll become a target if certain people find out some of the things you don't know. It'll reveal things best not revealed quite yet."

"And let me guess, next you're going to promise to tell me everything I need to know to—"

"Can you *please* stop being so antagonistic for once?!" He had raised his voice and turned to leer at me as he reprimanded me. I wanted to retort and give my usual defensive, leave-me-the-fuck-alone type of response. Instead, I lowered my eyes and nodded. As far as I could tell Briar was my only way home. And I still had my doubts about whether or not he believed I truly was going to be leaving his today.

"Commander, back so soon?" A honeyed voice carried our way, eliciting a hushed curse from Briar. "You've missed Madam Medela. She left shortly after you this morning. Furlong again. No surprise there." The man walking towards us as he spoke had an olive complexion and gorgeously curly hair with the faintest graying at his temples. He wore a long white jacket that resembled a lab coat, but instead of the typical lapel there was a collar that covered most of his neck. His beard was short, neat, and trimmed, and he stood almost as tall as Briar. Despite his graying hair he looked to be a few years younger than Briar, but maybe that was his smile. It was welcoming in a way I hadn't seen since arriving in this world. When he got closer I couldn't help but notice his velvety brown eyes that were yet to leave me. Then I noticed it, that floral scent from Briar this morning. I had been right and the vice around my heart again tightened at the realization.

"How unfortunate. I was hoping to introduce her to my companion here." I looked up at his dubious use of the word companion. I suppose he was accurate in a literal sense, if no other. "We'll take a quick look around the greenhouse and be off then. Thank you, Sir Agustín."

"You should at least introduce *me* to your lovely companion!" His mock outrage at being brushed off didn't sit well with Briar. Nothing about this man did. It was clear they weren't the best of friends. Sir Agustín's eyes had a glint of mischief that I didn't quite trust, even if it did intrigue me.

Reluctantly, Briar relented. "Sir Agustín, this is Draca Francesca. Draca Francesca, this is Sir Agustín Medela, he is the next head of the Medela Family for Furlong. He's finishing up some work for us here before he unfortunately has to leave us. His mother is Madam Medela, current Head of the Medelas."

"And you, my dear, need no further introduction. The Commander here is quite smitten with you." Agustín's warm eyes sparkled, waiting for my reaction.

I laughed lightly at his insinuation. "As smitten as a child with their pet," I said as he held out his hand for me to shake. I extended mine and he quickly turned it over, kissing the back of it. I'd seen this in movies but couldn't believe anyone would actually pull this move. It felt like his lips lingered but I couldn't be sure. Briar was certainly bristling.

"Children often care very deeply for their pets. Often more than we care for one another. Perhaps being a pet wouldn't be so bad?" He winked at me as I shook my head. "Come with me, dear pet. I would be honored to show you around my green-house." He offered me his arm and Briar intercepted, placing himself between the two of us.

"We're already behind our own schedule. We couldn't take your time like that. I merely wanted to show her the Dragon Heart and our investment in them."

"Ah. Taking her downstairs next?"

"This evening, actually."

"It was lovely to meet you Draca Francesca. We should have dinner sometime soon. Our worlds have a lot of plant species in common as well as ones that rival one another. I'd enjoy a little mind to mind. Owjen taught me more than I can say. I believe you were quite close with her at the end?"

"I was, yes. She taught me, well, she taught me what she thought I should know, I suppose." He looked tenderly at me for a long moment. "And please. Call me Frankie." I smiled at him maybe a bit too sweetly. He was a smooth talker, but it was nice to have someone, anyone else to talk to. Or at least, someone who hadn't abducted me.

I may have imagined a little color in his cheeks as he returned the smile. "And you must call me August. I insist. Sir Agustín was my father." Briar groaned quietly beside us, making his annoyance unmistakable. Agustín's eyes brimmed with laughter, and I took a step back, having not realized how close we were still standing.

He left the same way he'd come. Briar waited until he was gone before he spoke again. "Yes, I was with Madam Medela most of the evening, but it isn't what you think."

"I know." Somewhere between realizing how deep his hatred for sorcerers ran and how clearly transactional his relationship with Agustín was, it had become clear he hadn't been out with Madam Medela in the way I'd imagined.

"Frankie- were you doing that just now to make me jealous?" His incredulous tone was almost endearing.

"Honestly?"

"Honestly."

"A bit." I was beyond entertained. "Did it work?"

He grumbled, "A bit," as he headed towards the same door Agustín had disappeared behind and I giddily trailed after.

I had been expecting some kind of sterile whitewashed lab, this was more like a jungle. I wished Agustín had stayed, I had so many questions and Briar had very few answers. For genuine lack of knowledge this time. The greenhouse with the Dragon Hearts entailed far more security than what was typical for any medical lab I'd heard of. Though it was far closer to the sterile lab I'd been expecting. The plants looked more like bushes standing almost as tall as me. They had fruit that resembled pomegranates, but they looked almost swollen with a red nectar that was slowly dripping from the tips of them.

"They're not ready until they've released all of their nectar.

It takes a very long time, and their medicinal uses aren't nearly as effective if we do anything to speed up the process."

"How many dragons are you healing?" I asked, having to stop myself from giggling at my own question.

"The plan is for two. But we like to have a reserve."

I looked around and saw no one within earshot. "Hey, what was with that name thing earlier? When you introduced me?"

"I have something to show you." He was forcing a frown, but I could see the corners of his lips curling up. "We need to go back to the Mountain."

CHAPTER
TEN

Briar's house was nearly a fifteen-minute walk west of the Spires. The queen's Mountain was a little over a fifteen-minute walk north. I was trying to get my bearings of the place and gain an understanding of the layout. Briar knew what I was doing and wasn't subtle about how he felt about it. He was also still being indignant about Agustín, so I was taking everything he said, as well as his attitude, with a grain of salt.

I was nervous about seeing the queen again. Especially now that I knew how much she wanted me dead, or had wanted. Briar's demeanor changed as he dragged that explanation out of me. To his credit, he made a sincere effort to comfort me. "She doesn't still want you dead. She gave me her word. You're safe here. I keep telling you, you are always safe here with me."

"Do you believe her? Do you trust her?" His answers didn't come quickly enough.

. . .

WE ARRIVED at the castle they called the Mountain. It looked just as cold as it had that first night. A few guards were positioned around the base of the stone monolith. I was surprised at how few were there. They were dressed just like Briar, minus the cloak, clad in the same deep gray leather. The front of their armor had straps of leather crossing over the front in thick diagonal strips. I wondered if there was any practical reason behind the design. Everything here had a type of beauty all of its own, but it all seemed to serve a purpose.

We went through the main entrance instead of Gale's secret side one. (No surprise there.) The whole place was a polished slate gray- the stairs, columns, outer walls, even the flagstones in the courtyard were all the same cold, intimidating gray. We ascended an obnoxiously imposing outer staircase that led up to a grandiose landing, bypassing what looked like a mountain of well laid rocks. To say it made me nervous about the stability of the castle itself was an understatement, but as I'd seen far more impossible things in the past 24 hours, I wasn't going to question it.

Something felt off being here though. I could feel it under my skin. I shouldn't be here. I wanted to talk to Briar about it, but I knew better than to invite trouble by asking something I should already know. When we finally made it to the top every guard bowed their head to Briar. He ignored most of them, giving only a curt nod to a handful. I annoyed myself by being impressed.

Up here the level of fortification, at least as far as guards went, felt more on point for a castle. Briar said something to one of them and they were off. I wasn't paying too much attention. I was busy marveling at the marble-like columns that marked a magicked environmental boundary between inside and out. The barrier existed despite the lack of wall or anything else substantial. I stepped back and forth over the threshold, outside-cold, inside-warm, outside-cold, repeatedly experiencing this drastic change in temperature. Briar was watching me now, a smirk across his face. I was about to ask him what he was smiling at when her voice dug into me.

"So nice of you to come for tea!"

I scurried in past the columns as Briar answered for us. "Helen. A pleasure, of course." I was surprised he was allowed to call her by her name like that. They seemed very comfortable with one another, and I couldn't help but wonder if they'd slept together. *Why do you keep doing that?* I asked myself.

The queen takes her tea in a small, gardened area lush with plants in the depths of her cold Mountain. The room is entirely encased in glass with gold accents along the support structures. We were like figurines in a gilded terrarium. I watched the coming and goings of the people outside, silently, the glass walls apparently soundproof, as Briar and the queen discussed some formalities. Looking around at the plants I wondered if this was what Heartwood looked like in the warmer months. I hoped I wasn't around long enough to find out.

There was actual tea this time, which was bitterly strong. We discussed what I'd seen since arriving and how I was finding it all. It came across as more of an interrogation than an amiable well visit. Briar told her what he'd managed to tell me so far. She was indignant I didn't know more but was sated when he asked about one of the caves. He stood to apparently examine said cave and she followed. I watched them as they both went to leave, unsure if I was supposed to follow until she called back to me.

"Draca Francesca, this is for your sake. You will need to be present." She said it warmly enough, but with her clipped accent I wasn't sure if she was amused or annoyed. I hurried to catch up, embarrassed that I'd either misunderstood or zoned out.

They walked together, side by side, talking like old friends. At one point my ears caught him talking about Agustín being his typical self with a pretty girl. It was amazing how much that actually bothered him. It'd be cruel for me tease him like that again. Really, I was flattered that he felt so threatened. At least that hungry look he kept giving me wasn't a lie, even if he was a bit cheesy.

We descended countless steps and traversed a plethora of hallways. We had to be travelling down into those stones, and likely further. The first few sets of stairs were grand and illuminated. The last few were hidden, narrow, and dark. The queen went first with Briar behind her. I was a little surprised how comfortable she was navigating these places. She clearly knew them well. More than once I'd swear I felt something land on me, and I'd given a little whole-body shake. This place definitely creeped me out. Briar held my hand on particularly treacherous sections, giving me a reassuring squeeze before letting go each time. I was guessing that our use of this room wasn't to be widely known.

We finally reached our destination, at least I hoped we had. There was a door made out of what looked like solid stone that Helen and Briar had to move together. Helen said a few hushed words to him before turning to me. "I will return shortly. You will not be alone." And then she was off.

Briar turned towards me and offered his hand, which I hesitantly accepted. I eyed him suspiciously as we walked further into the room with a door I couldn't open by myself. The rest of the cave room looked like, well, a cave. Briar used his energy to kindle some lights high up on the walls. It still amazed me to see it done and he knew it. His eyes smiled at me as I marveled at the lit lanterns that hung too high for anyone to reach on their own. Claw marks, deep and ragged, embedded in the stone floor and climbing up the walls kept catching flickers of the light.

I asked slowly, unsure of whether or not I wanted the answer. "Briar, what happened here?"

"I'll show you. But can I ask you a favor first?" His nervous energy was contagious.

"Sure," I answered slowly, unsure of my answer.

"I would like to kiss you."

"Are you asking permission? Or are you just stating the obvious?" Acting far more confident than I felt was a well-honed skill of mine that had kept me alive. It had clearly not diminished. I expected him to tell me to forget about it or to get annoyed at my inability to not be an ass.

"I am asking." His voice was steady and sincere, surprising me.

My stomach was turning to knots. I believed the only thing keeping him at bay was that we hadn't physically reconnected. And now he was asking, rather politely, if we could. I didn't want to have the feelings for him that I did, and if I'm being honest, he wasn't the only one between the two of us that I was trying to keep in place.

"It's not going to change anything. I'm still leaving in the morning."

"I know," he said steadily. "I'm still asking."

I thought about it for the hefty moment it required before giving a thoughtful, yet timid nod.

He stepped carefully and deliberately towards me, closing the slight gap between us. I stood still, watching him, waiting. He took so long I thought he was going to lose his nerve. Why was it so much more intense now? All at once he put one arm around my waist, pulling me flush to him as he put his other hand behind my head, losing his fingers in my hair as his lips met mine. The kiss deepened until I relaxed and my arms went up around him. He backed off just long enough to bite my lip and make my whole body shudder, before sinking back in. I couldn't believe how much I had missed these sensations. Missed feeling him under my fingertips. Missed his smoky leather scent washing over me. Missed... *him*. I allowed myself to get lost in him in that moment. It had only been a few days, but it was like reigniting a fire.

Helen clicked her tongue and we froze. Our lips parted but we held onto one another. Our foreheads touching, I didn't know what to say as I tried to catch my breath. He apparently didn't either as we continued to stand there in silence.

We slowly took a step back from one another. I turned to see Helen place a glass vial and an ornate box on top of what looked like an altar. "Plenty of time for that later, you two." But Briar was worried there wouldn't be a later and he was savoring every moment. I looked into his eyes and saw his worry. I reached up to cup his face with one hand as I gave him a small smile.

"Hey, I'm not going anywhere, okay?" I said, surprising even myself.

"Honest?" The desperation in his voice should have warned me.

"Honest." I gave him a bigger smile and his eyes rejoiced.

I shouldn't have promised when I didn't know what was coming. But I knew where my fire wanted to be. Whether or not I should want it there be damned. Coma, afterlife, dream, whatever was going on- I was done fighting it. I was going to start living in the moment and doing what I wanted to do. The promise of pain be damned.

He kissed me again, holding my head in both of his hands then quickly let go and took a few steps back. Helen firmly grabbed me, too firm for her little frame, and pulled me back towards the door. "What are you doing?!" I tried not to scream at the queen. It all happened so quickly I didn't know what to do. Turning to Briar for any kind of answer I saw him rapidly undressing. "Briar, *what* are you doing?"

I turned back to see Helen's smug expression. I didn't have time to register any of it. None of it made any sense. Sounds of snapping and the crackling of crunching bones echoed off of the cave walls. I felt them in my bones as it sent a shiver throughout every bit of me. Trying to find the source, I saw Briar's skin turning a dark copper as it twisted and contorted, growing. His face was full of unimaginable pain. A howl that started as a human noise filled with agony, quickly escalated into something I'd never heard before. Deep and dangerous and drawing me towards it.

Helen held fast as I tried to go to him. She was right beside me but had to yell to make herself heard over the sounds of anguish reverberating around us. "You need to stay clear until he is done. He has very little control as he changes. If he hurt you he would never forgive himself. Nor me."

"*Are you insane?! He's in pain! I need to help him!*" I couldn't believe her strength. I thrashed with everything I had and wasn't able to budge an inch. I could do nothing but watch. But like a shooting star, I blinked, and it was done. Where Briar had been there now stood a dragon. Not the gigantic, size-of-a-house dragon. But one that was seven or eight feet tall at its head, with molten gold eyes. I watched, stunned, as it opened up its wings, taking up most of this cavernous space. It looked like all dragons should- glorious and deadly. And it was staring at me.

It began to approach us, its wings relaxing by its side. I tried to move, to get back, to get away. But Helen held me steady. Panic set in when it was only a few feet away. The dragon stopped in its tracks and sat back on its haunches. Bringing its tail around itself in a relaxed manner as it sat there, watching us. Its scales shone of copper and I was trans-fixed, powerless to look away.

Those molten gold eyes…. Did I recognize those eyes? I knew. I'd witnessed it. Still, I had to ask. I had to ask because it wasn't possible. "I know what I, uh, saw. But, well, that can't be…. Uhm…. Did Briar just turn into a dragon?"

There was a voice that sounded like Briar's, though an octave or two lower with a timber that reverberated throughout the cave. "Don't be afraid, Frankie. I'm not going to hurt you. It can be dangerous when we transition. With the pain we have little control after we start the process. But I would never hurt you."

"Briar?!" I barely managed to squeak out his name. Helen let go of my arms after making sure I was able to stand on my own.

The deep din of his voice came again. "Yes, Frankie. It's me." A wave of lightheadedness overtook me and I broke our gaze, focusing anywhere he wasn't. Helen stepped back in to steady me for a moment until I could right myself. I was amazed and incensed.

"This definitely counts as you lying to me. This is kind of a big thing to keep secret. Did you really think—"

"That would be my fault," Helen interjected. "As queen, the safety of my dragons is my only priority. We do not hide what we are. Not in this world. But we do not go about telling strangers such things, either." I turned to look at her, confused and frustrated. "I think I will take my leave then. Frankie, Commander, I hope you two have a productive evening." She gave Briar a nod as she turned to leave. I could feel his golden eyes boring into me the entire time.

Dragon Briar spoke to me again. "I wanted to tell you before."

My eyes found him and kept washing over him. I couldn't

believe what I was seeing. A dragon. That had been Briar. Or rather, was Briar. Briar was a dragon. A fucking dragon....

"Explain." It was all I could say. My head was swimming. Nothing made sense.

"I am dragon. But was born in human form. It's akin to a long-standing curse for our kind. If you believe our legends, that is. I can change between the two forms, but my dragon takes exponentially more energy to control and maintain. Owjen was also dragon. There are many of us, but dragon being in your blood does not guarantee you can change. There are some who only carry it. You need to be able to access your energy to change."

I knew what he was going to say, but I didn't believe it. I couldn't.

"Frankie, you *are* one of us. I hope you can understand now why I had to bring you home." I'd begun to circle at a distance, wanting to see more of him, but my body stiffened at his words.

"You're telling me I can... that I have a dragon inside me?" I scoffed and his eyes locked on me, holding my gaze as my heart raced.

"You can touch me. I won't bite." I walked toward him, and he lowered his head. Gingerly I reached a hand out, inching forward. He puffed out some air, making me jump as he chortled heavily. I exhaled nervously and glared at him as I gathered my courage and stepped a little closer.

He lowered his head and pushed it into my palm. Warmth. Of course he was warm. I rubbed my hands over his warm scales. They felt like smooth, hardened leather. He had horns on the top of his head that flared backwards and felt more like bone. My hands trailed down his neck to his chest. The scales became much larger and harder, more unmoving. I looked at his front feet and talons. Of course that's what caused the marks inside this cave. But.... "Why are there claw marks in here?"

"We go through a phase where we can't control ourselves at first. We need a more experienced dragon to help us. It can get rough."

"At first?"

"When we are born in human form, we cannot turn into our true selves for quite some time. We need to be nearly grown as humans before our bodies can handle the transformation. We need to be able to instruct our energy and build it up. I can take years of practice."

"Does that mean I won't be able to change? If I believe any of that."

"It's difficult to say. Your first time is different. Needs to be triggered. You could choose to stay as you are, never needing, or being able to transform."

"You *need* to transform?"

"Your energy changes once you accept your dragon. You can't control it the same way, but it is heightened. That's part of why we handle our ire phase the way we do, to reclaim control. Feel for my energy. Tell me what you sense."

I wasn't sure if I should. But how does one argue with a dragon? "Is this why you called me Draca before?"

"You are Draca Francesca. Helen is Draca Regulus. I am Draco Legatus."

"Regulus, queen. Legatus?"

"Commander."

"Is Agustín one of us?"

Briar growled. His derision evident. "No. He is a sorcerer. Sirs and Madams. We don't mix."

"What do you mean, *don't*? He seemed to want to mix this morning."

"You're stalling. Feel for my energy. You'll be alright."

I sheepishly leaned against him and closed my eyes. It was instantaneous. Copper swirls flying everywhere off of the dragon shaped Briar I was touching. I gasped as I opened my eyes. If a dragon could smile, then Briar was smiling at me.

"If I wanted to..., to do this," I began to ask, gesturing at all of him.

"You *are* a dragon, whether you want to be one or not. The question is can you take on this form."

"If I wanted to take on this form then... what would that entail?" I asked as I continued to run my hands along his scales.

"There's a formula from the queen that helps to trigger the change. It strangles your energy and initiates the transformation. Your guide will help the first time. You would transform in a room similar to this so that you can be contained."

"What if my body can't handle it?"

"If you begin to transform and your body can't handle it, you would not survive."

"Is there a way to know? If your body can handle it, ya know, beforehand?"

Again, his answers came slowly. "No. It is something to consider with a clear mind. The queen has left a vial with us. She would like you to use it tonight. Please trust me, now is not the time. Despite how she feels. She may have promised to not harm you, but I don't know that she has our best interests at heart. And when the time does come, I cannot be the one to guide you."

"What?! Why not?" I was surprised by his answer and backed away to get a better look at the gambit of expressions rotating in his golden eyes.

"As I said, it can be rough. Your guide needs to be rough with you. I'm not sure I can be that for you. I won't hurt you. I'd sooner let you burn down our world."

Another bone crunching noise rattled through the cave and I backed further away. It took less than a minute, but it felt interminable. When he'd finished, he was on one knee with his hands on the ground, panting. He stood up slowly and raised his head. "It'll be easier to talk like this."

Stark naked, he was looking at me curiously as he realized I wasn't quite used to all this just yet. He began to move closer before I cut him off in his tracks. "Briar, put your clothes back on," I snapped as I turned around to give him some privacy.

"You don't need to be so coy. Like I said before, it's nothing you haven't already seen."

"Well, I guess it's Madam Medela's to look at now, isn't it?"

He snuck up behind me and whispered into my ear, "You know it's not." Jumping, I put a hand on my chest to stop my heart from flying off like a bat. "And you need to stop calling me Briar." I snorted in response. That was definitely not going to happen.

"We should go," he said. I didn't want to agree, but I did very much want to get away from this place. It was... oppressive. He grabbed the vial and the box that Helen had left us. We didn't talk along the way, not about what we needed to. He told me about an envoy from another kingdom that was due to arrive any day now, and that he'd be quite busy with them. "They're honestly more like savages. They let their changelings wander about until they come to a kind of interdependent relationship with their other form. I've seen it. I know it can be done. But they're brutal when they change. And sometimes they don't turn back at all, and they lose their minds. Whatever benefits they think outweigh the harm, they're fooling themselves."

"Why would they then?"

"They have little respect for anything outside of themselves. Dragons are their only priority. But as a kingdom we're obligated to interact with them, to be *civil*. It's complicated."

"Can I meet them?"

He grumbled for a bit before answering. "It can be arranged. I need to speak with Helen about it first."

"Oh! Does that mean they have their own queen or king? Will their commander be here, too?"

"Yes, and yes. I haven't dealt with them in quite a while. They're smaller than most of the others. Their queen is very young, and I'm told she and her commander are quite, uh, close. That sort of thing isn't done. It isn't safe. For them or their kingdom." He scoffed in disgust. He was clearly not looking forward to spending time with these people, but I couldn't help my curiosity, and he was being unusually open. Maybe he thought that was only fair, considering the bombshell he'd just dropped.

"Is it always a queen?"

"No. Kings don't last long though."

"Yeah, that makes sense," I said, nudging him as we walked. He put his arm around me and again, I let him. He was ridiculously warm. Even warmer than usual. "Are you okay?"

"Hmm?" he asked, not yet understanding my concern.. "Ah, yes. It's from the transformation. It takes a significant amount of energy, which results in our bodies throwing off heat for a time. And your size as a dragon is related to the energy you're able to cultivate."

"So do you have a little or a lot of energy?"

He looked down at me with his eyebrows raised as though I'd just asked a terribly impolite question. "My dragon is larger than most." He smirked at me as I bit the inside of my cheek and tried desperately to not blush.

"Is that why you're the commander? Because of your energy?"

"Not quite. There's a lot that goes into being a commander. Yes, you need to have an impressive amount of energy, but you also need to be strategic and disciplined. It's a complicated trial."

I put my arm around him as we walked in silence for the last few minutes until we were at his home.

"Did your changing today... how badly does it hurt?"

He plopped down on the couch after adding some more wood to the fire. I joined him at the other end, sitting sideways so I could face him. Staring into the fire he finally answered me. "For a minute, it is excruciating. But it's only a minute. It's not so bad when you know what to expect. And it's worth it. You also don't remember the pain. You know it happened, you know it was bad, but you don't remember it."

"Do you want me to see if I can handle it?"

He let out a heavy breath as he continued to stare into the fire. "Yes and no. It's a connection to yourself I can't explain. You would be able to feel what I feel. But the idea of you not being able to...."

"Briar...."

"I told you to stop calling me that."

"Briar," I teased. He turned to look at me. I couldn't quite tell if his annoyed countenance was put on or if he was actually bothered. I leaned forward and in my sultriest voice I repeated his name, "Briar."

He growled my name, "Frankie." I wasn't sure if it was a warning or an invitation.

I laughed playfully and called for a truce, the tension between us clearing slightly.

"It's unfortunate timing with the envoy. I can't take much more time away from my duties. Not until after they're gone anyway."

Slowly I reminded him, "I am still planning on moving out tomorrow."

He said nothing and turned back to glower at the fire.

"It doesn't feel right, me staying here. I still want to see you though. Just, on more equal footing, that's all."

His voice had the barest hint of anger. "I had no problem being indebted to you. Letting you take care of me."

"You had been attacked! Here you've abducted me from my world and have me living with you. It's a little different."

"Are you ever going to forgive me?" He looked at me now with pleading eyes. I didn't know if I actually could. I wanted to, my body, my fire, every part of me wanted to forgive him. Except for whatever nagging part of me kept telling me he was going to abandon me too. That he wasn't the one to trust. After moments I had lost track of, he grabbed the small box Helen had left and offered it to me. I eyed it, and him, suspiciously before taking it.

I opened it slowly to find Jen's ring, now attached to an almost ethereal chain. It was a soft gold that looked to have something swimming inside the metal. Whatever it was had a copper tint to it that offset the ring beautifully. "Be careful wearing it. You don't yet know its value, and I don't have the energy to explain it tonight."

We both went to our rooms in short order afterwards. I was determined to sleep in not-his bed tonight. After all, I'd be on my own tomorrow. So of course sleep was even farther away than it had been for the past couple of nights. I left the room to head downstairs.

As soon as I stepped out into the hall, he called from behind his closed door, "Frankie, save us both some time and just come in here."

CHAPTER
ELEVEN

I shouldn't. I knew I shouldn't. But I also knew I hadn't been able to sleep anywhere else and I was desperately tired. Eventually a frustrated exhale escaped my body as I opened his door. He was already laying down and looked at me when I opened the door.

"I didn't know if I should," I meekly offered as way of explanation.

He answered softly, "I don't know either. But I do know I want you to."

I walked over to the bed and crawled in beside him, careful not to touch him. We laid there, staring up at the ceiling. Briar broke the silence. "I don't want you to go," he said as he laced his fingers with mine.

"I know."

"Are you interested in Agustín?"

"I'm not moving out so I can see someone else."

"That's not why I'm asking."

"Why are you then?"

It was his turn to let out a long sigh. I smiled thinking

about this shared idiosyncrasy. "Would you get dinner with me?"

"When? Wait, what? You mean ... like a date?"

"Yes, Frankie, like a date." My cluelessness exasperated him.

"Oh." Was all I could say.

"Oh?"

"Yes, *oh*. You came to my world and stole me away. Then I find out all this crazy stuff about you and me- a lot of it I still don't understand, which is to say nothing about whether or not I believe it. Today you kissed me, and it was the first time in a long time that I was... happy. As if I was okay letting happiness win, even knowing what that's going to mean sooner rather than later. And my gut is trying to tell me something but I don't know what. You're asking me to dinner. You're asking to date me. Right? Every bit of me wants to scream yes. But something isn't right. There's a restlessness. Something I don't know yet. I'm sorry to be dropping all of this on you but yes, *oh*, because *oh* is all I can think to say. I don't know why you want me, and I don't trust it."

"Is it really that hard to believe?"

"I don't know!" Anything I could think to say would make me sound too needy, but I didn't know why he was interested in me. He was handsome, powerful, and kind, even if he did seem to have a bit of an anger problem. I'd seen how others looked at him. I knew he was aware of all of this.

And I knew how he looked at me.

"Sleep now. Tomorrow is going to be busy, moving you into your own place and all." He turned towards me and wrapped his arms around me, pulling me into him. "Is this okay?" I snuggled into him in response. Whatever may come, I was going to miss his heat.

~

WARM LIPS on my neck woke me up. He was behind me, kissing me, holding me to him. Arms wrapped around me, one of them grabbing a breast from underneath my night shirt, the other one slipping into my bottoms. I tried to turn around, but he held me tight. When I couldn't move I began to panic.

"Briar," I called to him and was met with a soft moan. "Briar, stop. Let me go." Something was crawling under my skin as he held on so tightly.

"Such a brave one, calling me that," he growled into my ear.

He kept kissing and groping me until I yelled for him to stop. My whole body was shaking as he let go. I moved away quickly, sitting up on the edge of the bed as far away from him as I could, biting my tongue to stop myself from crying. I didn't know what was happening. Why was I shaking?! My back was to him as I wrapped my arms around myself. After a few moments he broke the silence.

"I thought we both wanted—"

"I... it didn't feel right. I'm sorry."

"Don't be sorry. I—" A noise came from the front of the house, and he cursed under his breath. "I'll be right back." I thought about going to my room to get dressed, but worried he'd be upset if I left before we could finish our conversation. He hadn't meant to hurt me, or scare me, or whatever the hell that was. Not really.

Before I could decide what to do, he came rushing back up the stairs. "The envoy will be here sooner than expected. I've let the necessary people know you're moving into the apartments today." I was surprised he didn't address what happened, but I guess it was better to let it go and move past it. "I'd like to help you move in."

"Sure. That'd be nice," I said, doubting myself.

Packing a mere handful of items took very little time, though I couldn't seem to do it fast enough. "The place comes with the essentials, but if there's anything else you need, just ask. I mean it, Frankie. You're not alone here." He was clearly concerned, which did mean something to me.

Walking to the Spires together was a bit awkward. Briar was distracted, and I guess it's fair to say I was as well. Briar directed me to the LaFaye Spire, the one we had visited on that first day, with all the shops and the pleasant attendant. We were taken up to the apartments and exited onto a busy lobby. There was minimal paperwork that Briar mostly took care of, and then I was given a small stone with some kind of rune on it. My apartment was several more floors up and when we exited the elevator, past the moderately sized foyer, there were only four doors on the whole floor. Briar had to show me how to use the stone.

"It's a lock stone. It's your key. You hold it up to its corresponding rune, and it locks and unlocks the door for you. Much like a hotel key card on Earth. Although these are much more secure and take more work to create."

"And how hard are they to duplicate?" I asked, working with the stone to get the door open.

"The right sorcerer could do it. But there are checks and balances and security protocols. You're safe here. Not as safe as you would be at my—"

"Briar.... This is *not* just an apartment," I said, surprised at the penthouse we'd just entered that had to have more square footage than the whole of my parents' house. "This is too much." He refused to look at me, the grander accommodations clearly his doing. "You shouldn't have. Really." The calm sage green of the walls, with every color, piece, and textile complimenting one another was doing nothing for my anxiety.

"It's embarrassing enough that you're not staying with me. Let me give you this." The hint of exasperation in his voice more than conveyed his disappointed, so I acquiesced. Having a couple of extra rooms to soothe his ego wasn't going to hurt me.

As I explored, he stood at the floor to ceiling glass 'window' that made up the curved, outer wall. There were segments of thick drapes, currently gathered together every few yards. I imagined having them all pulled to one side would create quite the view.

I thought that's what he was admiring as he looked out across the kingdom. But not Briar. The man was perpetually 'on,' taking care of everything and anything.

"You'll want to see this," he called as he continued scanning the horizon. "You see those three dark marks in the sky? They're the envoy. Headed for the Mountain. I need to be there when they land. Are you okay?"

"I'm okay. A little overwhelmed. But when haven't I been over the last few days?" I half smiled as I laughed it off and looked for the dragons flying towards the Mountain. They looked miniscule in that moment, like little pencil knicks against a white sheet of paper, but I imagined they must be quite large to be making the time that they were. The one in the center flew a bit higher than the other two. It also seemed the largest. Nervously I asked, "Can I come with you to greet them? I know you have work. I'll try not to be a bother."

He smiled warmly at me. "I love that you're curious, it bodes well that you might, possibly, think about staying. But this needs to be nothing but strict protocol. It's best if we keep things simple for right now." He chastely kissed my lips before leaving. And all at once I was alone. I looked back at the dragons, surprised at their speed given how much more visible they already were. I'd been right, the one in the middle was substantially larger than the other two. It and the one to the right were a dark green, almost black. The third one had more red to it, but still quite dark. I wanted to learn everything I could about these beautiful creatures. But I'm sure Briar was right. This was not the time for it.

They were headed towards the Mountain, but the larger one was clearly scanning the kingdom. I was fidgeting with Owjen's ring around my neck when it looked my way. For just an instant I would have sworn it was actually looking *at* me. It almost looked like it had paused in midair, right before they all began their descent. My stomach fluttered in that moment, surprising me. I must have been worried about Briar because I felt that flame inside me spark.

After they were gone from sight I looked around the place, *my place*, for quite a while, trying to figure out what to do. The person who gave me my lock stone had mentioned something about amenities and services for newcomers. I decided to go ask the elevator attendant. The place seemed like a utopia, and I wanted to find the dropping point. It's what I was best at.

The kingdom required we give back and contribute, but we had time to settle in before committing to anything. In the meanwhile, we were encouraged to explore and become acquainted with life here. There were all sorts of recreational sites, gardens, libraries. They even offered tours of most of the greenhouses and other facilities. Plenty enough to keep me occupied until Briar could tell me everything he needed me to know before taking me home. I didn't want to get too comfortable, after all.

Agustín would likely be in the Medela Spire. It would likely bother Briar though, if on the same day I moved into my own place I went looking for someone that made him feel threatened. I probably shouldn't care, but I did. Besides, I really had no place being in the Medela Spire.

So I explored here instead, starting on the first garden floor. The buildings were massive enough and the garden levels were designed at such a modest incline that as you walked, area to area, in a circular direction, you'd go from level to level without really noticing the incline. The medicinal greenhouses we'd visited the day before mostly weren't like this. They were sterile, secure, and the levels were entirely separate.

To call this place an ethereal Eden would be an injustice. It was an extensive, open, and elaborate multi-tiered botanical garden with something alive and growing everywhere you looked. Even the footpaths were covered in a low grass and some type of clover. It was the most crowded place I'd seen here besides the courtyard. Given its beauty and serenity, it was easy to understand why.

A few trees even made their way up the levels through the floors, magically I imagined. One of the levels I walked through was littered with giggling and blushing teenagers as they weaved in and out of a hedge maze that offered ample privacy. The elevator structure ended here, leaving only the incline. It soon became much less populated.

For what felt like at least a few levels (it was hard to tell without the elevator structure as an anchoring point), there was just the strip of foot path and then a thick glass wall that circled along with you. It wasn't narrow enough to make you feel claustrophobic, but if you leaned that way, and thought about it for too long, it might. Through the impossibly heavy glass walls you could see that the space that had been so open and lush with plant life on the lower levels, was now packed with dirt. It was as if you were in a lighthouse, with a corkscrew walkway instead of the narrow steps, and outside of the safety of the lighthouse walls, was who knows how many tons of dirt. Every now and then, like a window pane, you'd come across a view of these complicated networks of roots- an array of sizes and shapes interweaving with themselves.

The incline became noticeably steeper as the glass walls of dirt began to sharply lower until they leveled off completely. It quickly opened up into a lush tropical forest, complete with overgrown vines, singing birds, and a pressing humidity. Here, like at the Mountain, it was a matter of steps, and you went from one climate to another. This was the first time I'd truly felt warm since being in Visnatura. There was no one else in sight and I began to wonder if I was allowed up here. Seems I'd finally come to the top of the Spire.

A barely worn path weaved in and out of the trees and foliage. The undergrowth was so overgrown that I could barely see the outside walls. I wanted to see if I could still see the ground below. After fighting with the flora, and losing more often than not, I eventually found it. The whole kingdom lay before me, the forest that surrounds it, the animal sanctuary, and it looked like another wall a fair ways off still. I knew that if I could see the animal sanctuary I was looking west.

As I tried mapping out more of my surroundings, a familiar and honeyed voice came through the foliage from behind me. "I must be coming into some kind of luck, seeing such beauty two days in a row." I turned around to see Agustín walking towards me holding a stack of folders. His crisp lab coat exchanged for a kind of suit that had likewise clearly been tailored to him.

"Sir Agustín, how are you?" I was a little anxious at his sudden appearance, but it seemed he wasn't here with the sole purpose of running into me.

"Better now." He smiled broadly, although it seemed strained. "And *please*, call me August."

Returning his smile, I asked, "Is everything okay?"

His smile took on a sly, somewhat aggrieved state as he

looked away. "Your beau wouldn't like me talking to you about the work he has me doing."

I was becoming aware of how deceived I felt. Even if Helen was taking the blame, something was off, something my gut was still trying to tell me. They were keeping something from me. It was easier to listen to my instincts without Briar around.

"He's not my beau," I said frostily.

"Does he know that?" Agustín teased. At least I think he was teasing. For all I knew he was sincerely asking.

"You're right though. He'd be angry enough knowing I'm talking with you. He certainly wouldn't want us talking *dragon* business." I fumbled over the word dragon, trying not to laugh.

"He is unusually protective of you, isn't he?" He very clearly wanted to say more.

"It's a little disquieting if I'm honest." A feeling of helplessness came over me. I was beginning to realize how truly trapped I was.

"He can be a bit intense at times," he said, laughing lightly. "But please understand, the poor boy simply doesn't know how to behave with you. He's only like that because he's never really cared about anyone before you. At least not that I know of. And just so you know- Sorcery families know everything. And that goes doubly for the Medelas." Good to know.

"Are you two close?" I asked.

"We work together often. Your kind are a challenge to heal. I specialize in challenges."

"Aren't dragons impervious? What is there to heal?" I was going off of nothing but myths. Realizing this could be dangerous and that I knew nothing, I could only hope Agustín wasn't too terribly curious. If Medelas really did know everything, he'd already know that I knew nothing.

He eyed me questioningly, and answered slowly. "It's unlikely for your kind to get hurt, but when you do, it can be useful to heal without using too much energy on the spot. Tell me, you can use your energy and give to plants. Have you ever tried *taking* energy?"

I stared at him, dumbfounded. "It never really occurred to me to try." One more thing I hadn't been told.

"Let me talk to Thorn. I think you'd benefit quite a bit from some lessons. If you take to it like I imagine you will, I have a project I think you'd be interested in. I could ask my sister to teach you. If you'd like? I would never say this to her, but she is vaguely better with some things than I am. And maybe Thorn won't be such an ass if Lily is the one teaching you."

"I would *love* that! When Jen started teaching me, it... well, it saved me. I would love to learn everything you and your sister could teach me. Anything to take my mind off of whatever this is." I gestured with my eyes to the world outside the window. "If it isn't too much of an imposition? I imagine your family is quite busy. It takes work to know everything, after all."

"Not as much as you'd think." We exchanged cheeky smiles. It was a relief to have someone I could actually talk to. "Besides, Lily would leap at the opportunity to teach a dragon. You didn't hear this from me, but she is slightly obsessed." As he was saying this a mousy little man had come up behind him. The man's face fell as he saw me, and Agustín must have noticed my concerned expression looking past him. He turned and the tips of his ears turned crimson. He cleared his throat as he addressed the person. "Yes? What is it?"

"Your sister is looking for you, Sir."

"Of course she is," Agustín groaned. "Take these. Deliver them to my office." He watched his assistant, or his sister's, leave before turning back to me. "We really should have dinner sometime. Do you have any time that Thorn hasn't already claimed?"

"I told you he... he is a friend, maybe not quite that anymore. I actually moved into my own place this morning."

"I know," he said, flashing his devilish grin again. "I'll need to send you a gift! I'm assuming you're in this building and not the Mountain since you're wandering around. Feel free to wander around at the Medela greenhouses and libraries as well. I'll have you listed as one of my personal guests. Just use your official title. And be careful what you touch."

He came up to me and took my hand. This time when he kissed it, he held my gaze for a moment before taking off himself. I could understand why Briar would want to keep me away from him, but he needn't worry. Agustín was a flirt and a charmer to be sure, but that wasn't what he was after. He was a people collector, nothing more. I wondered if he knew how easy he was for me to read.

DIFFICULT DOES NOT BEGIN to describe how hard it was to find my way out of that jungle. Too easy to get turned around, too tempting to want to lose yourself. By the time I did manage to find my way back down and to the elevator, I'd made up my mind to learn everything I could of this world on my own, more or less. It was clear that no one with answers was going to share them readily.

I found one of the Spire libraries on my way back to my apartment. If universal centers of knowledge exist across worlds, surely they exist as libraries. I mostly wanted to acquaint myself with the politics and hierarchies. It constantly felt like there was some kind of grand joke being told with me as the punchline. I explained my situation, what I felt I could anyway, to the librarian. She wordlessly disappeared, returning moments later with a stack of books. I checked out a few history books on both dragons and sorcerers and another about magic beasts. The information on dragons seemed dismally generic, but I'd take what I could get.

By the time I got back to my apartment I was actually missing Briar. What was wrong with me?! Maybe that was the issue. We'd spent so much time together so quickly and with everything that was happening, maybe I was simply projecting my negative emotions. Or maybe he was an asshole, and I needed to get away.

I laughed to myself at my own indecisiveness, a lifelong trait unfortunately. Lark would have had a field day! These psych buzz words were from her after all. Some had partially stuck with me from when she was going through this phase of diagnosing everyone around her. Not that she wasn't still doing that, but still.

Remembering her was like a punch to the gut. I wondered if I could get a letter or something to her. Anything to let her know that I was more or less okay. I didn't want her to put her life on hold to look for me when I knew she'd never find me. I knew that's what she'd be doing. I knew this because it's exactly what I'd be doing.

I was crying by the time I walked into my apartment.

His voice rang like daggers flying through the air, "What's wrong? What happened?"

CHAPTER

TWELVE

"Briar?! Why are you in here?! How did you get in?" My anger may have been misdirected, but these were legitimate questions.

"I came to see you! The door was unlocked and I was worried. I came in to check, everything seemed fine, so I assumed you'd not thought to lock it. I know you're not used to the stones. I didn't think you'd mind me waiting. Why are you crying? What happened?!"

Anger dissolved as my tears returned. It had been years since I had cried like this back home. I hadn't completely bought into the whole 'different worlds' thing. Not yet at least. But all I wanted in that moment was to crumple and fall to the ground. As though he was reading my mind he was there, holding me. Handing me a handkerchief and wrapping his arms around me as I let myself fall onto him.

"It's too much. This is all too much! I need to go home." I sobbed into his chest, unsure if he'd be able to understand anything I'd said.

"Frankie, what happened?" his soothing voice implored, and infuriated.

"I miss my sister! I miss things being normal. And no, it is *not* okay for you to let yourself in like that! I need to have some space. Some place or thing that I have some modicum of control over. Even if it is bullshit."

It wasn't quite a whisper as he begged to soothe my nerves, "I won't do it again. I'm sorry. You have to know how much you mean to me. Please."

I looked up at him through my tears and realized he wasn't giving me a line. He looked terrible. And he actually did care about me. Wiping away my tears I tried to right myself. "I need to shower. It's been a long day."

He gave me a sad smile and slowly nodded. "I'll leave you to it then. When you're ready, please come find me?"

"I thought you wanted to go to dinner?" I asked.

He was stunned for all of a minute. "YES! I mean, would you like me to wait here? I can wait in the hall. I can come back?"

My arms went around him, hugging him tightly. He was nothing if not endearing. "Wait here, silly. I'll be out soon." I kissed his cheek quickly, any longer than that flutter of contact and I wouldn't be able to stop. I wish I wasn't so flaky in my own emotions, desires. But I am.

I planned to finish crying in the shower, let all of my tears out, drown their song under the water. But no more tears came. The day had overwhelmed me. It was that simple. My outburst had oddly settled me, and I began to look forward to dinner with Briar.

Thinking about actually dating him allowed curiosity to get the better of me. With the water turned off, I couldn't hear Briar doing a thing and wondered what he was up to. Wrapping a towel around myself, I opened the door just a sliver to see. He was nowhere in sight. I walked out looking for him, not willing to believe he'd simply leave. The back of the sofa faced the bedroom door and as I walked past I saw him lying there, fast asleep. Of course he was exhausted. This had to be a bit of a whirlwind for him, too. I bit my bottom lip and slowly approached him.

For a commander I couldn't believe he was so careless with where he fell asleep. I knelt down next to him and studied him. His strong jawline all the more prominent from a recent shave. I wanted to run my fingers over its outline and through his nearly black hair that had grown slightly longer. I moved to touch him when his eyes opened. For a moment we just stared at each other. I could feel my face and chest turning red. The things I'd already done with this man, and I was still blushing.

"I wanted to see what you were doing, and then I didn't see you. So I started looking around, and...."

"I wasn't able to get much sleep this past week. It's been difficult, you know, sleeping next to you and keeping my hands to myself. Which is to say...." There was a heavy pause as he looked at me with a somewhat dismayed expression. "I can't say I'm sorry enough about this morning. I was being selfish." My heart fluttered. I either needed to love this man or hate him, and I needed some damned consistency. For me and for him.

I was still wrapped in nothing but a towel as I looked down at him laying on my sofa. I stood, holding his gaze for another moment before promptly dropping the towel. His eyes widened and he tried to sit up. Pushing him back down, I straddled him right there. He readily laid back under my direction, placing his hands on my bare hips as I moved my wet hair to the side and leaned down to kiss him.

He tried to let me take the lead, but as his fingers dug into me, I blissfully succumbed to his thirst. The way his body reacted to my slightest touch was intoxicating. Our kiss deepened as his hands grabbed my sides and pulled me flush against the coarse texture of his armor. As a moan escaped me he used the opportunity to kiss me elsewhere- my face, then my neck, then lower as his lips trailed down my chest.

The sensations his tongue elicited made me weak. I found myself wishing I'd pulled him into the bedroom before we started. The sofa wasn't big enough to roll around on, and my damn leg kept slipping off the side. He pulled away from my breast to look me in the eyes. A husky voice that made me aware of how much I needed him asked, "Tell me what you want?"

"Bed," I mumbled. Not quite the answer he'd been expecting. His eyes laughed as he asked if I was sure, if it was really what I wanted. When I nodded enthusiastically, he kissed me with enough force that I wasn't aware of him picking me up until he was putting me down on the bed. His lips remained constantly on one part of me or another as he deftly removed his armor.

His eyes were wild, needing, and for the first time I truly saw how he worshiped me. In that moment, with the glowing golden hue of his eyes reflected, we both needed one another just as desperately as the other. I kissed him deeply, passionately as we held each other and he fully entered me in one swift motion, eliciting an embarrassingly lewd moan. He very much enjoyed that move. My body had certainly missed it.

He held himself up as we fucked and I watched as he freely allowed himself his expressions. Every twist and contour of his face was a direct result from the pleasure we were deriving from one another. I'd rarely seen him with any kind of emotion displayed outside of moments like this and I treasured them. My breathing was becoming more ragged through my movements and moans of ecstasy as he maintained his steady and fulfilling pace. My lustful vigil was more and more difficult to maintain. I reached up and put a hand to his face. He grabbed it and kissed every inch of it, his golden eyes meeting mine.

Our held gazes sent him into a frenzy as his movements became erratic. I could feel myself getting close when he grabbed my hips and changed his angle at the perfect moment, sending me over the edge. As my body began to convulse he thrust in hard one last time, letting out a loud, ragged moan of his own. Feeling and hearing him come as my own body still shook nearly brought another tear to my eyes. I couldn't believe how much I had missed his warmth, even if it was excessive.

I WOKE up with his arms around me again, both of us tucked in under the blankets, no light yet protruding into our peace, no realistic idea of what time it might be. I'd been a little surprised at his vigor and wondered if it was a dragon thing to have his level of stamina. As a commander I imagine a few nights of restless sleep weren't something new to him. Snuggling back against him, I could still feel the weight of my tiredness as I soundly fell asleep.

He seemed to still be asleep when I later woke beside him, still with no idea what time it was, but wide awake and restless. He looked so content, and I knew he must be exhausted. Not wanting to wake him I went to use the bathroom and thought I'd slip into that smooth red nightgown with the dragon embroidery. Now seemed as fitting a time as any.

Moving out to the main area to let him sleep, I picked up a book on dragon history from the top of the pile and skimmed through it. There was an origin story that broke my heart more than anything. I think it was the one I'd seen the painting of at the Mountain my first night here. Well, first night conscious anyway. Whether or not the legend was true, it helped lay out the different types of dragons. It seemed to be elemental, genetic, and could help trace lineages. That is, if you knew what you were looking at and for while examining one's energy. This might make for a good conversation with the queen. I'd had little to say at our last tea.

There was a chapter on prophecies I was particularly interested in. Nostradamus had been a weird high school fascination of mine, and these reignited that. I had just began to read through it when I heard him call out in a blood curdling panic, *"Frankie! Frankie?!"*

The book fell to the floor as I ran to him. "I'm here! I'm right here." I jumped in next to him and enveloped him in my arms. "You're okay, I'm here."

He wrapped his arms around me tightly and buried his face in my chest. I absently ran my fingers through his hair as I rubbed his back. "I thought... I don't know what I'd thought. I'm sorry. You're the one going through hell and here you are comforting me."

"It's not hell. Besides, you're always there for me. Even when I don't want you to be." We both let out a small laugh. I think for different reasons. "I want to be here for you, too." I pulled his face from my chest, kissing him. His hands started exploring my body again and he noticed I was wearing something. He was looking at it with an expression I couldn't read. "Do you like it?"

His eyes shot up to meet mine. I'd never asked him a question like this before and I felt vulnerable. "It looks beautiful on you."

His hands started exploring again and my nightgown ended up on the floor as I showed him how much I had missed his touch, again.

~

I was resting on his chest, as I had back on Earth, as he held me and ran his fingers through my hair. I was drawing patterns between his scars and enjoying his occasional happy sigh.

"How was the envoy? Does that sort of thing even phase you anymore?"

"You're the only thing that phases me anymore." I knew he was being facetious, but I still smiled against his chest, relishing his adoration. "It was fairly routine. They'll be gone tomorrow."

I sat up, a bit disappointed. "Already? Is there time for me to meet them?"

"Why would you want to? They're brutal. Claiming whomever they want for their mates, using energy in unnatural ways, refusing to live within limits so our world can continue to flourish. We deal with them as a matter of national security. That's it."

There had to be more to it. They didn't have the numbers to be any kind of threat, at least that's what I'd been told. I settled back down on his chest and snuggled into him. He made an approving moan as he asked, "Would you like me to claim you? Do you want to be mine?"

I couldn't tell if he was being serious. I wasn't sure what it all entailed, but right now I didn't want to know. I just knew my answer was no. I knew how to stop this quasi-proposal before it got any traction. And if he was going to change the subject like that, so could I. "I saw Agustín today."

He groaned in mock pain. "That is a horrible response!"

I laughed enthusiastically enough that my whole body shook, and I could tell he enjoyed the movement. "He mentioned his sister Lily might be open to teaching me a few things. Sounds like a dream to me. But I wanted to run it by you first. You know, as Commander and whatnot."

"You don't want me teaching you anymore?" He seemed genuinely wounded. I sat up again to get a better view of him.

"That's not it at all! The Medelas might have some work I could contribute to. I appreciate everything you've taught me, you know I do. But I want to learn everything I can, and you have other obligations besides just me." He thought about it for a moment as he looked at me, his hands on my hips.

"You don't need to contribute. You are my responsibility and I'll take care of you. You can do as you please."

"Why am I your responsibility? You know I can take care of myself. Besides, isn't it up to the queen to tend to her people? And why am I default one of hers? How do you know I don't belong to one of the Wilds? And don't you dare say you'll answer all my questions later because you keep saying that and for every question you do answer there are three more you don't!"

"I was going to say I had a surprise for dinner, and we could discuss it then. But it seems we might have missed that window. Still, if I can pull myself away from you long enough to get dressed.... Although I imagine it's probably breakfast by now." He sat up, sliding me down to rest on his thighs. He looked at me for a while as I glared playfully. I was determined to get some answers. "I know these words sound like a line. Believe me, I do, but you're special."

I scoffed at his answer and moved away. I wanted him to pull me back but given what had happened this morning I understood why he was being cautious. Sitting on the edge of the bed, he sat next to me, his leg against mine. "We're not sure why your mother took you from our world. Or what happened to her afterwards. My mother had abandoned this world. She'd committed some minor atrocities and couldn't stay, but she was also ready to leave. She did what she did to end a war. I hated her for leaving me when I was so young, but I can't hate her for the sacrifices she made for our world. She barely kept in touch, and I never cared to find out why.

"You know she wrote to me about you. Told us that you had gilded eyes when your emotions would escalate. Although admittedly muted, almost unnoticeable, most likely from your time in that world. That you could utilize your energy, but that you didn't know what you were. Helen ordered her to get close to you, to keep an eye on you. My mother became quite fond of you. She started writing to me frequently with news of you. She told me all about you, your personality, your habits, she told me more than she needed to. Maybe more than she should have."

His words had this excited apprehension to them that set my nerves aflame. "You may hate me for this, but I was in love with you before I ever even met you. I grew much closer with my mother over the few months before she passed, because of you. When two scheduled updates were missed, I was sent to find out why. And to find you."

I wrapped my arms around myself and kept my eyes on the floor.

"I may have already been in love with you, but when I saw you that first time I panicked. I needed more time to gather myself. I wanted to tell you everything, to show you, to convince you. Being so physically close to you, I needed answers. When I kissed you, my mind felt like it was on fire. I couldn't believe it. I know I was just a passing thing for you then. I hope now I can become more. But you need to trust me. I told Helen about you. About your energy. It's different, Frankie. You and your energy are special. It's unique and could be useful."

And there it was.

I could be useful to them. That's why I was still alive.

"Maybe you do belong to one of the Wilds. I can't say. I can't find anything about your parents. And I've tried. I've had as many people as I trust working on it. I tried when I first found out about you. Then, as I was falling in love with you, I became obsessed trying to find any scrap of information or clue as to.... Well, I hoped when I finally met you that maybe there would be something to help track your parents down. But I'm still not able to find anything and at this point I believe the information has been intentionally destroyed.

"I'm sorry I fucked up and brought you back before we knew why you were taken. That sort of thing isn't done. But it really wasn't safe for you there. I wish I knew what had happened to your parents, so I'd know where you belong. I know you've never felt at home anywhere and I want to fix that for you. I'm trying to. If nothing else, please believe that." I doubted I'd ever believe another word he, or anyone, ever said again.

"You're my responsibility now because I want you to be. You're a mystery and for the sake of our world we need to know why information is being erased. Stay here or you could have a room in the Mountain if you'd like. You would normally have fallen under her purview. That's why that first night was so rocky, she wanted to keep you there with her. She thought you'd get the wrong idea, like I had just captured you to bring you back to be with me. I can see there may have been some wisdom in her counsel." He stopped for a moment, letting what felt like a confession filter through to me.

"This is a lot. I will do whatever I can for you. Always. Just tell me what to do. I didn't know how I could tell you any of this before. I don't know if now was the right time either, but you deserve to know. I'm sorry I don't have more to tell you."

I couldn't believe what I'd just heard. They'd been spying

on me, manipulating me from the start. Jen had started all of this. She'd always been a bit cranky, but she'd been different with me. I thought she cared about me. And to know what I was and to not tell me? To befriend me, just to give me up to her son? To a kingdom she'd abandoned? It didn't feel real. What awful thing had I done in life to bring myself so much pain? Not just this and all of them, but even before any of this began. I didn't understand.

"If she hadn't told you about me, my eyes, my abilities, would I be here now?"

He didn't want to answer. Of course he didn't, and he didn't need to. He'd told me that first day she'd written about me, but not like this. Now I knew I was only here because of her. She used me. He used her. And now I was a world away from any reason I had to live.

"Is there anything else you need to tell me?" My taciturn tone cut through the air like a bladesmith's sword.

"Frankie...." He had the audacity to sound as though *he* was the wounded one.

"If there is nothing else you need to tell me, take me home."

"Talk to me," he pleaded painfully.

"TAKE ME HOME!" I screamed as more tears impossibly fell. How could I have been so stupid?! The manipulations and betrayals... I was beginning to see red.

"I'm sorry, but that can't happen. Not right now." His words turned emotionless.

My eyes burned as I turned to him. The words came out in more of a growled hiss than I'd ever heard before, **"You promised!"**

"I can appreciate your anger. Again, I couldn't tell you before."

"Before *what?!* Before you *fucked* me again?!" My once

strong and rage filled voice began to crack, just as the rest of me did. *"How could you?!"*

Somewhat impassioned he confessed, "Frankie- I love you!"

"You are such an.... You don't! You love the *idea* of me. They are not the same thing. If you won't take me home, then leave. I don't want to see you. EVER AGAIN!"

"You don't mean that, you're—"

"LEAVE! NOW!" My voice had changed to a growl that would have surprised me if I wasn't so vehement.

He dressed wordlessly and I kept my back to him, my arms wrapped around myself. I needed to see Helen.

I needed to get home.

THIRTEEN

The sun had completely risen when I arrived at the Mountain. Unable to even think of sleep, I'd mulled over every possible outcome and implication I could before setting out. Still, it took much longer than I expected to get to the queen's residence. I had a general direction. I'd made the trip before. But by no means was I able to find my own way. Upon arriving at the front entrance, I'd tried to explain who I was. It wasn't until I used my title that there was any recognition and someone went away and returned a quick moment later to escort me.

A guard guided me to the same little glass garden terrarium we'd been in last time and told me to wait. There was a small commotion as the door opened and closed again too quickly. Helen was staring Briar down just outside the glass doors as she stood between him and the entrance. All the fury I'd felt early this morning resurfaced. I'd hoped to have a civil conversation with Helen. Now it seemed I'd end up a mess again, yelling, because someone was to blame for all of this and I needed to know who and why.

I glared at Briar, unwilling to look away and seem the weaker of us two. False sorrow blanketed his face and for a moment, an instant, nothing more than a flash, my heart hurt for him. Maybe he did love me, but it wasn't the real me. What had happened was wrong, and for me, unforgivable.

Helen came in a moment later, alone. She was as elegant and posed as ever, as if nothing odd had happened. Her black gown had sweeping golden feathers embroidered from her hem to her bodice. Gold flattered her in a way that let you know it belonged to her. It was as if she had a connection with the metal, and, seeing her, you were made aware of that connection to her yourself. As though she had a birthright to gold, and it wanted to be hers just as instinctively. It was a pet of hers that wanted nothing more than to linger on her.

"Draca Francesca," she used my title as she extended her hands, a gesture I reciprocated despite myself. She pulled me in closer as she proceeded to kiss first one cheek, then the other, ending with a kiss on my forehead as she bowed my head down. I wasn't sure if this was a normal greeting or if she was queen and simply did what she wanted. She hadn't done it before, but this was also the first time I was meeting her alone. "I am so glad to finally have tea with you alone. You know, as queen, I never ask for anything more than once. Briar wasn't supposed to accompany you last time, but I thought it was what you wanted, so I allowed it. He is right about one thing. You really are special." She winked at me playfully then pouted seeing my gloomy demeanor and reaction.

"Ah, not in a good place with it yet. I see." She waved to the door and a slender young woman in a golden slip dress carried in the tea tray. Last time a guard had brought the tea in. I had to stop myself from noting the difference aloud. "Come then. You have questions." The young woman brought the tray to the table and poured ceremoniously. The porcelain set was as heavily accented with gold as the queen. Helen picked up a small golden spoon and fidgeted with it between her fingers incessantly. The young woman smiled pleasantly enough but never once made eye contact with either of us. The queen's eyes never left her, even as I spoke.

"She's quite lovely," I interjected as Helen watched her leave.

"She really is," Helen sighed, finally turning her attention towards me. "But she is not why you are here. Tell me what happened." Her usual clipped accent sounded harsher now, colder.

"You already know," I huffed, my eyes shifting to where I had last seen him.

"Yes and given your reaction I wonder if you did not think things through. Or if possibly there was a miscommunication. For the second, and last time, I shall repeat myself- tell me what happened." The queen was the type of person to lower her voice when many would raise theirs. For the first time, though certainly not the last, I truly felt how frightening she could be.

I cleared my throat nervously and began explaining. Helen kindly nodded at all the right moments and listened tentatively before giving what can only be described as her decree. "I cannot control the actions of my people. What Owjen did seems wrong to me as well. She should have told you. However, she was there, I was not. It was her call. There may be factors we are yet unaware of. Though I do know she wanted to prove to her children that she loved her people. I think the love of a mother is something not to be understood by any but a mother. I do not believe she meant to hurt you. She wanted to bring you to a home where you would know you truly belonged. You said yourself you never felt like you belonged as you did when spending time with her.

"Right or wrong, I do not believe you can hold Thorn responsible for the actions of his mother. As far as your bumpy transition, I bare the blame. I gave in to his request, which now seems to have been made with more emotion than was wise. At the time I did not know that he was in love with you."

"He doesn't *love* me. He loves some imaginary, idealized thing from the reports his mother sent. Who knows what they even said?! He's only spent a few days with me. That isn't enough time to know if you love someone!" I scoffed and rolled my eyes. She seemed amused at my reaction, making me all the more livid.

"You do not think so?" As she spoke she continued to hold and fiddle with her golden spoon, using it as a comically miniature scepter as she waved it about, pointing it at me.

"No! Absolutely not! I mean... for the most part, no."

She laughed a warm, bubbly laugh. "Maybe you should figure that out for yourself first. And you should not underestimate what Owjen would have had to say about you. That woman was misery incarnate. But you do not seem to despise her. Of course I only knew her before she was banished, but I doubt she changed simply because she was on Earth."

"He should have at least told me all this... before."

"Before? Before you came here? Would you have believed any of it?"

"I don't know, but telling me when he did was not okay." I could feel my cheeks flushing.

"When did he tell you?"

Burying my face in my hands, I murmured, "After we slept together last night."

"Ah. And that was the first time you two reunited? Since you have been here?" I nodded, still hiding behind my hands. "You should ask yourself why that is so consequential to you. You slept with him after a day in your world. You are not what one would call... *old fashioned*, for your world. Why now does this matter?”

I grumbled as I pressed my hands over my eyes, trying to soothe myself. “Boundaries! Trust! That’s why.”

A gentle smile was waiting for me when I looked at her. “I have had to retrieve four dragons throughout my entire reign. You are the first that did not know what you are. I can only imagine how difficult this must be for you.”

“With all due respect, how long could your reign possibly be? You can’t be much older than me. Thirty five? Maybe?”

Her eyes shone with excitement and an odd appreciation, “My darling, I am nearly three hundred years old.”

My laughter was short-lived as she stared me down. “Wow. Is that a, uh, dragon queen sort of thing?”

Her stare turned into a half smile. “That is a dragon in its own world sort of thing. Think over what I have said. Your training with Madam Lily is approved. Tell Sir Agustín as I am sure he will be the one arranging it all.”

“Can I go home?” I pleaded pitifully.

She sighed. “I truly am sorry. Until we know more about you- who you are, what you are, you cannot. Briar has been thorough and diligent in his efforts to uncover that information for us, for you. Heartwood is a wonderful place to call home my little dragon.” She stood and touched the side of my face, staring into my eyes for an uncomfortable moment before leaving me with my thoughts.

As I was leaving I couldn’t help but notice that she’d swiped her own spoon.

～

I spent the next few days in my apartment, alone. I’d fallen back into that emotionally numb realm. Not depressed, not sad, not happy... nothing. I wasn't even angry anymore. I just... wasn't. But the beginnings of restlessness were stirring under my skin. I didn't know what day it was when Agustín stopped by to check on me. No doubt sent by Briar. At least he knew not to deny it, and if nothing else he convinced me of his genuine concern.

"Of course he asked me to check on you! But that's not why I'm here. I was worried, my dear. You need to pull yourself together, find your fire, even if it's only an ember right now. No one else can do that for you and it clearly needs a good sparking."

Easier said than done. But I'd been here enough. He was right. I needed to keep moving through the motions. Though said motions were a world apart this time. Something would slowly spark. I agreed to lunch and began to get ready. I only had a few outfits. Something I'd like to see about changing since it was clear I wasn't going home now. At least not anytime soon.

But first, I needed to fix something. Their style of dress was exquisite, yes, but for me, impractical. I couldn't move in the damned things to save my life. The skirts were too thick, too heavily lined. My legs constantly felt encased, weighted down, restricted. I'd had to shorten my stride to keep from tripping and I hated it. It took too long to get anywhere.

Agustín had some work to do before lunch, so I was meeting up with him later. There was no one to ask if I could alter the dress. Probably for the best. I'm not sure I would have listened if the answer had been no. Heartwood seemed particular about who was allowed to be peculiar.

They'd given me a small sewing kit in one of their welcome boxes. I'd loved sewing when I was younger and was fairly confident I remembered how. At least I hoped I did. For all the wonders this world had, I was humbled by how they repurposed and salvaged nearly everything. Hence the supplied sewing kit, with mending in mind. Resourceful was an understatement here.

I laid the skirt out and cut an upside-down V shape out of the front, careful to leave enough material intact at the top. I made a makeshift bias tape, thin strips of the skirt material, from what I'd just cut out, and bound the raw edges. This little touch of finesse looked nicer than a plain hem, not to mention it made it more manageable to sew up, given the layers of lining. There was very little skirt in front of me anymore. My legs could move, and I no longer needed to stunt my steps. The skirt still mostly twirled and flared around and behind me. Their version of leggings would keep me warm enough. And I blissfully wouldn't look like all of them anymore.

I didn't register too many odd looks as I made my way. Once there it was undeniable though. I didn't really care. Finally moving how I wanted was enough, for now. Agustín's own surprise was short lived.

"Aren't you stunning?" He'd initially seemed somewhat taken aback, as though he wasn't entirely sure how to handle it, or me. But it had only been for a fraction of a moment. Clearly he'd had practice withholding emotions from his face as he did so, and we exchanged greetings and pleasantries.

He quickly steered the conversation towards Briar, and I was grateful for the chance to vent now that I was feeling up for it. "I thought it was what I should do, reconnect with him. I also wanted to. I wanted to be done being rational. If even for just a moment. I thought he had my best interests at heart. I thought maybe he actually did... No, it shouldn't have happened. I didn't know all the relevant information. How could I when they've been withholding it?! They've been lying to me since the moment we, since *before* we even met! Fake it 'til you make it, go through the motions until it's real, right? So that's what I was doing! I think, anyway. I don't know! Maybe there was something more."

"Frankie, that's not how love works!"

"But he made me *feel* again! I can't tell you... And it *was* different. It really was something physical in my chest. A warmth. More than I've ever felt before. And then I find out they were just manipulating me too. Now I don't know what to do. Or who to trust."

"For better or worse, that boy loves you with all the passion and darkness that comes with such an endeavor. That doesn't mean you have to reciprocate those feelings. Especially if they aren't actually there. But don't lie to yourself just to stay angry. Figure out how you actually feel, without faking anything for anyone's sake! Including yours."

I stared off, not knowing how to respond. I hated it, but I believed Agustín. I could fathom reasons why he'd lie to me, but none of them felt true.

"Besides all that, you've been approved from both sides to work in my Dragon Heart greenhouse with me. Fair warning, I won't be going easy on you because you're cute." I gave him a polite half-smile. He was a sweetheart and fun, but he was also hiding something from me. I had no idea what or how precarious it might be, but I needed to figure it out. Not knowing around here was dangerous.

"You'll be using your energy to help the Dragon Heart along. Then we'll process it into Dragon Cor. I'm researching the effectiveness of the medication when pushing the plant along. Historically it's had some fairly adverse effects to its potency. But I think a dragon moving it along might fix that. This will also help you build up your strength. I understand you're a bit behind the curve compared to others your age.

"That being said, we'll start slow. Briar has informed me that you don't always know your limits. Or how to listen. I won't babysit you. If you overdo it you'll end up in one of the med wards, you'll miss work, and Briar will threaten my life. I will kick you out of every one of my greenhouses and you'll never touch a medicinal plant in Heartwood again. Medelas don't give second chances." Given his genuine smile I wasn't sure if he was kidding or not. Best not to push it.

~

THE NEXT MORNING I headed to the Medela Spire shortly after dawn. I still couldn't seem to sleep well here, and early mornings were almost a relief. Though this didn't seem to be a particularly busy time around here. The nine-to-five didn't seem to have the same predominance in this world.

I told the elevator attendant I wasn't sure where I was going, but that I needed to see Agustín. I doubted I'd be given the same access as I had before, not to mention I had no idea what I was actually doing, so finding him only made sense. Still, the attendant, a bit grumpy, mumbled to herself as she moved the elevator. It opened into a lobby with several uniform doors. Before I could ask her which door, she was gone.

I knocked on the closest door and found the mousy assistant from the jungle garden at the top of my spire, Cifelli. He apparently was a morning person, very pleasant and wonderfully helpful. I was amazed by his kindness given the overall impression of the people I'd encountered so far. Which, in all fairness, had been limited.

"There are symbols on the door, but you have to know what you're looking for. It's all a bit much if you ask me. But they're a very protective bunch and these symbols mean different things to different families and lineages. It's a way for them to quickly glean a lot about you. The symbols luminosity depends on abilities. I'm from a line that doesn't have a house here and I can barely see them. As a Draca you should be able to see them at the right angle. Here's Sir Agustín's offices. Stand like this and you should be able to see what I'm talking about."

"Just some weird scribbles, right?" I actually had no issue seeing them at any angle, but it seemed rude to rub that in.

He snickered lightly. "Yes. But to them it's their name in their mother tongue along with a few other honoraries and tidbits." He shrugged as his eyes rested on the information on the door. "His assistant is usually in Furlong, but now you know where to find me." I thanked him and he headed back to that first office.

I knocked on Agustín's door. No answer. I wasn't exactly surprised. Cifelli was already back in his office. I wasn't sure if it would be okay to enter, but I figured I would wait Agustín out. The door was unlocked, and I let myself in. There was a small room with nothing in it. No chair, nothing on the plain white walls, simply a wooden door at the other end. I walked over to it and again knocked. Thinking I heard something this time, I let myself in again.

Warmth and light and green enveloped me. Everywhere you looked vines traversed the room. Leafy tendrils criss-crossed from shelves to walls and hung from the ceiling. It encircled the room back and forth slightly above eye level. I had to duck under different parts of it a few times as the denser vines crossing back and forth dipped lower in places. Some-thing caught my eye on a nearby vine. Staring at it for a moment, unsure if I'd seen what I thought I'd seen, I timidly poked at a curled-up leaf. It unfurled itself slowly, revealing a primed fountain pen. It had some beautiful curves to it, and I loved the deep magenta color. Lark had dyed her hair that shade one summer. I thought about picking it up and decided better of it. Not my pen, after all. I stepped back and the leaf curled back up, securing it once more. There were several leaves like this throughout what seemed like miles of vines.

This room was significantly larger than the bare waiting room and although it was very warm, I saw no fire. There was an oversized desk covered in books, roles of parchment, and piles of paper. One wall was lined with mismatched and disorganized bookshelves. The whole room was overflowing with books. There was a well-loved leather chair behind the desk, likewise buried under a pile of books.

I walked the office, mindful of the vines, and found another room off the one wall. It opened into a more traditional greenhouse. Several tables with different levels and shelves had trays and trays of plants all in clay pots. Windows for the outer wall of this spire were on the far wall letting in an abundance of light. Whatever was creating this warmth, it was coming from that room.

I knew how Agustín was about his plants and knew better than to trespass, at least more so. A nearby and ancient looking book caught my eye. Mostly because of the material the book was bound in. It looked as though it had been made of a large leaf that had been worked into a book or at least made to look as such. I began to thumb through the leaf book. The cover was surprisingly cool to the touch, but it was the title that made me freeze- *The Stone and the Sap: An Ancient History of Heartwood*. It was handwritten, but not by someone trained in doing so. It was all about building the kingdom from the ground up, and it seemed more like someone's personal journal than anything else. This gem might be my only way to escape, since no one was up to keeping their promises in this world either.

I was reading a chapter about their sewage infrastructure the House of Pherrius had installed with great forethought from a seer. 'How convenient that would be, knowing the needs of a city before laying everything out and building it?' I thought to myself, letting out a small snicker.

"Something funny about a sewer system?" Agustín's sudden interjection made me jump.

"Why would you do that?!" I was about to tell him off when I remembered where I was, and what I was doing.

His tone was as calm and honeyed as ever, "Why would you intrude into my office and pick up *that* particular book at *that* particular time? These are questions and they have their answers. But ultimately, it doesn't much matter. And before you ask, no, you cannot borrow it. I am curious about you just letting yourself into my office though."

"Well..., I was looking for you. You told me not to be late but never said when that was. Besides, you should lock your office if you don't want people walking into it at will."

"Most people know better," he snapped and then sighed either at his tone or my rudeness. "Come on. Best get an early start I suppose. We'll cover a few useful glyphs as well. Thorn warned me there may be some... complications."

The Dragon Heart greenhouses were emptier than before. Agustín took a moment to fill in the guards about my new position. I assumed there would be more red tape around this, but no. He and one of the guards created a glyph on a side door I hadn't previously noticed. A pinprick to my finger, a smeared drop of blood in the center of the glyph, and access was granted.

Behind this side door was the processing of the Dragon Heart into Dragon Cor. I was now the third person with access that could enter this room at will. Agustín and Helen being the others. I wanted to ask why Briar didn't have access but thought better of it. While I knew he was still going to come up, I didn't want it to seem as though he was always on my mind. Still, I was a little taken aback that I was given this level of access. They seemed to really be trying to prove something to me.

"The majority of your work will be out here with them." He motioned towards the bushy trees that Briar had shown me. "They take forever to ripen. Then we have to wait for all their nectar to flow out before we can harvest them. It's a long process and nothing seems to effectively speed it up. However, we have reason to believe a dragon should be able to do it, if they have the right... demeanor. We haven't had the opportunity to try before now. Your kind isn't often willing to work with ours. Even when there is something in it for them."

We moved along rows of these trees as he spoke. I trailed behind, getting somewhat lost in my fascination with the fruit they bore. It seemed to be *turning* towards us when we got too close. "Frankie?" He called to me when I was clearly not paying enough attention for him. I blushed as I straightened up and turned towards him, leaving the attentive fruit to its own meandering.

"You'll be directing your energy, but this will be different. You need to *encourage* the fruit to squeeze that nectar from itself. It's kind of a self-drying out process. We need them completely dried out before we can process them. That nectar, fresh and still fluid, is beyond toxic. Do NOT touch it." He glared at me as he gave me that warning. As if I were a small child barely paying attention, instead of a grown woman barely paying attention.

"Agustín, is everything okay?" My question seemed to surprise him. He literally snapped his head back as he evaluated either me or my query.

"It's been a long week." He crossed his arms over his chest as he looked away from me. I thought about pressing and I was about to tell him he could talk to me, that it's not as if I had anyone to gossip with anyway, when he came out with it on his own. "Lily is more reluctant than I expected to teach you. She's... busy. But our mother asked her, and you don't say no to Madam Medela." He sneered as he said this, and I couldn't help but ask.

"She's Madam Medela, but you're Sir Agustín. Why isn't she Madam whatever her first name is? I'm sorry if that's a rude question." It didn't feel particularly important to me, but something was bothering him, and I wanted him to talk.

"The head of the family will be known only as the family name, such as Madam Medela. Besides being head of the family she is also Head of Heartwood. When I become the head I will no longer be Sir Agustín, but Sir Medela, and I will need to return to Furlong. A different family will claim the title of Head of Heartwood for a time. That won't be until after Mother rests, mind you. And always just August to you, my dear. My sister is Madam Lily. If something were to happen to me before an heir is named, she would become the next Madam Medela. Simple enough.

"And I do know what you're doing, my dear. Getting me to talk- you think I have some kind of wall up, but I don't. I'll tell you everything I can. For instance, I can't help you escape. Well, I could. But where would you go? I don't know how to manage the way between our worlds. Even if you could get back, they'd come for you. You have to know that. Make your peace with this, Frankie."

I clenched my jaw shut as I nodded. He was right, after all.

He walked me through the theory of what I was to do with the trees. We were starting out small. He couldn't guide me, not the way Briar had. Our energy was different enough there wasn't any point in trying. After struggling a bit to pinpoint the fruit's energy (*it kept moving, how amazing is that?!*), I managed it. "Start small. Just a handful for today. I'd like to teach you a water glyph before you go as well."

After I'd worked through several pieces, obviously more than he liked, we stepped back from the plants. He apprehensively showed me the water glyph I'd need to commit to memory. For now he brought me a few pieces of fancy paper with lines that were as complicated as the one Briar had shown me back at Jen's.

"I was told you somehow managed to overdo it with a simple fire glyph. This water one is useful for basic maintenance with these plants. You will need to be able to get this. Now my dear- do NOT drown them. We'll try it here before I let you use it on them. Try not to drown yourself either, hmm?" It took an inordinate amount of effort to not roll my eyes, but I managed as he handed me the first piece of parchment with the water glyph. "Find your energy, trace the writing, be careful to enclose the glyph. Visualize it. Try something a tad different this time. Pull water from the air, from the humidity around you. Not too much, just enough to help water the plants. Release it when you're ready."

I followed his instructions. Meditated, covered the writing, tried to not do as much as last time, but still complete the markings and connect them where needed, enclosing the glyph. I used the same word as before to release it.

Agustín's eyes conveyed his shock as his body darted into action. Everything seemed to be moving in slow motion. My mouth was filling with water from the inside. It was everywhere, most notably my lungs. As horrifying as that was, I registered it just as slowly as everything around me seemed to be moving. In a word- painfully. Sluggishly I dropped to my knees as I tried to cough it out. My muscles contracted violently trying to expel it. It was gushing out, but not enough. Agustín placed his hands on me just as Briar had done. He pulled the water out of me, but I still couldn't breathe. It felt like an eternity before I was able to gasp for air and actually find some.

"Well, my dear dragon, or whatever you are, it seems as though more research is required before we try that again. I'll need to recount this to your commander of course. He won't be happy and naturally I'm over the Sister Stars grateful to you for that." He glowered playfully at me. "Tell me, what was the word you used? I heard you say something, I'm sure of it. No shame in needing a word to release."

I glared, not playfully, at him as I continued to take deeper and deeper breaths until my breathing regulated. "Fine. I said fine!"

He chuckled as he shook his head. "Well, you've certainly made a *fine* mess." He winked at me as we both sat on the ground, thoroughly drenched, and I removed his hand from my chest. He made a face before letting out a raucous laugh with me soon joining him. He might be a sorcerer, but I appreciated knowing him. He wasn't ever going to be completely real with me, but he was the closest I'd gotten to having a friend since arriving here.

"You should rest. That likely took more out of you than you realize. I'll deal with Thorn."

I didn't feel like resting though. I wanted to know more. At this point I *needed* to know more. After my first day working with the Dragon Heart and nearly drowning myself, I went back to my apartment and changed. I was off to the library again. There was only a nominal din, but it was better than the deafening silence in my apartment. I was trying to find every morsel of information about dragons that was out there. The available materials seemed limited, so I asked the librarian. He suggested I ask Queen Anumonwo, but he'd keep looking in the meanwhile.

Apparently she kept a tight rein on who knew what about

her dragons, and she likewise wanted to know who wanted to know what and why. It seemed excessive, but then again, so did she. I thanked him and told him I'd check in next week. Given what I knew of Helen, I didn't have high hopes that he'd be successful.

I planned on talking to Helen about it at our next tea. She'd asked that I meet her for these little dragon finishing school curricula once a week or so. I'd like to say I didn't mind. That anything to break up the monotony of my imprisonment was welcome. But it wasn't. Something drew me to her Mountain and concurrently repelled me. There was a pressure in the air when she was unhappy. Palpable and suffocating. Without realizing it I found myself trying to do what I could to make her happy. That seemed to help.

Over the weeks my work with Agustín began to intensify and my hours in the greenhouse increased. I was clearly building up my stamina, and he was beginning to trust me more and more. Agustín was always a bit of a charmer, but there was something else. He was hiding something from me, and we were both painfully aware that I knew it. I didn't push. I wasn't going anywhere, because I couldn't, and at some point I'd made peace with that. This greenhouse was a far stretch from my open fields, gardens aplenty, and country cottage dream. But it still felt good touching the soil, feeling my energy flow through the earth and bind me to the world's tapestry. I was connected and whole while I worked, and in those moments I couldn't ask for more. I knew not to expect more.

My afternoons were usually spent in the library. I couldn't find out much more about dragons. Helen constantly pushed off the subject and became visibly irritated if I brought it up. So I focused my attention on the world itself. Its history, cultures, geography. Not so much the people. Either they avoided me, or I avoided them. I'm not sure to what extent Briar was involved with that, but I didn't dwell on it. No one was particularly rude, but few were friendly.

Lily eventually stopped by the greenhouse. I'd met her briefly before and she didn't seem to enjoy the interaction. She looked a bit more sullen now. Her dark hair braided in plaits over her head like a crown, just as she'd had it before. She had the same perfect skin as her brother, although he was a fair bit older than her. Where he was svelte she was curvaceous and had such vivid gray eyes that always seemed too intense. Or maybe that was just Lily.

Agustín was in the processing room while I was out with the trees, as was typical in the mornings. Lily nodded to me as she approached the room. She tapped on the nearly transparent barrier that would have been a door on Earth. Agustín came up to it and wiped a hand over the embedded glyph in the not quite invisible screen. It disappeared and after a few hushed words she entered the room and he put the barrier back up. But not before winking at me. We'd been working with each other enough that he knew how much I hated it when people winked at me. His smile beamed as I scowled at him, even as my stomach twisted in anticipation.

Lily was here for my first lesson, whether she liked it or not.

CHAPTER

FOURTEEN

Neither Lily nor Agustín looked terribly delighted as they left the processing room. Agustín noticed me watching and did that thing where he washed any trace of genuine emotion from his face. He looked at me directly and gave me that politician's smile that made my stomach turn. Something was wrong. Well, *more* wrong than usual.

They stopped as they came across my path. Lily was wearing a simple black dress with buttons that went from just under her chin all the way down to her knees. I'd gotten to know the Medelas, and this all-black, prim-and-proper outfit generally meant one thing. She'd been in a meeting with Madam Medela. She looked between me and her brother anxiously. Where Agustín was poised, Lily was honest. You knew how she felt about you. Always.

"Lily will be beginning your lessons this afternoon and then as her schedule allows." Agustín looked at his sister with an expression I couldn't entirely read. There was sympathy and censure and some indefinite sentiment, which was rather typical of him. "Which it will allow," he said, making sure we all understood where we each stood on the matter.

Lily cleared her throat and found her own composure, submitting to whatever will was being forced upon her. She looked at me with a blankness that was unsettling at best, as if she was looking through me. "We'll be meeting in the forest outside of the main kingdom. Follow the path towards the sanctuary. It's a walk for a dragon. Don't be late." With a curt nod to her brother she took her leave. Agustín sighed heavily as we both watched her make a hasty exit.

"Wow, she seems super excited about it." I tried to quell my cynicism. Agustín quirked an eyebrow at me. If I had a degree in sarcasm, this man was a tenured professor in the field. He was clearly debating how much he should tell me.

"She's nervous. She hasn't been given much responsibility, and she feels this is too much for her. She's also afraid of your queen."

"Everyone's afraid of Helen. At least you know where she stands. Is this too much for Lily?"

"The task is not too much for her. She's afraid of failure, just like the rest of us. But she lets her fear paralyze her to the point where she doesn't act. Unacceptable for a Medela, and Madam Medela has chosen to snuff it out of her, using you."

"Why? Because it won't matter if she fails?"

He looked at me for a moment before letting out a cynical laugh and crossing his arms over his chest. I scowled at him for a minute before taking off my regulation Medela lab coat. It was made with precious fibers to facilitate a hygienic atmosphere. The Dragon Heart was from much further south and almost impossible to retrieve anymore. As such they took every precaution to keep their supply alive and well. It also had a couple of layers of magicked protection for us, just in case.

I hung my coat up and was starting for the exit before Agustín noticed. "She won't fail with you! She can't. But she doesn't know that, nor should she. Do you understand?"

"Yes," I called back as I continued to the exit.

"I explained everything you need to know! Where are you going?" he called after me.

"Back to my apartment. It's freezing outside, and I need some more layers if I'm going to be frolicking in the damn woods with a sorceress that doesn't much care for me."

"Yes, I suppose that could be a little chilly," he practically yelled. He didn't see me rolling my eyes as I left the greenhouse, but he knew. Soon enough he'd be heading out himself. He always left at roughly the same time for his daily meeting with Briar. That was all I ever cared to know about it.

It was a short trip back to my apartment, and despite Lily's demeanor I was in unusually high spirits. Until I saw him. He was headed towards the elevator I'd just walked off of. The attendant waited for him expectantly. He ignored her and merely gaped at me. It took all my grit to not stare at him. He looked ragged, thin, and pale. But even with his gauntness, or maybe because of it, I still felt myself being pulled to him.

"Commander," I said flatly as I walked by. He turned with me, his body following mine. A book rested against my doorstep. For the first week he'd left flowers and plants, which I promptly disposed of. I didn't want them, not from him. After that he started leaving books. He knew I wouldn't get rid of those. But I never even read the titles. Instead I dropped them at the library. Books weren't as plentiful here as Earth, likely why the few libraries throughout the Spires were always decently populated.

"Don't give this one away," he called after me as I unlocked my door. I turned my head to the side, listening but not willing to engage further. "This one is different. It's from Helen's library. It's yours though. You'll want to read it. I promise." I could hear his smile and feel his hope. He was proud of whatever he thought he'd done for me. I stood still for another moment. He thought he had me. "I miss you, Frankie. I—"

I slammed the door shut, leaving him and his book outside. I heard him set it back up against the door. He might have whispered another apology through the door. I wasn't sure, but I was done wasting my time.

Adding a pair of wool leggings under my linen pants, I put on my sturdy boots, and grabbed the heavy, long jacket I'd picked out when I first arrived. It hadn't really been all that long ago, but it felt like I'd been here for years. I wasn't what I'd call happy. I was essentially imprisoned after all. But I wasn't unhappy. I was in a fantastical world, using abilities I'd only ever dreamt of, studying cultures and creatures before unknown to me. And oddly enough, everything felt so natural anymore. Except when it came to Lark. I still missed the hell out of her.

By the time I finished dressing I'd forgotten the book. I'd be lying if I said my interest wasn't piqued as it again hit the floor with a thud. Briar was thorough, as always, and knew what he was talking about. The extremely worn book was a thorough history of dragons with an emphasis on prophecy. *Of course* I wanted to read it. I wanted to burrow in and get lost in the damn thing!

Notes and scribbles littered the pages like a well-loved, or at least well-used, textbook. It wasn't just one person's handwriting either. I was instantly obsessed with finding out who had written what and why and when. Now wasn't the time to sit around with it though. I threw the book into my knapsack along with a light lunch to eat on the way to meet Lily.

The walk itself was lovely, cold and lovely. Which pretty much describes Heartwood. I should have bothered Agustín for a heat stone, but my mind had been elsewhere. I ate my lunch mechanically. I couldn't even tell you what I had. I just kept thinking about that damned book, and Briar.

I knew he had people that watched me. Either he or Helen did, anyway. The librarian never did have any luck with my request, which hadn't been a surprise. I still couldn't quite figure out Helen's reaction when I asked her about it. The first time I'd asked her, well, the details are fuzzy, but I left that day with a sense that I should have never bothered her about it. That I'd somehow burdened her simply by bringing it up.

My mind wandered, trying to figure out what exactly had happened with Helen when I was pulled from my muddled thoughts. "This way, dragon." My head jerked at Lily's voice, a good distance behind me now. I hadn't been paying attention and walked right past her. I was more than a little surprised and worried at how distracted I'd been.

She smirked as I stalked towards her. "I cannot even imagine the entitlement dragons must have to be so careless with their situational awareness. You never know what could be waiting for you." I grumbled something not worth repeating as she spun on her heels, leading me further into the woods. I wanted to ask her what I needed to worry about, what she thought might be waiting. I had a few ideas before the thought occurred to me that it was her, and I kept quiet.

Lily, still dressed in her somber clothes, led me into a clearing where sections of a tree trunk had been cut and arranged more or less in a circle. There had at one time been a decent sized fire going in the center, judging by the ashes. Lily sat on one of the sections of tree trunk facing me. Her thin dress fluttering about her legs as she crossed them. I was surprised the cold didn't seem to bother her. Then I noticed the stone she was fidgeting with in one hand as if she was practicing a coin trick.

"I don't even know if you're able to do what I've been tasked with teaching you. So I suppose we should start there. How much energy have you used today?" She looked at me as if she was expecting a literal measurement. I'd only learned to not push it. Not after last time at least.

"I'm not sure. Not too much? I was only working in the greenhouse for an hour or so before you came by." Her shoulders fell as she closed her eyes out of exasperation.

"We'll assume *not too much* then, shall we? I'll walk you through what I'm doing as I show you. *Pay attention.* I won't do it twice." She carefully knelt on the ground, tucking her dress under her knees as she did so. Leaning forward, she placed a hand with splayed fingers on the muted green grass that had gone dormant with the winter.

"I'm going to pull from the grass. I'll take its energy and hold it within me. Then I'll use it elsewhere. For you, you'll store it alongside your own energy. Whatever you're taking from will be clearly different from your own. You'll see it exist with yours. It shouldn't blend unless you've taken too much. *Don't. Do. That.*

"You won't be able to take too much here, but I'd be remiss if I didn't warn you. While there is an interconnected network, it isn't so connected that you'll take it all. Really, it's not an easy thing to do. It's not an easy thing to watch someone do, either. It takes more effort than you'd believe. When you use too much energy and you've depleted yourself- you'll pass out, lose your ability to self-regulate, all of that. When you take too much, you've done just that. It has to go somewhere. You'll expel it in the usual ways, vomiting, diarrhea, that sort of thing. But it's worse, it can come out as pure energy, and you can't control it. You've seen what energy can do controlled. Imagine what it could do uncontrolled, loose, searching for a purpose." I could imagine. It would be chaos, unimaginably unpredictable chaos.

Lily closed her eyes as she sought out and pulled the energy from the grass. The color waned from its dormant green to a dead brown, starting at her fingertips and stretching out like ripples of color in an otherwise still pond. She pulled an almost perfect circle of energy, about six feet in diameter. It seemed simple enough. My concern was with my own control.

When her eyes opened they shone an even more brilliant sheen. "I'm going to release that energy now. It's not the worst idea to have a buildup, but that's a lesson for another day."

She placed her hand on the cut piece of wood she'd been sitting on. As she closed her eyes she let out a soft breath. I was watching her so intently that I didn't notice the small sapling starting to grow out of the center of the piece of wood. The new tree was about two feet tall before it stopped growing. Lily stood and smoothed out her dress before turning to me. "Your turn," she said calmly.

Kneeling, I began meditating. Feeling for my energy. I watched it move. Lily began speaking to me more softly than I imagined her capable. "Find the light of the grass." I'd heard Agustín use it enough that I knew most sorcerers called energy light. I'd begun using them interchangeably given how often I was around sorcerers anymore. Helen didn't love that, and so I was careful not to do it around her.

I obeyed Lily and placed a hand on my own section of grass. Slowly I felt out its energy and saw what she meant by an interconnected network. "Once you have a feel for it, instead of letting your energy flow out to it, pull at its light.

Pull at it as though you're pulling at fibers to wind them up. Steady, but loose. Controlled, but unhurried."

I began winding up the energy of the grass. "Don't be timid. It's just grass. Take it and keep moving outward." I didn't love it, but I was able to take it easily and at first, slowly. I watched as this clumpy green energy stuck together and swirled amongst my own smooth flowing golden energy. I'd seen plants' energy plenty of times before. But it changed once it was inside me, possibly from being somewhere it didn't belong. Now it looked like curdled green milk, and my stomach turned slightly.

"Slow!" Lily snapped. "Slow down! You're going too fast!" I tried to slow down, but it was like slipping on an icy driveway that led downhill- everything slows down and speeds up at the same time and the next thing you know you're on your ass and not entirely sure where to go from there. And that's exactly what happened. I felt as though I was finally going slowly again when I felt Lily kick my arm away, breaking my connection. The jolt was too much for me, and the next thing I knew I was throwing up my lunch.

"Release it. *NOW!*" she shrieked. As scared as she sounded, I felt worse. I scrambled to the nearest cut log and hurriedly placed my hand on it. I closed my eyes and desperately looked for some modicum of life inside this dead log. "Find any tendril of life," Lily said with a nervous, frantic energy. "Release it, slowly. If you're capable of actually doing so." A growl seethed from my lips at her words, followed shortly by the rest of my lunch. There was no vitriol in her tone this time, but I was still furious. Frightened and furious.

I found the tendril of life I'd been desperately seeking and let the chunky green energy out of me into what was to become a sapling. I went as slowly as I could, painfully so. Every inch of me exhaustingly sore as I pulled back as much as

I could while still letting the energy trickle out. The nausea was overwhelming and I felt wretched. The desire to let it all slide away in an instant and curl up in a ball was powerful. But I didn't dare. Not here. Not with her.

Once all of the foreign energy was out of me, I took in a huge breath. I hadn't been breathing. Something a more weathered teacher would have caught. I was on my knees still, gasping, on the dark, frozen ground. I snapped my head around to scold Lily for her failings. My words stuck fast in my throat seeing her paled face.

She was gawking at something high above me. I looked up to see my sapling had become a tree that looked as though it belonged in the great forest that surrounded the kingdom. The original slice of wood had broken apart in the wake of this new tree. Its impressive regeneration already budding leaves.

Standing in an attempt to fully take in what I'd done, I noticed something else that sent a shiver up my spine. For as far as I could see I'd taken the energy, the life from the grass. Taken it completely and where there had once been a blanket of muted green, now was nothing but crunchy brown death. "How far do you think it goes?" I asked.

"I don't know. And that's exactly what we say. About *all of this*. You know nothing about it. Any of it. Understood? We didn't know if you'd be capable of this. But given the interest Helen and Briar have in you, it only makes sense that you... You could be in real danger. Do you understand? This isn't normal for your kind. If they find out you're capable of this kind of destruction, never mind the creation... Well, if you think you don't like them now, you'll see what it really means to be at odds with one's own." She was terrified and not hiding it as well as she thought. I needed to talk to Agustín about this, but for now Lily was absolutely correct. No one was to know about any of this.

"I won't be telling anyone. Believe me."

"Come on. I need to speak with my mother. And we need to get away from here. Your commander has people trailing you, so they'll have some idea, but he won't know the whole of it. I'm assuming you can keep him off your back." I glared at her as she headed back to the center of the kingdom through the woods, impatiently gesturing for me to follow. "Never take the known route when you can avoid it. And don't even think about trying any of this until we meet again. You clearly have no sense of control."

THE LAST BIT of light from the sun's rays filtered through my wall of a window by the time I got back to my apartment. The grass had been deadened for at least a mile around, and I was pretty drained myself. The adrenaline had been my fuel to get back here. Now I wanted nothing more than to pass out and forget everything for a while. The layers of sweat and the lingering stench of vomit compelled me to rinse off the day though, and then my muscles pressed me to draw myself a bath. Every bit of me needed all the help it could get to relax and heal. I had one foot in when I heard him at my door. One misdeed attracts another, I suppose.

"Go away, Briar. I'm taking a bath."

"Draca Francesca, this is your commander at the door." His words sent a chill through me. Shit. This wasn't going to be good.

I wrapped a towel around myself and answered. I'd expected it to just be Briar. There were two guards with him, they were all wearing their leather armor with the diagonal strips across their chests. Their hands were clasped behind them with their shoulders back. I knew this was their more relaxed stance, but it was still rather intimidating to me. "We have questions for you." He was yet to look at me. Instead, he stared blankly ahead. A behavior his companions mimicked.

"Let me get dressed quick." I began to shut the door and one of his guards grabbed it, stopping it from moving. I was surprised, somewhat unsettled, and slightly alarmed. I looked to Briar. His face was still cold and emotionless. "*Fine*. Come in." I was determined to not be the only uncomfortable one here. I motioned to the couch, but they all remained standing.

I knew I wasn't in any actual danger, not with Briar here, even if he was acting the part. I sat down with just my towel on, not terribly concerned with modesty given they couldn't be bothered to allow me any. "Well? What questions?" They still hadn't so much as glanced at me.

Briar's tone was as cold as his demeanor. "Early this afternoon there was an occurrence in the woods west of this kingdom. During our investigation we found something that belongs to you. We have reason to believe you were involved with this incident."

"What *are* you talking about? I don't have any idea about any incident. Thanks for asking. I wasn't even out in the woods today. I was with Sir Agustín. You can ask him yourself." I knew right away I'd said too much. Briar made a clicking noise, and his companions turned around on their heels and left my apartment. I watched them go before relaxing my shoulders.

After we heard the click of the door Briar ran his hands through his hair before grabbing it roughly. "Frankie," he hissed as he whispered, "For fucks' sake, don't lie to me! I know what that means to you, and *please*, not with me."

"Excuse me? Are you fucking kidding me?!" I yelled. He tried to stare me down, but when it was clear I wasn't having any of it, he moved with a speed that startled me, placing a hand over my mouth. I bit down, hard. He glared at me but didn't move his hand.

"If they think this is anything but regulation we'll have Helen to deal with. You know she'll find out, Frankie. I need you to keep it down. Understood?"

I could almost feel my eyes bleeding from the rage inside as I fought it down. When he'd lunged at me he'd dropped my knapsack with the book in it. I'd taken it assuming I'd be waiting on Lily. Earlier in the woods, in my amazement and fear, I'd forgotten to pick it back up.

"What happened out there, Frankie? Be honest with me. I'll know, and I don't have all evening."

"Oh? Hot date?" I hissed at him under my breath after he'd slowly removed his hand. He fumed at me, but I rolled my eyes and explained as best as I dared. "I don't actually know, okay? Lily was teaching me... something. I don't know, but I didn't do what you think I did." He bought it. At least he seemed to or was willing to pretend to. He picked up my bag and handed it to me.

"I wasn't kidding about not getting rid of this one, okay?" His eyes washed over me, hesitating where I expected them to.

"Obviously, I didn't mean to drop it. Why do you think I was carrying it around? And what was that? Trying to get your goons to intimidate me? That's new for you." He moved in close, leaning over the chair and me, my chest heaving as I tried to control my breath and near panic. His face brushed up against mine, but I wasn't about to give in and lean back.

His lips were practically on my ear as he whispered, "It's different now. When you give me the truth, I will too."

"Like last time?" That was enough. He backed away and straightened himself, his eyes never leaving mine. There was a different pain behind his callous expression. He was fighting something and failing. My heart ached for just a moment wanting to console him. It was enough that I almost forgot his trespasses.

Almost.

"Queen Anumonwo will see you tomorrow morning for tea. You know the drill." He looked deeply into my eyes one last time before leaving. Again I thought I heard him whisper his sorries before leaving, but again, I wasn't going to dwell on it.

CHAPTER

FIFTEEN

I was so desperate for sleep that night I actually started to miss Briar's warmth. Maybe it was just his bed. When sleep did come it didn't stay long. Horrible visions haunted me. The red elk was still after me, but it looked nearly rabid. It was horrifying. But I wasn't afraid. Not of it anyway. We were being chased, and something inside of me was changing or bubbling up. I wasn't sure if it was just in the dream, but something was brewing.

After some deliberation I decided to wear one of my altered dresses to tea with Helen. It was a deep earthy brown with copper silk embroidery and accents. I'd had to take my time altering this one to match up the embroidered designs that had gone into it before I ever got my hands on it. I was sure I'd get another lecture and feel the literal pressure of her disapproval. In for a penny, in for a pound I suppose.

Nothing seemed amiss as I left the Spires and headed for the Mountain. Heartwood was a tight-knit kingdom. When something happened out of the ordinary, either everyone knew about it or no one did. It depended on who found out first. For no one to know about this when Briar and his goons did, no one else was going to. That worried me more.

Even the Mountain seemed at ease. If anything, security was slightly lax. Helen was expecting me though. It had occurred to me before that this style of entrance on the second floor was likely a strategic choice. Higher ground and all that. As I ascended obnoxious step after step to a waiting queen, it wasn't even a question.

"Frankie, right on time!" I hadn't been aware of a particular time. Helen moved things around as she saw fit and everyone else worked with her ebb and flow.

"My queen," I said as I extended an arm and we kissed each other's cheeks before I bowed slightly, allowing her to kiss my forehead. I'd been schooled on the niceties and while this was a bare minimum, it pleased her that I was giving her any honorific at all.

Helen was wearing an unusually light and flowing golden gown adorned with colorful embroidered flowers. It flowed like a sundress that had been poofed up by too much happiness. Her usual lock of braided hair had golden silk weaved into it, and she seemed eerily happy. The air felt lighter. It was as if I could breathe deeper, easier around her today.

As we walked to her glass terrarium she made a point to walk beside me. I generally trailed after her slightly, as was custom. "I love what you have done with this gown. It suits you. It is you, and it is also us. And that is exactly what you have done here." I smiled nervously at her compliment. She beamed at me, making me feel all the more nervous as her warmth encased me.

She paid unusually little attention to her hand maid that day. And she wasn't fidgeting with her golden spoon either. Something was wrong. If I didn't know it, I could feel it. "Talk to me of your work with the sorcerer, Sir Agustín?" I imagined her eyes glowed slightly as she used his title. She knew I didn't have the distaste for them the rest of my kind did, and she was wise enough to show them their due respect. Even if it was clear she didn't want to.

"It's been going well. Agustín says this new method seems to be about seventy percent as effective as letting the fruit dry itself out. And given how much more quickly we're able to process larger quantities of them, it's worth it. Not perfect of course, but still worthwhile. And I can feel my energy growing every day as I'm working. It feels good to put in this kind of effort and be tired at the end of the day. He's also shown me how to process the Dragon Heart, but I haven't done much of that really."

"You two must be growing close. You have been working in his lab for some time now."

"It doesn't feel all that long, really. Most of the time, anyway." While this was true, Helen breaking out into what seemed to be a genuine laugh was unsettling and put me even more on edge.

"I can imagine spending that kind of time with them could be a bit draining." Her choice of words made my body stiffen slightly. She noticed and gave me a kind, almost whimsical smile.

"He's a great teacher, really," I said. "And I feel as though our respect for one another has grown. But I don't know that I'd say we're becoming close. It's a working relationship. I might not have the same temperament that most of my kind has, but he knows to keep his distance from a dragon." Complete and utter bullshit. Exactly what she needed to hear.

"Speaking of dragons, have you decided when you would like to go through with your transformation? We could bring in a commander from another kingdom to assist? Given the unique situation we find ourselves in, I believe everyone will be more than understanding and accommodating, at the very least." Her eyes again glowed slightly as she peered at me over her teacup.

"I still haven't decided if I even want to yet. So no, I haven't decided when, your majesty." I knew she'd get bristly at this point. This was a topic that came up at every tea, which had been slightly more than weekly. Still, I was a bit shaken by her response this time.

"Well, take your time. But remember, as your energy grows, so too does your dragon. If you keep it up, Thorn will *have* to be the one to assist you. He still says he will not. But I cannot really think of anyone better for the job. He is one of the more impressive dragons in our world."

"Nothing has changed between us. I still very much want him to keep as much distance as he can from me. I can't... I don't trust him."

"I do think you are being a bit harsh, little draca. He is young, naïve. You are a connection to his mother he never had. It may be a rough, peculiar love. But what real love is not? You think you have had real, burning love before. Did that not turn out to be nothing but ashes? My advice would be to stop *thinking* so much, and to start *feeling* more. What does your body, your inner dragon, tell you? I am not saying to trust your gut alone and abandon all reason, but let them work together, hmm?"

I let out a long sigh as we held each other's gaze. I nodded slightly, acquiescing in the moment, vaguely. Again, she beamed at me. When Queen Anumonwo really smiled at you it was as if the sun itself had chosen to shine for you. Just you. As stifling as her disappointment could feel, this went the complete other way. I couldn't help but return her smile, that soothing warmth steadily embracing and suffocating me.

"Besides, you have no idea what that boy has done for you.

Not really. Other than persuading me to not kill you, I mean. He will not tell you, but you are a smart woman. It will come as no surprise that he should have ordered some of his to keep tabs on you. When I tried to follow up with his duties, enforcing what needed to be, he outright refused! Can you imagine? The sheer willpower! It is quite impressive. He was determined to not let anyone interfere with you. Well, anyone besides himself, I suppose." She chuckled lightly to herself. I didn't believe her, but I was still enraptured by the palpable feeling of happiness from a moment ago and simply shrugged it off.

"He has also convinced me to..." She turned to her ladies in waiting. There were two of them today in front of the glass door by the hallway. "Ladies, leave us." She waited until they were standing in the hallway, facing away from us before she continued. "He has convinced me to give you access to my personal library."

She gave me a moment to let that wash over me before she started to reinforce what that actually meant. "I do not let just anyone in there, my draca. It contains information about us that could have a rather pernicious effect. Do you understand? I need you to be wary with who you speak to regarding our secrets."

"Of course!" I stumbled over my words as I stumbled over my emotions. "I've only ever wanted to know more about who I am, *what* I am, and where I come from. Even if I don't precisely know where that actually is. Besides, who would I discuss it with?" She gave me a knowing look. We both knew she meant the sorcerers. They collect information like a bee collects nectar, constantly and desperately in preparation for what they know is too soon to come.

"How is your training with Madam Lilith progressing? I heard you recently began learning some interesting techniques." Helen was grasping for her own nectar. She knew bits and pieces, they all did. But they didn't know everything, but they'd be damned if they'd admit it. It was easy to forget how dangerous this world was at times. But not here. So much always unknown but not knowing who I could or should trust always set me on edge. The sorcerers knew everything. Why shouldn't the dragons? Lily's warnings kept ringing through my head.

I cleared my throat, about to ask some dangerous questions. I imagine my own dragon's gold flitted across my eyes because the next moment Helen was waving her hand in front of her as though to clear the metaphorical air. "Worry not, my draca. I was merely being polite and doing my due diligence as your protector, and the protector of our people. Your time with your sorcerers is your own. I do not need, nor do I really wish, to be privy to its intimacies."

Her implications weren't exactly polite, but I wasn't going to press. I had enough to digest from today as it was. We said our farewells with a promise that she'd soon give me a tour of her private library. One more thing for me to catastrophize and wonder about. What would I owe Briar if I accepted? I would have time to think it over while I worked. My activities yesterday with Lily had put me more behind than I liked at the greenhouse. I hadn't even opened the book from Briar yet. What might I owe him for that one? How would he know if I kept it or not if he really didn't have people keeping tabs on me? But then again, I guess he didn't really. Not until I told him.

SIXTEEN

The day's tea with Helen, as bizarre as it had been, kept replaying in my mind. I didn't understand why she was pushing me towards Briar. My biggest issue was his lying about taking me home. But how honest was that? Maybe I should have mentioned his promise to take me back. If Briar had ever intended on going against Helen though, I didn't want to be why she didn't trust him. You never know what might happen someday. And that was probably giving my word far too much credit. It likely would have just been one more thing she'd tell me to forgive and forget. It felt like this entire world was conspiring against me. My grandiose rumination resulted in me losing my way as I was trying to leave. I had taken Gale's side path, hoping to avoid any possible encounter with Briar. But I'd taken the stairs down at least one too many levels.

The hidden stairwell with its tight, quick steps had given me a headache and I jumped at the first exit I came upon. Judging by the dark corridor before me, I must have gone down a few too many levels. There was an odd, sterile smell adding to the discomfort in my head. I wasn't supposed to be here. I knew that. I could feel it. But there was something else. Something propelling, or pulling, me forward. It was one of the few times I'd felt secure in who I was and what I was doing since arriving. This was the way I *needed* to be going. I'm sure the tea had something to do with that, basking in Helen's golden rays of love or whatever that bullshit was. I knew better than to be *this* absent minded. Being under this overbearing Mountain played tricks on you. About to ignore my gut and turn around, a heart stopping wail curdled my nerves and froze my steps. Except, I didn't actually hear *it*. I heard its echo- something similar to the visions I'd been having, in a room I could sense not far from here. All I could experience was pitch black and that scream. It made my blood run cold.

I took a few long steps towards the room, telling myself I was definitely *not* supposed to be here. And knowing I was *not* supposed to have heard that. Our queen used practices I didn't agree with, but I believed her and Briar when they told me she did what was necessary for her people. I believed her to be a good protector. They'd both been lying to me though, and Helen's recent intrusions and abruptions pushed me to need to know what was going on. I needed to know how dark this might get.

My intuition from this auditory vision guided me as I crept down the hall. A whisper of footsteps seemed to be leading me, but whenever I'd stop, they would too, making me question if I wasn't just hearing my own steps. Light filtered through a line in the wall and I began to feel around for a door, hoping all I needed to do was push in the right place or find some lever or latch. Running my hands over the wall, something sharp cut into me. I jerked my hand back from the pain as a glyph flashed across the wall. The sliver of light grew larger as the wall gave way slightly. I listened for a while, trying to anticipate who or what would be waiting inside. All I could hear were faint hints of erratic whimpering. I squeezed myself into the gap, hoping to be inconspicuous while also trying very hard to not freak out.

It was almost as dark inside, save for the solitary lantern on the far wall that had illuminated my way. I hurried over to it, afraid of what might see me that I could not yet see. I picked up the lantern and quickly put my back to the wall. The whimpering had stopped, and now all I could hear was the racing of my heart, some shallow breaths that were not mine, and nothing else.

I took a few breaths to build up my courage before following the worrisome breathing. Before pressing on, I closed the bit of wall that I'd passed through to get into here. Guards patrolled every level of the Mountain. This one would be no different. If anything was out of the ordinary they'd alert Helen and likely Briar. I needed to find out what was going on before they could lie to me again.

Even with my slow and deliberate pace, I quickly stumbled into a massively solid door. A thick metal bar that I couldn't lift held it in place. Whoever had been making the pained noises earlier was now quiet, and I hoped desperately that they'd simply recovered. Placing the lantern down a good ways back, I returned to the metal bar.

Lifting the bar was an impossibility, but I could push the damn thing out of its holder and then it was just a matter of hobbling and walking it out of the way from the door. It'd do me a world of good if I just slowed down sometimes and gave things a little thought. Still frustrated with how quickly I was able to move it once I thought about it, I inched the door open to find that I could actually see in there, but just barely.

A dragon lay covered and weighed down in chains. She was shades of an ancient forest, such a deep and primordial green she was almost black. A shudder began in my spine and worked its way out to the rest of my body. I don't know how, but I could feel her energy, what little of it there was left, even from here. She was weak, nearly dead. I wasn't sure how she was managing to remain in this form. Her body was curled up around herself, her head hidden from me. Inching forward, I held the lantern out a ways in front of me hoping to see some sign of whether or not she was conscious or aware of my presence. I stepped warily into the room, needing to understand.

When I saw someone resting against the side of the dragon, I reflexively jumped back, ready to turn and run. He wore nothing but threadbare and torn strips of stained fabric, his skin was caked in what I could only presume was blood, some of it dry, some of it not, and his long, dark hair was matted and wild. When he didn't move I started forward again, slowly. As I got closer, the devastating smell of blood and death and decay stole my breath and made my skin crawl. The man had chains around his wrists and ankles somewhat securing him. There was an odd black cloth wrapped around his hands tightly enough that they almost looked gloved. It was a safe bet the material was covered with glyphs to render his energy feeble at best. His head was slumped forward, and I saw no sign of him being aware of my trespass. Guardedly I moved to the side, needing to see the dragon better.

Regardless of why they were down here or what they may have done, this treatment was horrendous and beyond unacceptable. My legs felt weak and wobbly from the shock of finding such a scene, here of all places! I could only imagine the explanations that awaited me. I wanted to help her. I *needed* to help her. But I had to touch her to really see what was wrong. My hand reached out shakily to rest on her tail as I closed my eyes. Needing to sense what was wrong with her, I moved as quickly as possible. Both the dragon and that man could reach me, and I had no idea who they were or why they were down here. Neither of them had moved, which was uncannily more disturbing to me than not.

She was closer to death than I had realized.

My eyes flashed open the instant I saw her damage. Looking over at the man, I jumped seeing his eyes- two stormy blue worlds with shards of glowing gold, boring into me. There was something primal about him. And wretched. They'd tortured his companion to the brink of death. I didn't know the extent of what they'd done to him, but his broken lip and deeply bruised body worried me. Only a couple of feet separated us as he held my gaze. There was a fierceness behind his gold as he stared into me, startling me for reasons I didn't understand. I stood up quickly, unsure of what was to come. My heart felt as though it was about to burst.

"She needs help," I said in earnest. He kept staring, wordlessly. Something felt off with him. He was dangerous. Even as he sat there, nearly crumpled over, I could feel his strength. I wanted to help her, but I'd never attempted anything like this before. My lesson with Lily had severely drained my energy, but I knew I could make her okay. It was what he could do that worried me, especially while I was preoccupied with healing her. Though it didn't take much time for me to realize I didn't actually care. She was dying. I could help her. If he killed me- so be it. End this cycle of flickering hope and drowning numbness.

I was aware of his eyes upon me as I knelt down by her side with a huff. Placing my hands on her smooth scales, maybe I imagined it, but she felt colder already. It made me nervous. Taking a moment to gather my energy, I became aware that I'd never struggled quite so much to clear my mind. I'd never healed a dragon before, not like this, and it was taking a considerable amount of energy.

There was a stillness, a different kind of quiet, as I gave her the energy she needed. Hers was sluggishly building up as I gave to her. Her body slowly warming under my hands. She wasn't where I wanted her to be, but I had to stop. I was exhausting myself, and this was the last place I wanted to pass out.

She needed only the tiniest bit more. I gathered what I could and did what I had to. But it'd been more than I realized. The familiar drain on my body and mind engulfed me like the morning sun, imperceptibly steady until suddenly- it's there. I was blacking out. I felt my body collapsing as she began to move under me. Something enveloped me like the darkness. The last thing I remembered was smelling something ancient. I have no other words to describe it.

And then I was gone to the world.

WARM, firm arms nestled me in their embrace as I came back around. We were away from the other dragon, but I could feel her heated vehemence filling the room. I didn't care. He was a steady comfort as I lay against him. His scruffy and bruised face was staring straight ahead, distracted. I should have been fearful, but there was no such emotion. There was some left-over braveness from before, or idiocy, whichever the case may be. I wanted to know if this was real. I reached up, and my fingertips grazed his overgrown beard.

Those stormy blue eyes shot down to meet my gaze. It wasn't so much as butterflies in my stomach, but fireworks in my chest. It was exhilarating and terrifying and the sensation filled me with a sense of the sublime. I slowly moved away knowing I needed to leave, soon. He freely let me go, and a part of me cursed him for doing so.

The rest was a blur. Agustín came through the door, dropping some of the Dragon Cor at the sight of me. This resulted in some impressively large puffs of red smoke. Then he was dragging me away, ignoring all my questions. We made our way back through the stone tunnel, replacing the heavy metal bar. He was careful to hang the lantern back precisely as it had been before.

"Show me how you got here," he demanded through clenched teeth. I wanted to argue and preserve my secrets. But I knew that wouldn't go well. Besides, I'd drained myself, and I needed his help.

"Only if you answer my questions about them," I countered. He scowled at me but yielded easily. It wouldn't be that simple, but even I knew we shouldn't be having this conversation in the Mountain. I walked back up the tight steps and exited back into the palace with him following. Briar was nowhere to be seen, thank the gods.

As we exited he took the lead, and my arm, leading us back to my apartment. "Frankie, what were you thinking? What were you doing down there?!" He helped me lay down on the couch as he gathered some food to help build my energy back up.

"I was leaving from tea... I got lost. My mind was elsewhere, and I just kept walking. There was a sound.... It was a kind of vision thing I have sometimes. I followed it... to them. Who are they, Agustín? What happened to them? Why are there dragons being held captive in the queen's Mountain?!"

"Frankie, promise me you won't go back down there?! I don't know what Briar would do if he found out. Unfortunately I *do* know what Helen would do. You need to stay away. Promise me?!" He was terrified and begging.

"They're both involved? Who are those dragons and why are they down there? I'm tired of all the fucking secrets,

Agustín! Please?! I know it's not your fault, but please, don't leave me in the dark like they are."

"It's not for me to tell. This is all to do with your own people. I am just the one that heals them when they need it." His arms were tightly crossed in front of him as he began pacing the room, frustrated and clearly concerned. Concerned for whom I wasn't sure.

"You're healing them? Why are they still down there then? Why were they down there in the first place?"

"How could you understand? It's not your..." He paused for a moment, staring at me as he nervously bit his lip. "Promise me- promise that if I tell you what I know, you won't go back? It's for your own safety, and let's be honest, mine as well. Briar has spent his life on this and if—"

"I promise! It'll be okay. *Please*, I need some answers. All they do is lie to me. Please, just tell me what you know!" It was my turn to beg.

He looked away, unsure, before turning to me and staring me down. "They are from one of the Wilds that live outside of a kingdom. The recent envoy. Their way of life- it's dangerous, for everyone, not just them." He paused for a moment. I could tell he was wondering what all he should say. "They're the bad guys, Frankie. Briar is getting information out of them. Information he needs to keep the Wilds in check and keep all of Visnatura safe. They're different. They're dangerous for a whole plethora of reasons, in more ways than you can imagine. They'll end our way of life. You have to think of the people of this kingdom, this world. And I'm not just talking about the dragons." He was aggravated and irate, but it was clear that his anger wasn't directed at me. "I don't even understand it all myself. I just know your queen is doing what she needs to in order to keep your people and this kingdom safe. That's the bargain after all, they're given free rein and they protect us all."

I had to look away. "You're healing them so Briar can continue to torture them."

"I don't ask questions. I supply and administer the Dragon Cor. Then I leave."

Realization dawned slowly. "I think I'm going to be sick. Dragon Cor. That I've been helping with? How could you let me... Without telling me what it was for?" He couldn't even look at me. He just shook his head at nothing in particular. "How much longer do you think they're going to keep them down there?"

He did look at me then, peculiarly for a moment before his confusion washed away, slowly replaced with sympathy. "Hon, they're not going to be leaving there alive. Once they aren't useful they'll strip the... they'll take what is useful and be done with them."

I knew the kingdom used their animal sanctuary as a front to propagate certain species of magical beasts to harvest what they needed. They did a lot of good work as well, both for the people of the kingdom and the beasts. But as they say, you don't want to see how the sausage is made. To harvest a dragon, *their own kind*, it had to be more savage than anything those in the Wilds have ever done. I felt ill again, for an array of reasons. I laid down, shaking my head in disbelief.

"What were you even trying to do? Don't you know you can't really heal a dragon in its natural state like that? That isn't how it works. She clearly had preserved more energy than Briar realized..." His words trailed off as he became lost in thought. I trusted him to an extent, but if he thought I couldn't heal her, I saw no problem in letting him continue to think as much. It wouldn't be the only thing I was keeping from them all. Ever since I started working for Agustín my energy had been increasing drastically, much more than I'd been told to expect. It even began to recuperate faster too. Something I'd been told didn't really happen.

His attention suddenly returned to me. "Frankie, you promised. Remember that, draca." My inflamed, gilded eyes shot up at him. I couldn't believe he was okay with this. Then again, Agustín was nothing if not practical. He was a Medela after all. I nodded slowly, knowing what he needed to hear from me too. "Let me see your hand. If Briar sees that cut, he'll know."

I should have thanked him for healing me. I didn't. "If I keep disobeying, if I keep angering them, will they force me to turn and lock me up like that?"

He looked over and his genuine emotion had been replaced with his usual, placating demeanor. "Oh hon, gods no! Briar loves you. Through all of this, believe what you want, but he really does love you. Those two are a threat you could never be. He would never let that happen to you."

"Would you stop it if it did? If Helen or Briar told you it needed to be done. Would you still go along with it as readily?"

He looked at me for a long moment before looking away.

"Good to know," I mumbled to myself. I'd just found out these people were torturing others and would be capable of torturing me too. It was only a matter of time before I did something to upset them that they wouldn't forgive. I needed to escape, and soon. The imprisoned man's face flashed in my mind, and I felt a painful stab through my chest. My need to flee was a selfish one. Impractical too.

I sat up and attempted to smother my own emotions. I wasn't as practiced as Agustín, but I made it work. "Why don't we get dinner tonight? You've been asking since I arrived. Why not now? And I can tell you how my lesson with Lily went."

He smiled at me shrewdly. "I could believe that. I could pretend I don't know you better. That I'm not painfully aware you're plotting something. I could go ahead and make dinner plans with you. Or you could tell me what you're thinking." He sat down in one of my chairs and leaned back with a practiced ease.

"You know, I think this is the first time I've seen you ever really relaxed."

"Frankie..."

I looked at him squarely. "Can I trust you? I feel as though we have a certain amount of respect for one another, and with that has to come some modicum of trust, yes?" It was a loaded question, and I expected a throw away, dishonest answer that would help me pinpoint exactly what I could and couldn't discuss. I did not get that answer. Instead, I got an honest one for the first time since I'd arrived. "Agustín, can I trust you?"

"No."

"Fair enough," I said, only allowing some of my surprise to surface. "I need help finding out about who, and what, I am. I know I'm dragon, but you know I'm more. Something is off and no one is telling me anything. Helen invited me to her private library. But I know she'll only let me know what she wants me to. There's something bigger going on, and I don't think even you know everything about it."

He made no reaction. As a sorcerer they went through a lot of training, from birth practically. It was ingrained in them that they served their families, then the kingdoms, always in that order, and they took it seriously. They were the pillars of this world, the ones who made most of the big decisions. Having a dragon government in the kingdom was an honor, and it added an extra level of protection. More and more it seemed to me as though the kingdom was more so paying thugs for protection rather than having an honorable Dragon House.

I had one other method to try and get to him. He'd see right through it of course, but that didn't mean it wouldn't work. "Sorcerers have a right to know what's going on. But I understand. You don't ask questions, not of them. I should let you go. I'm sure you have a busy day." I sat up to say my goodbyes and insisted I was well enough that he could take his leave. I looked over at him, his arms across his chest again, biting his lip, staring off out one of my windows.

"I don't have a busy day. My existence is merely a busy one. There is a difference." There was my in. I needed to learn what I could.

"Well, you still have to eat. Let's actually have dinner then. We don't need to discuss anything if you don't wish to. I can meet you at your office?"

Again, he made no visible reaction. Almost anyway, his lips twitched almost imperceptibly. Slowly he agreed, "Maybe we should see if Lily will join us. I haven't heard from her since yesterday."

He knew something was off from the lesson, but I owed him no explanation. I was done being the plaything of the people of this kingdom. They were going to teach me what I needed to know, one way or another, and I was going home. But I couldn't leave those dragons down there. It wasn't right. They wouldn't be hiding them like that if what Agustín had told me was true. This world may be no kinder, no fairer than my own, but that doesn't mean I should turn a blind eye.

Nor would I.

SEVENTEEN

Agustín had gone back to his greenhouse and retrieved another vial of the Dragon Cor. I'd never so much as smelled the finished product before, and now he was forcing a tube of it down my throat. The smell itself was floral, but the elixir had an almost gamey taste to it. The juxtaposition was enough to make you gag, never mind the physical effect.

"I'm not yet sure where your energy went, but you should feel better soon. You will still be completely drained. DO NOT try to use it. *At all.* Do you understand?" I scowled at the taste, the physical reactions, and him as I nodded my acknowledgment. "Rest. I'll take care of things in the greenhouse today. Remember your promise, little dragon."

And with that he left me to a fitful sleep.

My dreams had been awful. Just terrible enough to wake me, but not so memorable as to keep me that way. When I finally did stay awake, I couldn't remember a thing about them. One more thing to anxiously wonder about I suppose.

For my own sake I needed to keep busy. I thought about

diving into the book from Briar, but he was the last person I needed to be thinking about at the moment. For a moment I wondered how necessary his work in that dungeon might be. Maybe Agustín was right and it needed to be done to keep us safe. After all- what did I know of this world, really? Then reason crept back in. Why weren't there guards posted there? How many actually knew about the dragons they had imprisoned and were torturing? There was so much I didn't know. Too much. But it wasn't like I could just go ask Briar or Hellen. And whose fault was that?!

The rest of my afternoon was spent in the main library of my spire. It occupied a couple of levels and like everywhere else had rounded, outer walls. The walls here were all lined with books. The librarian was a sweet, tall woman that rarely smiled, although she was always pleasant enough. The free-standing curved stacks lined the floor like tiger stripes and offered a fair bit of privacy. There were plush chairs for those wanting to relax as they read. And desks with uncomfortable chairs for those that had work to do. I'd spent many days here since settling in, more often than not in an uncomfortable chair.

This library had most of the infrastructure books I needed. You couldn't check these out, but I didn't want to. I didn't want word of what I was reading getting back to anyone. They knew I wasn't happy, but they thought I'd settle down. They didn't actually know me, didn't know how much I needed my home, my family. And they didn't know what I'd recently discovered.

I had always been someone who let everything simply fall to me. I was told I'd be a good nurse. So, I went to nursing school and was offered a job. I was told I needed to get out of the house one difficult summer, so I volunteered at a local garden. I met Jen and was taken down this fucked up path. I never sought out any of this. And this? This was different. This time I needed to know where *I* wanted to go. And I had to be the one to actively get me there. I just needed to figure out where *there* was first.

What I was reading wasn't all that helpful though. Maps and blueprints were somewhat, but they were all from a few hundred years ago. I couldn't exactly ask someone if they were still up to date or if everything was still in working order.

After struggling with attempts to formulate a plan all afternoon, I'd nearly forgotten about dinner. Walking back to my apartment I thought about which of my few outfits to wear. A wave of grief and longing for my overly abundant closet back home hit me and I had to steal myself. I knew thinking about which dress to wear was silly, but I still thought about it and was done judging myself for it. Lark would have been proud. I could have cried when I got to my apartment and found that Agustín had sent a gift. I'd almost thrown it out thinking it was another peace offering from Briar.

Briar knew better than to let himself in to my place without my permission again. Even so, I always entered my apartment with a hesitation and did a search of all the rooms to make sure I was alone. Once I'd performed my checks I opened the gift box.

It was clearly a dinner dress, but he must be taking me somewhere a little unexpected. If I'd been wearing dresses, this was a gown. Silky silver-white opalescent fabric, slightly shorter in the front and tapered to be floor-length in the back, sleeveless with intricate embroidery on the bodice trailing down to the long skirt- it seemed a bit much really, but I loved it. He'd even blessedly thought to include a pair of silver flats.

I had to hurry to get ready. I was always hurrying anymore. It was exhausting. What I wouldn't give to be back in a garden that was all my own. With time that was mine. To live in the woods enjoying a garden of my own, to rejoice in napping under a tree dappled with sunlight as it perforated through the leaves, that was what I wanted- what I would work for. But I couldn't think of that now. Now I needed to hurry. I was even hurrying from my spire to the Medela Spire.

I'd worn my hair up with a few curly tendrils strategically down, mostly because I didn't have anything to put in it to stop it from turning into a giant frizz ball. There were products, natural oils and magicked items that could bring the comforts of my home to exist here. I just hadn't made any effort to acquire them. This wasn't home, and I didn't want to adjust. More than once I'd heard the comment about how I couldn't be a dragon because I wasn't vain enough. I didn't feel that was accurate. I had different priorities at the moment, that was all.

My hair up left me feeling rather exposed around my neck and shoulders. But I dealt with it the same way I had dealt with everything else, mostly by ignoring it. The elevator was busier than usual, and I assumed the go-between would be as well, but perhaps it was always this busy at this time of night. It was customary here to eat dinner very late. Well, late by my standards anyway. The stolen glimpses were beginning to make me uncomfortable. Maybe it was because the gown was a bit too low cut, but that was normal for most of their clothing. The ethereal chain that Owjen's ring hung upon was long enough that it kept the ring rarely visible. With this gown you could see the top of it, and that was saying something.

No answer at Agustín's office, again. I debated letting myself in and decided to, once the lobby started to get populated with other Medelas that cared for me about as much as Lily did. The first room was still as empty as last time. Agustín's actual office was not. I opened the door to find him and Cifelli hastily putting themselves back together. I smiled wickedly at them both. Agustín loved teasing me incessantly, and now I could return the favor. "I never thought I'd see the great Sir Agustín looking so guilty!" I was tickled and overjoyed. "Were we being naughty during work hours?!"

He gave me a stern look before trying to reason with me. "It's not the same here, Frankie. And it's not what you think. Cifelli, he's not..."

"He can't give you an heir," I said thoughtfully, thinking I understood his predicament.

"What?! No! I mean, literally no, yes. But that's not the issue. Wait- do you have any idea how many sisters I have that will produce heirs?" He shook his head at me as he refocused himself. "No, it's... he can't read enough of the glyphs to appease my mother. She'd never allow it. Do you understand?"

I was torn between being perplexed and genuine abhorrence. "He isn't strong enough for?"

"Prestige, Frankie. And when it comes to the Medela family, that's the only thing that means *anything*. It'd be seen as an embarrassment, a loss of power. I'm begging you..." I'd never seen him like this. He was always a little too full of his own bravado. And here he was, nearly fearful of his mother finding out about his... well I guess I don't know what he'd consider him. Cifelli himself had turned to face away from us both. My heart broke for a few different reasons.

Lily came up behind me calling for her brother, "Agustín, have you seen Cifelli?" I turned on my heel at the sound of her voice. She smiled coldly as she looked me up and down, evaluating my attire, and, well, me. "Have you seen my brother? You're blocking the way to his office so I'm assuming he's in there."

A nervous laugh bubbled out of me as I fidgeted with my hands and repositioned my arms. She was always a tad intimidating, but this damned gown made me feel all the more vulnerable. "He is, yeah. I was just talking with him. I didn't know Cifelli was your assistant! We were talking about our lesson." She looked me up and down once more, clearly trying to figure out what was wrong with me.

She winked at me as she began speaking louder this time. Her message clear- keep your damn mouth shut. "You know, Frankie, I don't teach Agustín's strumpets. Did he get that dress for you?"

Agustín yelled from behind me. "She is NOT one of my strumpets!" I moved aside to let her pass, following at a safe distance. "And you're the one who pointed out that dress the other day!"

"HA!" she squawked. "I knew that'd get you going. And yes, so you could get it for me as a birthday gift." She seemed only playfully annoyed. "Cifelli, he doesn't have you working for him again, does he? Auggie, get your own assistant!"

"I have one! He's just never around when I need him. And it isn't my fault you used up all your credits on other dresses. Oh, and I hope you don't mind; I'm bringing a dragon to your birthday dinner." He grinned mischievously as he winked at me. For as much as I hated being winked at, the Medelas loved doing it. The last thing I wanted tonight was to intrude on a family affair, especially with a sorcerer family, particularly *this* sorcerer family.

Yes, I'd had an agenda around dinner. Yes, Agustín likely knew that all along. Yes, he'd ended my plan before it ever started. "Come on now," he said. "Wouldn't want to be late!"

Cifelli snuck out while Agustín finished packing up from the day. He tapped one of the leaves along the endless vines in his office, and when it opened up he placed his pen inside. The leaf promptly wrapped around the pen and stilled itself. I'd seen it enough times before, but it was always mesmerizing to watch.

Remembering myself, I turned to Lily, "I'm sorry, I didn't

know it was your birthday dinner. I'm the one that asked about dinner, and he said tonight. We'll reschedule."

"Nonsense," Agustín inserted flatly. "It's just dinner. Besides, we have business to discuss. Come along, ladies." Lily gave me a terse look as she gestured for me to follow him.

I was worried it would be a big family dinner. The Medelas were a large family after all- Madam Medela herself had produced four daughters and one son. Not to mention the countless aunts, uncles, cousins, nieces, nephews, etc..

But this dinner was just the three of us. It was the same place Briar had taken me to that first day, but it wasn't our own private room. The dinner crowd was also a world apart from those from lunch. I wasn't exactly out of place here, though I still felt as though I was.

We'd ordered drinks before Lily started in again. "Agustín, are you planning on asking mother if you can marry her?" Lily had a habit of talking about me as if I wasn't there. As if I actually was Agustín's strumpet. (She knew full well I wasn't his type.) But she relished any air of indignation she could have with me. I wasn't sure what I'd done, but she seemed to delight in it. It occurred to me more than once that I likely didn't have anything at all to do with it. Still, it was hard not to take it personally.

"Oh, that's an idea!" Agustín chimed in. "Can you imagine? A dragon sorcerer! I've read the powers don't blend well though." He was clearly trying to provoke some sort of actual conversation.

"Has there ever been one?" I joined in with what little information I had. "I've been told dragons don't breed with non-dragons." I could practically feel Lily's eyes light up. I continued with my line of thought, although I didn't know if any of it was actually true. "I recently read that when dragons take on non-dragon lovers, they always end up in unfortunate situations."

"Any experience with that?" Lily asked, trying to sound as disinterested as possible.

"You know- I'm not really sure. I've never exactly been 'lucky in love,' but I've also never turned. So that's probably just been me." I hoped my melancholic nostalgia wasn't too evident.

"Turning doesn't matter," Lily said too quickly, before trying to tamper her excitement. "Or so I've read. Apparently this is one of the few things it doesn't affect. It's different from their heat, strength, all the things that usually come with transforming. It's more of a blood thing. Evidently those who don't or can't turn still have all of the consequences of a dragon that has turned, like your eyes." She really did have a fascination with dragons. I thought Agustín had been lying. She was also slightly too proud of her knowledge.

"Can I ask- where did you read this? I've looked at every book I can get my hands on. I'm disappointed with how little I've been able to find. Everything is either second or even third hand knowledge. Helen recently invited me into her library, but, and no offense here, I can't imagine she'd ever let a non-dragon in. Especially not a sorceress. How do you know these things?"

"Well, it's not really my place..." Medelas outright refused to deal with third hand knowledge. They had a funny little quip about it that I never could remember. But they'd under-stand and appreciate my interest in source materials.

"Answer her, Lily." Agustín's tone was so sharp and demanding I couldn't help but glance up at him.

Lily looked at him suspiciously as she began to answer my question. "Your queen has a private library..."

"Yes, she's invited me—"

"No, no…" She seemed to be thinking something over. I had the distinct impression she had started to tell me something and changed her mind. "She doesn't allow books with too much information to be out in the other libraries. I had a small collection, and she *persuaded* me to strategically dispose of it. Into her care, of course."

It was obvious that I wanted to know how she could have possibly done that. Agustín cut me off before I could. "Don't bother. She won't tell you any more than that anyway. Although, Lily, I do believe you owe me a favor for covering that little *escapade* of yours a few months ago?"

"We're not talking about that now, dear brother." She smiled tightly at him.

"Of course not, *dear sister*. But I am calling in that favor. Tell Frankie what you know."

"I can't! I'm not a dragon. I… I don't know enough to tell her."

"Frankie's a clever thing. She'll figure it out. None of them are going to tell her. You know they won't let her read about it either. Give her the information. That's all I'm asking, and I'll forget what I know."

"I need to think about it. If she found out I told her… you know what would happen." It was clear she was worried about Heartwood's dragon queen. I wondered how it mattered when it wasn't her own kind. What *could* Helen do to her? And while there was some distance between us and the other tables, it wasn't the separate room I'd been in with Briar, and I began to become more aware of those around us.

Clearly it was a big ask, and that I was dying to know what she had to tell me. Lily spoke in a demanding but bright voice, "That's enough of that now. Let's stop with all this cloak and dagger talk. So, Frankie, I know it's a bit of a personal question, but… what is it that you hoard?"

"Excuse me?" I choked out. I had no idea what she was talking about.

"Are we *sure* she's a real dragon?!" she asked Agustín. "Hoard? Collect? Covet? Whatever you call it." She was wide eyed and curious. I hated to dash her spirit, fearing she'd think me even less of a dragon- although that only seemed fair.

"Do dragons actually do that? I don't collect, well, anything that I can think of really." She grumbled a bit as she and Agustín shared a glance I didn't understand.

The rest of the conversation was about their family operations and the pressure on the greenhouses. We spoke briefly of my first lesson with Lily. She and Agustín spoke mostly in code. I didn't follow everything, but it was clear he understood what had happened. He was more puzzled than impressed. I knew I had destroyed quite a lot, but I'd also created something rather notable as well. My pride was a little dashed that no one commented on that.

After dinner we went back up to the go-between. Naturally they'd have apartments in their own building, but Agustín insisted on walking me to my door. As we said goodnight to Lily, she again eyed me up and down. This time with a slightly less sour look than she had all evening. "That dress does look nice on you. It compliments your eyes." She gave me an uncomfortable hug and held me close to her. She whispered quickly in my ear, *"She will show you one library. There is another. It has the information you're looking for. She shows it to her lovers, to trick them into believing she trusts them. I don't know how to open the entrance, but it's within her regular library. Get her to let you spend time in the one, and I'm sure a* clever thing *like you can find your way into the other."* She released me from the hug but wouldn't look at me.

"Thank you, Lily." I tried to convey my sincere gratitude through my expression and tone, but she wouldn't meet my gaze. She simply nodded and walked away. In that moment I realized I had no idea what she was risking.

"Let's get you home," Agustín said, offering me his arm.

"If only," I sighed. Half smiling, I put my arm in his.

We began walking towards my place, and I felt I needed to convey my gratitude to the only person that came anywhere close to being a friend. "Thank you for everything, really. I don't know why you're helping me, but I can't tell you what it means to me."

He didn't miss a beat. He never did. "The expectations on us all- it can be difficult at times. You are someone who knows what difficult truly is. Maybe that's why I like you. If I may be so self-indulgent, there's a sense of camaraderie in those who have known true suffering."

I thought about it for a moment, knowing that wasn't the whole of it. "I don't know. Everyone has their own version of difficulties. Besides, you won't say it but there's something else, some other reason you're doing this. I don't know what, but I know there's something." He patted my arm in silent acknowledgment. Far more than I expected.

"Ah, you have company," he said grimly as he stared ahead.

My eyes shot up at his words. "Briar, why are you here?" I asked as I slid my arm from Agustín's. I kept kicking this man out of my life, and here he was, again. I desperately wanted to ask about his prisoners, but I didn't know enough to throw around accusations yet. (At least that's what I told myself in my cowardice.) Agustín was right about one thing though, it wouldn't go well for me, or their prisoners, if they knew I'd been down there.

"I didn't plan on running into you. I wanted to leave these." He gestured towards a bouquet of wildflowers that reminded me of home, clearly hand-picked. I know he thought it was a sweet gesture, but they only made me homesick.

"You thought you'd give me flowers again? Why?! To remind me of what you took from me?! The home you promised to take me back to despite having no intention to actually do so?! Or did you want to check in to see if your latest tribute had been well received? What do I owe you this time?"

"It's not about the book or the library- you don't understand. I want to take you back, but I can't. I'll explain once *he* leaves." He snarled towards Agustín.

I was about to light into him again when Agustín spoke softly behind me. "Frankie, what would you like of me?"

I turned toward him. He'd helped me so much I couldn't ask any more of him. But I needed to, and it seemed we were beyond keeping score at this point. "Stay, please." His face had a kindness I hadn't seen in quite some time as he gently nodded and tucked his hands behind his back. I turned towards Briar, pointing towards him and then the elevator as I said, "You, GO!"

His hurt expression turned to one of anger. "You have to talk to me at some point!"

"Is that coming from someone who thinks he loves me? Or is it an order from my commander?!"

"I *know* I love you!" he entreated. "And I know you love me too." I scoffed at his words as I folded my arms in front of me. He rubbed his face with his free hand as he always did when he got frustrated. He put the flowers down by the door and headed towards the elevator. As he walked past me, I was aware of Agustín's pose going from relaxed to defensive. Briar paused when he got as close as he thought I'd let him. Looking up at me and holding my gaze, he whispered, "I miss you, and I *do* love you."

Frustrated, I made my way to the door. I looked back at him and knelt down to pick up the flowers. A glimmer of hope flashed across his eyes as the elevator door closed. I turned to

Agustín and shook my head, unable to explain the helplessness I felt.

"Does he do this often?" He seemed worried, reasonably so.

"No, well, not as much anymore. Recently he seems fed up with giving me my space though."

"Are you going to be okay?"

"I'm sure. I don't know what to do about him though."

"I'm not in any place to give advice, as you know. Do let me know before you do anything rash though, yes?"

I hugged him good night. "Thank you again for everything." And I meant it.

"You can thank me by keeping your promises." He winked at me and headed to the elevator. He was aware I needed to know more about the dragons under the Mountain. But I had promised. And it did only make sense that they were a threat. I spent a lot of time that evening in the bath, thinking about everything. I only wish any of it made any sense.

I decided to try and have a civil conversation with Briar. As much as I could anyway. If nothing else, he was my commander and that entailed certain responsibilities he had towards his people. Helen had been right. I couldn't hold him responsible for the things a desperate mother had written about me. I'd wanted to get home so badly, and he had promised. All of it still felt unforgivable to me. But I could have a conversation with someone whom I couldn't forgive fully. And I needed to have that conversation.

EIGHTEEN

The next morning Cifelli was at my door, handing me an envelope adorned with emerald-green filigree. "Have a pleasant day, Draca Francesca," he said, leaving before I could ask what was happening. I wanted to apologize for when I teased Augustín, if I'd brought up anything painful. But he was already gone.

Written in a sloppy sort of script:

Medela Arboretum. Now.

-L. M.

I DRESSED and headed over to the Medela Spire. Their arboretum was in the same place as every spire's- the absolute top. Anxious and curious, I walked quickly through the lower gardens, grateful for the alterations I'd made to the dresses that allowed me my full stride.

Lily was sitting under a giant tree, her usual braided plaits laying in their perfect crown against her head. A substantial ball of something black and fuzzy was in her lap, and she was running her fingers over it. I was embarrassingly breathless from the hasty walk up here. Trying to hide my attempts to catch my breath, I quickly greeted her. "Morning, Lily. How're you?" The black ball of fuzz jumped and climbed up her, hiding behind and clinging onto her shoulder for dear life.

She shot me a dirty look as she replied, too snippy for my liking, "I'm here. And you owe Purpura an apology for scaring him so." She coaxed the creature out from behind her. For such tiny, fuzzy feet, they appeared webbed as it moved, its toes spreading, nails catching on Lily's dress as it climbed. As it was moving, I could see what must have been even more webbing—from its front to its back feet, there was a thin layer of skin, thin enough you could see the veins running through it.

"What is it?" I asked as I sat down beside her, my eyes never leaving the ball of fuzz as it hid its long face from me.

"It's about as friendly as I am, so don't get too close. His name is Purpura, he's a baby optera." She smiled down at him as she scratched his chin. He made a kind of chirping noise in response and moved his head to match her affections, much like a cat. I'd never really cared for cats. To be accurate, they'd never really cared for me. They always seemed to stay clear. I smiled to myself, wondering now if it was because I was a dragon.

When she stopped scratching him, his eyes popped open. Two large, mesmerizing purple spheres began looking about, annoyed at the sudden lack of contact. He crawled back up her looking for a spot to roost. This time as he stretched out his arms they reminded me of bat wings. "Can he fly?"

She laughed at my question before answering. "No, not for quite some time yet. He does glide though. They're climbers.

They climb up rock pillars and glide back down, catching their food off guard from above. Purpura here is really just a baby-baby. His mother was being housed in the animal sanctuary and passed recently. He needs a warm body to attach himself to for now. They grow quite large, but it takes a very long time.

"We're not here to discuss opteras though. We're here so I can teach you things I'm not entirely sure you should know. Do you know the difference between my abilities with light and a dragon's ability with energy?"

"I understand the concept. I think. It has to do with our heritage or blood or whatever and how that allows us to manipulate energy. Dragons manipulate using our heart, our source of energy. A sorcerer pulls from around them, it goes through them, but it doesn't reside in them. You're careful not to let it touch your hearts."

She nodded subtly before adding her own dictum. "A dragon can build up their abilities by building up their source. By working and practicing and building a deeper core of energy. By making their heart stronger. A sorcerer can build up their stamina to pull more energy, but it's never from within us, not the same way as a dragon. This allows for different types of use. Your abilities are limited because it is coming from within. It's finite. My abilities are limited because I bring nothing from within myself. I always need to pull. Limited only by what's around me and my own stamina. I could pull from an ancient tree, and my ability could be nearly limitless, if I had the stamina. Right now, you can only give so much of yourself before there is nothing left to give, and nothing left for you to do. Well, that's the case for most dragons. Do you know why you're different? Why you're unique? Special? *Especially* to them?"

"Do you?"

She sighed heavily as she looked off into the distance.

"Agustín can't tell you because of his position. If they find out I've told you- I would likely be married off to a family in a kingdom even further north. Or killed. I do owe my brother, but I don't know if I can trust you. I can't see it. And I don't know if now is the right time. Do you understand?"

"No, obviously not. I have no idea what you're talking about."

"Are you stupid because you're a dragon or is this just a Frankie thing?"

"Oh, I imagine there's probably another reason altogether." I stood to leave. Agustín would just have to tell me whatever she was supposed to. I had enough going on without adding her attitude into my pile of anxiety.

She looked me up and down before shaking her head. "You know you're not just a dragon. You were taken from this world for a reason. I don't know much about that. Agustín and I were told to watch over you. That the level of interest she has in you... it's telling. This is far bigger than you can realize. It doesn't feel right to me, getting involved in the affairs of drag-ons. Given there is more to this, my brother may be right this time.

"Listen to me closely, dragon. I will continue teaching you how to use your energy like a sorcerer. The way your people, and mine, have instructed. Figure that out or not, *clever* thing."

I shook my head at her and paced around. This arboretum modeled a different ecosystem altogether. The smooth bark of these very distinctive looking trees was peeling, exposing a sickly dark blue ooze. I steered clear of it as I ambled about before asking a question I wasn't sure I wanted the answer to.

"How is that possible?"

"There is no information on your lineage or origin."

"Yeah, Briar looked into it too and—"

"No. You misunderstand. We aren't simply *missing* a file or

did promise, I will keep your training going. Work on pulling energy and transferring- with *control*. Get yourself some house plants, break a few bits and fix them. No life exchanges. You're not ready for it. Not yet."

AGUSTÍN WAS off attending to some family business in another kingdom for a week or so, giving me the time off guilt free. We'd have to discuss a different assignment when he returned. I refused to work with the Dragon Heart any longer. Given my newfound free-time, I was likely going to be making some poor choices.

After a long day debating my options, I decided to try and find my way to Briar's house to have that dreaded conversation. I needed to leave this kingdom, but there was still a sort of pull towards him. I'd felt something similar to the dragon with the stormy ocean-blue eyes. Maybe it was all related and it was destiny. That, or the danger and vulnerability of it all. I couldn't explain it. I didn't understand it. I had hope that I could find some answers with Briar.

Annoyingly I easily remembered the way to his home. I knocked and after a moment Gale answered, her golden locks perfectly framing her face. "Oh, it's you," she drawled, not exactly surprised. "He isn't home right now. I suppose I should ask you to come in and wait. I was making dinner."

"Thanks. When did you get back? If that isn't a rude question."

"I've been back. There's always something that needs addressed with trade agreements and civil treaties. Not to mention, if I don't make my brother eat, then he won't. I have you to blame for that- me having to play mama bird while he's like this, instead of being out, enjoying the warmth here."

Winter was in full effect, but Gale lived in Furlong. Unbelievably even further north than Heartwood. Although it had warmed today, you could nearly feel the storm dancing in the air.

Regardless of the impending weather, I ignored her insinuation. He was a grown man and could take care of himself. "When do you expect him back?"

"I don't. I'm usually gone by the time he drags himself home. He trains until he can barely move at night. It's the only way he can get any sleep."

"Did you know he promised to take me home. Then after we slept together again he told me he wouldn't?"

She opened her mouth to say something and quickly closed it again. After a moment's thought, she answered, "I did not. He shouldn't have promised you that. And it's not wouldn't, just so you know. It's can't. He can't take you home. She'd never let you leave. She can't keep you safe there."

"Helen?"

She looked at me as if I was stupid, something I was getting a little tired of. "Of course Helen! As queen her will literally cannot be defied. If she tells you to jump off a cliff, your body does it. And it's not just your body, your mind *wants* to do it, for her. She tells Briar he can't return you home, he can't return you. Even if he wanted to. Not that he'd want to." She shrugged. "It takes an unimaginable strength to disobey one's queen. It's an ordained *gift*, essentially. It helps them keep us safe."

I sat down on the sofa, trying to understand all that, wishing I'd brought Briar's book to read and cross-reference. Gale finished up in the kitchen and came back out to leave. I wasn't comfortable waiting alone there. "I shouldn't be waiting inside when he gets home. I yelled at him before for kind of the same thing."

"If he comes home and smells you and you're not here, he'll lose his mind. Don't think about it. He understands why you needed your own space. After I explained it to him anyway. He knows to leave you alone; he just can't seem to. I'm sorry this is all so messed up. You must miss your home, but this is a good place, with good people. You could be happy here, if you let yourself."

I nodded, not wanting to fight, and sat back down to wait. After an hour or so running imaginary scenarios of how this conversation might go, I figured I should find a book to pass the time more productively. He had a few history books, some on folklore and prophecies, nothing with any new information about dragons of course. I picked one up and started to get lost in it. At some point I must have fallen asleep because I woke to the last embers of the fire fading in and out. I put some more wood on and decided to head back. The streets would be well lit enough by the nearly full moon, and it was generally safe enough here to walk back alone at night.

I'd bundled up and was opening the door to leave- and of course, there he was. Just sitting there on the cold stoop, his back to me as he looked off and away. He must have mistaken me for his sister as he nodded his head in my direction as acknowledgment of my presence. I wondered how often this happened, how often he sat out here in the cold letting his thoughts haunt him.

He'd clearly been lost in thought as it took him a moment to register that it wasn't Gale after all, but me coming out of his house. His jaw slacked and a second later he was scrambling to stand up, to tower over me. My lips twisted into a grimace as I looked up at him, trying to figure out what I should do.

Turning around, I walked back inside. He didn't immediately follow. "Well, it's your house. I'm not going to invite you in. Hurry up and shut the door."

He was stunned, and it took him another minute to do as he was told. He still hadn't said a word to me. I took off my boots and coat, placing them back where they'd been. "Your sister made you food. You should eat. Apparently it's my fault you're not taking care of yourself."

"You're here..."

"Yes, I'm here. Now come on, we need to talk. Get some food."

"*Fuck* the food. You want to talk?" Between the shock and hope in his voice I found my vitriol breaking down even further.

Letting out a long sigh, I shook my head back and forth, mostly to myself. I walked up to him and hugged him, my arms around his waist and my head against his chest. He hesitated, shocked I'm sure, before he wrapped his arms around me, holding me tightly. He buried his face in my hair, inhaling deeply as if trying to convince himself that this wasn't all just a dream.

After some time, I pulled away from the embrace and he reluctantly let go, his eyes a little red. "Why did you promise you'd take me home knowing you couldn't? Be honest."

I saw his chest heave up and down as realization dawned on him that we were actually going to have this conversation. "I wanted to be able to do whatever you wanted of me. Had I been able to find out if you belonged to one of the Wilds or another kingdom, I'd be obligated to return you there. Helen would have to relinquish her say over you. I've spent years trying to find out where you're from, only to come up with nothing. I assumed after spending some time here, albeit against your will, that I'd be allowed to return you since we couldn't find your real home."

"My real home is back on Earth." I eyed him crossly for forgetting that.

"Of course," he said kindly, or perhaps patronizingly. I couldn't quite tell. He may have wanted to argue, but he wasn't an idiot.

"I'm not mad at you for the things your mother did. Although I am still hurt she was only kind to get me to you and this world. But that isn't your fault, and I'm trying to remember that."

"Frankie, you have that wrong. My mother loved you. It's very clear in her reports. I have them all at the Mountain. Come with me tomorrow. I'll show you."

I thought it over for a moment. Hope, that life stealing bastard, began to creep back into my heart. One quick, short nod and I could practically feel his jubilation. "Don't get too excited! I was already going to be there to check out Helen's library." It made my heart ache to see him so happy. I didn't want him to misunderstand. Hell, did I even understand?! He had bags under his eyes, and his cheekbones were even jauntier than the other day. "If you eat something! You look awful, dummy." I mumbled as I stared at the floor, "You need to take care of yourself."

"Are you worried about me because you care, or because someone asked you to?" His morose face told me something else had happened in the meanwhile.

"Who would ask me to? I'm worried because I care. Why would you even ask that?" His eyes searched my face, looking for something. "What's going on?"

"You forgive me then? Does that mean we're okay?"

"I am trying to forgive you. But it's too complicated for there to be a 'we' anymore."

"Frankie, please, I'm begging for another chance. We'll

take things slow, go on actual dates. We'll have fun, I promise! It'll be how it should have been."

"There was nothing wrong with how it started. Sometimes things happen fast. You lying to me- that's where it went wrong. Which I suppose is how it really started... But I will think about it, okay? But don't get your hopes up. I can't ever completely forgive you." He looked a little broken, but he smiled through it.

Maybe I did love him. Even when I hated him, when I thought he'd manufactured everything himself, I *still* wanted him. With him, what wouldn't I forgive? A vision of the dragons in the Mountain crossed my mind, making me shiver. I couldn't believe Briar was capable of doing that.

"Meet me at the Mountain tomorrow for lunch? I'll show you the reports. We can have a little picnic."

I looked at him for a moment, not even knowing what I wanted. "That does sound nice." He gently tucked a wild lock of my hair back into place, and my eyes closed at the familiar sensation. He cupped my face with his hand, and I placed my hand over his, leaning into his touch. I could feel myself wanting more, and I stepped back, clearing my throat. "I will be off then. Have a nice night. Don't forget to eat."

Incredulously, "It's late. I'm walking you back."

"Excuse me, Commander. I can handle myself," I scoffed at him.

"You can either walk with me, or I can creepily follow behind you to make sure you get there safe. Your choice." There was my old Briar.

I eyed him with a fake annoyance that he instantly saw through. "Fine!" He smiled broadly at my use of our word.

As we walked I gingerly told him about how work with Agustín had been going. He politely commented at all the right moments, although I could sense him tensing up here and there. I smiled to myself. It was nice, being near him again.

"I wanted to ask, what do you know about Helen's private library?" He'd either understand and all I could do was hope he'd tell me, or he wouldn't, and it'd be what it is.

"I can't help you get into her secret library. She rarely lets anyone in there, and it's not something I can ask. No one is supposed to know about it, but she's been sloppy for the last decade or so." After a silent moment he cautiously asked, "Do you still forgive me?"

"Again, I'm trying to. You know that none of this, us, is related to her library. I don't use people like that. Okay? Besides, I'm sure I can find it myself." He grunted his assent but made no comment. I was also thinking about trying to sneak back in to see the dragons. I wanted to believe Agustín when he said it was a security issue, that it was necessary. But part of me knew better. I knew something else was up. I couldn't shake the question of why they were so hidden away if what Agustín had told me was true? Things with Briar had just taken a turn and I couldn't ask him, not yet. I needed to know some more things first. One thing I knew, my Briar wasn't capable of torture. Not like that. Not without a good reason.

When we got to the Spires, he insisted on walking me to my door. He knew I was safe, but he said he'd take whatever time with me I would give him. "I don't want to press this grace you've given me, but can I hug you?" I could feel myself blush a little as I nodded.

He held me for a while before I kissed his cheek. Then he pulled back to look at me. I stared into his eyes for too long. He wanted to kiss me, and I wanted him to. I was disappointed when he let me go. I think he knew that.

We said goodbye again before I finally went inside. I was looking forward to tomorrow, but angry at myself for letting it happen. The plan had been to return to an amiable state. NOT set up a fucking date.

CHAPTER

NINETEEN

Heavy gray clouds were leisurely dropping large, lofty clumps of snow when I woke up. I was actually surprised it didn't snow more here. But it was drier than I was used to, and it was always so damned cold. Looking out at the kingdom from my apartment, the beauty of this snow-laced world lifted my spirits. I wondered if it was a sign. Of what? I wasn't sure.

Between lunch with Briar and my clandestine mission to infiltrate the queen's secret library, I was a bit of a nervous wreck. It wasn't the library I was really worried about though. Briar kept popping up in my mind. I felt stupid for agreeing to his little picnic idea yesterday. I should have known to give it more time. He had this effect on me, and the flame weakened when I didn't see him. At the very least I didn't think about him as much when I didn't see him. Not that he ever really allowed that to happen.

I went through the Mountain's main gate, trying very hard to not recall how Agustín had dragged me from that dungeon last time. Briar's second escorted me to his office to wait for him. The guy was gruff and grumpy and there was something about him I didn't trust. He wore the standard uniform, as did most of the people we passed. Briar had been wearing it every time I'd seen him recently. I couldn't help but think about how well it suited him. *Stupid girl*, I chastised myself again, realizing I had actually missed him.

His office was unsurprisingly unpretentious. Basic desk with one moderately comfortable chair, a few plain chairs on the other side, standard wooden bookshelves that had files upon files and a plethora of maps piled on them, and very few books. I sat in his comfortable chair a while before opening the top drawer of his desk just a smidge. Thinking about being nosy, well, *nosier*, and going through it when a square fridge magnet caught my attention. Some of the technologies in this world were antiquated, with magic making up a good share of the difference, but a fridge magnet was not something I'd expect here. Looking at it closer I recognized it. It was from the pizza place back home.

Unable to take my eyes off of that damned magnet, I barely registered the door opening. Such a silly thing, but it was a piece of home when I had none. I didn't even have the clothes I was wearing when I was stolen. Seeing this piece of familiarity, it was too much. His voice finally cut through. "Frankie, what's wrong?" Looking up at Briar, there were tears in my eyes, yet again. My fingers shook and I dropped the magnet as he shut the door and came rushing to me. Kneeling down before me he held me as I cried. How many times had this man held me as I fell apart?

Whimpering my sorries countless times, I let my pain flow from me. Each time he'd say the same things- I didn't need to be sorry about anything... It was all his fault... He was sorry... He wished he could fix everything...

At some point I slid off the chair and onto his lap. Sometime after that my head was resting on his chest as his arms held me tightly to him. I'd have occasional reverberations of sobs and he'd hold me tighter. My heart felt as though it'd been shattered and was slowly being hodgepodged back together.

"I'm sorry I ruined our picnic," I whimpered as I wiped my nose on his handkerchief.

"Nothing's ruined. And there's nowhere I'd rather be than here with you right now." He kissed my temple and hugged me tighter.

"You really mean that. Don't you?" I sat up a bit. I wasn't the type of person to be comfortable sitting on a lap, but as often as he had me do it, he had to enjoy it.

"I do." His eyes wandered slowly over my face as if he was trying to read a map and had lost his place.

I laid my head against his. "I really want to kiss you right now, but I don't think I would stop. And we keep jumping in, and it never goes well. I want it to go well this time."

"Me too," he whispered into my ear, sending a shiver throughout my body that forced me to sit up again. "We still have a picnic, if you'd like?"

"Are you sure I haven't kept you too long?"

He groaned, knowing I was right. More than once we'd heard someone walk up to his door and walk away without disturbing us. I didn't know how much longer that would last. "I hate to ask, given how many times you've told me no, but... dinner?" I bit my lower lip and nodded. He asked slowly, apprehensively, "If I were to send over a dress, like he did, would it be well received?" He wasn't being vindictive. He seemed genuinely vulnerable. I wasn't sure what was going on, but he needed to know that I valued him.

I nodded again, smiling a bit bigger for his sake. He let out a nervous sigh and a huge, genuine smile lit up his face. His vulnerability and that smile, it did something to me. Against my better judgment I kissed him. He hesitated. I had literally just told him I didn't want to move too fast. I'd kill to have a little damned consistency inside my own head, or heart, to actually know what I wanted, *for once!*

I started to pull away, and he kissed me back with an intensity that made me forget the last few weeks. Until he bit my lower lip a little too intensely, and I ended up pulling away. "Hey! Too hard," I grumbled, nursing my swollen lip, when I noticed he was looking at me with that hungry look of his.

"You're killing me, you know that?" he said, clearly pained. I was still sitting on his lap and knew exactly what he meant. I looked away, trying not to smile.

I carefully stood up and turned around to see him watching me from the floor. I loved catching him looking at me like this. It made me feel like he actually wanted *me*. I'd never felt so sure of someone wanting me before. Not just making do or good enough or filling a role, but actual desire, want, *need*. We stayed like that for a few minutes, maybe more, I'm not sure. Watching the need build in one another's eyes.

A knock on the door stirred us from our tense reverie. Briar called from the floor through gritted teeth, "Yes?"

"Draca Regulus is asking for you, Commander."

"Tell her I'll be there in ten," he grumbled and reached his hand out, asking for mine. He held it, looking at our intertwined fingers for a while before standing up wordlessly.

"Do you work with her a lot?" I was trying my best to not sound jealous. I was failing.

"Unfortunately. We're on our way to inspect some dragons that are up for promotion."

"What does that have to do with Helen?"

"To protect her people she needs to know that I'm doing my job well. My troops and their abilities are proof of that. She's an integral part of that process."

"Does it take long? Should I wait maybe? She was going to show me her library, but I wouldn't be surprised if her golden handmaid was tasked with it now." I sincerely hoped this to be the case. It'd make my mission exceedingly less risky as her handmaid, Claire, was an absolute angel.

"A couple of hours I'm afraid. But dinner tonight, yes?" I nodded, somewhat wistful. He pulled a wooden basket not entirely dissimilar to a picnic basket from under his desk. "I put it together myself. It's not exactly gourmet, but I think you'll enjoy it."

"Oh! That reminds me, you actually kept that fridge magnet?"

"Of course. That first night, they'd stuffed it between the menu they shoved in the box. Remember? You said you didn't mind. I wanted something to remember that time." He was staring at the floor, undoubtedly remembering fond memories before everything got so muddled. I hadn't remembered until just now, not really.

It was a stupid thing to do. Stupid, stupid, *STUPID*. But it felt right in that moment as I teased, "By my calculations, we have nine minutes…" Briar needed no further encouragement. He wanted us to go slow because I wanted us to. He was ravenous and knowing his insatiable tendencies when it came to me fueled my own desire.

We tore at each other. Pieces of clothing pushed up or down, pulled this way or that, anything else ripped out of the way. We didn't care. I wanted him and I wanted to be as close as I could, for whatever time he had to give me just then. We both seemed to have forgotten where we were. I don't know how long we spent like that, but no one dared knock.

· · ·

"I REALLY DO HAVE to go. Frankie, I..." He wanted to say he loved me, but he thought better of it in the moment I suppose. He kissed me deeply, holding me flush against him. I bit his lip this time, and he pretended like I'd seriously wounded him. And then he was gone.

I waited about ten minutes, recovering, still a bit overwhelmed by it all, before I grabbed the picnic basket and headed to Gale's staircase. I needed to find those dragons again, needed to know how involved Briar was with all this before I fell too hard. Again. How could Briar- *my* Briar be as entangled as Agustín had led me to believe? Not that I believed he had intentionally lied to me, but I knew he wasn't being entirely honest either.

Last time I'd passed out before I could really ask anything, but I needed answers. 'Security' didn't explain everything. Hell, it didn't explain *anything*. Especially not with all the hush-hush that was going on about them. Though why wouldn't Briar have had guards posted if he was involved in all this? It made no sense. I needed their side before I dared question Briar. I didn't want to question him at all, but I wasn't stupid enough to just go into that conversation blindly. Of course I knew not to trust anything the other dragon's said either, but that wouldn't be anything new around here. I'd take what I could get and see what I could make of it.

First... I had to find them again.

Of course I mucked that up right off and had to backtrack. I'd gone up one too many levels, apparently. Trying my damnedest to not be suspicious, I snuck back to the main staircase and as casually as I could manage- went up another level before finally finding it. Being this nervous and making these kinds of mistakes was how I was going to screw myself over, and I knew that. As I went back down the hidden staircase, after finally finding it... I don't know, something was telling me

I needed to collect this knowledge. That I *needed* to know the precise details. These odd little 'visions' really should come with a user's manual.

And so I counted how many levels I had to go down before I found the right floor. This took a little extra time as I had to look around each, nearly identical level for a couple of minutes before I knew. But retracing my steps down the dark and frigid hallway, I knew I was onto something, and I was where I needed to be.

I again had to move my hands over the wall when I came to where I knew the door would be. Feeling for it, I moved my hands much more slowly this time, now aware of the trigger. When it cut into me I still felt it, but much less severely. Just a drop of blood this time. I imagine that was how it was supposed to work. A pinprick would be easy enough to hide. Briar would never know and Agustín wouldn't have to either. It'd be healed well before he returned. A pang of guilt gripped me for being back here after I'd promised him, not to mention it wasn't a great way to start fresh with Briar either. But I knew they were all still keeping something from me, and I was determined to get ahead of their game for once.

Nearly everything was as it had been before. The notable exception being the table was now adorned with a great deal of blood. Fresh too. The scent of iron lingered like smoke from a snuffed out candle. I nearly froze up, just as I had back then. That felt like a lifetime ago now and also as if it had been yesterday. I hurried down the stone tunnel, afraid of what awaited me. Relief washed over me as I saw them both, though it was short-lived. She was lying flat on the floor as if she had nothing left, her head resting on his lap.

He made a guttural, growling noise at my arrival, and I stopped short. When our eyes met his auditory threat silenced instantly. My attentions turned towards her as I became more worried than I thought I could be for a dragon I'd never properly met.

Speaking with a harsh and hoarse, but penetrating voice, he said, "She is alive, barely. They have not been killing her the same way these last few days. Tell me?" His worry clear- he feared her end. His accent was unlike any I'd ever heard, gruff but flowing. The effort from each word clearly pained him.

"Agustín is away at the moment. Let me heal her like I did last time," I pleaded, unsure if he'd let me. I closed the distance between us and came alongside her, across from him. I put the basket and lantern down as I knelt, ready to do whatever was needed.

He looked at me resignedly. "She cannot take more of you just yet. It would only cause her to lose what little of herself she has left."

"I have food, but it's for humans. I don't know if she can eat it as a dragon? I can go get whatever she needs and come back. Please, just tell me what I can do?" I'd always been able to keep calm, but now I didn't know what to do. That had been my trick. I had always known what to do and I moved it along. You do one thing, and then the next, and then you simply keep going, keep doing. Don't think. Just move. Now I was lost and trying desperately to not panic.

"You are dragon." He wasn't asking, but he seemed surprised. It was clear his words were becoming increasingly painful for him as he struggled through them.

"I'm new." I shook my head at how absurd I sounded. "I mean- I only found out a few months ago." I watched his face, waiting for a reaction that never came. "Who did this?"

"Truly? He is on you." I could feel the color drain from my face. Helen doing this or commanding someone to do it made sense to me. But Briar? *My* Briar?! I'd convinced myself he wasn't capable of such a thing. I placed a hand on her and saw it. A flash of Briar torturing her, ripping off her scales, blood splattering on his face. I was grateful I hadn't eaten yet. My disbelief and disgust must have been clear. "Your commander is killing her."

"Why would he do that?!" I whispered mostly to myself, horrified, afraid of the answer. I pulled over the picnic basket and pulled out all the food for them. There was a folder at the bottom of the basket. I knew what was inside, but I couldn't have cared less anymore. I wasn't entirely sure what these visions were. If they were visions of the past, present, future. If they were real, imagined, likely. I didn't know. But I knew to trust what they showed me. I knew it was some part of myself that was showing them to me, allowing me to see what I needed to see. And it was time I trusted myself.

As my fingers grazed the papers another vision seized my body. This one was different. My entire body froze up as I saw a ghost. Jen. Talking to Briar inside her home. Her home that I'd come to think of as a second home myself. She was excited, her eyes dancing as she showed him a few plants I recognized. They were some of the first few plants I'd healed.

I felt my stomach drop. Jen really had betrayed me for the sake of getting back into the good graces of her son. "It's her, Bri. I'm telling you! She's the Impossible Child! Why else would she be here?! How else *could* she be here, unaccounted for and all?! Have Helen to look into it. That's all I'm asking."

Whatever I was seeing trailed off after that. Frantically I grabbed the folder, rubbing my hands all over it trying to spark something more, but nothing came. That's when I realized his eyes were still very much on me, very much aware that something had transpired.

He looked at me with a peculiar sense of worry for someone who'd been being tortured. "I... I'm sorry. Drink!" I handed him the water and tried to forget what I'd just seen. There were more pressing matters at hand.

He drank half the carafe of water before answering my question. It seemed to sting his throat, but his voice smoothed afterwards. "They think we are lying. Or maybe they think we shall end their abominations. Or perhaps they merely enjoy it. Take your pick. Their reasons matter not."

This man trusted me enough to drink freely of what I offered him, and to let me heal his companion, but he wasn't telling me the whole of his durance either. Not the heart of it anyway, but he'd told me enough. I didn't know if I should, or could, trust that.

Briar had always been keeping something from me. He'd tell me these half-truths when he'd needed to appease me. Only for me to later suffer through overwhelming revelations on his schedule. It had happened time and again, and he was *still* keeping secrets from me. I felt like such a fool. I was done. I needed the truth.

For now though, I needed to go. I'd been there too long, and it wouldn't do to linger. In coming to them I'd made a clear choice without even realizing it. I could have gone to Helen's library. Maybe I could have even found her secret one. Prioritizing this knowledge had surprised me. I needed to know if these two were okay more than I needed to know who or what I was. Without noticing it, I'd pulled myself a certain way, and for the first time I realized that it was *my* way. The way *I* needed to go, the way I *wanted* to go.

His eyes still weighed on me. "You are his. Why help us?"

"I am not *his*!" I don't know why it bothered me as much as it did that anyone would call me his. And I couldn't explain why I was helping them, other than my sense of humanity. I didn't know if I should believe any of what I'd just discovered. But I needed to find out more. I could come back tomorrow to ask Helen about her library, feigning ignorance of the day's schedule. She wouldn't like it, but she was being nicer lately for some reason. This would be a good test of that newfound kindness. Tonight- I needed to find Lily. She had more answers and might know more about the Impossible Child Jen mentioned. Something I knew better than to ask any dragon in Heartwood about. "Is there anything that can help? Anything I can do?"

He'd finished the water. The unconscious dragon had taken a few sips after he'd held her mouth open and let enough fall into it, but she never truly woke. His husky voice had taken on a euphonic quality, and I could feel my body react. "It's the Dragon Cor. It sustained her life as they've continued pulling her scales off. They've used it too much. She is reacting as though she's been poisoned. Her body is exhausted. She needs to return to her human form for her energy's sake. These chains won't budge for anyone but that damned wizard. Short of a miracle from the Mother herself, there is nothing to do but let her get what rest she can."

Agustín hadn't been lying about the Dragon Cor then. I'd had a couple of drops, and it had felt like I'd been brought back from the dead. I imagine to actually bring one back from death's door, or close to it, you'd need a substantial bit more. And that was exactly what Agustín had done.

I took the empty carafe and placed it back in the basket I'd picked up. I left everything else with them, hoping the food would help. I'd have to tell Agustín I'd broken my promise when he got back. He would have to do *something* for her. I could only hope she'd hold on that long. I didn't know what else I could do that wouldn't put them in worse danger.

Turning to leave, I grabbed the lantern, and his voice sent a chill through me. "Who are you?" I turned back to look at him, only for a moment, before walking down through the stone tunnel. The gold had long vanished from his eyes, leaving only a dark blue ,like a murky ocean after a storm. They were wild and striking and left a lump in my throat. I couldn't stop seeing them.

I had no idea how long I'd been down there. It was still snowing when I left the Mountain, and the world had darkened from the clouds. I hurried through the emptying streets clutching Briar's picnic basket, though nothing in it mattered to me now. Still, I clung on to it for dear life. I was having dinner with him tonight. How I was going to make it through a meal without asking how he could be so kind and gentle with me and then turn around to torture our own, I did not know. He didn't think of them as our own though. I knew this now, but I didn't know why, not the truth of it anyway.

Back at my apartment I had a couple of hours to kill before he'd arrive. Dinner needed to be short for me to still make my meeting with Lily. I'd sent a note to her that I hoped hadn't been too cryptic. Cifelli had assured me she would be there. I could only hope that she would know what she was risking.

Briar's dress for me never came. I had felt silly when he asked about it. I didn't need more dinner dresses than daywear, but now it felt like he was playing games. Or maybe he'd forgotten having been otherwise preoccupied. I didn't like either possibility. I used to think I could read him, now I didn't know. Knowing his mother had given me up to him made this all the more tenuous, and now I *knew* not to trust him. And as dangerous as he'd felt before, not being able to read him felt insurmountably perilous.

The evening dragged on. It was about an hour before Lily would be in the arboretum for our meeting. I decided to make dinner. Sitting down to eat, I thought I heard him. I'd heard steps, no knock. I didn't know for certain it was him. I thought about ignoring the sounds, but I didn't have a lot of time for this discussion either way.

"Open this door." His voice was cold, beyond frightening.

I barely unlatched it before he was pushing his way in. I couldn't believe his audacity. "Not okay!" I yelled. "You flaked on dinner, and you're mad at me?!" I assumed the offensive would be the safer position from which to feign ignorance.

He whispered it at first, seething, "Do you have any idea what you've done?" I cocked my head to the side not knowing what he was talking about. I looked at him then, really looked at him. He was standing in the middle of the room, face ashen, hands, arms, everything... covered in blood.

"Briar, what happened to you?" His eyes shook in anger. He never wanted me to meet his other half, *this* other half.

He pursued me as he spat out his questions, backing me up against a wall. "How did you get in? Why? Why would you go in there? What were you doing?!" There was no point in denying any of it.

"Me?! What were *you* doing?!" A sudden fear overcame me, and my tone shifted, quivering, "Briar, what did you *do*?"

His eyes locked on mine. There was nothing there but flowing fires of gold. His dragon was taking over. "I showed him what happens when he thinks he gets to protect you."

"Briar, what have you done? Are they..."

"THEY are none of your concern! You should be more worried about yourself!"

I wasn't sure what he was implying. "Are you going to lock me up then? Tear me apart? Am I next?!"

Shocked at my insinuation, much of the gold in his eyes fell away at my words. As he gathered himself, his anger came back. "I knew it was you the instant I walked in there. I would have been lenient if he would have told me. He thought he was protecting you." Briar's voice had been steadily rising to a near scream, "He doesn't get to protect you! Only I get to protect you! I am your commander, NOT HIM!"

I winced reactively hearing him yell like this, feeling it, mere inches from my face. But it was the implications that frightened me. I needed to know if they were okay. My voice shook as I asked, but still I asked, "Are they alive?"

"You are never to go down there again. *EVER!*" He started to leave and I reached out for him, begging him to tell me what was happening. I asked my questions. 'Why were they down there? Why was he torturing them?' He wouldn't answer any of them. Not even to lie to me about how he was the good guy. He wouldn't even look at me.

Nearly to the elevator I grabbed his arm one more time. I was determined to not let go until I knew if they were okay, still desperately trying to get him to look at me. It all happened so quickly. He grabbed me and pushed me up against the wall. His eyes raging gold, his fingers, sharp as talons, digging into me as he held me against the wall. He was staring into my eyes as I managed to squeak out his name. Snarling out some angry noises, he let me go and I fell to the ground. He grimaced seeing me crumple to the floor, then he quickly retreated to the elevator.

I needed to see those dragons again. I needed to know.

There would be guards everywhere now. I had to hope they at least didn't know about the servants' stairwell, or that I'd known about it. I needed to beg Lily for her help. I'd have gone to Agustín if he were here, and I cursed my luck that he wasn't.

She wouldn't be at the arboretum yet and this couldn't wait. I needed to find her. I knew there was no reason why she should help me, but I had no one else to turn to. I was standing outside of her office before I even realized my feet had started moving. I barged in and thanked my lucky stars that she was still here.

And there *he* was.

CHAPTER

TWENTY

"Agustín!"

I thanked the gods and wished on the Sister Stars for this to not be my last lucky turn of the night. He was here! Leisurely sitting on a couch, reading that ancient leaf-covered infrastructure book he'd refused to let me borrow. I'd asked him before what he was doing with it, and his only answer had been that he didn't know, but he was told to hold onto it. He was shocked at my appearance, but I couldn't be bothered with that now.

"I need your help!"

"Frankie, you're covered in blood!" He'd stood at the sight of me and was now checking me for wounds. Lily stood silently, taking everything in, watching her brother.

"It's not mine, mostly. I went back! Briar found out. He hurt them, I... I don't know how badly. They may already be dead. It's all my fault. Please, Agustín! I need your help." My voice was weak and faltering, but he understood. He didn't criticize or chastise me for having broken my promise. And for as wretched as he looked from my confession, he kept up.

"Lily, go. Frankie, with me." He led me over to his office. I never did see Lily leave, but she didn't question her brother in the slightest. "What's next?" he asked peremptorily.

"I need to get them out of there."

"You don't know why they're—"

"Neither do you! But you take part in it. How can you?!"

"It's the price we pay, Frankie! I... gods damn it all," he paced the room anxiously, angrily, "It's what we do! It's what we've always done. We trust you dragons as much as we have to. And here, I had- have no choice." The remorse hung from his face like kudzu vines on a tree in the deep south, heavy and invasive. "My aunt lives an hour outside of the central gates. She intercepted me today. Said I'd be needed here tonight. *You* are why I'm here. Not them, I'm certain of it. I can get *you* to her, not them."

"I don't care about me! It's not me that needs to be rescued."

He laughed painfully, sardonically in my face. "You've needed rescuing since the day you arrived. You're only standing here now because Helen doesn't know, yet. Briar is risking his own life by not telling her. He will eventually, he'll have to, and then you're done. Unless you leave this kingdom. They have little authority outside of their own walls."

"I'll do it without you then." I didn't mean for it to sound like a threat, but it still took him aback.

"You're going to get yourself killed! If they find out I helped you..." I moved to leave. I hadn't thought about him, something the next head of the Medela family wasn't used to. But my need to save those dragons from what I'd done didn't supersede Agustín's life, not to me, and so I would figure it out without him.

Quickly striding past me he locked his office door and then turned on a dime. "You asked why I have that particular infrastructure book. I have it because my aunt gave it to me shortly before you arrived. She told me I'd be needing it. You don't ask Auntie Sabina what she means. You thank her for telling you whatever crazy thing she's said."

After grumbling to himself and letting out some kind of frustrated grunt he seemed to have found peace with his decision. He went to one of his bookshelves and dug through a pile of books to reveal an inconspicuous little lever that he now pulled. There was an almost inaudible click, and he pushed the bookshelf back, revealing a dark passageway.

He motioned for me to follow him as he promptly disappeared into the darkness. As I followed him I reached my hands out to brace myself. He reached back, pulling me along with him. By the time my eyes had adjusted to the dark, a light appeared along the passageway. The light had been coming from a room filled with ancient and dust covered boxes and trunks. Handing me a black cloak Agustín instructed, "Put it on. I'll be back in five minutes. Wait here."

The cloak was a marvel. It was blacker than any fabric I'd ever seen before. It didn't even seem like cloth, it looked more like a nothing, an emptiness, a void. Looking more closely I could see some sparse light reflecting from within this nothing cloak. A complex glyph had been embroidered into the nothingness. I would never have seen it had I not been ogling it.

After what felt like an hour he finally returned carrying a small box with several vials of Dragon Cor. He stashed it into a sack he'd grabbed from one of the many boxes and again disappeared. This time he didn't go far, and I could still hear him. "If they're still alive we'll heal them as much as we can. I'll take their chains off and... best not say it aloud I suppose. Sabina's place isn't too far, but they'll need to be gone by morning. I can't go with you. I'm putting my life at risk as it is. He'll know I was the one that helped you."

"What will happen to you?" I asked as he reappeared.

"Banishment. That's all, as long as he doesn't find me alone. Madam Medela will likely reassign me to Savisa. They don't have a Dragon House. It's a harbor kingdom that if I'm honest I'd prefer over Heartwood or Furlong anyway. When this is all said and done I just might owe you one." He smiled at me with far less sincerity than I knew him capable of mustering.

"Why are you doing this? Why take this risk?"

"What they've had me doing...," he sighed heavily, "I'm doing this for me. That's all you need to know. Don't mistake this for any kind of altruism or kindness. This is nothing if not selfish, understood?" I nodded grimly, understanding far better than he realized.

He grabbed two more cloaks and placed them on top of the vials inside his bag. He grabbed another bag that looked already filled, ready to go. We went back out to the dark passageway and continued on the way we'd been going. It is possible that I may have lost my bearings, but it seemed we were out alongside the far wall.

We came to a split in the passageway and slipped into a cramped room that looked like a narrow cupboard, barely enough space to stand side by side. He held up a piece of paper to a panel on the door. There was a flash of light and the paper was gone. I had to bite my tongue to stop from screaming as we went practically freefalling for most of the one hundred or so odd floors. I eventually caught my breath and turned to glare at him as the room gradually slowed. He knew this was coming, he'd braced for it. He continued to stare straight forward, lost in thought. I couldn't blame him for being preoccupied. Though a warning would have been nice.

When we finally stopped, he backed out of the room, and I

slid over to do the same. He was already a good distance ahead of me, and I hurried to catch up. Opening another door, he walked in, making enough room for me to stand next to him as he impatiently motioned for me to do so. He shut the door and used another sheet of paper that again lit up and disintegrated as this room fell backwards, catching me even more off guard. I reflexively grabbed onto him to steady myself. He held me securely almost as a default, mindlessly. I would have given anything to know what was going through his head at that moment.

The movement stopped and he slid a panel of wall away to reveal a small doorway that opened up out of the back of the Medela Spire. We stepped out, and I took a second to find my footing. Meanwhile he was already moving quickly. We took different streets than I was used to. This route took at least twice the amount of time. Finally, the Mountain came into view. Only now did it occur to me this may all be a ruse to see which side I would take.

He was headed for the main entrance. I put my hand on his arm, needing some answers. As he turned to face me, too quickly, I flinched terribly. He looked bewildered. I didn't have time to explain I was reacting from what happened the last time I grabbed someone's arm. Struggling to regain my composure, and catch my breath, I asked, "What are you doing? They're going to be expecting me, right?"

He shook his head. "If Briar had alerted anyone the queen would know, and you'd already be in custody, if not dead. He doesn't want that. He knows it won't end well. Briar is the only variable we need to be worried about right now. Given the blood on you, I'm assuming he went home to wash. Is he likely to look for you again tonight?"

"I don't know. He was furious, he... he was rough. I saw the other side of him. The side he's kept hidden from me. I don't know how he's going to react now. But he usually gives me my space for a while after anything big."

"Best not to hope. We need to keep moving."

We continued through the main entrance. The night guards were alert but paid us no mind as we walked up the ostentatious stairs, and with his usual confidence Agustín simply kept strolling along. The snow was still coming down. Heavy enough now that the stairs should have been slippery, but they weren't. Even as our shoes dug in, our prints were quickly being filled in behind us.

There were a few guards patrolling the hallways, but Agustín walked around as proud and annoyed as ever. They never stopped us. Briar wouldn't have been able to put them on alert either, not without an explanation. And one never knows who is loyal to their queen over their commander. I walked closely behind Agustín with my head down casually, the cloak hiding my disarray and bloodstains. We didn't generally roam the Mountain together, and I didn't want any hint of something odd getting back to anyone just now. I hoped none of them would recognize me, but I had no idea if any of them did or not. They all seemed to be looking through me, not at me.

We reached the staircase and descended as quickly as we could. Agustín had been right- no newly appointed guards. We stood in front of the door, Agustín taking a deep breath before moving his hand over the door. Nothing. Again he slid his hand over the blood lock. Horrid stillness.

He turned to me, impetuously. "He changed the damned lock. I suspect only dragon's blood will open it now. And quite possibly only his." I still wasn't sure if I bought being a dragon, but this safeguard at least made sense. I didn't have time to sit with the thought. I threw my hand all over the door where I thought he just had, trying desperately to find the lock, hoping my blood would suffice.

He must have tired of my looking because he mumbled a word and a shining orb snapped into his hand. It lit the hallway painfully, and I forced my eyes open to see the blood lock glyph for the first time. I quickly pressed my hand against it firmly and felt it pierce me, deeply. I wasn't sure if Briar had adjusted the lock or if my sweeping motions had made it hurt less. Now it stung with a force I had not been expecting. I muffled a scream as the pain seared through my hand, up my arm, and to my chest. The glyph illuminated. The door opened.

Despite the pain my mind was elsewhere. I was grateful for Agustín's orb. Especially so when we saw the lantern was missing. No light was coming from the end of the tunnel, and I hoped against the gods that they were still alive. Agustín's expression told me he was thinking the same thing.

We ran down the tunnel. I was terrified of what we'd find and grateful he was in front of me. If it was as horrific as I'd imagined it to be, I wanted someone here to shield me. Now was not the time or place for me to go numb again. I shook my head at my foolishness. I used to work in a trauma center. Gruesome had been my daily routine, before. I wasn't sure why I cared so much about this, here, now. But I needed to take care of this.

When he hesitated as we entered, I pushed past him. There was so much blood. More than I'd ever seen. The dragon was splayed out. More of her scales were missing. Too many. Then I saw him. He was slumped over a few feet away from the dragon, unconscious, arm outstretched as though he was trying to get to her.

I ran to him and checked him over. Still breathing, but painful, shallow breaths. Placing my hands on him I checked to see the damage. A few broken ribs, dislocated jaw, a broken nose, and some bruised organs. He also had some deep cuts that could become a problem. I rolled him onto his back and began trying to pull my energy to heal him.

Agustín had gone to the dragon. I'd told him she'd been given too much, that it was having a poisonous effect on her. He only nodded grimly and assured me that it would be okay. That once she could preserve energy in her human form that she'd heal. I knew so little. I didn't know if I should believe him. But what could I do? He was administering vial after vial of the Dragon Cor into her, and I knew first-hand how difficult that was to cultivate and collect. This use of a resource would likely be his biggest crime as far as the queen was concerned, or his mother.

I continued to pull more and more energy. I knew Agustín was saving a few vials for him, but I was hoping he wouldn't need them. I went to work on the tapestry that was this damaged man under my hands. It took nearly four times the amount of my energy to heal him than I would have expected, but it *was* working. His breathing had already started to return to normal. I worked break by break, damage by damage. Starting with his collapsed lung and other vital organs, then moving on to the bones. The bones nearly wiped me out, but I knew I needed to save some energy. I'd been replenished myself by Dragon Cor the other day, but still, it wasn't *that* much of a miracle drug, not quite. And we had a long way to go. I refused to stop until I could tell his heart-beat and breathing had stabilized, but he was still unconscious.

When I finally opened my eyes, I saw Agustín staring at me. I didn't have time for whatever he was thinking. I moved my hands to the dragon. She was still badly damaged. Without really having a clue as to how or why, I knew Agustín was hesi-tating with removing her chains. Similarly, I knew that was exactly what needed to happen next, and he needed another push.

"Take off the chains!" I commanded in a voice I thought I'd lost. I didn't need to say it twice. Pulling a large key from his pocket he inserted it into the lock. Then he scratched in the final lines for a glyph onto the oversized key, muttered something under his breath, and with a final turn of the key- the chains that held the dragon in her form fell off.

I watched, waiting for her to turn human. She didn't. Maybe she was too far gone. Her body jerked a few times, then stilled again. This terrible pattern, reminiscent of a death rattle, continued on. The man made a painful groan that diverted my attention to him as his own chains fell away. His eyes shot open, gold glowing bright enough it added light to the room. He laid still for a moment. I could almost hear his erratic heartbeats. His voice was weak, pained, "Why does she not turn?" A question I wanted answered as well.

Agustín looked her over tormentedly. "She's missing too many scales. If she turned now, she'd have too big of a hole in her chest. Her body knows she'd bleed out instantly. A Mother's scale is the only thing that will save her now. I'm sorry but there's no other option. We need to leave her."

"NO!" The man and I said at the same time. His, a pained hiss. Mine, unwisely loud. I could feel the man's eyes on me as I lifted Jen's signet ring from around my neck. I'd felt a peculiar connection to it ever since Briar gave it to me, and I'd never let it too far out of my reach. Especially after I found out what it was.

"What do I do?" I had learned the value and power of this ring. Helen had confessed it during one of our teas. She made it seem as though she didn't mean to let it slip. Queen Anumonwo never did anything without intention, and I spent days trying to figure out why she'd want me to know when

Briar clearly didn't. One thing I still didn't know was how to use it though. It was clear Agustín didn't either. And the man could barely speak as he fought for every word.

"It has its own energy." I wasn't sure if I understood. But I would try. We should have long been gone from here. Briar could very well be upstairs. Or coming down the hallway.

I positioned myself in front of the dragon's lacerated chest. Holding the ring in my hands, I rested them just above the gaping wound on her chest. I began to meditate and couldn't believe how low my energy was. I'd used more of it than I realized. My left hand, the one that I'd used to open the door, had gone completely numb. It was cold to the touch, and I could barely move any energy through it. I began pulling from the copper-colored energy of the ring. It took a lot more of me to pull from this ancient scale than anything else I'd ever done before. But at least I didn't have to give any more of my own energy. I didn't have much left to give. Now it was mostly about effort and stamina. Neither of which were too plentiful at the moment, but I could push.

I'd never experienced an object having this kind of usable energy. The energy coming from the dragon before me barely had any color left to it, a muted earth green. It hummed more than shone. I continued to pull from the ring until I could no longer feel it in my hands. It hadn't come apart like energy usually does, like yarn being moved, wound. Instead, it crumbled away. I had flaked off copper chunks and began meticulously laying them on her from the inside out. We didn't have time, but I needed to be careful.

I laid as many scales as I could, but she was still missing a few. Carefully I spaced them out as strategically as I could. I even tried using my own energy, but it didn't work, not for this. Even with the vials she was in dying need of her own energy. Desperately I tried to give her some of mine. It was as though it wouldn't reach. Hers seemed too far gone for mine to be able to connect. I used the open spots left from the three remaining scale wounds. As I touched her unprotected, pulsating flesh with my still functioning hand, her body flinched. I stole myself and pressed down firmly, forcing my energy into her and she sucked it up like a sponge. It didn't replace the scales, but it seared over some of the wounds that had been there, cauterizing the flesh.

I used too much, not quite falling away when Agustín caught me. The man was more aware than he had been, coming more into alert consciousness as his body adjusted from the energy I had given him. He went to his partner as she began to transform. The bone crunching and crackling sound barely penetrated my ears. In another moment the dragon was in her human form. Dark olive skin like the man, dark hair, slender. She was barely moving, but she was alive. Good. It would be easier for two humans to escape than one dragon and one human. "Frankie! You stupid goose!" Agustín grabbed one of the few remaining vials, and I clenched my jaw shut.

"No," I was able to murmur weakly. I knew he heard me, but he kept insisting, moving without hesitation. "She needs it. They need to get away."

"He can't save you now. Drink!"

Again I gritted my teeth and forced myself upright. "Her… give it to her… now." She was only barely conscious. Her body reacting to its circumstances. Even if I could only drag myself along, it was better than carrying someone completely.

He groaned in frustration as he moved over to her, forcing the contents down her throat. For the first time I heard a sound other than faint breathing from her as she choked on the liquid. I heard Agustín murmur, "finally" as he grabbed one more. She was awake and frightened and jumped, as much as she was able to, behind the man. Clearly still fearful of Agustín and me, rightfully so. The man knew who I was, in a way, and knew Agustín was here to help, this time. She must have been shocked they were still alive.

They spoke in hushed whispers, and she acquiesced, very cautiously. Agustín grabbed the satchel, pulled out the two cloaks, and handed them over. The woman huddled naked underneath hers. I had a shift dress and leggings on underneath my wool dress. Struggling against a numb hand and overall exhaustion, I partially disrobed. It was one of the warmer styles of dress, a gray knitted thing I'd left unaltered. I offered her the dress, the man having to take it as she refused to get closer to me. Agustín had turned his back towards her. Time and again he'd healed her so they could destroy her again, and now he was showing a level of modesty that seemed out of place. Something felt off.

She cleared her throat when she'd finished, and as she did, she clutched at her chest. The places where I couldn't heal her now had scars that looked like fresh burn wounds. The man quickly helped her cover herself with the cloak as well as my dress (it was only a few sizes too big for her), hiding her wounds completely. If I gave anything else, I wouldn't be able to walk. I wasn't terribly far from that now. I was considering it, ready to be done. Today could be my last, if that meant giving them a tomorrow.

Agustín read and interrupted my thoughts, whispering harshly to me, "You can't. I won't leave your body here for them. You need to be able to walk. She can handle pain. Believe me, I've seen it." I scowled at him, then nodded in surrender.

I'd never heard him so authoritarian as when he turned to address us all. "We need to move, now. Can you all walk?" She could barely move. The man could stand up, just, while leaning against the wall. And I was ready to give the last of myself in order to not weigh them down. What a sorry bunch we were.

His voice shook me. It was deeper than it had been earlier. It was freer now, alive. "I can walk, but I cannot carry the queen, and she cannot walk on her own." Agustín unceremoniously picked her up and slung her over his shoulders. I suppose it was easier than carrying her in front of him. The gruffness surprised me, but not as much as how silent she remained through it all.

"We need to go. Now." Agustín turned to me and asked, "Are you okay to walk?" I was holding myself up against the wall as well. I removed my hand and nodded to him, as if to prove I could. He took off and the man and I looked at each other for a moment before stumbling after them. His eyes were still that stormy blue, but there was a streak of something else. Something new.

We went back to the narrow stairs. Agustín had headed down at a much quicker pace than I expected for someone carrying someone else. I had Blue go behind them. If anyone was going to buy anyone time, it was going to be me. He wanted to argue, but he didn't.

I could see him stumbling every few steps and I was grateful for the distance between them and us. We finally got to the bottom, and Agustín took off again. Blue waited for me and offered to help support me. He could tell I was struggling. "We will help each other," he said when I hesitated. Reluctantly I went to his side, and with an arm around each other we hobbled along trying to catch up.

It was cold and quite dark. We were still in the Mountain after all. Under it now, perhaps. I could hear the slow movements of water and smell the musty aroma that comes with such places as it cooled my skin that was now covered in a cold sweat. Agustín had stopped at something that resembled a stony, shallow creek bed that seemed to run under the Mountain.

"They used to believe these springs had healing properties. They've forgotten them over time, and from knowing better. There's not enough room to walk along the banks. We'll have to get in. It shouldn't be too deep."

He went first, still carrying the silent queen over his shoulders. The water came up to his waist. I let go of Blue and tried lowering myself into the water. I slipped and went completely under. The shock of the frigid water took my breath away, making me inhale the painfully cold water. My left hand had begun to turn white, something I'd been trying to hide. I could no longer feel past my elbow, and I floundered trying to right myself without the use of both hands under the water-soaked cloak. I had a moment of dread when I couldn't feel anything but cold until his hands found me, righting me. It was Blue, and he seemed genuinely frightened as he helped me stand and pulled me close to him. His grasp on me now noticeably firmer. Panting, chest heaving, I worked desperately to catch my breath as our eyes searched one another's. For what, I do not know. We started to shuffle down the stream, chasing after Agustín for what felt like hours.

Time passes differently in some spaces.

I hadn't asked, instead trusting that Agustín knew what to do. "Agustín?" He mumbled something and his light orb appeared. He'd stopped and we were now facing a stone wall that the water ran up against and under. There was no room for us to pass. We'd been traveling long enough; we had to be out from under the city at this point.

"Give me a minute," he grumbled, panic rising in his voice. He set the queen down along the narrow stream bank and began pacing back and forth in front of the wall. Occasionally rubbing his hands over the stones. He was getting frantic until he stopped dead. "Frankie!" He didn't take his eyes off of whatever he'd found. "Let me see your hand. The one that opened the door before." I stretched it out towards him only to pull it back, seeing the ghastly pale that was creeping further up.

"Figures he'd do something like that." Agustín shook his head but offered no word of comfort. "Run your hand over this." He pointed to a particular line in the wall. "It may hurt." I quickly ran my hand over where he indicated and felt nothing. Examining the hand, it had indeed gotten sliced, deeply. But no blood flowed. Agustín tried to heal the gash to no avail. He whispered sadly, seeing my worry and pain, "It needs blood." I whimpered involuntarily.

"Let me," Blue insisted. My relief, laced with guilt, was short lived.

"It needs to be her." Agustín wouldn't look at any of us as he said this. Our silence urged him to explain. "It needs to be someone under the queen's direct protection. Or Briar's. I don't know how everything works with you all, how you can claim each other. But... if I'm not mistaken, you've been with him recently. That will be enough."

My face flushed. I didn't want *him* to know. But of course he already did. I was foolish for caring. He'd smelled him on me before. He knew, but I didn't want it said aloud. It was my imagination, but I thought I saw Blue clench his fists when Agustín explained. "As unsavory as it may sound, it need be only a crumb of ownership by one of them, and, like it or not, that's enough." I turned back to the wall and ran my non-poisoned hand over it. Feeling it this time when my hand was slashed open, along with the gush of blood to attest to my pain. Agustín tried healing this one as well, but again it was ineffective.

It didn't matter. My blood had worked. The stone wall moved. But as we continued the water deepened substantially. I worried about my open wounds in the water. At least it was running and not stagnant.

Blue helped me into the water this time. He was even gentler than before. I suppose he was worried because of my wounds too. I felt guilty but I definitely began to lean on him more than he was leaning on me. His energy seemed to be getting stronger, whereas I could feel myself getting weaker. It didn't make sense. My recuperation time had been improving recently. Now it seemed to be at a standstill. And the water kept getting deeper and deeper.

I could feel my breathing getting more and more ragged. I tripped in the water, and his arms were around me again. His eyes... such a storm, such chaos, contained in such order. I was getting lost in them as the world began to lose me once more.

TWENTY-ONE

I woke thoroughly drenched and being carried. Things wouldn't connect. Agustín's light showcased a steady cascade of snow through the darkness. We were outside of the tunnel. There were muffled words. A woman's voice I didn't recognize. "We leave them and run. There is no other way."

The one holding me spoke, his vocal timbre making me quiver. "She saved us and doomed herself. I will *never* leave her." I leaned into his warmth, hoping to take some of the chill off of myself. His hold on me tightened in response. I looked up and saw tumultuous oceans staring back at me, worried, affectionate. I smiled at the kindness of such a vast phenomenon, still not completely aware of the situation.

"Good. She's finally awake. Now stop making those faces and let's move. We'd have another hour to go on a clear day. This snowstorm may cover our tracks, but we're just as likely to die in it."

"We need to dry our clothes, wizard. Start a small fire. We will beat some of the water out of them and warm ourselves.

We may survive in damp clothing. We will not if we stay drenched." He said this with such authority and weight that my exhausted mind knew he had enough control over the situation that I could rest again. I started to allow my body to sleep when he spoke to me softly, rubbing my shoulder where he held me, "Not yet, Little One. We still need your help."

No one had called me little anything since I was about eleven or twelve. Right before puberty hit me square in the hips. I was still nuzzling into his chest as I opened my eyes against him, recalling that we were still fleeing. Hopefully Briar didn't know that yet. I sat up, lightly pushing off of Blue. "What..."

"You lost yourself for a while, Little One. We have far to go before you can rest. How are you fairing?"

I took a moment before answering. "I can't feel my left hand. My energy isn't coming back. I'm soaking wet, and I'm freezing." He'd put me down but now pulled me back to him, rubbing my body with a gentle aggression.

Agustín kept glancing over at me as he busied himself with a fire. He may not trust Blue, but these dragons were from the Wilds. They'd know better than us how to survive out here, and I was happy he wasn't arguing. "Your hand was poisoned from the glyph. I don't have what I need for that. My aunt, Dryad's willing, will. It isn't stopping at your hand. I'm not sure what he's done. I imagine by now it's past your elbow. Be careful, you won't feel it get damaged. I gave you the last vial of Dragon Cor that all of Heartwood had. Not that it seems to have done much."

I wanted to yell at him, but I was too weak. Still, he could sense it. "Before you chastise me for using it on you, we wouldn't make it far with you unconscious. I didn't do it for you. I did it for them. We'll listen to Rinn and dry our clothes. I have a spell that can help dry them out, but unfortunately they do need to be off of us or else it'll suck the moisture out of our bodies too. I can't do anything about the cold just yet. We'll be alright." He didn't sound convinced.

We all turned our backs to each other and handed our clothes to the center of our huddle where Agustín stood next to the fire. He worked to dry our clothes one at a time. His spell would help them along, but it would be more effective if they weren't completely soaked through still. I felt bad I'd given the queen a knitted wool dress, it must have absorbed quite a bit of water and been difficult to dry out. She wasn't far from me, none of us were far away from each other. I heard her grunting from the effort. She'd been through hell, but she was still very much alive.

"Mine is as dry as I am going to get it. Let me see yours," she said, surprising me. She held a hand out, looking sideways in my direction. I stopped trying to press the water out one handedly and begrudgingly handed her my shift dress and wool leggings I'd struggled out of. I was grateful for the effort she put forth on my behalf as she worked the water out.

We set out again in nearly dry clothes. The queen was walking on her own now, keeping close to Blue. He asked me if I needed help. Agustín chimed in before I could answer. "I'm here if she does. I'm still the best off, after all." He was trying to be helpful. I think.

We didn't waste energy talking as we trudged through the storm, our breathing quickly becoming labored. The night was eerily still. I heard only the faintest sounds of the queen and her commander conversing. At one point I thought I heard her chastise him for not helping with her dress. She'd been torn apart, and it seemed that Briar had left him comparably untouched. Until that last day. They'd both been through it, really. But what did I know? They'd been there for weeks, months. I could see how she would feel worse for wear.

I spoke as quietly as I thought I could to Agustín and still be heard, "Will your aunt be okay with this? Does she know?"

"I wasn't able to send her a message, but she'll understand. She probably already knows. She'll trust me, if nothing else. We seem to stick together better than you dragons." He gently nudged my shoulder. He was giving up his home for us. As much as he said it was his penitence, it still had to be nerve wracking. "She's the one who sent me back after all. And she was the one who gave me that book that shows the under-workings of the Mountain. She knows. Something is unwinding."

I looked back every once in a while to check on them. After an hour the queen seemed to be fading, she started leaning on Blue. "You should have used that last vial on her. Briar would have found me there sooner or later. I could have escaped another time."

Agustín shook his head at me. "You've seen him angry once. I've seen him kill more times than I care to admit for more years than I care to remember. He loves you, but monsters have their limits, too." Briar would never really hurt me. I knew that, even know. But there was also this side of him that I never before knew.

"We'll be there soon, I think." I could hear he wanted to grumble, but he had been right- he was the best off of all of us. And he knew better. I turned back to tell them and saw they'd fallen even farther behind. I stopped Agustín and he ran back to them while I tried to catch my breath.

They appeared to argue for a moment before he picked the queen up as he had before. She seemed slightly more indignant about being carried over his shoulder this time. Blue kept up but stayed a step behind. I joined him, safer to travel two by two in case another one of us became wary.

His eyes found mine, and I nodded as I joined alongside

him. He insisted I be the one to follow in the path of Agustín's steps. I followed closely, but they were quickly being covered up as the heavy snow continued to fall. Blue seemed to want to say something, repeatedly looking over at me, over and down. He was about a foot taller than me, stocky too, even after being in that damned place. *Well-built*, as Lark would say.

After he'd glanced over at me a few times, I returned the look sharply, catching him in the act. "Yes?" I asked curtly.

"I should not have been staring. I am sorry." I looked at him, annoyed. That wasn't it, not all of it. I shook my head, and we kept walking. He began to lag behind. Not much, and I matched his pace, backing away from our travel companions. "Do you trust him?" He asked so quietly I wasn't sure he'd said a thing until I looked up into eyes full of suspicion.

"I do. But I trusted Briar, too." I looked away. I didn't want to show anyone the pain I was feeling over someone who could do this. I stumbled as I was looking away. Blue reached out and caught me, only letting go after we walked a few paces with his arm around my waist.

"I was harsh before, about his scent on you- I am sorry."

I kept my eyes in front of me this time. "You don't owe me any kind of apology. You should hate me."

Agustín's aunt's house came into view, but not until we were nearly on top of it. She must have had something protecting it. It should have been visible a ways off, not only now once we were practically walking up to the door.

We didn't knock, and it seemed as though there was no lock whatsoever. The snow was coming down in wet clumps as I looked out at nothing but darkness. The blizzard should play to our advantage, now that we weren't in it. If nothing else it should cover our tracks. Dragons had heightened senses after they'd transformed, but a few feet of deep snow should, if nothing else, help mask us.

Agustín had put the queen down to open the door. She huddled next to her commander, and I noticed his arm go around her as they whispered together. I felt a pain in my heart, wondering what Briar was doing. Was he on his way to kill us? Did he even know yet? Had he left flowers on my doorstep again?

Opening the door, we were flooded with warmth and a comforting light. I'm not certain if you would ever see this light if it wasn't meant for you to see, and no one seemed worried about still being inside the kingdom, besides me. The place smelled of freshly baked bread and relief. We funneled into a large room with a roaring fire and two very plush and welcoming sofas facing one another with a low table between them. A pile of blankets had already been laid out, as well as sets of wool tunics and pants.

"You said you hadn't gotten a message out?" I asked, growing more and more uncertain of where I'd put my last strands of faith.

"I didn't. And don't look at me like that. Auntie Sabina has a gift for sight. She's our Seer, not that she falls in line with family business. It comes from her father's side- Maias. That book she gave me was the only reason I knew there was a waterway out of the inner kingdom from the Mountain. I told you before, she *knows*. Though I am bothered that she doesn't seem to be here."

We had little choice but to trust him.

The queen was such a petite thing, I was not, and the commander was so tall, it wasn't hard to distinguish whose pile belonged to whom as we hurriedly turned our backs to one another again, removing our frozen and still damp clothes, and quickly dressing into the well-made, warm, and dry ones. The queen ended up helping me, wordlessly, as I struggled with my arm. It seemed we were more than expected as everything fit as though it had been tailored to us.

"I'll check her supplies and see if she has what I need for your arm," Agustín said. It was nearly at my shoulder now. The queen had made no reaction when she saw it other than to glance over at her commander. I assumed they were planning to take off at the next opportune moment. I had no sensation in the arm, and it felt like nothing more than a heavy weight hanging off of me. And the whole thing, at least what I had seen, was an ashen gray-white.

The three of us went to sit by the fire as Agustín disappeared into the house. There was a large stone hearth at the base of the rounded fireplace and the three of us could just fit. I was closer to Blue than I liked, but I was so exhausted and so very cold. I wanted for nothing but to be warm. He spoke to the queen in a language I didn't understand. Normally I would have been quite intrigued, but now I was just cold. And I wanted to be left alone, the weight of the day crashing down on me. They carried on for a few minutes until he stood and left the room.

The queen was watching me, wanting her attentions to be acknowledged. "You are colder than I, but be careful with your arm. You cannot feel it, yes?" I nodded slowly, my eyes still transfixed on the fire. "It is very close to the fire. It would not do to burn that cloak, or the fresh tunic, or your flesh, even if it is dead."

"Why do you think I am colder?" I asked, somewhat matching her accent unintentionally. She smiled lightly, almost piteously at me. The thought of my arm being dead not something weird enough to ask about, not after seeing it.

"You have not yet taken to your dragon. You do not yet have your dragon's heat," she said softly. I moved away from the fire, sighing heavily. I was probably better off under a blanket that had been warming by the fire than being cooked myself. I grabbed one with my right arm and went over to the overly plush couch. I sat down and struggled to spread it over myself.

Blue came back carrying a tray of food. He sat it down on the table in front of me and grabbed my blanket, spreading it over me and tucking it in around me. I was so unnerved by his actions, and exhausted, that I didn't bother stopping him. He looked at me for a moment as I stared out into nothing before asking, "Would you have another blanket?"

"No," I mumbled as I watched his queen come over to the couch opposite me. He had brought back three bowls of a thick stew and several slices of fresh bread that had been heavily buttered already. I couldn't see any possible way to eat the stew without making a mess, and I wasn't looking for any more help. I grabbed a piece of bread and ate it slowly. The queen had already dug into the stew, but he kept watching me. I ignored him as best as I could.

By the time Agustín came back into the room, complete with his own outfit change, I could feel myself fading again, my body asking for permission to sleep, to close my eyes for just a minute, to fade into that comfortable abyss of nothingness. They exchanged a few words I didn't catch until Agustín started talking about me. "I'll stay up and keep an eye on her, if it moves up to her shoulder, we'll have to remove it."

"Not yet, Little One." I had started slipping away when Blue called to me. "You must eat first. I will feed you." I groggily opened my eyes to glare at him. He chuckled lightly and the sound made my wearied heart crack and flutter all at once. I was grateful that the heat in the room had already made me flush.

"Just hold the bowl, please," I groused. Of course this didn't work nearly as well as I hoped.

"Just let me feed you, please." I reluctantly gave in. He took the spoon from me and sat on the low table with his legs spread around mine. He moved nearer to feed me, the closeness and attention waking me quickly. He kept his eyes focused on me the entire time he fed me. The heat was becoming bothersome. I tried my best to look down or to the side or anywhere but on him, my face growing redder by the spoonful.

When I finished he brought a hand up to my face, and I instinctively flinched. This was the second time I'd done this since Briar had dug into me. It had been an aggressive enough act itself, but it'd also brought up some things from my past. I bit my tongue as I looked away, angry at myself for reacting like this.

His hand stilled for a moment. "I will never hurt you," he whispered before moving in closer. Our eyes locked on each other. He used his thumb to wipe off my lips, and taking his hand from my face, he put his thumb between his own lips to clean it off. The shade of red on my face deepened as I looked away, breaking our gaze.

"You aren't the first one to say that to me... well, recently. I believed it then." I hadn't meant to cause him pain, but sure enough it was there in his eyes when I dared a glimpse. I had to look away. The queen had fallen asleep almost the instant she finished eating. Agustín was silently pacing along the hallway. I would see him every few minutes, walking mindlessly, his arms across his chest as he bit his thumb. Blue was still sitting very close, watching me. I still couldn't look at him again.

"You should eat and get some rest," I said. "I imagine you two have a long journey ahead of you still." I glanced at him as he shifted his body.

He looked worried. "You will come with us."

I shook my head. "Maybe I can slow Briar from here. If he

doesn't have power outside of these walls then we just need to get you two out. You never know what kind of a difference an hour or two can make. I know it's not much, but it's all I can do."

"You like it there?" he asked, no intonation in his voice.

I laughed caustically. "It isn't, hasn't, always been awful. But it's not home. I don't think I can ever actually go home."

"I am sorry, Little One. My people would welcome you. You are a hero to them already."

"Don't you apologize! And your people would hate me as soon as they found out I'd been sleeping with the one who nearly killed you two."

"He has claimed you?"

I hesitated before answering. "No. At least I don't think so. I guess I don't really know."

He smiled at me, amused, and I could see a hint of red on the tips of his ears. "You would know," he said suggestively. I leered playfully at him. "At least, if I had claimed you, you would know." He finally started to eat. Likely, I imagine, to keep himself from saying anything else that might get him in trouble with his sleeping queen.

"What's your name?" I asked him. I'd heard Agustín use it before, but just the once. For all I knew it was a snide nickname, the way dragons used the word wizard. I didn't want to repeat it if that was the case.

He eyed me with interest as he chewed his food. "Rinn. For now," he said as he glanced over at the queen. He kept looking me over for just a moment, waiting for me to ask what he meant. I had a friend that played those games. She would laugh hysterically out of nowhere, waiting for you to ask her what was so funny. When you didn't ask, she'd become furious and storm off. I wondered if he'd do the same thing if I didn't play into his game.

We sat there for a while as he watched me. I closed my eyes for a bit, close to letting myself fall asleep. The sound of his bowl being placed back down on the tray forced them open. He was still sitting on the table, looking around the room. Now trying pointedly to not look at me. "Aren't you going to ask me what my name is? It's not Little One, in case you weren't sure."

He gave the question space as he beamed at me. I hadn't meant to be that familiar, I was just so tired. "Tell me your name, if you wish. But I already have one that suits you."

I'd been given plenty of names, not all companionable. I tried desperately to squash my curiosity. It didn't work as well as I'd hoped. I was exhausted but still asked, sleepily, "And what might that be?"

I watched him lean in closer as he worked to decide if he should tell me or not. He was close enough I caught a whiff of his own natural, earthy musk underneath the overwhelming warm yeast smell from the bread. The underground springs had done wonders to wash away the smell of torture and agony. His lips began to part to answer...

The queen, still laying on the sofa facing away from us, answered for him, "He calls you Little Rose."

I felt a shiver go through me as I felt her words brush over me. Awareness hitting me instantly.

Lark and I had gotten these little line tattoos on her eighteenth birthday. I got a rose, and she got a lark. It wasn't exactly somewhere that everyone would just see it. *How* had he seen it? Maybe I was being neurotic, and he was just a romantic? What are the chances of that? What did she mean, *he calls you*? How often had he been speaking of me?

We held each other's gaze again, and I lost track of my reasons for blushing. The way he was looking at me... I knew he was grateful for what I had done, but a part of me wanted to mistake it for something else. I couldn't argue with the attraction I felt towards him, but really, I hadn't even started to unpack everything from the last twenty four hours. Yet, the way he kept looking at me, the way he kept moving...

"It's actually Frankie," Agustín interrupted from the hallway. He raised his hands in submission and retreated as my eyes shot daggers at him.

Rinn had turned to look at him and turned back to me as he left. I shrugged and sat back, closing my eyes. "Little Rose it is," he said, and I could hear him smiling. I liked how it sounded. When he said it.

He stood up to cover the queen with her blanket that had fallen down when she repositioned herself. "This is Anthea. She can be rather cold, as you know. I'd say she warms up. But that would be a lie."

He turned back to me. "May I see your arm? Before you rest?" I nodded and tried to move the blanket. He sat next to me and smiled kindly as he pushed it back and carefully removed my arm from the tunic to examine it. I turned my head, not wanting to look at my decaying appendage. He ran his hand over where my unaffected flesh met the ash gray and I unwillingly trembled at his touch. I turned my head further back, not wanting to see his reaction. He covered my arm back up.

"Sleep now, Little Rose." I didn't argue with him. I hobbled around as I tried to lay down, ignoring his offer of assistance. He didn't ask if he could tuck me in, again he just did it. I'd wanted to say thank you, but I was out before I could.

～

I'D NEVER DREAMT in black and white before. My dream from that night wasn't exactly in black in white either, but shadows. There was a dragon, immersed in shadow. It had wrapped itself around a blinding white spot. That was how I knew there was a dragon at all, the shining white spot darkened only by the moving outline of the dragon. I'd see glimpses of this white spot. It hurt to look at it, but I couldn't stop. I looked longer and inched closer. The white spot became a snow-white egg. I reached out to touch it. The dragon was either unaware of my presence or didn't care. I touched the egg and could instantly sense the energy.

CHAPTER

TWENTY-TWO

I woke with a start, struggling to catch my breath or calm my anxious heart from what had to be some unremembered dream. I heard their voices- Agustín and a woman, his aunt I was sure. I couldn't make out most of what they were saying, but their tones did nothing to alleviate my disquiet. With an embarrassing amount of effort, I struggled to turn over on the sofa, barely managing it. Rinn was asleep on the floor next to me. I wouldn't be able to stand without stepping on him. Why hadn't he slept next to his queen? She was likewise still sleeping soundly.

I looked at his resting face, his features softer now. His dark olive skin glowing from the firelight. I couldn't believe I'd been bold enough in that dungeon to reach out to him, to feel his strong jaw through that beard. I wanted to run my fingers through it again. "You should stop looking at him that way if you aren't coming with us."

I snapped my head up to look at her, not loving her implications, "And you should stop pretending to be asleep and spying on people."

"We do not sleep around your kind," she commented nonchalantly.

I scoffed, "My kind, hm?"

"You know she is not one of them, Thea." I started at his words and looked back down at him. "And you both should let the tired rest." He had a small grimace across his face now, but his eyes were still closed. Anthea groaned at his defense of me and rolled away from us.

"Sorry," I mumbled softly and laid back with some difficulty.

He sat up suddenly, as if remembering something important that had been left behind, and he looked over at me. "Your arm, Little Rose?" My face paled. I was having some trouble breathing, but I was still able to manage it. Not that I was about to tell him this. He must have seen the worry in my eyes because he leapt up and out of the room without another sound. A few hushed but hurried words to Agustín and his aunt and they all stormed back in.

Agustín looked at me uneasily. His aunt seemed less than happy with the whole situation. She gave off the impression of being perpetually busy, even when standing still. A short, plump woman with gray eyes and matching hair that rested in a loose bun. She was wearing a dark lavender dress that gathered at her waist and then puffed out. It buttoned all up and down the back and I wondered how she ever managed to get it on or off. "Madam Sabina, this is Draca Regulus Anthea from—"

"The arm," she cut him off with a tired and impatient tone. She walked over to me, and I struggled to move at all, let alone sit up. Rinn came over and pulled the blanket completely off of me. Putting an arm underneath me, he pulled me up to him. He looked worried. Sabina looked annoyed.

"Put her on the table in the kitchen," she said with an air of exhaustion as she headed back the way they'd come. Before I could try to stand, Rinn scooped me up and headed down the hallway. If I wasn't afraid they were about to cut my arm off, I might have blushed. He set me down gently on the kitchen table as he leaned onto it a bit himself, supporting me from the side.

Sabina sounded irritated. "I found what I needed alright. Though you'll likely not be able to use it for your energy anymore." I understood. It was better than dying, or so I thought. And Rinn felt so warm. I was happy to have him there, stabilizing me physically and emotionally. I let myself lean into those emotions temporarily, knowing he'd be gone soon with his queen. I could let my mind pretend, for just a little while. I'd been pretending so much as it was already.

"The pain'll be too much for you." She looked at me objectively. I was hopeful she was going to knock me out first if it was going to be that bad. A foolish dream, quickly dashed. "You'll need to fight to stay conscious. The longer you can stay with us and move your energy, the better its function will be after. You're going to need that for what's to come." She didn't wait for me to express any level of understanding. Which was for the best. I didn't have much, and I probably would have insisted on taking time I didn't have on an explanation I wouldn't have gotten anyway.

She addressed Rinn without looking at him, "Hold her steady, Commander. She'll fight her way free to escape the pain. The salve needs to rest on her arm for a good while."

Anthea slowly made her way into the tense kitchen. "The wizard should be the one to hold her down," she quietly suggested from the corner of the room. She looked uncomfortable and ready to make a run for it. Agustín nodded in agreement and understanding at her words.

Rinn lifted his head, his eyes glowing at his queen. "I will hold her." I looked over in time to see her silently look down and away.

"Pin her down best ya can." Sabina instructed. "Believe me, child, she *will* do anything. I don't need her kicking and clawing, managing to run away to scrape this stuff off before the job's done." I was starting to get worried about how bad this was going to be, but my labored breathing was getting worse.

Rinn removed my dead arm from the tunic, exposing the entirety of the affected area. I would have been embarrassed with how much of me was laid bare if I hadn't been so terrified. He saw my fear as we looked at how far it had spread across my chest, both sets of eyes pausing on the fragile lines of ink that made up my little rose. I looked over at him and our eyes met, he put a hand up to my face, "You will survive this, Little Rose."

Letting out a breath I hadn't realized I'd been holding, I nodded and leaned back into him. He smiled tenderly at me as he rubbed my cheek with his thumb. For whatever reason, I believed him.

He slid onto the table and pulled me back to him. He did as Sabina had instructed, wrapping his legs around mine, pinning me against himself. He wrapped his arms around me like a pretzel, holding my good arm down against me while my dead arm lay lifeless on the table in front of Sabina. "Comfortable?" she asked as she chuckled and put a wooden spoon in my mouth. "Don't bite your tongue. Or him. At least not on my table." Again she laughed at her own humor. Agustín looked terrified standing behind her, still biting his thumb.

Readying herself next to my arm, she brought over a bowl of a foul-smelling salve and placed it in front of her. There was steam coming off of it, and my eyes watered when the toxic vapors reached me. "You won't want to watch," she said flatly, offhandedly as she moved my arm about. I turned the other way to see Rinn's face right next to mine. I wanted to look away, but there were so many emotions flickering through his eyes right then. He was hiding his worry, but it was there. The blue of his eyes seemed to swim as it swirled with flecks of gold. I was captivated. And thankful for the momentary distraction.

She began placing the salve on my arm, starting at my chest. The fetid smell singed my nose. I tried to look back at it, but Rinn awkwardly put his face over mine, covering me, preventing me from looking around. He whispered in my ear, "The pain will be less if you do not see." His breath tickled my ear as my body jolted from the surprise of the salve settling in. I couldn't feel the heat, not at first. Then a warm tickle on the skin began to creep out, suddenly it felt as though a fire was working itself down to my bones. As if I was being burned down past my skin and muscle and into every part of me. The spoon helped to muffle my screams, if nothing else.

He began repeating "Little Rose, Little Rose" over and over again in a cooing, singsong, soothing sort of chant. The pain continued to rapidly increase in intensity. It was my arm, yes, but it was now a vengeful inferno that was coming for the rest of me. I needed to run, to get away. He'd been holding me firmly before, but it was different now. He wasn't just holding me. It was as if he was willing the pain from me as he embraced me, my pain, my past, as he forged a connection through this trial by fire.

No longer was it my pain alone, to suffer in isolation.

Sabina began giving me orders- "Use your energy, girl. Push it from your chest through your shoulder, down your arm, out your fingers. Move it around. Circulate it. Recreate the pathways." She had said this before, and now kept saying it on a loop, aware that I was struggling to do so. I was grateful for something to do, I thought it might help with the pain. Nothing helped. Nothing but him.

Sabina continued on, but it was his voice that soothed me enough so that I was able to think and to actually find my energy at all. I was still very weak from draining myself yesterday. It hadn't recuperated in the slightest, and I could only hope this arm had something to do with that. The pain worsened, and I kept thinking about how it would have been better had they left me there to die. Or worse, to be found by Briar. His face when he grabbed me kept flashing in my mind. My father always told us not to judge someone based on their worst day, their worst moment. But Briar had done so much worse, on so many days. Judgment had nothing to do with it, I could never forgive him.

I began to fade in and out of consciousness. Every time I'd begin to fade Rinn would nuzzle me with his nose and tell me I couldn't rest quite yet. It was foolish for them to still be here. They should have left at daybreak. I was angry at myself for not thinking of this sooner. For not telling them to go when I first woke up. I began to cry, thinking of what Briar might do to them, to all of us, if he found us now. But really, I might have just been crying because my arm felt as though hydrofluoric acid was eating away at it from the center outwards.

Slowly it began to feel like an arm again. Not just an appendage of pain. But it was hot, too hot. I couldn't see but the skin had to be badly damaged, likely flaking off of my body now. I wanted to run outside and plunge it into snow that would melt from the firestorm that was now attached to me. The pain never lessened until it ebbed ever so slightly, and then all at once it was gone. My ragged breathing slowly began to calm down as I took deeper and deeper breaths. I hadn't realized it before, but now I could feel how tightly Rinn was pressed into me as I felt our bodies move together whenever mine would quiver from my sniveling.

I felt Sabina and Agustín wiping the salve off of my arm. Rinn still wouldn't move his head to allow me to look. Sabina moved him to take the spoon. "You're tougher than I'd seen. Odd." She wasn't speaking to anyone but herself, and she sounded concerned. They wrapped my arm in a linen cloth that smelled of sage and aloe. It finished cooling my burning arm, and I started to let myself go. "Take her upstairs. The room on the right. She needs proper rest now that her dragon heart can convalesce."

Rinn carefully untangled himself from me. His body leaving mine left a painful, cold emptiness where he'd been a moment ago. I'd be bruised where he'd held onto me so tightly, but I didn't care. Something to remember him by once he left, I suppose.

In a heartbeat he scooped me up again. My now mobile arm lay across my lap and I rested my exhausted head on his shoulder. I was so drained I didn't even mind him carrying me upstairs.

I barely registered the room besides the plethora of drying plants, but I could smell Sabina everywhere. I was grateful she was letting me use her bed. He laid me down gently and knelt down at the side of the bed, resting his head at an angle so he could look at me straight on. He brushed my matted hair out of my face as I studied him. I could feel sleep once again taking over. "Can I rest now?" I teased.

He smiled sweetly. "Rest now, Little Rose. We have a long journey ahead of us."

His words roused me from my imminent slumber. "You need to leave! Both of you. Now. You've stayed too long as it is. It isn't safe here."

He shook his head at me as I started talking louder. "We are not going without you. Your wizard assured me it is safest to travel by night. We are hidden here. We are safe, for now. Rest. Tonight, the three of us will leave, together."

"Rinn..." I trailed off.

"Call me Perrin." His voice was comforting but dangerously sultry. He was still running his fingers through my hair, a soothing touch that was putting me to sleep. I wanted to ask about the different names, but now wasn't the time.

"Will you stay with me?" This level of exhaustion has a way of altering inhibitions. "Just until I fall asleep? I don't want to make trouble with your queen."

He looked amused and satisfied, moving onto the bed to lay next to me. It wasn't a small bed, but it felt tiny with Perrin in it. After he'd settled down next to me, he started running his fingers through my hair again. I couldn't help but close my eyes. He moved closer and whispered, "She may be queen, but she is not *my* queen, not that way. Anthea is my sister." My heart quickened at his words. But it didn't matter. They needed to leave. Without me. I could sense Perrin was as stubborn as I was and wasn't going to leave unless I did. But that didn't mean I needed to leave with them. Love only brought pain after all. I'd had enough of both.

But he did feel nice.

CHAPTER

TWENTY-THREE

I dreamt of the dragon of shadows and their single, blinding egg again. There was another overwhelming energy this time, watching me, surrounding me. The voice was familiar and not at the same time. It was calling to me, but I couldn't make out what it was saying. I was trying to turn towards it as a fire was building inside me. I was close to squaring up with it when the luminous egg cracked, spilling out a darkness that came rushing towards me. A darkness more true, more nothing, more void than even the Medela cloaks we bore for safe passage.

Perrin's soft snores saved me from being engulfed by that darkness. I wondered if I should tell his sister that he had actually fallen asleep. Now that exhaustion didn't cloud my mind, I could take in the room. Quaint, nothing extravagant. Only one window, from which I could see dusk approaching. I wasn't surprised that we had slept most of the day. At some point Perrin had moved closer and wrapped an arm around me. His warmth was distressingly comforting. I knew I shouldn't be this close to him, but I didn't want to move. And I was tired of doing what I should.

The realization that the attraction I felt towards him reminded me of a similar attraction I'd felt towards Briar didn't upset me as much as it should have. For a flicker of a second I wondered if it was just another dragon thing I didn't completely understand. I'd been around and met plenty of other dragons in Heartwood and hadn't felt this magnetic pull towards them. Whatever it was, I can only describe it as feeling drawn towards an embodiment of fire. I wondered if this was how moths felt. If so, maybe they didn't much mind being burned. Still, there was so much I didn't understand. And now that I'd never get inside Helen's library, I wasn't sure I ever would. I could waste time and energy worrying about the choices I'd made. But why? Instead, I decided that my choices were fine. Or they weren't. And that I'd deal with whatever came of them as they came to me. There wasn't much else to do. Right in that moment, there wasn't much else I wanted to do.

Perrin's face was dangerously close. Not as close as on the kitchen table, but now I could see his soft features again. I said screw it and began tracing the line between bare flesh and shaggy beard. His nose twitched after a moment, and I ran my fingers through his beard on his chin. His snoring stopped. As though he was afraid the rest of the house wouldn't let us be once they knew we were awake, he whispered, "You really do not like to let me sleep."

I whispered back, "I don't. You better leave me here." I felt his face move under my fingers as he smiled, and I bit my lower lip to stop myself from saying something untoward. He opened his eyes, and his tempestuous oceans made my breath catch.

"You will be surprised by my home. Your people... *these*

people do not know what they think they know of us. You need to see it, but I will not make you do anything you do not wish to do."

It may not have been the time to ask, but I needed the answer before trying to figure out where I should go. I stopped moving my fingers across his cheek. "Is that why he was torturing you? Answer me honestly this time, please." I felt as though, after what we'd gone through together, we'd grown to trust one another enough that he'd actually give me the real answer now.

He nodded somberly as he stared into my eyes. "Their queen heads a special council. It is unusual that they asked all of Visnatura's regents to take up with such a thing. We were interested, given that aspect alone. But these kingdoms, they are selfish, foolish beyond reason. They believe a prophecy can be forced. It is nonsense to manipulate such a thing, and their efforts come from a time shortly before my sister's reign began. Our people chose not to take part, largely due to the required bloodshed. Therefore we are not privy to many of the details. We did not mind until we were informed that due to our lack of involvement they would require remuneration. All territories that were not willing to take part had to give. We came to negotiate the fee. They did not wish to negotiate." His smile had faded into a grim expression.

"What was the fee?" I didn't want to know, but I needed to. This was a completely different reason than I'd heard from anyone before, including him. Although not a word of it surprised me.

"A dragon's heart. It is a priceless thing to any dragon, not just its dragon. Our people do not bargain with the body parts of our deceased."

My face paled, and I removed my hand from his beard as it occurred to me. "There were three of you."

"They killed her the day we arrived." He grabbed my retreating hand. "You are not them," he assured me as my tears threatened to fall. "Tell me how you came to be here."

His request surprised me. My mind raced with questions of prophecies, requirements, manipulations, whatever information he did have. But right now it was clear he wanted to think of anything else. I suppose it was my turn to share my misery. "I'm not quite sure. I thought I was human until a couple months, er, lunars ago."

He chuckled lightly and explained, "We are familiar with your measurements of time. We have several humans from Earth that live in our Mountain. You will meet them, if you wish. After you've settled."

I glared at him before continuing, "I met a woman who taught me to control and use my energy on plants. She passed away, and I was taking care of her gardens. I met her son a few months later. He was looking for her ring. She'd put it in the fire, and it had been taken out with the ashes for the garden. I..."

I looked deeply into his eyes. I didn't want to tell him about Briar, not everything anyway. "Her son and I grew close. I found the ring. There was a red elk that was after us. He knocked me out- Briar, not the elk. And I woke up here. That's when they told me what I do know. Which, as time goes on, I'm finding out is less and less. I've been here for a few months now. I miss my family. I just... I miss home." I turned over in the bed to face away from him. "I want my quiet, uncomplicated life back."

I felt the bed move as he shifted positions. I was surprised when he wrapped his arms around me. He pulled me tightly to him and placed his head in the crook of my neck. He said nothing and simply held me as I grabbed onto his consoling arms and cried as silently as I could. I'm not sure how long we laid there like that.

Sabina knocked on her door. I'd stopped crying by then and had simply been laying there, running my fingers across healed over scars on his forearm. I imagined most dragons must have these to some extent.

She told us dinner was ready and we should eat before she kicked us out of her house. I thanked her and he growled playfully into my shoulder when I told her we'd be right down. I reluctantly rolled back towards him to lay on my back. He'd refused to let go of me and had propped himself up on an elbow, his other arm still holding me. I looked up at his almost pained face and traced his cheekbones. He shuddered at my touch, closing his eyes for a moment. When he opened them again, I propped myself up too, realizing my arm only tingled now, the rest of the feeling in it had returned, more or less. I watched his eyes wash over me.

Anthea called from the other side of the door, "Rinn! Now!" We listened to her stomp back down the stairs.

"Why doesn't she call you Perrin?"

"She knows not to with these people around."

"You didn't tell me."

"There is much I have yet to tell you."

"Anything I need to know before deciding if I'm going with you or not?"

He seemed to genuinely think it over. Then his eyes focused on mine, and he kissed me. Deeply. Taking his hand off my waist only to lose it in my hair a second later. I let myself melt into that kiss as our bodies molded to one another. I recognized the fire from my dream instantly as it took my breath away. It was a long kiss and feeling that fire from my dream... surreal doesn't do it justice. It just couldn't *be*. It had actually, literally, taken my breath away, the way you see it happen in those old *film noir* movies- gritty and impassioned. I looked up at him, slightly out of breath as my chest rose and fell against him. I could tell from his wild eyes that it had done the same for him.

As exhilarated as he seemed to be by this, I was mortified. I should have pulled away from him before our lips ever touched. I should never have let it happen. I pulled myself away from him now and stood up. "I'm sorry. That shouldn't have happened, I shouldn't have asked you to stay with me. We shouldn't have—"

"Little Rose!" His voice was full of surprise and dismay. He jumped out of the bed after me and stood in front of me. "I don't know what that was, but I *know* you felt it too! That was unlike anything... that was destiny! What is going on? What is wrong?" I said nothing but kept shaking my head side to side. "I *know* you felt that too."

I looked him squarely in the face as I lied, "That was nothing but pain." Shaking my head, I left the room. He followed and I could only hope he'd let it go once we were around other people. Destiny? How stupid.

He kept following behind me as I walked hastily into the kitchen where the three of them were eating. Sabina's kitchen put Agustín's office to shame when it came to dangling plants. Everywhere you looked there was this succulent or that fern or an ivy hanging from copper this or that. Shelves lined with copper pots, pans, plates, cups, everything and anything. It was like a mosaic of greens and copper on top of white washed shelves. I'd been too preoccupied earlier to notice anything other than the table I nearly died on. The table which now had people about it and food upon it.

Agustín looked up at my flushed face as I worked to regain some degree of composure. He chuckled loudly as he asked, "What were you two doing?" I glared at his wicked smile. His laugh must have been contagious because Anthea was clearly trying to hide a smile herself until her brother walked in behind me. He cleared his throat as he came in and gave them both a look that shut them up instantly.

At least Sabina was still focused on our impending doom. "Eat, you two. We have much to discuss and then you all need to get out of my house."

I took a seat as she handed me a bowl and Perrin followed suit. I refused to look at him. Something I'd wanted to keep up but knew would become quite difficult since he sat directly across from me. Agustín took charge, as he'd been groomed to do his entire life. "Auntie rounded up a few horses for us, as well as some more travel worthy outfits. This will be the safest way for you all to travel. They'll be expecting you in the skies and while they shouldn't move outside the walls, we all know what they're capable of. They shouldn't follow outside of the kingdom's reach, but still, I will ride with you for a ways past that. From there I will be leaving you for now."

"Agustín, I am so sorry." I didn't know all of what he was giving up, but I knew it pained him.

"Don't worry about me, Frankie. It's still not enough to make up for everything I've done. My sisters and mother will send my things that they haven't confiscated. Dragon Houses and Sorcerer Families rarely outright oppose one another. Even in this- they won't go against the Medelas. I'll be safe in a kingdom free of you lot." He winked at me.

I wasn't sure how to ask this, so I did so outright, "Can I go with you?" I was aware of Perrin clenching his fists at my question, but he said nothing. I saw Anthea glance at him and quickly look away.

"Frankie, it won't be safe for you in an inner kingdom. Not now. They all still acknowledge the Dragon Houses. They all want a branch to call their own and would never outright defy one. If they ask for you, every kingdom will give you up. You'd be better off walking up to the front gates right here. For my part in all of this, I truly am sorry." I shook my head, telling him no sorry was needed.

I sighed, contemplating. "Maybe that's what I should do. Briar might not chase any of you if—"

"He nearly killed you!" Agustín was angrier than I'd ever heard him before. I was stunned. "If Sabina didn't have Maia tendencies from ages past, she would never have started making that salve before we arrived. It would have gotten to your heart. Do you know how useful a heart is that has no blood?!"

Sabina broke the tension, kinder than I'd yet heard her. "He's right, perdita draca. You only know one side of him. He only shows you that side. He loves you, but the rest of him would never let you live without him. He knows you're not his. Now more than ever. If you aren't his, he won't let you be. Or be anyone else's."

"Then how is that any different? Won't he keep chasing me? Regardless of who I go with? Or where? I'm putting whoever I go with at risk." No one had an answer for me. Not for this, not that they wanted to say anyway. "I just want to go home," I murmured quietly to myself.

Anthea spoke up for the first time, "I do not like you, Frankie." My name sounded weird coming from her and I flinched imperceptibly. "But you saved my life and that of my commander. You used a Mother Scale to heal me. I can never repay you, not in the same way. But you are welcome and have a home in my Mountain forever further. I will not say more here in front of them, but do not fear that monster when it comes to him infiltrating *my* land."

She seemed too sure of herself for someone who came from the Wilds. How long had she been tortured? And none of her people had come to her rescue. Her forces can't be that tactful or grand. I shook my head. "I can't."

Perrin's voice cut through me, "Why not?!" The angry, pleading tone made me look up at him for the first time since upstairs.

"I don't belong there. Your people will hate me. Up until yesterday, literally, I was sleeping with the monster that killed one of you and was torturing you two! I'm tired of being thrown around wherever someone else thinks I should belong. I just want to go home!"

A kind voice came from Sabina, again surprising me. "You belong here, child. You belong in this world, for now. Don't fight it. You will find your place, in time."

I'd finished eating and slumped back, helpless. Aware that I would never again have any control over my own life. What did it really matter? What had I been doing? Passing time in my little gardens, surviving, hiding.

Agustín's voice was tender as he spoke after several minutes. "Wear the cloaks. They have glyphs to keep you out of sight to those seeking you harm. Auntie has packed some things. I'm not sure how far you're traveling, but I hope it will be enough."

Perrin's deep voice filled the room. "You have done enough, Sir Agustín. I cannot forgive you for your part in all this. But mine will have no ultio with you. We are grateful to you for your part in saving us." Listening to Perrin speak it was no wonder he was a commander. When he spoke, you listened, and you felt assured of your place.

I looked to Agustín for some clue as to what an ultio was. He nodded grimly at Perrin but said nothing. Sabina interrupted the silence. "Go. Prepare yourselves and the horses. I need to undress her arm." Perrin and Anthea thanked Sabina ceremoniously. She looked twenty years younger as she listened to their appreciations and blessings. Agustín gave her a solid hug and kissed her cheek. He thanked her for everything and said something in an unfamiliar language that somehow felt restful to my bones.

As they walked out Perrin looked back, catching my gaze. He looked forlorn as he turned away quickly. "That one will be trouble for you," Sabina said as she took off the wrapping from my arm. She wiped it down and looked closely at the scars that had formed across my chest where the deadness had reached. It looked like wild and savage lightning connecting as it circled around me, over my chest, across the top of my shoulder, under my arm. I couldn't see it, but knew it connected along my back.

"I don't know how to repay you. But thank you."

"I don't need your thanks, or there's. We will see each other again child. Sooner than you'd like, but you will be ready." I didn't believe her, but I wasn't going to be rude either.

"Can you see the future?"

She laughed a huge, hearty laugh, and I watched her, unamused. "No child, and no one from this world would have asked it that way. I see patterns, much like you do with your energy, your visions. I have a particular gift for seeing patterns in time. Our magics are not so different. We just use different materials to patch the patterns."

"Sure. Why not." I said, not sure if I believed her. Four months ago I knew dragons didn't exist. Now I'd seen and touched two. I still doubted if I was actually one of them, but it didn't matter. I had no plans of ever finding out. "Is Briar done with us?"

She sighed heavily as her arms fell to her side. "You know the answer to that. Fight against it as you may." I nodded at her bleak assessment and walked to the door. "Don't fight against him, child, your connection with him is not something to squander. It will make you into something stronger than this world has seen in ages, if you let it." I almost asked her if she meant Perrin or Briar, but I didn't need to keep playing into her riddles.

"Let it? Do I have a choice?"

"We all have a choice. Though we can't always manage to make it ourselves."

"I... I had a vision. Kind of. It was more of a flash of the past. Everything happened so quickly I kind of forgot it a bit. It was Owjen and Briar. She called me the Impossible Child. She was quite certain that she'd found me, or at the very least that's what I was, am, I don't know. Does that ring any kind of bell for you?"

"Not one you need to worry about now. Keep your head about you. That's the best advice I can give you. Anything else wouldn't much matter right about now anyway. Now hurry and ready yourself. You've got a bit of a journey to get on with yet."

Swinging my cloak around myself, I secured it as I walked outside. There were only three large horses that reminded me of Clydesdales. I'd worked in a stable every summer during high school and still helped out occasionally when they asked. I'd never been able to commit to owning my own horse, but this led to me getting to know several different horses and learning to be able to adapt to their personalities. I was yet to meet a beast I didn't like.

All three of them mounted quickly. Leaving me to either wonder who I was supposed to ride with or choose for myself. After a few minutes of me staring them down Perrin's voice cut through the air. He'd mounted the largest horse, making him look all the more intimidating. "Come, Little Rose, you will ride with me."

I walked over to them. "Agustín, I'm riding with you."

"Really, Frankie? You're going to throw me into this? After everything I've—" I shot him a look he cringed under. "Gah!" he groaned. Agustín offered me his hand and I ignored him, instead using a nearby stump and the saddle to mount this beast of a horse myself. I hoped everyone else was as impressed with me as I was. Agustín whispered back to me, "You're going to get me killed one of these days, you know that?"

"You'll probably never see me again once we part ways. I wouldn't worry about it."

"Oh hon, you should know you can't actually get rid of me that easily."

CHAPTER

TWENTY-FOUR

We rode until dawn, passing through the outer kingdom wall. Sabina had ways to travel in and out of the kingdoms without using the check points. Agustín told me she didn't care for the societal structure, but loved her family. And she knew where she was needed.

We were a few hours outside of the wall as the sky began to lighten. Agustín was leading our group and came to a halt in a small clearing in this forest of oversized trees. "We'll rest here today. Tonight, we'll travel for a while more and then part ways. I believe you two know where you're going from here."

Perrin was scanning the sky as he asked, "How long have we been outside of Heartwood's reach?"

"About a turn or so. We should be safe now, but I suggest you keep traveling by night for the next few days."

I dismounted behind Agustín before anyone could offer any assistance. They tied their horses in a way that allowed them to move about. The snow had stopped, leaving behind frigid temperatures and too much accumulation in the wide open. I wasn't sure how I was going to be able to sleep in this cold. Perrin and Anthea would be fine. They ran hot since they'd transformed. Agustín and I didn't have that advantage.

The siblings were talking together far enough away that we couldn't make out what they were saying. Agustín was shamelessly watching them. "If you don't cuddle with him, you know- for warmth, do you mind if I do?" He winked at me as he teased. "Just on the off chance you decide to stop getting in your own way that is." I rolled my eyes as he shrugged his shoulders, flashing me a grin and another exaggerated wink. "She doesn't seem so bad either," he added.

"She's the one you have to watch out for. By the way, ultio?"

"It's similar to a duel or a grudge. A vengeance of sorts. He won't be coming after me or any of mine because of what I've done to him and his. It's as close to forgiving me as he's likely to get."

I nodded my understanding as I unsaddled his horse. We didn't have any brushes for them, but I patted the beast down by hand. He seemed to appreciate it. I noticed Perrin doing something similar a moment later. "You should talk to him. Whatever you have going on in your head, stop it." Agustín seemed to genuinely care as he scolded me. I think he was involving himself so he didn't have to think about his own situation.

"You don't understand. I'm clearly too damaged. It won't work out well. I'll just end up hurting him because I have no idea how to have a normal, healthy, happy relationship." I'd said this enough to myself, yet it still stung to say it out loud, "I'm not good enough to make someone else happy."

"Happy? Who do you know who's actually *happy*?! Besides,

did it ever occur to you that you need to be involved with someone as fucked up as you are so you can both be actually, genuinely, if not happy... content, joyful, at ease? That maybe you could take away each other's pain, or if nothing else, understand it for one other? See one another? Maybe for you, someone with a significantly different level of pain simply won't be able to matter as much in the relationship. That maybe that sort of inequity wouldn't work."

"You're saying I need to find someone as fucked up as I am?"

"Yes and no. That seems almost impossible at this point." Agustín's tone was so apathetic and matter of course that it'd be cruel if it wasn't so comical.

"Hey!" I laughed as I called him out.

"You know I'm right." He half smiled at me. "But don't stop caring about people because you're afraid. Don't let that darkness become you. You can thrash against it all you want. You can sit there in your void numbness and let it envelop you all you want. But if you *become* that darkness, then there's nothing stopping you from becoming someone else's darkness. Don't do that, Frankie. There's already too much of it. Keep thrashing. Let yourself be okay."

"I'm too tired of the pain. Deep in my bones I'm too tired. And that's all it is anymore."

"There's nothing else?"

I shook my head. "Not enough."

"Well hear me now, little dragon- that man knows pain. And I'm fairly certain he wants to take yours away." He sounded fairly convinced.

Sighing deeply, I untied the horse and walked him over to the small stream we'd passed a little ways back. It had a fast enough flow that it hadn't completely frozen over, but we still needed to be wary. Agustín had called after me to not go too far. As I stood by the stream allowing the steed to drink, I heard Perrin come up behind me. He wasn't trying to be quiet. He looked at me as he held the reins of their horses. Standing a few feet away he nodded at me. A gesture I reciprocated. He wasn't trying to push.

I walked back to where Agustín and Anthea were rationing out some food, the last of the fresh bread and some jerky. I tied the horse back up and took a seat next to them in the area they'd cleared. "Don't you sorcerers have some kind of smokeless fire?"

"We have hot stones." He pulled one out. Just one. A smooth rock with complicated and ingrained ruins. "Unfortunately, I only have the one. Auntie Sabina must have forgotten you don't have the elevated body temperature." As though that woman had ever forgotten a thing in her life... We ended up sharing the stone that day. Anthea and Perrin didn't sleep terribly close to us, but I imagine they could hear what we were saying. I never heard Perrin snoring and wondered if they really didn't sleep while around us. I felt a little tickle in my heart realizing he had actually fallen asleep beside me yesterday.

Whispering, Agustín seemed worried about me, "Are you going to be okay? I know they'll take good care of you. You'll likely get some of your answers."

"I don't want to be taken care of." I was a little curt, but it was how I felt. "I want my life to be mine again. I'm not so unaware of my surroundings that I think for one goddamn minute that that can happen anymore. I'm sure they'll be kind, I have no question about that, but I want more. Is that so wrong of me?"

"No, it's not. I'm sorry any of this has happened to you." He meant it too. I didn't think I'd be able to sleep in broad daylight like that, but the oversized trees offered plenty of shade.

"Why is everything so much bigger here?" I mused, mostly to myself.

∾

I woke up shivering so violently that it must have been my chattering teeth that roused me. I'd turned away from Agustín in my sleep and lost the connection with the heat stone. When I opened my eyes, I could see Perrin a couple of yards away. He was still laying on the ground, but our eyes met, and I wondered if he'd been watching me sleep. I rolled onto my back, looking up through the needley branches. It was midafternoon. We couldn't travel quite yet, but I knew I wouldn't be able to sleep being this cold. I searched for the stone and found Agustín clutching it tightly to his chest. I smiled at the sight; it was like his little teddy bear the way he was holding it. He only had the one and he'd be traveling by himself. He'd have to take it with him. I didn't know where he was going, but I was sure he'd need it.

I sat up to try and get off of the cold ground a bit more. I pulled the cloak around me, futilely trying to get warm. Needing to get my blood flowing, I decided to get up and move around. I was a few yards away from everyone when I realized Perrin had followed me.

"What are you doing?" I called back to him.

"These woods can be dangerous. I want to make sure you stay alive."

"You should be resting."

He didn't respond immediately, considering his words. "Come lay with me then." So much for him not pushing. I let out a cynical snicker and shook my head in frustration as I kept walking between the trees as he called after me. "I mean nothing by that. You are too cold to sleep, yes? Your wizard is hoarding what you were using for heat. Being near me... you will be warmer."

I didn't want to be considering his offer. But I could feel the fatigue in my legs. I decided to change the subject. "I thought it was dragons that hoarded, not wizards."

"Some of us, yes."

I turned to face him, surprised he'd answered me. And that I'd been right. "Do you?"

He looked around a bit uncomfortably. "You do not know, but that is a private matter. We do not ask."

"Is that a yes?!" I laughed lightly watching how uncomfortable he was about whether or not he had a weird collection of gold hidden somewhere.

"Do you?" He asked me, his eyebrows raised seductively.

I shrugged and walked on, looking back at him every once in a while. He kept back a few feet. "I used to collect bird nests when I was little. I had shoeboxes full of them. One of my brothers teased that I'd stolen a bird's home. I thought I'd always been so careful to make sure they were abandoned first. But the idea that I may have stolen safety from something crushed me. I ended up borrowing my mother's sewing kit and spent all day trying to sew all the nests to this old tree in our backyard. It was a dying pine tree that had almost no needles left, even fewer after I'd spent the day climbing and sewing dozens of nests into it. It looked ridiculous. But I felt like I'd made the birds a refuge. A place where they could belong. I was so proud of it." I smiled sadly to myself, remembering that day, and my family.

I no longer heard his steps and looked back to see him standing there, watching me with an expression I couldn't read. He clenched his fists and locked his jaw, and it was gone.

I started walking again. He mumbled something behind me. "I'm sorry. What?" I asked, turning to him.

"Rocks! I said rocks! I hoard rocks!" He was charmingly cute, vulnerable even in his confession, and I couldn't help but excitedly smile.

I tried my best to keep the laughter out of my voice. "Rocks? Like... you see a shiny rock and want to add it to your hoard?" He threw his hands up and started walking back. I scrambled to catch up to him. "I didn't mean anything by it! I'm curious," I said as I grabbed his arm to turn him to face me. I flinched again. He didn't see it as he stood still, and I scooted in front of him. "Tell me?" He folded his arms and looked down at me, clearly uncomfortable. "Please?" His eyes softened and we slowly began walking again, side by side.

"It's not because they're shiny," he said defensively. He was quiet for a while and I nudged him, hoping he'd go on. He looked down at me, and I smiled up at him. He let out another long sigh. "They have been around so much longer than we have. Each with their own place in history, their own journey. How can that not fascinate you? I am reasonable though. They are never so big as a boulder. Well... once." I laughed lightly hearing his happy tone. "And sometimes, yes, damn it! It is because they're shiny! Or rough. Or colorful. Sometimes I find one at a particular place because it reminds me of what I went through there. My story became part of that rock's story. I'm altering its path, becoming part of its ages old story. They have so much more time, worlds' worth even, compared to us, and how does that not stagger the mind? They are so much bigger than us, and we never think of the effect time has on anything but ourselves."

"Aren't you the romantic?!" He stopped and turned towards me. I looked up at him as a million things happened in his eyes all at once. There always seemed to be. He again shook his head and started walking. "What was the last rock you picked up? For your collection, I mean."

He grumbled, "You don't want to know."

"Oh, come on. Tell me." He made another grumbly noise. "Please?" I asked again. It was beginning to feel like this was an actual magic word with him.

"The last rock I picked up was from the day I realized who I wished to claim."

"Ah." I couldn't think of anything to say to that. I didn't want him that way, or at least I shouldn't. But I also didn't want to hear about his love at home waiting for him. Instead, I asked more about the claiming thing Briar had condemned right up until he'd asked if I wanted him to claim me. I'll admit it didn't sound great. "How do you claim someone? Can just anybody claim anybody?"

"You really do not know?"

"Really. I was kept in the dark about basically everything." I wrapped my arms around myself. I was still cold, but I was also ashamed that I hadn't tried harder to find my answers sooner.

"I am sorry." He stopped to look at me straight on. I shrugged and tried to keep walking. It was his turn to take ahold of my arm and gently directed me. "Let me hold you for a moment. Simply to warm you." I eyed him suspiciously, but my chattering teeth convinced me. I nodded and he took a step closer to me. He unfastened his cloak and wrapped me in it as he pulled me to him. He was delightfully warm. I unfolded my arms and laid them on his chest as I rested my head against him. His body stiffened under my touch. He rested his chin on top of my head as he tightened his grip on me. I could hear his heart beating. It was the most reassuring sound in the world. It sounded like him. I'd been close to him before, but this was the first time I really smelled him, his actual scent, not from the dungeon or Sabina's, just *him*. I'd been under some stressors earlier, but I couldn't believe I hadn't realized before. He smelled like the forest, earthy and ancient. It was intoxicating and I inhaled deeply. His body stiffened again as he cleared his throat.

"No one can claim another that does not wish it. Both must desire to be claimed by the other. The connection does not work if both parties are not invested. In my world there is often a public celebration either before or after, but the ceremony is done in private. It can be as intimate as they wish. Some claim one another without any interest in a primal connection, but that is generally a part of the ceremony. You see why it is generally done in private.

"It creates a deeper connection between one another. Even when not physically close it feels as though they are near, as though they are only a room away when they may be across an ocean. It is difficult to fully explain. It is more than a connection. It is a belonging. A place you have in this world. An unbreakable bond. A destiny."

There was that word again. We stood there in silence. I didn't like what being this close to him was doing to my body. But I couldn't manage to pull myself away. He kissed the top of my head as a signal. We both knew we needed to get back. "This way, Little Rose." We stepped away from one another and walked back in silence until I saw Agustín and Anthea.

"Thank you for telling me about your hoard. Your secret is safe with me. I promise not to take it for granite." I was certain he heard me, but he didn't respond, he wouldn't even look at me. I didn't think my joke was *that* bad. Lark would have laughed anyway.

"There you are! We were getting worried," Agustín said as he rolled the heat stone around in his hand.

"I wasn't," Anthea chimed in as she took another bite of a roll, nodding at her brother.

"We should leave soon. Frankie," he said as he held out the stone to me. "Take it. It'll help with... it'll help."

"You keep it. You'll be traveling alone after all." A curt nod, and he quickly pocketed the stone.

We were about to mount the horses when Agustín pulled me aside. "I know what I said before about you not coming with me. But I have some sway where I'm going. It would still be dangerous, but if you really can't stomach the idea of going with them..."

I thought about it for a moment. "It would make things harder for you. I can learn more about what I am if I go with them. I think that's the next step in me being able to take my life back, figuring out what I am, ya know? Thank you, though. You're a good friend, and I will miss you."

He mounted his steed and looked around. Anthea and Perrin were already waiting. Anthea's back was to us, but I could see Perrin had a smile and a glow to him as he spoke with her that made my heart happy. He must have been excited to get closer to his home.

"For what it's worth, I like him for you a lot better than I ever liked Briar. He's open. He has scars, but I think he'd tell you everything you ever wanted to know. I also think he'd let you go, if you asked him to."

"I don't need to know everything about anybody else's scars. I just want people to stop giving me new ones." I plastered on a smile as I said our last private goodbye and then walked up to the other two.

They looked between each other. Perrin asked me, "Would you prefer to ride with one of us, or would you like to ride alone?" His expression and tone were void of any emotion, allowing me my choice unhindered. I thought about riding alone. But I was so cold.

I tried to sound as unaffected as I could, "Riding with you will be fine. How are the horses?"

Apparently I amused him, judging by his tone. "These are stallions from the Narrows! They can handle this cold, us, and more. Come!" He reached out an arm and for some reason unbeknownst to me, I took it. I had ridden behind Agustín, but Perrin pulled me up and placed me in front of him. It was a little awkward. I imagined Anthea rolling her eyes at us, but I didn't actually see her do it. I was preoccupied by Perrin wrapping his arms around me to grab the reins in front of me.

"Ready, wizard?" He was trying to restrain the excitement in his voice. He was not successful.

Agustín took off, and we dragons followed. I was glad Perrin couldn't see my flushed face. It had been years since I'd ridden for any length of time and my muscles were sore. I was grateful for how he held onto me, and for the comfortable pants from Sabina.

Agustín came to a stop at a peculiar tree in the middle of a clearing. "Dragons, here is where I leave you. For my part in all of this awfulness, I am sorry. May the Oracles judge us all. I cannot ask for forgiveness, nor will I. From you or them." They nodded solemnly and he returned the gesture. "Frankie, I'm sure I'll see you soon. Be well. And let yourself be happy. No one else can do that for you. And it's a rare enough thing."

"Goodbye, August. Be safe." He smiled and shook his head at me finally calling him August. He took off at a run, and we watched him go for a few minutes.

Perrin whispered in my ear, "Little Rose, are you sure? Are you ready?"

"Of course," I said, waiting to find out where we were going. We curiously headed southeast, and I had to ask, "I thought your territory was called the western territory?"

"We do not tell them anything they do not need to know. Is there anything you would like to know? I will tell you everything." I wondered if he could feel my racing heart. He didn't need to whisper or get so close to me, but I enjoyed it, nonetheless.

"How much farther until we get there?"

"By sky? No more than a day. It is difficult to say on horseback. The wizard was right. It will be safest to keep to the nights for now. We will ride southeast until we come to the Scissura River, at least two days. Once we pass, we will follow it south until we come to the Narrows. We will take that pass for another day or so before it opens to the Flatlands, a few days there possibly. Cross the Flatlands and our home is at that mountain. A week at the very most to get there." I absentmindedly leaned back against his chest. This was going to be a very long week.

He nuzzled his face into the side of my neck again now that he could reach it. Suddenly I sat up, remembering myself and pulling myself away from him. He straightened his stance, and I was careful not to lean back again. I was still close enough to him that I was warm, warm enough. I didn't need to get burned again.

We rode until we met the sun and found some shelter inside of the tree line we'd been following. Agustín seemed to have left us with most of the food. I hoped he took enough to sustain himself for however long he needed to. I wondered if we had enough to last us a week. "Tomorrow it will be safe for a fire. We will hunt and have fresh meat. Do not try to ration your food so strictly, Little Rose. It is still quite cold, and you need your strength."

"Isn't that risky? To assume you'll be successful at hunting? Shouldn't we, I don't know, gather berries or something?" They looked at one another and laughed lightly. I asked, "Dragon stuff?"

"Dragon stuff," Perrin confirmed for me. "Come now. It has been a long night, and we need our rest. Anthea will take the first watch." At his words she quickly scaled one of the nearby trees, knocking snow off the branches as she went.

"Why didn't you do this yesterday?" I asked as I watched her ascend.

"Neither of us slept yesterday. We had been taken prisoner and tortured. Our precautions were not enough. Now we can rest a little easier, so one of us will keep watch. Come now, Little Rose." He had cleared a small area and laid down, clearly marking the space he'd made for me as he held an arm out. I tried to lay farther away but ended up scooting back against him before I felt warm enough again. I was still a bit cold as I pulled my cloak tighter.

"You are still shivering, Little Rose. May I put an arm around you? Nothing untoward, I promise."

"Promises, promises." He made no movement, nor did he ask again. After a few moments of dreadful silence, I answered, "Yes, please." He placed his arm down my side, dropping it in front of my waist. "Thank you," I whispered, unsure of why I felt the need to.

"Sleep now, Little Rose." And so I did.

THAT DREAM HAPPENED AGAIN. But this time the egg was inside a fire embodied by Perrin's energy, incubating, protected. I felt safely warm, and I suppose that was my real world adding to my dreamworld.

I HADN'T SLEPT that well since Earth. Not anywhere. I woke and Perrin still had his arm around me. He wasn't snoring so I asked, "Did you get any sleep?"

"I did." He moved his arm and laid on his back. I stood up, dusting myself off. I could feel his eyes on me, and I looked up to see Anthea steadily climbing down. "Any news?"

"Lone dragon, around midday. North to south and did not waiver."

"That's good, right? They were searching and went past us. So, we're okay now?"

"One can hope." Anthea looked nervous still. She'd been tortured and had the marks to prove it. I doubted if she'd be comfortable anywhere. "I'd like if we could start moving now though."

"Aren't you going to rest?" She didn't seem to appreciate my concern for her.

"Tomorrow."

We didn't argue and instead ate while we rode. Perrin told me what to expect over the next day or so. "We will reach the river by dawn. It may be difficult to pass given the snowstorm. And more dangerous given this cold."

"What do we do?"

"I will try to find the safest place to cross. But if there are none, we may leave the horses and fly after all. My fear is that they are still scouting. If that is the case they may spot us rather quickly. I cannot imagine him letting you go so easily."

"I've never turned before." He was silent for an uncomfortable moment. I'm not sure what he wanted to discuss, but Briar wasn't high up on that list for me.

"I know. I will try, but I do not know how you would take to being carried as we fly. You could ride on my back. Though Anthea may not care for that."

"Why? Is it forbidden?" I giggled at the idea of it all.

"Very little is forbidden, Little Rose. But it isn't something we do unless it is absolutely necessary. Like looking at another's energy. You can tell how strong someone is from doing so, and that is discouraged without an immense amount of trust."

"Ah, well, let's hope you can find a safe place for us to cross. And I'm sorry for sensing you and your sister's energy before."

He wrapped an arm around me and pulled me back to him. "You saved me. And my sister. Do not be sorry. Besides, most have a general idea once they've seen our true form." He took his arm away from the embrace that was holding me to him, but I didn't move. I liked how he felt against me, and I missed his arm around me. He held the reins in one hand, his other hand rested on his thigh. Against my better judgment and without thinking too much, I reached for his hand and wrapped it back around me. He held his arm where I put it without really holding onto me. Either confused or thinking it over, he hesitated, then all at once grabbed me and brought his head down next to mine again.

My breath caught from the sudden movements. "Little Rose...," His tone seemed despondent, and I expected he'd question my sudden intimacy.

I pressed back against him and put my hand on his thigh. He was close enough I felt more than heard him groan softly. We rode like this for hours until the forest started to thin out. Still mostly dark, all I could hear was rushing water. The river had to be nearby. "We must have made good time," I commented.

"I wanted us to rest before crossing. After the river we can travel during the day." He dismounted and instead of his usual hand to help me, he grabbed me by the waist and tenderly pulled me down, holding me to him. He stared into my eyes as my hands rested on his shoulders.

Anthea was only a few yards away, but it was still fairly dark. I didn't know what she could see. She called to us, "There's something wrong. Can you feel it?" I turned my head in the direction of her voice, getting a sense for the place. She was right.

Perrin cupped the side of my face in his hand and softly turned me back to look at him. He was staring at me as he said loud enough for Anthea to hear, "There is something wrong, we can feel it too, but do not yet know what." Then he whispered to me, "Whatever it is, it is not *this*." I knew what he meant, and I knew he was right.

"I am sorry. But I do not think a fire is a good idea. You were right, Little Rose. Your instincts may be better than we thought. I am sorry for not listening." I rested my forehead against his chest, and he kissed the top of my head as he held me tightly. "Anthea, try to get some rest. We'll keep watch for a few hours."

"Watch of what though," Anthea grumbled. Perrin laughed silently into my hair, his chest rumbling against me. He held my hand and led me further to the edge of the forest. We'd traveled far enough there was no more snow on the ground. Though I had to imagine that was likely what had stirred the river up. The moon would be full in a couple of nights, and the area was well lit once we got out from underneath the thick forest canopy.

He suddenly spun to face me. Holding my hand he stared pensively at me. "Why haven't you asked why I call you Little Rose?"

I was startled by his movements and question. "Well, I don't know. I'm sure you have some reason."

"Possibly I saw something?" He looked at me nervously, I could feel myself blushing again.

"Perrin!" I wasn't really sure what else to say. Admittedly I'd wondered, I just couldn't fathom how.

"The day you saved Thea's life, the first time. I promise I was just trying to protect you. Your dress was a bit low. It...

caught my attention. A quick peek, I was curious about the markings, that was all it was, I swear it! I wasn't sure how to tell you."

He was so nervous it was adorable. I wanted to thank him for being honest with me. I *wanted* to do a lot more than just thank him for being the first truly real thing I'd experienced since being here.

"I like it. How it sounds, I mean. When you say it."

He breathily whispered his name for me then, knowing full well what he was doing.

"Rose..."

I found myself holding my breath again as he brought his other hand up to my face. "Rose, may I—" I reached up and pulled him down into a kiss with the ravenous hunger we'd both been denying. My hands stayed in his hair as he put an arm behind my back, pulling me into him. The familiar fire from before erupted. The sensation seismic and still surreal. I matched his zeal and my back quickly ended up against one of the giant trees.

He broke the kiss, leaving me breathless as he pressed his forehead against mine. "We are not doing a great job of keeping watch. Our timing is less than ideal."

"We'll be at your Mountain soon. I'm not sure what all that entails, but—" He kissed me again, his body molding to mine as he pressed against me into the tree.

He trailed kisses down my neck, a small moan escaping me as his hands wandered desperately over my body underneath my cloak. "I want to show you everything," he whispered onto my skin.

We spent the next couple of hours keeping watch, walking around, telling one another about our lives and worlds, stopping every so often to refuel the fire that was igniting between us until we'd inevitably come back to our senses. I was curious about our blaze, certain it was dragon stuff. I knew I didn't need to worry about feeling foolish asking Perrin questions. For the first time that I could remember, I felt as though I could truly trust someone. "Will you tell me about that building sensation? When we kiss, what is that?!"

"I have no idea." He was holding my hand and looked over at me, smiling. "I hoped you knew."

"It's not just normal dragon stuff?" I stopped, finding it hard to believe him.

"Not that I've ever heard of before. Or experienced. But we have cultural experts back home. We'll have them look into it when we return. I can't wait to show you their library." He was so animated as he spoke of his home. His eyes lit up differently, and he had this kind of wonderment about him. I suddenly had this need to kiss him again. I reached my hands up to him and gently pulled him down to me. He pulled me to him at the same time and I could almost forget the rest of the world. Almost.

The sense of impending disaster had become nearly palpable. But still nothing came of it. As the sun rose, we circled back to a seemingly rested Anthea. "Wait here with her. I need to scout the river," Perrin commanded the queen. I didn't want him to leave. Something was certainly off. "Anthea, be on guard." He kissed me again. "Little Rose, I will be back shortly. Stay alert." I could see the gold in his eyes as he pulled away.

Anthea stood beside me as we watched him ride out. "Something is wrong," I mused. "Maybe the river is too high. Can you hear it? It shouldn't be this loud so far away." Anthea nodded at me, knowing I was right. She went to saddle her horse so we could ride out to him and find a different plan. I couldn't wait. Something in me willed me toward the river, towards him. I started walking and quickly began running all out. Tears had begun to fall. I didn't know what was coming, but I was terrified like I'd never been before. I could feel it in my blood, and I would have given anything for one of those visions.

Perrin was pacing his steed up and down the riverbank. He turned to come back to us and saw me. He paused for a moment, surprised, before lurching his horse into a dead run towards me. I stopped, wondering why he was running his horse so hard. With the water so loud I couldn't hear anything else. I felt the air behind me move and turned.

CHAPTER

TWENTY-FIVE

Steam from its moist exhale hit me right in the face as I turned. Antlers loomed as I stared up into familiar golden-brown eyes. It sniffed at the air between us and barked, a loud, high-pitched sound. I jumped at the noise, as I had done months ago. The gigantic elk walked past me as Perrin rushed to my side. I watched it walk by while Perrin lunged himself between me and the great beast. It looked at him squarely, sizing him up, before continuing its procession.

I knew this elk. That deep red coat. The way it eyed me. "Perrin, I know this elk. It's from home. My home!" He looked at me worriedly from over his shoulder.

"My Rose, that is a dragon cursed..." The elk looked back at him as he said this, casually letting out a small bark. "Do you know who it is?"

"I didn't even know dragons existed until I saw Briar change." I had an idea of who it might be, a feeling, but all that would have to wait.

The elk-dragon continued towards the water. The already risen sun gleamed off of the swollen and swiftly rushing river.

Perrin and I mounted his horse as Anthea came up behind us. "I told you to be on guard! And you leave her alone?!" He was furious, and she couldn't bring herself to meet his gaze. I was curious how she'd gotten to be queen with such a submissive streak. She wouldn't even look at him. But at the end of the day they were siblings after all.

"Perrin, that isn't helping." I saw Anthea flinch at me defending her. I wasn't trying to. We simply had other priorities. "Look!" I pointed at the elk-dragon as it waited on the bank of the river. "It's watching us." I took the reins from Perrin and headed towards it.

"Be careful, my Rose. Too many unknowns."

"It's here to help. It tried to warn me before, but I had no idea what was happening back then. Jen knew who it was, Briar probably does too. There's more to it, but I don't know what."

"I trust you, my Rose." I wanted to kiss him, but we needed to get to the riverbank. The elk-dragon was still there, waiting, but I didn't know for how long. I lurched our horse into an all-out run, stopping abruptly short with Anthea right behind us. The elk-dragon stepped into the river.

"What is it doing?" I asked mostly to myself. Our horse began pacing back and forth nervously. The river was high, but it was only coming up a few inches on the elk-dragon. "Perrin, could it be making it look shallow where it's not?"

"I would never say such a thing was impossible. But it is not likely."

"You said you trust me, right?"

"With my life."

I turned to look at him. He was serious. I placed a hand on the side of his face and kissed him with everything I had. Turning back around, we followed the elk-dragon at his glacial pace across the fast-moving water. It wasn't magic or any kind of trick. There was a physical, albeit narrow path. One we would have never found had this elk-dragon not shown us the way. How he knew where it was, I can't say.

When we'd safely passed, the elk-dragon looked back at us and barked one last time before dashing into the woods up stream. We were headed down, but for all the world I wanted to go after him. Perrin could already read me, not that this one was particularly difficult. "Shall we follow?" he asked.

"If they wanted me to know who they are, I would. I will, when it's time." Perrin grabbed me around the waist reassuringly and kissed the side of my head. I never thought I could fall for someone so quickly, not this hard anyway. I wasn't even sure if that was what was happening, but I knew I would die before I'd let Briar hurt him again.

We followed along the river at a distance as Perrin continued to tell me all about his territory. Most of it seemed fairly unbelievable. The library, the markets, the courtyard where heated philosophical discussions took place, the public gardens. It sounded like paradise. But so had Heartwood. I wasn't sure if he was trying to impress me. He didn't need to; I'd go anywhere with him.

Around noon we stopped to rest. It was unusually warm, and I could feel my nervous system relaxing the farther we traveled. Perrin and I hadn't slept in almost 48 hours, and I was exhausted. There were some boulders along the river, and Anthea climbed up on one to lookout and sunbathe. Perrin and I were down a ways from the boulders, resting in the dappled sunlight as it filtered through some nearby branches.

My back was against a tree, again.

We should have been paying more attention. We should have been more guarded. There was some kind of ethereal connection between the two of us. Neither of us knew what it was, we didn't need to. Every time we closed our eyes, we could sense it. Every time he touched my body, I could feel this... inevitability. I could taste the sense of belonging I'd been so desperate for with him.

There was a bend in the river up ahead. That sense of danger that had been so thick had never really disappeared. Crossing the river had given us a false sense of hope. We heard it before we knew what was coming. The water in the river began rippling violently in the wrong direction. Perrin yelled for his sister. She had already started descending from the boulder when we saw them.

Half a dozen dragons came soaring up from the bend, countless more followed in the distance. I recognized the one in the lead- Briar. Perrin knew it was him, too. Before I had time to realize that I didn't know what to do, it was too late. The dragons were landing in front of us, paying no mind as Anthea ran up to join us. Perrin and I stood side by side, hand in hand, waiting for the inevitable.

Briar landed and in a moment had transformed back into a human. The sounds still made me cringe despite my fear and adrenaline. Before he could say anything, I saw how this was all going to play out. Literally. Another vision- multiple visions. They all played out before me, but it was different this time. I had a choice to make, and I was seeing snippets of my options. Only one was acceptable. It wasn't what I wanted, but that's how life goes sometimes.

I don't know how I saw them, these paths and their journeys. It was similar to watching my energy going into my plants. There was a tapestry. But this was more like watching an invisible hand embroidering, sped up to an unimaginable speed and seeing multiple designs being placed simultaneously using the same material. I could see each one, see the consequences of different strands, different words, actions, decisions. But I could only see so far. I had to trust that I really was going in the direction I wanted.

While Briar was changing, I had picked up a small red stone near my foot. Dust on the outside crumbled away to reveal an earthy red rock underneath. I continued to wipe off the dust that had accumulated on the rock as I spoke quietly to Perrin. "Don't argue, just listen. We don't have much time. I need to go now." I could feel his body tense beside me, but he said nothing as his eyes darted back and forth between me and the one he knew would take me from him. "I'm not sure for how long, but it's the only way. I will be fine. I need you to be fine as well. So you need to listen and do as I say. I know it will hurt, but it's what needs to happen. You said you trust me. Trust me now, and we'll see each other again."

"My Rose, now is not the time for riddles," his tone and his eyes pleaded with me.

Briar had started walking towards us. He opened his mouth to speak, and I cut him off, taking a few steps to place myself between the two commanders. "Briar, I will go with you and be yours. It will be like it was before, as much as it can be. I will live with you, and we'll spend every second we can together. But you *need* to promise me you will leave these two alone. I will know if you lie to me, and you know it. You need to leave them be. Everyone needs to leave them be. No one is to follow them. I will go with you now, and together neither of us will look back. We'll claim one another, if that's what you want."

"Frankie... that's all I've ever wanted." He had a sickly-sweet grin plastered on his face. It nauseated me, and I had to steal myself to hide how I felt. "And they've served their purpose," he said with a shrug.

"Give me five minutes to say goodbye. That's all I ask."

"You have until my dragon is back. Every minute after that

and I remove one of his limbs. I didn't get the chance to do anything permanent before. I won't hesitate now." There was no bravado or pride in his voice. I didn't know what to make of it. My face paled as I heard a deathly growl from Perrin behind me.

I nodded to Briar as he quickly began the process. "Perrin," I handed him the stone I'd been caressing, holding his hand as I explained, "this rock is from a very special moment in my life." He had tears streaming down his face and he was shaking his head, whispering *no* over and over again, begging me not to do this, to not go. I tried getting my words out as quickly as possible, despite the lump in my throat. There wasn't any time to explain. I had to hold my own tears back if this was going to work. Never again would I doubt Briar's savagery. He wasn't an idiot. I'd be under lock and key for who knew how long. After all, it was me he was after, not these two. "I was holding this rock the moment I decided who I wanted to claim. It's only right that you should have it." I handed him the rock, and he saw the dust I'd been removing. He understood. I'd never seen such a heartbroken smile.

He fumbled with his pack, taking out a delicate blue pebble. "You asked about this once, My Rose. This rock is from the moment I decided who I wanted to claim. I have had it since Madam Sabina's. It was not an easy thing to find under all that damned snow. It is only right that you should have it. Until the two can be together again." I covered my mouth to muffle a sob.

He took my rock, and I took his. I turned to Anthea. "Take care of him. Do not let him follow. Both of you, *go home*."

"Come now, Frankie. I've been more than generous." His gravelly dragon voice flowed through me like ice in my veins, freezing me, destroying me.

Dragon Briar knelt down on a front leg, waiting for me. I

climbed on, his rough scales catching at my clothes as I settled in, clutching my pebble. I was grateful he couldn't see my face. Perrin fell away as we took off. In his fury he raged and roared helplessly at the universe. I felt his despair wash over me as it shook our world.

~

They had set up camp a few hours west of the river. Dozens of dragons flew behind us. Once we landed and I dismounted they all transformed back into their human forms. The cacophony of bones crunching would have bothered me had my mind not been entirely elsewhere.

Briar said nothing as he stalked towards a cluster of tents. I followed, not knowing what was expected of me. Without looking he held the flap open to one of these oversized tents, and I obediently walked in. Inside was simple, practical. There was a large cot all made up, a small table nearby with two chairs around it, and a table on the other side with maps spread out over it. I wondered if he knew this was how it was all going to play out.

He dressed in his uniform in silence, still yet to look at me. When he finished, he sat down in one of the chairs at the small table. Running his hands over his face and through his hair roughly, he let out a haunted sigh. He motioned irritably for me to sit somewhere, anywhere. I was standing beside the makeshift bed and so I simply sat down there.

We sat in silence until a call from the tent flap pervaded the deafening stillness. "Come in," Briar grumbled. A shapely woman walked in carrying a tray of food and a pitcher of something. She placed it on the table and asked Briar if he'd be needing any other services from her. Clearly trying to insinuate that this had been routine. Briar casually told her, "That will be all. Don't come back in an hour asking again." I couldn't see her face, but I imagine it fell flat. She bowed her head slightly to him then turned to leave, sneering at me as she did.

"You must be starving. Eat. It's not poisoned. She isn't dumb enough to do that." I smiled at his gesture. I was here to play a part, so play a part I would. "Don't, Frankie, just *fucking* don't."

"How should I behave then?" I asked as innocently as I could manage without coming off as patronizing.

"Don't pretend. Not with me. Yell at me! Hate me! *React* to me! Honestly." He stood as he pleaded and screamed, beseeching for some truth. Words escaped me as his eyes bore into me. "Slap me again until your hand breaks if you wish, just please, don't pretend with me!"

His eyes were bloodshot, I'd never seen him so ragged. "When was the last time you slept?"

"How long have you been gone?"

"You need to—"

"Once I realized... my every thought has been about getting you back. Saving you."

"I didn't need... Briar, you nearly killed me with that arm bullshit!" I motioned to my scarred arm and his eyes followed. "Don't give me that crap about saving me. Now answer honestly, why were you torturing them?"

He looked me dead in the eyes and came over to me. He knelt down in front of me and sheepishly put his hands on the outsides of my hips. I desperately wanted him away from me, but I knew why I was here. "Frankie, that glyph was *never* meant for you. I'm begging you to believe me." He took a moment, looking at my arm again. He clearly wanted to ask, to know, but I was grateful when he looked away. I wasn't going to give him any information he didn't already have.

"I believe you never meant to hurt me like that." He looked back at me then. The necessary seed of hope clearly planted.

"You've spent enough time with *him*. What did *he* tell you?" He couldn't keep the vitriol off his tongue and try as I might, I flinched at his words.

"You required renumeration. A heart."

He nodded slowly. "A small price to pay when you consider they've been able to keep their hands clean up until now."

"A heart, Briar? A life?!"

"They had a choice. They had years to deliver and still they came up short. One life. When I think of all that I've... we've had to take." His thought trailed off. I wasn't sure where his anger wanted to go.

"You got your heart from them. Why keep them? Why torture them like that? Briar, that was beyond cruel, and I don't know that I'll ever be able to understand it."

He looked up at me with his own particular kind of sadness. As much of a monster as he was, I wanted for all the world to wash it away for him. "You're absolutely right. I don't understand it, either. All I can tell you is that certain events needed to be... triggered. We are the guardians of magic. It falls to us to keep these things in line. As commander of one of the most powerful Dragon Houses, it especially falls to me. If I could have had it any other way, I would have. It was nothing personal. I may not agree with them or their ways, but I'd never wish *that* on them." I actually believed him. Then in an instant his icy demeanor returned. "At least I wouldn't have. But then they took you."

"They didn't take me! If anything, I took them. I helped them. Well, we helped each other escape."

"How?" His eyes narrowed, searching my face. I knew what he wanted, and we both knew he wasn't going to get it. I glared at him, my refusal not needing to be voiced.

He moved some loose curls of hair out of my face. I flinched at his touch and an anger and sadness flared behind his eyes. "I cannot forgive myself for hurting you. For showing you that side of me. You need to understand- that side of me has to exist, in order to protect us. That's my role, my duty. Do you understand? It needs to exist so I can do my job and protect our Kingdom, protect you."

"Briar! You were killing those two, and you did kill their companion. But you're apologizing for... shoving me?!" I stood in disgust and moved to the other side of the tent. "How can you live with yourself? With hurting your own people?"

"*They* are not my people. *You* are. And I'd do that and many more untold evils to keep you safe. Speaking of- this conversation stays between us entirely. Helen doesn't want you to know more than you need to. Not until you prove your loyalty. Given everything that's happened I feel it's only fair for you to know. There are things you're involved in that you know nothing of. I should have told you sooner. I... I don't know how to act around you! I don't know how to *think* around you! I barely remember to breathe when I'm around you!"

I know he meant it to come off as romantic. A part of me felt that. But mostly I felt suffocated. I'd been lied to so many times, and here I was again, being held prisoner, again. About to have another world of secrets dropped on me.

"I told you before our gods have a much more physical presence than yours. Ours test us, much like yours used to. There is a prophecy that is soon to pass. An Impossible Child would have changed our world. Either drained it of its magic or infused it tenfold. The inner kingdoms chose to nullify the prophecy. Those in the Wilds don't believe such a thing is possible and kept their claws clean. Our work will benefit them all, so we required renumeration. Sometimes the world is dark, Frankie."

"How... how do you nullify a prophecy? That seems impractical at best."

"You trigger the starting events, then cut it off at its head, so to speak. On the rare occasion that doesn't work, other events need to be initiated to ensure its completion, and then to guide it."

"I take it you're not just talking about cutting the heads off of livestock or frogs or something." He wouldn't look at me.

"It's done now, Frankie."

"Are you sure?" He nodded grimly and I sat back down on the bed. I didn't have the energy for any more questions just then.

"It's a fair bargain. Freedom, prosperity, liberty, equity. These are nearly impossible ideals concurrently. But not when you have people like me around." I had my arms wrapped around myself, staring at the floor. "You should eat. You look weak." There wasn't any care in his voice. The void of emotion felt wrong.

"There's something else. I *saw* something. Owjen gave me up to you, didn't she?"

"If you have a question, ask it, Frankie."

"Am I the Impossible Child?"

He froze. My bluntness throwing him somewhat. I could see him searching for a way out or around. Anything but the truth. I could practically feel the lie spewing forth now.

"You are *an* Impossible Child." I was stunned. "And no, I can't tell you anymore. Not out here. Not yet." I knew he was telling me the truth. I was some part of this prophecy of theirs, and somehow I'd managed to keep my head. Sabina knew more. Briar would never tell me what I wanted to know until it was too late.

We sat in silence as I considered everything. At one point I wondered if Perrin would be rash enough to try to save me. I'd told Anthea to stop him from following, but could she? I made Briar swear to me again that he wasn't going to hurt them. He promised and I knew he meant it, for now. He wanted to gain my trust back, he wasn't fool enough to risk that right away. I didn't want to think about what he would do when he thought he could.

"Why have a camp like this? It seems a bit much."

"We have work to do out here. It won't take long," he said flatly.

"What work? What's out here?" my voice began to rise despite myself.

"Frankie, you are my priority. But I am still Heartwood's commander. I need to ensure its safety."

"Briar, what are you doing?"

He came over to me and put his arms around me as I stood motionless, my own arms still wrapped around myself. He kissed my cheek and rested his head against mine. "Get some sleep. I have work to do."

Before I could say anything he'd left the tent. I tried following, but he'd stationed guards outside. I yelled after him, but my cries fell on callous ears. Nothing was going to happen right now. But I needed to know what he was planning. I wasn't sure how these visions worked, but I had to try and see more. I'd be using my energy soon enough, one way or another. I was going to need more strength than I had, but I would try. Better to try and fail than simply watch the destruction.

I spent the day meditating, contemplating, worrying. Around nightfall I asked the guards how much longer Briar would be before coming to bed. My wording amused them, but they didn't have an answer for me. I asked them to tell him I was waiting up. He wouldn't come right away, and he'd know I was still acting the part, painfully obvious as it was. But I also knew he'd be tempted. Time enough to prepare, to kill the rest of my conscience, to become my own monster. I meditated, trying to reach out as far as I could, trying to *see* as far as I could.

I was surprised by what I could sense. I had a suspicion it had to do with that pivotal event, that moment in time by the river when I could vividly see paths strewn out in front of me, and I chose. So often in life when we make our biggest choices, just after the decision is made, we're given an invaluable amount of clarity. Mine had been literal.

Now I could sense the entire encampment. Four other tents besides the one I was in, surrounding this one equidistantly. He either wanted to make sure I didn't get out, or someone else didn't get in. The tent behind me was being used for their meeting. I couldn't hear or really see; I could just *feel* their bodies, their energies moving around. Briar was in there with three other dragons. There were two guards in front of me. Half a dozen on either side of me, and a dozen or so in the long tent in front of me. Even more were actively circling the encampment. A gratuitous number of Heartwood's army was here. Why would he bring this many for a rescue mission? Even if he planned on attacking Perrin and Anthea, this was overkill.

I let out a breath, opening my eyes. I knew damn well what he was planning. I had needed to confirm it though, for my own sake. This level of force told me what I needed to know. I asked the guards again where he was. They were annoyed, but that would help. I then asked for some more water so I could wash up.

The same woman from before delivered the water, thoroughly annoyed as she was. She hadn't bothered to warm it of course. It didn't matter. I undressed and washed up as best I could and crawled into the cot naked, careful to leave my clothes laying on the chair in plain sight. It wasn't a nice, warm bed, but it was better than the ground. Not the ground with

Perrin, but it eased my tired muscles, and somehow I managed a sort of nervous sleep.

I DREAMT of Perrin's energy, enveloping my own in a way that allowed me to let go of the weight of this world. An unfamiliar voice pulled me away from him. A wave of nostalgic energy arose for this voice I didn't recognize. It was familial, yet other-worldly, embodied as one. It warned me to choose my path wisely, that extremes were unwise. I told the voice to fuck off. That the dark can be extinguished, it had to be. The world may be gray, and it may be exhausting, but we do not have to tolerate the unknowns. I didn't know what I was saying, but some part of me felt it knew.

BRIAR'S TOUCH on my bare shoulder woke me. I'd slept facing away from the tent flap, he didn't see the flash of fear I knew had crossed my face. Steeling myself, I turned towards him. Holding the blanket up to my chest, I tried to hide my new scars and produced a soft smile on my face. "You're back," I feigned a sleepy voice. "I tried waiting up for you, but you were gone so long…"

"What are you doing?" His voice was pained. "We talked about this."

"What do you mean?" I was waking up slightly, my plans were sobering.

"I saw how you two looked at each other. You know I want you. But I don't need… I don't want you to pretend. You know how patient I can be, when it comes to you."

"I do." I looked down soberly. "And you know how practical I can be. I want to get past this. And I don't want to do it alone." I looked up to see a melancholy face. "I shouldn't have

TWENTY-SIX

His body went limp underneath me. All of his energy was within me now, demanding to be dealt with. I couldn't linger as I screamed into the dark, other-worldly void that was once home to the bright, warm energy of my Briar. Only an eternal echo of my own selfish pain accompanied me, at first.

Then it became more. My screams echoing back to me became words in their own, novel voice. Ominous and darkly ethereal. I knew this voice. It was mine, and that of hundreds before that had likewise ventured into the dark. A multitude of voices speaking, existing, in harmony.

I screamed at it, into it. *"What have you done?!"*

"We are Destined. We are Fate. We are the threads of time that will not be broken."

"He was part of something that... that can't happen," I sobbed into the darkness, foolishly trying to defend my actions.

The voices continued speaking as one, **"We will show you, Lost One. A decision must be made."**

"I know what I am. I decide! I choose! Now show me! Show me how to keep them safe!"

I felt myself, my energy, being pushed out of this void. I finally understood. I understood, but I wasn't done with them yet. I needed more. I knew we were in a sacred space. That even they couldn't linger long in this abyss shared by death and life alike. I kept pushing, trying to stay in that void, trying to hear, to question, to understand. I began to feel myself being pulled in, and I knew I'd stayed too long.

The rest of what I needed would come to me later. Signs from the universe, from these fated destinies, are not missed. They pester you until you acknowledge them. I'd just have to wait and think of the sacrifices I'd chosen for other people, and for Briar.

He once said he knew I loved him. I'm afraid he was right. But I couldn't let him keep killing. Something had happened when I killed Briar. I had acknowledged my tie to this world, to him, and to Perrin as well. Now I could feel a connection to all the dragons of this world, to *my* dragons. Briar had been killing them. Too many of them to make any sense. Someone, or something else was at play. Knowing I was right didn't help. I wish I could have been the light that put out his darkness. But we can't save everyone.

I moved over to the other side of the cot, eyes still forced shut and strangled my sobs as they rose and fell like ocean waves. Not long ago I'd break for chipmunks and possums. Now I'd killed a man I loved for a world of dragons I didn't even know.

That wasn't entirely true. Even if it'd only save Perrin, I wouldn't have changed a thing.

I was fighting the urge to throw up as I kept sobbing. I'd increased my capacity for energy greatly, but there was still too much from Briar inside me. I put my hands on the earth and let it work its way out. It started as small shoots from the worn ground, carefully staying just inside the tent, and quickly they escalated. They kept growing. Beginning to flower and weave around one another, everything fighting for space as I worked to force it all to stay within these confines. By the time I opened my eyes I'd made a flourishing Eden inside this tent of death.

I am no saint. I have no right to decide, to pick and choose. I have no excuse, nor will I imagine any. I will protect what needs to be protected. I will safeguard this world. And I will save my dragons. Even if it's from themselves.

I dressed and then arranged Briar's body. I strapped his armor back on him, folding his arms over his chest. That's when I felt it in his pocket. That fridge magnet from the little pizza place. I desperately wanted to take it, but it wasn't right. It belonged to him, and with him it would stay.

Finally, I looked at him, *really* looked at him. His heat had gone with his life, and it began to truly tear me apart. Hands shaking I lowered his eyelids, kissed his already cold lips, and covered the rest of him in a blanket of greens.

Sitting on the ground I meditated to get a feel for who was around and where, when I noticed a bag under the cot, underneath Briar, and now jumbled by my plants. I pulled it out and began going through its contents. The book Briar had given me was in there, the one from Helen's library. As well as the files from Owjen. I wasn't sure about those, but I knew I was taking the book. It would be my own little memento from all of this, from him.

A loose sheet grabbed my attention. The handwriting seemed familiar, the content cryptic.

Every dragon has a source of energy. Within that source is the dragon's heart. We may transform and look in every way human. This does not make us human. In human form, our dragon's heart is imperceptible to all, with the exception being our own kind. Searching another's energy is an intimate act. It makes one vulnerable. We are only vulnerable in that seeing another's energy tells us of their true strength.

Sorcerers have a similar energy. Similar, but very distinct in two ways.

One - we cannot see their energies, and as a result, a dragon may not be able to decipher between human and sorcerer.

Two — dragons can only give and push our own energy, whereas sorcerers can rearrange, take, and pull energy from all around them. We can't touch each other's energies, only that of our own kind. Dragons and sorcerers do not mix for more reasons than anyone can tell, or knows.

Both are power hungry, vain, and while our lifespans can be far greater than humans, we are very much mortal. We often feel the need to outlive ourselves. Offspring between the two is practically unheard of. When it has happened, they rarely have control over their energy and end up being abandoned, or worse... by one side or the other. Though it is often best to not deal in absolutes.

It was beyond timely, nearing the uncanny. But its significance would have to wait.

Again meditating to get a sense of who was around, I could see them all vividly, too vividly. Something had happened to me when I killed Briar. I'd chosen a path when the voice demanded it, and there was no going back now. I could sense everyone in the encampment. Perrin's army wasn't far off now. I could have kept going through this world. My connection to it now on a far deeper level. I was its newest guardian, after all. I wanted to keep going, to explore, but there were things that needed my attention.

Briar's dragons were all still milling around, completely unaware of the shift that had just happened in our world. I wrapped myself in the Medela's cloak, keeping the hood down as I walked out. They'd done nothing to keep Briar from finding us, well, me. He'd never meant me any harm after all. The two guards from earlier were gone, likely dismissed when Briar arrived. Only a few guards stood in my direct path as I walked away.

They were hostile, but I'd heard something unexpected in Briar's void. I now knew what I was. I now knew the biggest secret he and Helen and Owjen had kept from me. I also knew things they didn't. My heart felt as though it had been ripped apart thinking of what could have been... if he had only been honest with me. But now wasn't the time to fall apart again. Now was the time to tear the world asunder so it could be reborn.

A gruff voice followed after me, "Where are you going? Get the commander! His bitch is walking away on him again. Must have passed out after having his fun." They laughed amongst themselves as two of them grabbed me.

The voice that came from me was mine from the void. Mine, but an octave lower and eons older, *"GET HIS SECOND."* The few guards closest to me, the ones that actually had a hold of my body, released me as though they'd been burned and ran for Briar's second. There were a few guards further away that began to approach me. Some knelt, recognizing what I was. I made no attempt to move, and they kept their distance.

I closed my eyes to reach out. Perrin was returning with his army. Its size dwarfed Heartwood's. Briar's plan to decimate them all, save Perrin and Anthea, was foolhardy at best. I called to Perrin in that voice, a voice I didn't yet understand or know. He was closer than I thought and understood immediately. I could only see his energy, but that's all I needed. I could see everyone's energy now, even as they stood beside me. It was like a layer illuminated underneath them.

Every dragon heard it at the same time, regardless of where they were stationed. I wondered how high Perrin had gone to avoid being detected. The roar from directly above us continued to crescendo. In their panic the guards began to transform. All around me I could hear the ripping of cloth and crackling of bone. It no longer bothered me. I'd been hearing that sound since our world began. I stood still. Still looking up. Waiting as the winds blew through me.

Perrin's was the only roar I heard. He landed in front of me effortlessly, the ground around us shaking at the impact. In my periphery I was aware of dozens upon dozens of dragons following his lead, flying through the dark for the night. I could feel each one land in a flurry of wings and scales and snarls as I began to be surrounded by more and more of my dragons. My mind was elsewhere, but I was aware of the variations in size and color and the intent within each one of them, on both sides.

In Perrin's dragon form, a majestic, primordially green beast, he bowed to me. I walked up to him and leaned over to embrace his sleek and powerful head. He slowly rose and I leaned into his chest. He had his intuition, his suspicions about what I was. But it wasn't until he heard my voice moments ago that he knew. I was grateful to have him with me.

His dragon voice was frightening, fiercer than any I'd heard. There was an anger behind his that would have made my skin crawl if it wasn't on my behalf. Now I didn't feel anything. I didn't even register what he was saying. I only knew he was taking over and cleaning up. None of the dragons from either side moved. They all stood motionless, poised to attack. Briar's second was one of the few still not in his dragon form. He began to approach and froze when Perrin growled at him.

I turned to address him but couldn't be bothered to look at him. Instead I stared blankly past him, as he'd always done. I'd met him a handful of times. Briar trusted him, and that was it. He hated the man, but knew he could get the job done, whatever it was.

I knew how this was going to play out, but it was only right to give him his choices. "Take your army and go. No harm will come to any of you tonight, but you must leave now. Your commander is dead. You are pathetically outnumbered and outmaneuvered. Leave now and survive."

He said nothing as he inched closer to me. I could feel Perrin's growl growing in his throat next to me. Briar's second stopped when he was close enough that I'd hear him whisper, "What did you do? Did you tell him you loved him? Or did you get his guard down a different way? Did you kill him while his cock was still—"

It was the noise that made me flinch more than anything. Certainly the sounds of bones being snapped and crunched played their part, but it was the ripping of the flesh that stuck out to me. The familiar sickly-sweet smell of iron filled the air as Briar's second fell to the ground without his head. I saw blood pouring out of Perrin's jaws, and I hoped he'd spat it out. Silly thought to have, but still, I had it.

It was over in minutes. Perrin's army outnumbered them five to one. The dragons that hadn't transformed were left alive. They weren't fighters. They'd been brought along to do the menial tasks and bore no threat. Dragons, yes, but they were either too weak or too afraid to transform. There were a handful from his army that had bowed to me and remained still during the slaughter. They were left alive as well. Hopefully the right message would be conveyed back to their queen. And all of Visnatura.

Perrin's dragons cycled throughout the encampment as though they were looking for something. I was so tired. So numb. I rested against Perrin and put my hands up on either side of his colossal dragon head. He let me hold him there, outside of time. He wrapped himself around me, protecting me from our world. Time has a peculiar way of altering itself when you'd give anything to exist outside of it. Sometimes it makes allowances for you, for a while.

When my mind came back around, the world was beginning to brighten with the sun. I allowed myself a moment to look at Perrin. He was mesmerizing. Almost twice my height, scales that reminded me of ancient ferns. Kind eyes. I nodded, and he tenderly picked me up. A moment later we were in the sky. Barely off the ground before I saw hundreds of other dragons a few miles away take flight, speckling the morning sky. They were the rest of Perrin's army. He must have flown like a madman to have reached his kingdom and returned so quickly. It felt dangerous to have called on so many for me, but I would have done the same for him. As I relaxed into his embrace, I began to worry about the danger that I might be to him. Looking up at him, this unease was short-lived. I need not fear who I was, as long as I knew who that was.

CHAPTER

TWENTY-SEVEN

The sun was setting over their Mountain as we arrived. Cunab, a hidden city, one you would easily pass over it, completely unaware of it as it lay nestled amongst the mountains in a forest older than spiders. A monumental mountain range with the three highest peaks staggered off of one another, each blanketed in trees larger than sequoias. In between these peaks their city structures replicated the jagged natural shapes and layout of the surrounding mountains. If you weren't landing on it, you would think the city itself was simply another peak.

For what little part of the trip that I was cognizant, I'd merely laid in his arms watching him. I had felt Perrin relax when the city came into view, prompting me to take in the sight as well. Looking back at him, I couldn't take my eyes away. He was effortlessly regal as he regarded his home with a pride and belonging I could only envy.

He flew to the top of one of the towers and landed. Gently putting me down he held an arm out, telling a waiting attendant with a blanket to stay back. No longer wrapped in Perrin's arms, I was freezing. I couldn't understand why he had him stay back. They all had every right to be pissed at me, but I can't imagine they'd do anything about it with him right there. Still, for any of them to have put this kind of forethought into this moment- to be ready and waiting, as if my arrival was a given.

There were several other attendants of all ages holding armfuls of long robes and trying very hard to not stare at Perrin and me. I watched several of the dragons land mid-transformation. I couldn't imagine that. The sounds they made when they transformed, the pain they must go through, and to take a landing in the midst of that was, in a word, remarkable.

They'd transform and grab a robe before heading to a stair-well, laughing and talking with one another. As they cleared off of the roof more would follow suit. Some of the younger looking ones, as well as the much older ones, would land before transforming. There was no shame about it, nor bravado that I could see. No one teasing anyone. Just a jovial cama-raderie. I couldn't believe how amiable they all were, given they'd been assembled to come get me. I'd told him not to follow.

I was so engrossed in watching them, noticing that Perrin was the largest dragon of them all by a head or two, that I hadn't noticed when Perrin transformed or put a robe on. I only did notice when he wrapped the thick blanket around me, securing it with a pin. His worry was unmistakable as I sheep-ishly avoided his darkened eyes.

He didn't push. Instead he offered his hand, and I took it. We walked side by side to the stairwell. The inside had walls that seemed to have been carved out of the mountain itself, rough and cool to the touch. We went down three floors before taking a door that led off of the stairwell. It opened onto a hall, at the end of which we took a left, walking around to the door at the end.

Perrin opened it and ceremoniously gestured for me to go in. I walked into a mostly dark room. He flipped a switch, which I hadn't expected, and was quite surprised to find they had electricity. I kept forgetting they borrow from our world, even the Wilds. My body had warmed from moving around under the heavy blanket and I undid the pin. He took it from me and hung it over a chair by the door. The room reminded me of something from the 70s. Large and completely open. There were massive spans of windows on the far side reminding me of my place in Heartwood, except here they were interspersed with rock wall. A small but adequate kitchen with an island and chairs lined the far side. A few chairs and couches encircled an irregular coffee table made of a dark, worn metal. There was a hallway past the living area that I assumed I'd explore later.

I took a few steps as I circled around, situating myself, taking everything in. When I finished I turned to see Perrin, standing squarely with his arms crossed in front of himself. It reminded me of Agustín, and I hoped he was okay. The silence between us was becoming unbearable, and I needed to sit down, but I was filthy. I opened my mouth to ask about washing up when his voice cut through me.

"How could you leave me like that, my Rose?" The thorns in his voice cut through me.

I had to steel myself. "Do you know what I am?"

"It does not matter. Do not ever leave me like that again." He crossed the room in few strides and wrapped me in his arms. Whispering, begging, "Please?!"

"Perrin, I never left you. And I never will." I put my arms around him, realizing he was still only wearing the robe. He was holding onto me for dear life, burying his face in my hair.

We stood like this until a knock at the door disturbed our silence.

He maintained his hold, kissing my forehead, then my cheek. He pulled back slightly and then really kissed me, taking me by surprise and nearly knocking me off my feet. He held me as I faltered and pulled me close to him like he had in that forest. I didn't kiss him back. I couldn't. Not right then. He looked at me strangely for a moment. "Rose, I am so sorry." I shook it off as another knock came from the door.

"It's Anthea," he said as a matter of fact, but looked at me as though he was asking permission. I gestured towards the door, and he yelled for her to come in. She and a few attendants filed in, carrying all manner of food and drink.

"I wanted to make sure you were both whole. I wasn't sure if you'd want to rest or wash before eating, but I wasn't going to come empty handed." She and Perrin extended their right arms to one another, bringing their hands up to cup the sides of each other's faces as they pressed their foreheads together. She initiated the same gesture with me, and I awkwardly took part in it. "Is there anything you need?" she asked me, taking a step back. She was no longer in the clothes from Sabina, but a green silk dress that tied behind her neck and fell loosely down around her knees. I couldn't help but notice that her dress had a similar embroidered pattern to the lush red nightgown I'd worn not too long ago.

"Something else to wear? And to wash up. I am starving, but I need to scrub this day off of me." She looked at me without an ounce of sympathy, beaming at me with a sanctimoniously satisfied look. I wanted to slap her, but as queen, and given what she'd been through, I understood why she was pleased with how the night went.

"Perrin has a lovely washroom. I will send over a few options for you to wear. Would you like to stay here, or would you prefer your own place? Whatever may or may not be, it need not be rushed." It sounded like she wanted it to very much *not* be rushed. I glared at her, unsure exactly of her implications.

She waved at her attendants, and they quickly exited the room. "Do not misunderstand. I am only trying to make sure you are comfortable. And that the choice is yours. I do not know everything you have gone through. I ask that you give us an account when you are ready. In the—"

"Tomorrow."

"Tomorrow?" She was surprised but couldn't hide her excitement, not that she tried.

"The sooner the better," I muttered.

"My Rose, do not push yourself. It has been an awful trial. You should rest. You are safe here."

"I know, and staying in bed won't change anything. I will give you an account tomorrow. And I would like to stay here with Perrin." I turned to see a look of relief wash over him.

He flashed me a small, quick smile before thanking his sister and telling her to get out.

"The shower is down here. I will draw you a bath while you wash the day off." I wanted to tell him not to go through any more trouble for me. But I wanted him to, and he seemed to want to as well as.

Lovely did not even begin to describe this lavish bathroom. I eyed the tub with longing, but I absolutely needed to wash the dirt, sweat, and death off of me first. Despite having proclaimed our intentions for one another, we'd really only ever kissed, albeit passionately, and I felt a bit shy standing in his bathroom. It likely had more to do with me having realized that I actually had loved Briar at one point. And then I killed him. Maybe I killed him before I realized it. It didn't matter. It only took Perrin glancing at the expression on my muddied face to understand where my mind was at. "I will wait in the hallway until you are in the shower, and I will keep my eyes on the tub as I prepare it. I can wait outside once everything is all set."

I somberly nodded my approval, and he stepped out. I wasted no time stripping out of the old clothes, careful to set my clutched pebble aside on a table. I was hoping Perrin would take the old clothes and burn them somewhere, and I wasn't about to lose my pebble. The Medela cloak, of course, was something to be cherished. I folded it neatly and set it aside, not that it would be a question to him anyway.

The shower was like standing underneath a cleansing waterfall. I'm sure I was selfish with how long I stood under that water. Part of me expected to have my usual breakdown there. Hiding my tears and my anguish. But no. I wish that would have surprised me.

I finally turned the water off. Stepping out, the scent of lavender, mint, and chamomile embraced me, lightening my limbs and relaxing my mind. The tub was a huge chunk of rock with a carved and smoothed out center. I timidly moved into the tub. The water was warmer than I was used to, but it was just the thing my body needed.

"Perrin?"

"Rose?" He called from just outside the door, and my heart skipped a beat.

"I... the tub is deep enough. I'm okay if you wanted to come in? To the room, I mean." I wanted to see him. To know this was real. He opened the door and our eyes met. He was still wearing the same robe.

"I was thinking I would shower. I do not want to leave you alone."

"Thank you," I said, grateful the water was on the warmer side. I could blame the temperature for my flushed skin. I knew if I asked to be alone he would indulge me, despite how worried he'd be doing so. I had my back to the shower, and I looked down sheepishly when he made his way over to it. The water came up to my shoulders, but I still put my arms across my buoyant chest as he walked by.

He was only in the shower a few minutes. The water turning off surprised me. "I'm sorry, did I use all the hot water?" I called over my shoulder.

He laughed gently, "You are adorable, my Rose. No, you did not use all of the hot water in Cunab."

"My sister always used all the hot water back home, so my showers would always be short. I guess it makes sense that it'd be different here." I missed Lark all over again. She was starting to seem like a dream I'd had a long time ago.

"I enjoy my shower, but it is quite loud. I wanted to be able to hear you. If you needed anything." My back was still to him, so I wasn't sure what he was doing.

"Have you... I'm sorry, I don't imagine you've been able to clean up since you were taken prisoner. I'm sure you'd like something more thorough. You shouldn't go to all this trouble for me when—"

"My Rose, this is no trouble. I have been through worse. Though I cannot remember when. *You* have been through much. Calm your mind, please." I couldn't help but notice how much space there was in this tub still. As though he was reading my mind, or our minds were in the same place, he chimed in. "Besides, I have only the one tub. I do not think you feel like sharing just now, understandably so."

I said it before I realized it. "Okay." And with that one word I was doomed.

"Okay? My Rose..." He wasn't doing a good job of masking his interest.

"Okay," I said again. "I'll share." I thought he was going to argue or push me to take my time alone in the tub. Instead he walked up from behind, naked, past me to the other side of the tub. My hands instinctively went up to my chest to cover myself again as my eyes darted away from him. I didn't know what was happening to me. I used to go skinny dipping with Lark's friends. People whose names I didn't even know. Now I couldn't relax around a man who'd saved my life just about as many times as I'd saved his.

He stood there with his eyes on me, saying nothing. I looked up at him, careful to maintain eye contact. He patiently smiled at me. "My Rose, you do like to tease me."

"No! I mean, I know it seems like that. Because it keeps happening. But I'm not trying to. I don't know what's going on with me!" I buried my face in my hands, realizing only too late that I'd left myself bare. My breasts fit my frame, which was on the larger side. And my larger breasts floated along the surface of the water, leaving very little to the imagination. I plunged my hands into the water, along my side, giving up any hope of modesty, faux or otherwise. My face must have been terribly red. "See? Just breasts. Now please, can we stop talking about it and you just get in?!"

He stepped in with ease. I'd be lying if I said I didn't take another peak. I was not disappointed. I hoped he wasn't either, with me, not with himself. The tub was large, but not so large that we could avoid one another's touch. We both decided to take over the right side of our respective sides. He relaxed and leaned back, the water not quite covering the top of his chest. He had a few scars of his own, and I reflected on my new ones, tracing the indentations and disruptions on my flesh. He watched me, wanting to say something but keeping it to himself.

We relaxed in silence for quite some time. More time than I realized. The water started to get cold. I was a little disappointed when Perrin suggested we get out and have something to eat before resting. He was doing what he could to give me grace. For that I couldn't be more thankful. But a part of me felt shattered, and all I wanted was to be wanted and held. I'd felt this way before, but it was different now. I wanted to fall or fall apart and trust that someone would care enough if not to catch me, then at least to put the pieces of me back together.

I looked away as he stood and put a towel around himself. The tub was large enough it was a little difficult for me to navigate, but it gave him no problem. It had clearly been built for someone taller like him. He handed me a towel without looking back at me. When he heard me struggling to get out of the tub he turned around and picked me up out of the bath. At which I squeaked slightly, eliciting a chuckle from him as he put me down and turned away again.

He cleared his throat. "The bedrooms are to the right. The one at the end of the hallway is mine. There is a guest bedroom between here and my room. Anthea had the things she sent over for you placed in the guest room." I must have been in the shower longer than I realized. "She sent over some things you could wear at night too. Of course, dress however you will be most comfortable."

It was so easy to forget that we really didn't know each other well at all. "Thank you, I'm sure I'll find something." He nodded and headed to his room with me a healthy distance behind him. I stopped at the opened guest room door and stood in the doorway, watching him walk to his room. He had so many more scars than I knew of. I was curious about them all. Maybe he was messed up enough that we'd be a good match, but that wasn't why I watched him. He stopped at his door and turned to catch me ogling. I felt my eyes bulge at getting caught and slipped into the guest room while his amused laugh followed me from down the hall. I relished his different laughs.

There were several silk dresses similar to the one Anthea had been wearing. There were also shorter tunic style silk dresses, exceptionally shorter. I assumed those were for night-wear. I put one of the short ones on, a gray blue one that reminded me of Perrin's eyes. I tousled my hair a bit, but I could tell it was already embarrassingly untamed. I stepped out of the guest room to see him, leaning against the wall opposite of the door, wearing a black silk tunic and lounge pants.

"Cunab looks good on you," he said as he offered me his hand. I took it, quickly wrapping both my arms around his, clinging to him as we walked back to the living area. I wanted to be close to him, and he seemed afraid that he might break me. The food was cold of course, but still delicious. Perrin asked every few minutes if he could warm something for me, and I kept telling him no.

After we finished eating, everything became awkward again. He told me to let him know if I needed anything. He was waiting for me to go take the guest bedroom. I could have. I could have pretended this didn't bother me. And I could have kept pretending until we grew apart enough that I'd ask Anthea for my own place. That's what I would have done, before. I would have wanted him to tell me what I meant to him, instead of saying any of this to him myself. I wanted to hear him say he wanted me without me asking. I couldn't do that anymore.

"Perrin, are you afraid of me?" I'd killed Briar. Maybe that hadn't quite sunken in yet, but thinking about it now, it shook me. I'd killed him. I'd needed to, but in doing so a part of me died as well. And something else came to be. It would make sense for Perrin to be afraid of me, now that he knew what I was.

"My Rose?"

I looked at him with tears swelling. "You won't get close to me, you don't seem to want me near you, but the tub was your idea. I don't understand. What is going on? Is this payback for before? I wasn't trying to tease—"

He bent over and kissed me so softly and so tenderly I wondered if it had actually happened. I blinked, unsure of everything in the moment. "My sweet, sweet Rose. I do not know how to do this. How can I be here for you, be what you need of me, after what you have been through? Tell me, and I will do anything."

My tears threatened to overflow. Just when I thought I'd finally learned how to command them. "All I want is for you to hold me." As soon as the words left my mouth he was around me, holding me. The tears finally fell. He held me like that until my sobbing eventually calmed down. Then he scooped me up and carried me down the hall. He went by the guest room, and I leaned my head on his chest. He laid down with me in his arms, only letting enough of me go so I could lay beside him, and we could hold one another more closely. I was exhausted more than I could ever remember being. It wasn't the instant my head felt his warm chest underneath, but it was close.

I slept too peacefully for someone who had recently taken a life.

TWENTY-EIGHT

I woke still on his chest with his hand on my bare ass as my tunic had ridden up as I slept. I moved, somewhat flustered. He was still asleep as I pulled the tunic down. Actually asleep, as he was snoring lightly. I breathed a sigh of relief, having remembered no dreams from that night. It had been the most restful sleep I'd gotten since back home. I decided to be brave, or selfish, as I reached up and kissed him. Light was coming from the hallway, and I thought it best if we got up soon. He didn't stir.

I traced his face and smiled contentedly at the familiar touch. He had a decidedly more wild beard at this point. I wondered how he usually kept it, when he wasn't being tortured or leading his army on a rescue mission. I let my fingers trace down his neck, onto his chest, down his side. I wasn't *that* brave, and my hand was making its way back up his chest when his hand flew up to stop my progress. He growled playfully, "This is not my favorite habit of yours, my Little Rose."

I tried suppressing a laugh. "What habit? We haven't

known each other long enough to-" He gave me a quick kiss, pulling back but letting his lips linger. I had an internal struggle about whether or not I was ever going to let him sleep in. He left his lips on mine, unmoving. He was waiting for me to let him know if I was up for this. I wondered if some part of me wasn't. Most of me was, but thought maybe I shouldn't be. I let that voice go. It wasn't serving me, not anymore.

I kissed him back, surprising him for a moment. His heat was intoxicating as his hands found their way all over me. I let myself fall back as he moved over me, and his kiss, his scent, the weight of the moment took my breath away. My hands found their way to his sides as he leaned onto me. He kissed down my neck and the sensation as it stirred through my body was exhilarating. My hands grabbed onto his back and my body writhed with want as I arched myself into him, pressing more of ourselves flush together, gasping when his teeth scraped my neck.

He moaned in response for a mere second before Anthea called from down the hall. "It's after midday, you two!" Her tone was amused, but stern.

Perrin yelled back with more than a hint of a threat, *"Go away, Thea!"* I let out a deep sigh knowing this wasn't going to be going any further.

"The council is waiting…"

His head fell against my shoulder. I moved a hand to his face, smiling empathetically when his eyes met mine. The flecks of gold around his blue were back. I was awestruck. He kissed me and quickly pulled himself away. I whined at the sudden lack of him against my body. A need washed over his face as he let out another little growl. My turn to move quickly before the queen would need to command us again.

I could hear people moving around in the main living area as I scurried to the guest room to go through the proffered clothes. The only one with a color that seemed to soothe me was a dark blue one that tied behind my neck. It was lower cut than I expected, but I liked how it shaped my body and didn't hide my new scars. I didn't want to hide.

Perrin called to me from outside the door. "Rose, let me know if you need anything. I will be right back. I have some words for my sister."

I told him I'd be there in a moment as I tied my hair up loosely, letting some stray strands fall down my bare back and shoulders. As I walked by the bathroom, I remembered my pebble in a panic, worried it'd be missing. In its place was now a delicate gold ring. My pebble nestled and secured into the metal of the ring. It looked as though the setting had been molded to fit it perfectly. The stone itself was still the most prominent part of the piece, but it looked remarkably fluid. I couldn't get my smile to go away as I put it on, amazed at the perfect fit. I wondered how he'd found the time to do this. I decided not to ask right away and to merely enjoy it for what it was.

I walked out, intending to go straight to the living area. The view in the light of day stopped me as I looked out over a world of untamed wilderness. I could see the other towers similar to ours in between mountains and trees. Seeing the landscape before and beside us took my breath away. I turned to go share my amazement with Perrin, only to find him standing at the end of the hall. His eyes slowly traveling over my body. I felt different under his eyes. I felt like me.

He walked up to me, his eyes pausing for a moment on the ring. I kissed him as I whispered a sweet thank you. He whispered back, "We shall reschedule."

We shared this desire, but I also wanted this done, and Thea was desperate for answers. "Come on, how long can this take?"

He grumbled as he took a hold of my body, resting his head against my hair. "Do you like it?" I knew what he was asking.

"I love it. Thank you."

He growled in exasperation when Anthea called us again. He held his hand out for me, and I happily took it. They'd brought food for us again. It was still warm. He turned to look at me and smiled warmly. "We will eat first. They can wait."

It was Anthea's turn to growl as she heard him. He shot her a warning look, and she upturned her palms, bowing her head slightly in some unfamiliar gesture of submission. "I will go, but if you two are not there in thirty minutes I am sending Vette and the others to come get you. It will not take much- they are all eager to meet her properly." She shook her head as she left.

"Do they want to know if they should let me stay?" I couldn't fathom why else they'd want to meet me. He'd told me I'd be a hero to them, but that was before.

He cleared his throat, "Let us eat." Like the night before, he told me what each dish was, and I tried a bite of each. They reminded me mostly of Indian food. A plethora of spices and complex flavors that all seemed too complicated for me to figure out.

"Why don't you want to tell me why they want to meet me? What aren't you telling me?" I was genuinely curious, but I also enjoyed watching him squirm like this.

"Anthea may have told them we plan on claiming one another. I am their commander. Many of them feel it is a duty of theirs to make sure my partner is up for the challenge." I snorted and he shot me a befuddled look. I tried desperately to straighten my face.

"Do we need their permission?"

He comically copied my snort and shook his head. "No. But it goes without saying that you are most definitely up for the challenge." He winked at me with a devious smile as he took one last, long drink of something that resembled coffee, except it was thicker and cold.

We went back to the hallway we'd walked through last night and he opened the second door on the right. There were six people sitting around a table, laughing and joking with one another. I felt uncomfortable for a moment wondering if they were talking about us. It struck me as a little odd that they were all wearing gray. Gray tunics with loose pants or gray dresses, even Anthea and Perrin were in all gray. Perrin shut the door and they all turned and acknowledged him as commander. I thought about hiding behind him, but I stood beside him, where I belonged.

Anthea introduced everyone. They were all pleasant except for one quiet man that looked to be about my age, shorter than the rest with a little extra weight to him, like me. He had dirty blonde hair and a beard to match. Light blue eyes, almost a light gray, and they rarely left me.

We discussed my part in Heartwood since I arrived, how I found them, what happened once I did. I found out Anthea had told Perrin to kill me after I'd healed her that first time. I was a little surprised by this, but not terribly. She was queen, and they'd been trying to kill her. To her, she knew she was going to die there and wanted to hurt Briar any way and as much as she could. It wasn't lost on me that Perrin had defied orders from his queen for me.

I was invited to ask a few questions, and I surprised myself by being bold enough to do so. "Why did you go to a hostile land with so few, when you have so many?" I couldn't understand it.

Perrin answered. "We never dreamed they would attack us. Nothing like that has ever been done before. They specifically invited us to discuss other ways we could contribute. We were misinformed. They had the assistance of the sorcerers. A rather new development for Heartwood since we last visited. We were ill-prepared. It is a dishonorable truth, but one we must admit to in order to avoid it in the future."

I thought about telling them that they weren't misinformed. That Briar had used them in other ways for their contribution. But I didn't know who all to trust here yet. And I didn't think it would matter.

The portly man asked me gruffly if I had any more questions. Perrin shot him a look that made him flinch. "Tysek, you will watch your tone with my Draca."

"It's true then?!" A bubbly woman asked with an undeniable excitement. She had dark skin that reminded me of Helen, but this woman had her share of scars. They all had them. This woman was on the shorter side, surprisingly shorter than me, but just as curvaceous. She was looking at me when she asked, and I blushed, not sure what all the question entailed and unsure of what to say.

Perrin had a beaming smile when he looked at me. Our eyes met and I looked away from him quickly, my face now uncontrollably red. "Looks like it's true, Vette!" An older man that could have been her father called out, clapping her on the back.

My face felt like it was on fire. We'd definitely be talking about this later. "Vette is my second," Perrin explained. "She's very excited to see me matched."

"Only because we all took bets on how long it would take." Anthea chimed in. I wanted to know what she was implying, but it wasn't as though I didn't have my own past.

Tysek was clearly annoyed with the diversion. "Let's hope she doesn't kill our commander while she's bedding him as well, hmm?"

Perrin jumped from his seat and was at Tysek's throat

before anyone else could respond. Not that any of them seemed to dare challenge him. "You will watch yourself or you will find yourself with the Fates! You wear the color, the same as the rest of us. Do not put on solidarity if it is not part of your whole." Perrin growled into his face with the ferocity I'd felt after I went with Briar. I was glad he didn't hide this side from me, and I was also aware I didn't need to fear it. Anthea was visibly nervous and kept her head low. They all had their heads low. I stood, feeling their eyes on me.

I walked over to Perrin and took his hand in mine. His eyes were swirling pools of gold and glowed like fire as he turned towards me, meeting my gentle smile. His eyes didn't waiver, but they cooled. He let Tysek go, and the little man crumpled to the floor, gasping for air. I led Perrin back to our seats. Everyone's eyes were still on me with a range of bewildered looks.

"I did kill him. And I did love him. If there had been any other way- I would have chosen it. I did what was necessary to protect my..." I wanted to call him my Draco, but I wasn't sure what that may mean, so I continued honestly. "To protect what matters to me. I will always make the choice I need to in order to protect what is mine."

Perrin tenderly squeezed my hand at my words. When I looked over at him his eyes were back to the stormy ocean blue that I loved to lose myself in. Anthea had raised her head first, "Do not mind Tysek. It is his job to go against everyone and everything. It keeps us grounded. It helps us see every angle. It would be wise if he did not enjoy it as much as he seems to though. His comments are not supposed to be this personal, which is why I will not punish my brother for this incident. But both of you need to keep your idiocy to yourselves!"

"Is it always his job to be hated?" I wasn't exactly confused.

Anthea smirked at my question. "Not exactly, but it is not

as though it is a role he finds difficult to fulfill. The position rotates, but he seems to enjoy pushing us." She seemed relieved to be saying these things out loud. I doubted if it was the first time any of them had thought them.

"Would anyone else like to challenge my Draca's place in our home?" I doubted if Perrin was actually openly asking.

Vette spoke up, surprising me, "I am not challenging, Commander, but we would be amiss if we didn't discuss this further." Perrin grumbled and looked down at the table between us all. He was contemplating his next move.

I interjected. "I agree with you, Vette?" She nodded and beamed at me. I explained to them what happened in that tent. I spared no detail and offered no defense or explanation. I couldn't look at Perrin, but Anthea's eyes kept flashing over to him with concern. I hoped it was obvious why I had to do what I did.

When I finished they all looked solemnly to their queen. For the first time she looked at me with an understanding and warmth that felt truly regal. "Thank you for protecting us all, and for saving us in our most dire of times. It is in honor of your sacrifice and your loss that our Mountain wears the color of the struggles of mortality.

"As an aside if I may, I do think you and my brother work quite well together. I hope that you understand one another and make each other whole. Do you understand what you are? I did not, not at first—"

Perrin cut his sister off. "Now is not the time for this conversation. I believe the three of us have earned some rest." His voice was gruff and oddly lacked emotion. I felt myself wanting to panic.

Everyone walked out without saying another word to us. I still couldn't look at him. We sat in silence as my anxiety continued to build. After a few minutes I could no longer take this suffocating silence. I stood to return to the room and was only a few steps away from my seat when I felt him embracing me from behind. It was too much for me. The rest of the tears I thought hadn't been there finally came out of hiding. It was my turn to crumple. He held me as my body could no longer support me.

Again he gathered me in his arms and carried me back to his room. I cried until there was nothing left. He held me the entire time. Running his fingers through my hair, holding me tighter when a new sob would overtake me, kissing my forehead intermittently. I finally squeaked out the words, "I'm sorry." Crying with him like this, it brought back too much of Briar.

He shook his head, "No, my Rose. I could not protect you when you needed me to. I do not deserve you. I am not sure what this fire is between us, but I do not deserve its light, its warmth. I can never forgive myself. But there is nothing for me to forgive of you. I can only hope to one day earn your forgiveness."

There it was. His honesty and vulnerability set him apart. I searched his face for a while, not sure what I was looking for. I stood and walked to the bathroom. He followed me wordlessly. I untied the knot behind my neck and let the dress fall to the floor. I heard a heavy exhale as he watched me. I stepped into the shower and turned it on. My eyes were swollen, and I wanted the cool water to wash away the weight of what I'd done. I stood, letting the water cascade over me. He hugged me from behind again, burying his face into the side of my neck. I grabbed his arms and we stood for a moment as the cold water did nothing to dull our fire.

I turned around to face him as the water fell over us. He held me as his eyes searched mine. I'd wanted the cold water to lessen the red and swelling of my eyes, but that was no longer on my mind. I pulled his head down to kiss him as we crashed into the wall of the shower. Our fire once again ignited, in that moment he was the only thing that existed in my world. His lips trailed down my neck and now, uninterrupted, or perhaps before we could be interrupted again, he kept going down to my breasts momentarily before dropping to his knees and tasting me. It took everything in me to stay standing as I climaxed while grasping his hair in one hand and the stone shower wall with the other.

Aftershocks continued to rock me as he stood. His eyes darkened as he watched me panting for breath. He kissed me relentlessly, his hands digging into me. I reached down to grab his length as it pressed hard against me. His elicited moans were euphoric. Grabbing my hips, he lifted me up against the smoothed stone part of the shower wall and my legs went around him. I moaned into his kiss, feeling him against me, needing him. He pulled back, searching my face. "Rose?"

"Please," was the only word I could find. He placed himself in me, entering at a maddingly slow pace. His eyes locked on mine. I tried holding onto his shoulders, the water making it maddeningly difficult. I needn't worry, of course he had me. He began moving rhythmically with me, burying his face in my neck as he leaned my back against the shower wall. I was going crazy as he steadily thrust into me, his momentum building, sending ripples of pleasure throughout every inch of me. I could feel his breath on my throat as his panting grew huskier.

I needed more of him. I grabbed his hair, making him look up at me, and kissed him as I held his head. My other arm was hooked around his neck as I continued to try and stabilize myself. He was holding my ass and had complete control, which I offered up readily. He buried himself completely into me one more time, hard. I felt his body shake and heard his rapturous moan.

He warily put me down and kept his hands on my hips as he rubbed his face against mine. We stood in the water for a moment longer. I could feel my legs were about to give out. I turned to wash, and he caught me, holding me close to him. "I have wanted you since the moment I laid eyes on you. I have thought of this moment for so long. That night at Sabina's, the fire I cannot explain, it has only been building since." I pulled back enough to turn to kiss him. I knew exactly what he meant.

"Can you carry me to the bed? I can't stand much longer." He turned off the water and grabbed some towels. He wrapped one around me and picked me up. I never thought I'd get used to him carrying me around, but I was getting close. He laid me down on the bed as he sat on the edge, looking down at me, hesitantly.

I pulled him down and he rested his head on my chest. I played with his hair while I mused, "I want to know about that fire. If it's not a dragon thing, what is it? Without sounding disappointed, I thought something more would have happened with it when we, you know. And I get it. All of it. I've had similar thoughts."

He looked up at me with smoldering eyes. "Oh? You seemed to not want me not too long ago."

I propped myself up on my elbows. "I wanted to not want you. I don't want to hurt you. Everyone I get close to gets hurt. When I felt that fire, it scared me. But I, and don't judge me for this, I kept having these dreams. I can't explain them, but I know you just want to nurture me, to grow with me. My energy... my dragon's heart showed me that you want what's best for me.

"Being with you, I've been thinking of this moment too. I never saw it happening in the shower though." I laid back, smiling, recalling his face in the shower moments ago. Pleasure so overwhelming it was tinged with pain.

His husky voice roused me from my musings. "Where did you see it happening?" Before I could answer his hands were on my towel, pulling it open.

We spent the rest of the day in bed. Blissfully undisturbed.

CHAPTER
TWENTY-NINE

The next morning, after spending more time undisturbed, Perrin showed me around his home. I was amazed at the technological similarities from what we had on Earth. "We have many people from your world. Blacksmiths that do a lot of what can be done in your factories. Not at the same level of output, but a different level of quality, to be sure. Electricians that work with different types of magic in a sort of synergy. A few sorcerers even call Cunab home. Mostly those that disagree with the way the larger kingdoms operate, and of course there are those that have been exiled. All information is freely shared, and we live comfortably. Not that we didn't without them, but shared technology is a wonderful thing." He was so excited as he continued telling me everything there was to know about Cunab.

We followed a well-tended path that led away from all the markets and venues we'd been exploring at the base of the Mountain. As he led me down this path I hesitated to ask, but needed to know, "Where are we going?" I had his hand and was happy, but something about this path felt portentous.

He sighed deeply. "The Dragon Oracle should know where she comes from. And you deserve to know why what you did needed to be done." I nodded, not quite understanding, and looked ahead as we moved humbly towards answers I hadn't even fathomed to ask about yet.

The path led us down into the mountain, literally. The entrance had been crafted in a gilded art deco style, all metal and glass and romantic sweeping swirls. Amidst the swirls were four eggs inlaid as different metals. The first one was gold outlined with diamonds, the next was copper, then iron, and finally silver.

Stepping inside, the path continued up to a shrine in the center of a large open cavern. There were three dragons surrounding the shrine. "When on duty, our guards remain as their dragon," explained Perrin. They certainly seemed to embrace their dragon differently here. The loose fitting clothing that could easily and quickly be thrown off and back on again as one changed made more sense, even if it was still somewhat cold for it for me, as someone that had yet to transform.

These dragons watched us as we entered, and Perrin gestured for them to be at ease. Anthea was standing in front of the shrine. My steps slowed and Perrin matched my pace, squeezing my hand as he reassured me that he was here with me. There was water dripping nearby, and the air smelled almost fresher, crisp, renewed. I liked being down here, even if I was a bit on edge.

He ignored Anthea and we walked past her. The shrine consisted of a wooden archway over a statue of a painfully detailed onyx dragon wrapping itself around four golden eggs. "This is the Mother Dragon. Do you know her?"

"Not enough to say so. I saw a painting of her in their Mountain and I've read snippets. I don't really know what any of it means."

"*She* means everything. Our goddess. She is why we live in human form. You have a right to her. This culture. It's what started all of this."

"I'd asked for answers, but everything was restricted or in the queen's library and..." I didn't have the strength to tell them that I'd chosen them over that knowledge. It was never even a question.

"Mother Dragon fell in love. He was human and praised her endlessly. Many dragons still crave this attention. She quickly became pregnant and gave birth to four children while still in human form. Her lover's request of course. Some versions recall it as a conditional for his love. Regardless, this doomed them to be unable to transform, unbeknownst to her. She spent a great deal of her time, as well as her hoard, to find some modicum of hope for her children to be able to claim their dragons. At last she was given an answer. Remove a scale for each child, forge a piece of jewelry from this scale. When the child wears it, the scale will become a part of them, and they will have the energy, the heart of a dragon and be able to transform.

"She removed them all from one spot, unable to speckle herself with missing scales. She took them all from just under her arm so no one would be able to see. She crafted a ring, an amulet, a diadem, and an armlet. Many believe this to be merely legend and give it no merit. A fun tale to tell your children, a warning of sorts. The story doesn't end well. One of her sons fell in love with a human who was jealous of his ability to transform. The human thought if they had a scale they too could transform.

"It is nearly impossible for an ordinary dragon to remove

one of these primary scales and survive. They do not grow back, not even for her. Remove too many of them, and we cannot change back to human, as you know. Being born human, we cannot spend our lives as dragons. We do not have the capacity for that level of energy. Apologies my Rose, if I'm telling you something you already know. Our size as dragons is based on our energy and can grow as we train ourselves."

All I could do was nod at him. He was the biggest dragon I'd seen, and I'd seen two dragon armies now. He lightly squeezed my hand again. "The son used a poison arrow to paralyze his mother. His lover had told him the arrow's effects would dissipate once the arrow was removed. Our scales are impenetrable and hitting something in the space of one missing scale is nearly impossible, but since Mother Dragon had removed four scales from the same spot, she had made a perfect target. The lover was lying of course. Once the arrow was removed, Mother Dragon's life was forfeit. Some argue that she died from heartbreak. The son that killed her had been her favorite.

"The son flew into a rage, killing his lover and wiping out the entire village. The story claims that that is what cursed us to suffer the pain of transforming. Believe what you will. From that day on all children of dragons born human are unable to transform until their human bodies can endure the pain."

"I was told that not everyone can survive it."

"Death is very rare from a transformation. When it does happen, it is usually a result of an unintentional trigger."

"And the rage phase?"

"Myth, mostly. Manipulation really. If you beat down your dragon instincts, you are destroying a part of you. It makes you a weaker dragon. Both in dragon and human form."

"So, you what? Learn to manage it?"

"Yes. It is a crass comparison, but it is similar to puberty.

You learn to manage your emotions and your desires. Some are quicker studies than others. We provide guidance for all of those who wish to transform."

"If I choose to transform, would you be my guide?" I hadn't meant anything with the question. I trusted him and knew I was safe with him. I heard Anthea choke down a laugh and saw Perrin smile coyly. "What?"

"For you? Yes. But it isn't something that lovers usually undertake. It can get violent. We need to consider all of the Mountain."

"You wouldn't put me above the Mountain." I wasn't asking. It's what should be. Although I knew the truth.

Anthea cleared her throat, again, and came forward with a wooden box. She handed it to Perrin before opening it and taking something out. She offered it to me- a small, crownlike piece. It had the same coloring and pattern as Jen's ring.

"This is Mother Dragon's diadem. It is now yours." Anthea looked reluctant, but clearly determined.

"What? Why?" I didn't understand how they could give up such a precious artifact.

"You used Mother Dragon's ring to save me. It is now part of me until I leave this world." Anthea touched her chest where the copper scale had mixed with her flesh.

"These items have immense power. You can understand why he was after that ring." Anthea didn't like saying his name. "And are after this piece as well."

"But he let me wear it around. He said it was mine."

"And so it was." Perrin took over the explanation for Anthea. For a multitude of reasons this seemed difficult for her. "It was bound to you, as he seemed to be. And that was enough for them. This diadem was Anthea's. She has chosen to bind it to you, to will it to you. It is only right after all."

I shook my head, returning the ornate piece back to its box.

"That's kind of you. But it should stay here, with your Mountain. It belongs here." Anthea lowered her head and took back the box.

"Frankie, all of Cunab owes you a great deal. None more than I. I hope you and my brother find your happiness together." I'd never seen Anthea be so kind, or so sincere. Albeit briefly. Hesitantly, "You have someone requesting to see you. It's your choice, to see her or not."

"Sabina," I said flatly. Perrin held my hand a little tighter, and Anthea looked perplexed that I already knew.

THEY'D HAD her wait in the meeting room we'd used the other day. She looked as busy as she had back at her home. Even sitting this little woman looked busy. "Child, do you know why I'm here?"

"Is Agustín safe?" I asked, trying to mask my panic.

"That boy is fine." She eyed me with a bit of concern that confused me. "Something is not as it should be. A thread has been broken. You never found Anumonwo's second library?"

"I never made it to her first. Why?"

"Threads are missing..."

"Missing? What threads? Sabina, are you okay?"

"Oh yes, dear. Tell me, would it be possible for me to stay a few days? I don't think it will take longer than that. These old bones do get tired." I turned to Anthea, and she nodded slowly. She didn't love it, but a debt was owed.

Sabina took her leave, declaring she needed some quiet. I spent the rest of the evening with Perrin in their Mountain's library. Heartwood had several different libraries with different collections, but Cunab kept all of their collections together as one. It wasn't as immense, but it was warm, and I felt welcome. Where Heartwood lacked for books on dragons,

Cunab over compensated. Dark histories, prophecies, and troubled legends abound in their texts.

Perrin left me to my own devices as he had duties that needed tending to after his long and unexpected absence. I read until the information dump became too much. I thought I'd read something about god-go-betweens and how they'd been subdued and manipulated. I shook my head, clearly needing some rest and quiet of my own.

Perrin wasn't back yet, so I decided to lay down. I'd started to doze off when I remembered the book Briar had given me and brought with him. The one I'd found in the Eden of death. I'd clutched that bag to me, just as I'd clutched my stone, as Perrin had carried me here the other day. I didn't remember having the bag after that.

I checked the guest room. Beside the clothing Anthea had brought for me lay the bag. I pulled out the files. They confirmed some things but raised a lot more questions as well. No new spontaneous vision. That must be a good sign. As I pulled out the book, a letter fell out. It was from Briar. I thought about burning it. I wanted to. Every bit of me wanted to. But I didn't dare.

FRANKIE,

You asked me the other day if all dragons have hoards. I've never

known one that didn't. You may not realize it, but you do have one,

a powerful one.

You collect darkness.

Don't be afraid of it. Let it in. It will set you free.

. . .

I DIDN'T KNOW if this letter had been with the book the entire time, or if he'd slipped it in right before his misconceived retrieval mission. There was something wrong about his words. I kept thinking of them. And then I saw them in front of me. I saw them as he was writing them. And I saw what they would mean. The letter fell from my fingers as a wispy thought began to solidify.

He knew?

He knew...

I picked up the letter and ran. I ran to Sabina. It made sense now. Someone had manipulated the threads. They'd manipulated me. And I'd cut one... I needed answers and all I could do was hope that she could see the threads as they were meant to be.

I reached the apartment they'd put her in. I banged on the door with all the urgency of destiny calling. She answered without a bit surprised. I thrust the book and letter into her hands. "He knew! He knew I was going to kill him, and he let me do it. WHY?! Why would he do that?!"

A part of me already knew the answer. Sabina said nothing. Instead, she closed the door and motioned for me to have a seat. "You understand now that someone, something, is manipulating the tapestries?"

"What could even do that?!" Again, I knew the answer but didn't want to believe it. She gave me a sympathetic look. She knew better than I what lay ahead. "Tell me," I already knew the answer, but again, the question needed to be asked, "That ember of a flame that I felt for Briar, was that real? Or something else? Is the flame with Perrin real?"

"You know what's real, child. They've tried to create Oracles before. It doesn't work, no matter how many events they think they're triggering of their own volition. Oracles only come to be when the world needs them to be. That tapestry is one that cannot be tampered with, in any world.

"Whoever, whatever is doing this has the ear of a lost god. There are other ways, but... You understand what needs to be done?"

All I could do was nod my doleful acceptance. I could see the paths in front of me again. I wanted to scream.

"The sooner we leave, the better. Your commander won't like this. But you are not following the pattern. Manipulations be damned, there was a setback, something caught, and we've veered too far. You need to be taught how to control your powers if you're ever to reset a damned thing. The power to save or condemn us all for the Sins of the Son will be yours. But you need to learn to see. You cannot do that here."

"She is staying, wizard. Your welcome has ended." I turned to see Perrin standing in the doorway. His eyes glowing with a golden rage.

"Perrin..." Sabina was right. I could see the pattern, the threads. That alone told me I was different. I'd killed Briar to protect this world, to protect my dragons, to protect *him*. At least I thought I had. We couldn't know what may have started with Briar's death, but I needed to be prepared for it.

"My Rose?" I couldn't answer. I'd just found him. We hadn't even had a week together. I'd barely been in this world long enough to be comfortable, and I'd been through more heartache than I thought I could ever bare. I had to leave to save him. It wasn't fair. He came over to me and knelt in front of me, much like Briar had done. I put a hand over my mouth to muffle my sobs.

"Not again. Do not leave me again." His voice was a desperate whisper that cracked as he spoke. I could feel all of him cracking.

"I never left you, and I never will. I am so sorry." Tears were already falling down his face. He knew this was how it had to be.

"I'm coming with you then."

My heart dropped. We both knew he couldn't. "You have an army here that needs to prepare. I won't let you abandon them. I have given up too much for my dragons already for you to do that."

"Your dragons?! Rose, you owe no one!"

"You know that's not true. This world is in chaos—"

"You still get to choose! I don't give a Dryad's damn what you are. To Baratrum with chaos! You still have a choice."

"I do. And I've chosen."

"Then choose me! I need you!"

All I wanted in that moment was to hold him. To tell him that I was always going to be by his side. "I do not know how long of a journey this will be—"

"You will come back to me."

"I don't know where this journey will take me."

"Rose, no..." I took off the ring. I held it out to him. He shook his head violently. "I won't take it. It needs to stay with you. I'll wait for you. I'd wait an eternity for you."

"You'd be miserable." I kissed him through my tears. I kept kissing him. He grabbed hold of me. Picking me up, he carried me once more to his home and into his bed.

NEITHER OF US slept for a minute that night. I wanted to soak up every second I could. He wanted to make sure I wasn't going to sneak out. I hadn't planned on it. I didn't want him to be miserable. Not for an eternity, not for a minute. I woke and dressed sensibly for a journey. I didn't know what I'd need to prepare. But Sabina would know what I did and did not know, and she'd handle it. With what I had to do, I didn't much care about my future at the moment. I knew I wouldn't be able to do, to learn, to experience what I needed to in order to become what my world needed of me, not knowing he was miserable. And I needed to do this without him. I wanted for all the world to rage against the darkness that my anger was creating. But I knew it wouldn't change a damned thing.

I kissed him one last time. There was something about the way he kissed me- he knew.

"Let me claim you. You have not transformed, you would not be able to claim me. But this way I will always be able to find you."

"That's why I won't do it. Not right now, Perrin. You know how I feel about you. Don't ever question that. I'm leaving... I'm doing this for you. I hope you can understand that, please."

I mustered every ounce of my energy that I could manage. I summoned my voice from the void, my oracle voice from times untold. I could only hope it would work, **"Fall in love with someone who deserves you. Claim each other. Be happy. Forget your Rose."** His eyes flashed gold and he stood, motionless, as I left his world to save ours.

EPILOGUE

It had been almost three years since I left Cunab. We'd spent a large chunk of our time in Sabina's home near Savisa. I learned most of what I needed to know from Sabina and Agustín. I'd become more of what I needed to be for our world. Regrettably, I was still having difficulty integrating my powers. There was little known about what I was, let alone how to guide me to reach my potential. I'd never transformed, and we all agreed that was likely what was hindering my progress. Dragons rarely traveled to Savisa, so I had little help with the process.

I'd run into a handful while there, but they didn't know me. They hadn't heard of me yet. Though I had become a legend in other parts of our world. In Heartwood I was the *Harbinger of the End* and had quite a price on my head. Helen had gone oddly quiet, and Agustín had tasked Lily with keeping tabs on her, as much as she could. We'd recently been traveling extensively, and I was known as the *Dark Oracle* in other kingdoms and Mountains. Not that they ever recognized me. Songs were sung of what I would become to these people.

There were prophecies that many put quite a bit of stock behind. But it seemed I alone was in possession of the only book that actually foretold of me. Briar had given it to me, trying to tell me the truth without forcing me into it. That was, until he quite literally did.

This morning I was searching for a plant that only grew on these particular mountain tops. It was needed to help alleviate some of the side effects of transforming. Agustín knew of it but could never cultivate it. He had acquired quite the supply of Dragon Cor though. That was the only reason we'd traveled to the Southern continent after all. I was fairly confident I wouldn't die. I had too much to lose now, too much depended on me. We'd planned on triggering my transformation next month. Travelling out to a desolate area, just in case.

I was scouting the area now as I looked for the plant. It grew nearby, but it needed time to be prepared. Sabina had a little cottage out here, but she and Agustín wouldn't be back out this way for a few more weeks. So I was relaxing, soaking in the afternoon sun. It'd been a chilly morning, and it was just starting to really warm up. My mind wandered to Perrin, as it often did. I could try to find him, to sense him, and had done so a couple of times in my desperation. Too many times. It never did good things for me.

I missed him with a pain I couldn't explain and couldn't rid myself of. The fire inside of me hadn't extinguished as I'd hoped. Absence seems to have only inflamed it. Sometimes it would fluctuate, and I would be so afraid of what might be happening to him. I could only hope my voice had worked, and he'd forgotten me.

Agustín was sure it had. He suggested that something else, someone else was sparking the fluctuations I was feeling, a lessening of our connection perhaps. They were rarely very bad anymore, and this broke me in a way I hadn't been expecting. I didn't believe Perrin would ever have taken on a new mate if he still remembered me, and I took solace in the hope that I'd been able to give him that. All the same, it took me a month to forgive Agustín for suggesting such a thing. I knew he was probably right- that's why it had hurt so badly.

There was another dragon around here today. I'd been able to smell her faintly. She seemed familiar, but I couldn't place her. Had it just been me, I would have paid her no mind. But I needed to protect what was precious to me, especially when they couldn't protect themselves.

I'd found the ideal spot for this plant to grow and knew it had to be around somewhere. The conditions it needed didn't allow it to bloom in many places. But only dragons would be after it. I wasn't worried about this errant dragon being around while I was working through my transformation. She'd either be friendly and might be able to give me some advice, or she wouldn't be, and I'd deal with her.

More of the scent from this unknown dragon wafted by. I could almost place her. I still didn't feel threatened enough to find out though. We'd either run into each other or we wouldn't. She'd been around long enough that she could have sought me out if she wanted to as well.

As I had this thought, I heard her not too far behind me. "Hello?" I called out to her.

"Frankie? It is you!" I recognized her adorably shrill squeal.

"Vette?" I turned to see her running towards me. Transforming unbelievably quickly, a Cunab trademark. Rushing towards me, teeth and claws bared, eyes glowing gold with a familiar ferocity. When she saw the younglings, with their identical tousles of curly red hair behind me, she froze in her tracks, giving me enough time to do what was needed.

ACKNOWLEDGMENTS

All the thanks in the world go out to Betty and Buddy (Courtney) for their unstoppable and endless support. I cannot sufficiently express my gratitude for your encouragement and genuine belief in, well, me.

Thank you to my children. You made this take much longer, but you've all made it so much more worthwhile. And thank you to my husband for helping me find the time and nerve.

Thank you to all of my Beta readers for your insights and overall impressions.
Thank you for helping me believe!

And thank *you*, dear reader!
I do hope you've enjoyed your time with this world.
Frankie will be back.

9 798868 985